MW01241514

She was determined to find the truth, but at what cost?

Everyone was still laughing when the butler quietly sidled up to Emmeline. "Excuse me, Miss Kirby, this was left for you."

He handed her a manila envelope. Emmeline's brow puckered. "For me?"

"Yes, miss. I must apologize for not giving it to you earlier. There had been a minor problem downstairs that required my attention, and I had to step away for a few moments. It must have been delivered at that point. I found it on the hall table just now."

"It's quite all right." Emmeline stared down at the envelope. There was no return address. It had been hand-delivered. "It's very odd. Why would anyone be sending me something here?"

She slipped her index finger under one corner and slid it across. When the envelope was open, she shook it until its contents tumbled out. It was a single photo. Emmeline's face drained of blood, and her hands began to shake. "Oh, my God. What have I done?"

A looted Nazi painting…A former IRA commander…The tie that binds is murder

Emmeline Kirby is back in London, determined to make a success of her new job as editorial director of investigative features at *The Clarion*. Three months have passed since her trip to Torquay and the devastating revelations that surfaced about her fiancé Gregory Longdon. The whole interlude has left a bitter taste in her mouth, and she is keeping him at arm's length. But a suave and dashing jewel thief like Gregory is not easily daunted. After all, faint heart never won fair lady. It doesn't hurt that Emmeline's grandmother and her best friend, Maggie, are on his side. Only his shadowy past could ruin his chances.

All of these relationships are threatened as Emmeline stubbornly pursues a story about looted Nazi art and an IRA collaborator. When a stolen Constable painting belonging to Maggie's family turns up in the collection of Max Sanborn, the chairman of the company that owns *The Clarion*, her personal crusade brings danger close to home. To find the truth, Emmeline and Gregory must untangle a web of deception, betrayal, and dark deeds. But will they learn too late that justice can be cold comfort if you're dead?

Critical Praise for Daniella Bernett

Lead Me into Danger

"Adventure from Venice to London with an engaging cast of characters in this fresh, fast-paced mystery filled with jewel thefts, international intrigue, unexpected twists, and a lovely touch of romance." ~ Tracy Grant, bestselling author of *The Mayfair Affair*

Deadly Legacy

"Daniella Bernett weaves a complex and engaging tale of suspense and mystery in *Deadly Legacy*...The story [has a] Hitchcockian feel...[and a] shocker of a twist ending that took me completely by surprise." ~ Debbi Mack, *New York Times* bestselling author

From Beyond the Grave

"*From Beyond the Grave* is a tense thriller that had me hooked from the first page and kept my attention until the last...The attention to detail, the layers of deceit and lies between the characters, and the plot combine to make this an enjoyable read." ~ Bookliterati Book Reviews

Other Books in the
Emmeline Kirby/Gregory Longdon Series

Lead Me Into Danger
Deadly Legacy
From Beyond the Grave

ACKNOWLEDGMENTS

I would like to thank Acquisitions Editor Lauri Wellington, who continues to have confidence in my work; editor Faith C., who gives my books the extra polish they need; and Jack Jackson, a master designer who creates the beautiful covers for my books.

My continued gratitude to the Mystery Writers of America New York Chapter for its support, particularly Sheila and Gerald Levine, and Richie Narvaez.

I would like to thank bestselling author Tracy Grant, who has been on this journey with me from the beginning. My deepest thanks also go to authors Emma Jameson, Alyssa Maxwell, Meg Mims, and Sharon Piscareta, with whom I became friends via Facebook and exchange lively ideas about writing and life.

A
CHECKERED
PAST

An Emmeline Kirby/
Gregory Longdon Mystery

Daniella Bernett

A Black Opal Books Publication

GENRE: MYSTERY/WOMEN SLEUTHS/INTERNATIONAL CRIME

A CHECKERED PAST
Copyright © 2018 by Daniella Bernett
Cover Design by Jackson Cover Designs
All cover art copyright © 2018
All Rights Reserved
Print ISBN: 978-1-626949-43-0

First Publication: SEPTEMBER 2018

Published by Black Opal Books **http://www.blackopalbooks.com**

To my parents and my sister Vivian with love.
I would be lost without you.

PROLOGUE

Nice, April 1943:

Guillaume was careful to cling to the shadows. His footfalls barely made a breath of sound as he dragged himself from doorway to doorway. He propped himself against the solid bulk of the building, resting his forehead against the cool stone. He didn't have to look down to know that he was losing a lot of blood. The fingers pressed against his left side were sticky and wet. The waves of pain were becoming more intense, but he had to move. Otherwise, he would be caught. He had to get to the apartment.

Guillaume cursed his luck. The mist had cleared, and now a voluptuous full moon hung low in the inky cobalt sky. Ribbons of warm vanilla light drizzled down onto the warren of narrow, cobbled streets in *Vieux Nice*, the old part of the city. The darkness was softened by a moonlight kiss. At any other time, he would have found this scene enchanting. After all, he was a Frenchman by birth and a romantic by nature. But four years of war had changed him—had changed everyone. They had all lost their innocence. The old world was gone. It had been replaced by one where ugliness, brutality, and, above all, fear reigned. Everyone was afraid. Afraid of the *sale boche*, the dirty Germans, who strutted like peacocks along the Promenade des Anglais. Afraid of that knock on the door in the middle of the night. Afraid of being betrayed by a "friend." Afraid of *everything*.

Guillaume turned his gaze skyward once more. The moon, inherently capricious, was determined to expose all of the night's secrets, for better or worse. He shivered involuntarily. A single drop of sweat traced its slow, torturous journey between his shoulder blades and down his back. His heart was in his throat, and his mouth went dry. Nearly dying has a way of shattering one's self-confidence.

He patted his pocket and felt the reassuring weight of the gun bump against his hip. Swallowing hard, he did his best to shake the demons from his mind. He had to warn the others that the mission was blown. That, despite all their caution and planning, they had been betrayed. It was too late for Jean-Luc and Antoine, but he could still save Paulette and Doyle. They were waiting at the apartment.

A sudden searing pain shot through his side and left Guillaume gasping for breath. His legs felt as if they would buckle under him. However, he summoned every ounce of willpower in his body and dragged himself from the doorway like a drunk on his way home from a bender. The Germans weren't too far behind. He had to get to Paulette and Doyle. They had to get to the boat. London said that the boat would be waiting at "Zero one hundred hours." One o'clock. It was midnight now. There was no turning back. Time to *move*.

Another part of his brain took over, and his feet seemed to grow wings. Within minutes, he was up the steep street and stumbling up the cramped staircase. The corridor was dark. He fumbled in his pocket for the key and slipped it in the lock. But the door was wrenched open before he had a chance to turn the key.

He tumbled into the room and fell to his knees, panting.

"Guillaume, my God. What happened? We were getting worried." It was Doyle, the Irishman. He was the only foreigner in their little resistance group. Only they didn't really consider him a foreigner because he had a French mother and spoke French like a native because he had spent his summers as a boy in Lyon with his grandparents.

"What happened?" Doyle repeated, his very green eyes bulging with concern. "Bloody hell. You're hurt. We need to get a doctor." He put a hand under one of his Guillaume's armpits and tried to lift him to his feet.

Guillaume saw stars. The pain blinded him as he weakly shrugged off Doyle's grasp. "No…doctor." It was barely a whisper. "No—time."

"But—"

"Must go *now*." Guillaume clutched at Doyle's sleeve. "It—was a—trap. The Germans were waiting for us."

"My God. What about Jean-Luc and Antoine?"

Guillaume shook his head.

Doyle squeezed his eyes shut, and a tiny tremor shook his shoulders. "And the paintings and everything else?" he said at last.

"On the way to Goering in Berlin. Don't you understand? We were *betrayed*."

"I can't believe it. I *won't* believe it."

"Believe it, *mon vieux*. We must hurry. We've wasted too much time already. The Germans were not far behind me. The boat will be waiting for us at one o'clock. Where's Paulette?"

For the first time since he had entered the apartment, Guillaume realized that Paulette was not there. The hairs on the back of his neck prickled. "Where's Paulette?" he asked again.

"Why, she's right here," said a male voice, as the door to the bathroom opened. The voice belonged to an SS officer, who held a gun jabbed against Paulette's ribcage.

Tears were streaming from the corner of her eyes. "*Guillaume*." It was a choked sob.

"Quiet," the German shouted and slapped her across the face. The crack reverberated around the small room. A tiny trickle of blood appeared at the corner of her mouth.

Guillaume's brown eyes widened in disbelief. He shakily rose to his feet and tried to hurl himself at the German, who merely laughed as Guillaume tripped and fell flat on his stomach with a *thud*.

Guillaume lifted his head and saw Doyle staring down at him, a look of pity reflected in those green eyes. "*Mon Dieu*, it was *you*." His voice was low and harsh. "You were the one, the *only* one, who could have betrayed us. Why? This is your war too."

Doyle hunkered down on his haunches. A lazy smile tugged at the corners of his mouth.

"My war? Oh no, you've got the wrong end of the stick there, Guillaume. This is definitely *not* my war. Why would a good son of Erin fight for the bloody English? Oh no. They're the *real* enemy. And anyone who's an enemy of my enemy is a friend of mine."

Guillaume blinked. He couldn't believe what he was hearing. His gaze strayed for a moment toward Paulette. She mouthed *Je t'aime* and then crumpled to the ground. The German had shot her without warning.

Paulette, ma cherie, Guillaume thought, *at least you're out of this cruel world. At least you can rest now. No more fighting.*

The German loomed over him now, his finger on the trigger. Every muscle in Guillaume's body tensed. He held the German's blue gaze. He would not flinch. He would meet death straight on. He would not allow these vile creatures to see his fear.

"No, Johan." Doyle stepped between them and relieved the SS officer of his gun. "I can't let you do it."

Guillaume's body relaxed as that green gaze swept over him. Perhaps, there was still some good left in this man whom he had once considered a loyal comrade in arms.

"I couldn't let a stranger kill you. Not after everything we've been through together."

"*Mon vieux*," Guillaume replied hoarsely as he attempted to pull himself into a sitting position.

Doyle flashed one of those brilliant smiles that lit up his entire face. "We've been through too much together, you and I. So I'll do it myself."

Before Guillaume had a chance to react, Doyle had pulled the trigger. The shot hit him in the chest. Dead center.

Guillaume slipped slowly back down to the floor. *Bastard.* He'd allowed himself to be betrayed a second time. At least Doyle wouldn't get a third chance.

Everything went black. *Now, there would be no more betrayal.*

ငာင္း

Paris, May 1944:

Lieutenant Cyril Watkins took off his glasses and rubbed the bridge of his nose. His eyes were as gritty as sandpaper and burned with frustration. He pushed the ledger away and leaned back in his chair. The words had started to blur on the page. It was not surprising. He'd been at it for hours. He closed his eyes. What a hopeless, impossible task. They had to try, of course. But did London or the Americans, or *anyone*, really think that they would succeed? He very much doubted it. They were only going through the motions.

Watkins opened his eyes and sighed heavily. He pushed himself to his feet and crossed the room. He stared at the row upon row of neatly stacked paintings, porcelain, jewelry, and other treasures that the Allies had seized from the Germans. All of it was stolen. Stolen from Jews.

Watkins fingered some of the objects. He was part of a joint British and American military unit attempting to identify and trace the owners. It was a noble endeavor, but utterly hopeless. He shook his head sadly. In all likelihood, the poor sods were all dead. And their families were all dead too.

His perambulations, as always, ended in front of a beautiful country landscape. It made him think of his grandfather's estate in Hampshire. His parents had sent him and his three older brothers there for their summer holidays. A smile touched his lips. What heady days those were. Unfortunately, at the time, he had been afflicted with the arrogance of youth and had been too foolish to appreciate it all. If only he could turn back the clock. He would appreciate it now. Oh, yes. After five years of this stinking war, he wouldn't squander a single precious moment.

Watkins's gaze roamed over the delicate brushstrokes of the painting again, taking in the contrast of light and shade. He lovingly caressed the frame. It was so beautiful it brought a lump to his throat and made him homesick. A sigh escaped his lips. If only he could keep it. But, of course, that was out of the question. Then a thought struck him, and he straightened up. Why *couldn't* he keep it? Who would ever know? It would be just another casualty of the war. Lost. After all, the owner was probably dead. Right? He couldn't allow it to fall into the hands of some philistine, who wouldn't appreciate it. No, that would be a sacrilege and simply would not do.

And so, as a soft drizzle started to dance on the pavements of the Right Bank, Lieutenant Cyril Watkins turned up the collar of his jacket, pointedly ignoring the insistent whispers of his conscience, and slipped out into the night. With the painting.

CHAPTER 1

London, June 2010:

Betrayal. *Such an ugly word*, Emmeline thought, as she tapped her pen absentmindedly against the copy in front of her. *Work*, she reminded herself. *You do remember the concept, don't you?* She looked down at the article again, but it was no use. She had no idea what she was reading. Emmeline pushed away the copy in disgust. Disgust at herself, not at the article. It was written by one of her best correspondents and most likely only required a few minor edits. The trouble was she wasn't concentrating today. Her mind kept wandering back to the same theme. Betrayal and lies. *And secrets*. Why were there always secrets? Why couldn't everything be black and white? The world would be much simpler that way.

A mirthless laugh escaped her lips. *Silly girl, when was life ever simple?* Emmeline rose and walked over to the window. She had a magnificent view of the Thames and the back of Tower Bridge. *The Clarion's* offices were located in one of those gleaming new glass towers on the South Bank. Today marked exactly six weeks since she had become editorial director of investigative features at *The Clarion*. It had been a lot of work, and she was still learning, but she certainly had been up to the responsibility and challenge. During her brief tenure, the paper had garnered a new respect—not that it wasn't well respected before. But Emmeline brought a fresh perspective and had made several changes that had been spot on. And now her colleagues and the industry were beginning to take notice. She had many ideas percolating in her brain that she hoped to implement over the next few months.

She should be proud of what she had accomplished thus far—and she was. And yet…and yet one thing eluded her. *The truth about Gregory.* As a journalist, this rankled more than anything. It colored how she viewed everything.

Emmeline loved him. There was no use denying that anymore. She would probably go to her grave loving that dashing, charming, incorrigible, infuriating man. She had accepted that he is—correction *was* a jewel thief. He promised to find a new form of employment—*a legal form of employment.* With a supreme effort, she had come to terms with Gregory's relationship and betrayal with the now-deceased Veronica Cabot. There was that word rearing its head again, *betrayal.* However, what Emmeline still could not get past was the fact that Gregory was keeping the biggest secret of all from her—*the truth about who he really is.* And that disturbed her. It shook her confidence in herself and their relationship. They were engaged again, technically. But how could she even contemplate a life with him, if he couldn't bring himself to trust her?

Emmeline stood there staring out the window, watching the boat traffic on the river without really seeing it. The afternoon sun glinted off the water's surface. It was the first sunny day after two consecutive weeks of rain. Unconsciously, she fingered the gold bracelet with the tiny rosette knots that Gregory had given her long ago and which she wore all the time. She treasured it more than the pink sapphire and diamond engagement ring that he had given on her birthday last month.

"Ahem," a male voice said behind her. "I did knock, twice in fact, but you didn't hear me."

Emmeline swung around, startled by the sudden intrusion upon her turbulent thoughts. "Oh, Nigel. It's you."

"I must say that I've had warmer welcomes," Nigel Sanborn, the corporate counsel, said genially.

Emmeline returned his smile. It was impossible not to. Nigel was the most amiable of fellows. He immediately put people at their ease. He had a sharp mind and a great sense of humor. However, he could be a tough adversary when negotiating a contract or in court.

"Sorry, that was rather rude. I was a million miles away." Emmeline came to sit at her desk and gestured for Nigel to take the chair opposite. "How are you today?"

"I'm fine. But the question is, are you? I have a penny somewhere here in my pocket for your thoughts, if you'd like to share them, that is. If you'll remember, I'm a good listener." His warm brown eyes crinkled at the corners, and another smile curled around his lips.

Emmeline rested her elbows on the desk and leaned toward him. "Indeed, you are a good listener, but no. It's just something I have to sort out on my own."

One of Nigel's eyebrows quirked upward. "This doesn't have anything to do with Tob—with Gregory," he corrected himself quickly. "Does it?"

Emmeline's back stiffened. "Now, what made you bring up Gregory?"

Nigel shrugged his shoulders. "Nothing in particular," he responded slowly—ever the cautious lawyer. "I was simply being polite. We here at Sanborn Enterprises have a vested interest in our employees' happiness."

"I see," Emmeline said. Her dark eyes impaled his warm brown ones, making Nigel shift in his chair. "Well, you know what? I don't believe you."

He cleared his throat. "Of course, it's true. Naturally, as one of our newest employees—and I'm proud to say my discovery—I have a particular interest in your well-being. So it was only natural to ask about your fiancé. The two of are still engaged, aren't you? I mean, you seemed to have weathered everything that happened in Torquay."

Emmeline sat back in her chair and contemplated him for a long, uncomfortable moment without uttering a word. *Torquay.* What should have been a lovely holiday had turned into a nightmare. A nightmare of betrayal and secrets. There was no escaping those words today, was there? And Nigel knew something. Knew something about Gregory's past. Words overheard in the hotel's garden in Torquay— words she had not been meant to hear—came floating back to her mind.

'No, Nigel. For the last time, I'm not going to tell Emmeline. And neither are you.'

'Not my place, old chap.' Nigel had sighed. *'I suppose there's nothing left to say. Will I see you again back in London now that Emmeline works for* The Clarion*?'*

'I don't think that's such a good idea, considering everything, do you?'

'No, I suppose you're probably right. Take care of yourself at least and don't give Emmeline too much grief. You're very lucky to have her. Not many women would put up with you.'

Emmeline leaned forward again. "What do you know about Gregory?" she asked bluntly. "I *know* you're hiding something."

"Hiding something? Don't be ridiculous. What should I know about him?" This was the first time in the two months that she had known Nigel that she had ever seen him flustered. "After all, I only met him when we were all thrown together by that nasty business in Torquay."

"I don't believe you. When we first ran into you in Torquay, you thought Gregory was someone else. A Toby Crenshaw."

"What a memory you have," Nigel murmured under his breath. Then louder he said, "Did I? I can't recall."

"You know you did. Don't lie to me. I hate it when people lie to me."

"I—I'm not lying. It was an honest mistake. I got muddled and mistook Gregory for this chap I once knew."

"There's nothing honest in this whole business. *You* don't get muddled. You have one of the sharpest legal minds I know."

"Why, thank you, Emmeline. That's very kind of you to say," Nigel said, hoping to divert her.

It didn't work.

"Don't try to change the subject." Emmeline pressed her point like a dog with a flea in its ear.

"I'm not changing the subject," he protested.

"You know, I find it all rather strange." Emmeline tapped her pen on her desk in irritation. *Tap, tap, tap.* "At first, you and Gregory eyed each like a cat and mouse and couldn't stand to be in the same room together. Mind you, I acknowledge that this tension largely flowed from Gregory. Then overnight the two of you became very chummy, and, suddenly, you were representing him against a murder charge. Doesn't that strike you as being a trifle odd?"

Nigel swallowed. "No, I wouldn't say so. I would say that it was rather civic-minded."

"Ha." She threw down the pen in disgust. "Now, you sound like Gregory when he's being evasive. Stand warned, Nigel. I'm not going to stop until I find out the truth." She held up a small hand to halt the protest bubbling in his throat. "You can tell Gregory that the next time you see him."

"I have no intention of seeing Gregory." The name still sounded strange on his lips. "He's your fiancé. If you're so sure that he's hiding something, why don't *you* ask *him*?"

"Well, that's easier said than done," Emmeline replied obliquely as she straightened some papers. "Was there something you wanted when you came in here?"

"Now, who's changing the subject? I only wanted to give you the Harper story. I vetted it. It will pass muster in any court, if you make the revisions I indicated in the margins." He handed her the copy and pushed himself to his feet.

"Thanks, Nigel. I appreciate it. Sorry for the grilling." She smiled up at him and then asked, "Can't you just tell me what you know?"

For a brief instant, the plea in her dark eyes made him waver. But Nigel recovered himself. No, it was not his place. Emmeline and Gregory would simply have to sort things out on their own. He wouldn't interfere, although he believed Gregory was a fool to keep things from her.

Nigel grinned. "Have a nice afternoon, Emmeline."

She watched as he quietly crossed to the door and let himself out of her office. Emmeline balled her small hands into tight fists and pounded them against her desk. "Ooh, men.

They all stick together. Fine. If that's the way they want it, the gloves are off."

The shrill peal of her telephone interrupted her next course of action. She snatched up the receiver. "Hello, Emmeline Kirby," she snarled down the line. "This had better be important."

"Is that the way I taught you to answer the telephone?"

Emmeline's face softened. "Gran. Hello there. How are you?"

Helen, her grandmother, was the dearest person to her in the whole world. Her grandmother had raised her from the age of five, after her parents had died while on assignment in Lebanon. Emmeline's father was a well-regarded correspondent for *The Times,* and her mother was a photojournalist. They were a team, in life and in death. Emmeline had been devastated when they died. But her grandmother had swept in, and she never wanted for anything, especially love. Always love. Emmeline grew up in Helen's lovely Tudor house down in Swaley in Kent. No one could have asked for a more wonderful childhood.

The woman that Emmeline was today was all due to her grandmother's nurturing. Her love of art and classical music were all learned at Helen's knee. Her grandmother also instilled in Emmeline a love and an appreciation of the written word. She became a voracious reader. Emmeline always had her head stuck in a book. Biographies, the classics, spy thrillers, but especially mysteries. Some of her fondest memories were of being curled up on the sofa with a mug of steaming cocoa on a chilly winter afternoon as she and Helen read Agatha Christie novels. Emmeline's love of reading also led to her interest in history. For her, delving into the past helped her to understand all the interconnections that made the world the way it was today. With this background as a basis, it was only natural that Emmeline should follow in her parents' footsteps and become a journalist. She hoped that they would have been proud of her.

"So, Gran, to what do I owe this pleasant surprise?"

"Don't think you're going to get around me by going all sweet and coy, my girl. That didn't work when you were five, and it's certainly not going to work now when you're a grown woman of thirty-one," Helen remonstrated. "You know perfectly well why I'm ringing. I want to know when you and Gregory are going to set a date. It's taken you long enough to make up your mind. I'm sure Maggie feels the same." Maggie was Emmeline's best friend since university. Maggie and Helen had been plotting to get Emmeline and Gregory back together ever since his sudden reappearance in her life in February—this after vanishing for two years. Well, now she had an explanation for *that*. Bloody Veronica Cabot.

"Emmy, are you still there? Did you hear what I said? I can feel you not listening."

"Yes, Gran. I'm listening to every word. As always."

"Ha. Now, I *know* something is wrong. When was the last time you saw Gregory?"

Emmeline twisted the telephone cord around her finger. "Oh, I think it was…Yes, when we came down to Swaley for my birthday."

"That was over a month ago. Why are you keeping him at arm's length?"

"I'm not. It's just…It's work. You know that my new job as editorial director here at *The Clarion* is consuming most of my time these days as I try to take the paper in a new direction."

"Rubbish. You *make* time for the people you love. Something happened in Torquay. I could see it in your faces when you came down here. If you don't want to tell me—although it would be the first time that you've kept secrets from me—that's your prerogative. It's your life, and I won't interfere."

Really? And what's this grilling in aid of? Emmeline thought.

"However, you and that good-looking devil better sit down and hash it all out. Nothing will ever get resolved if you don't talk to each other."

"Yes, Gran," Emmeline responded dutifully. It was the only way when Helen was in full vent.

"Good. I'm glad to see you're finally seeing sense. So when do you plan to speak with Gregory?

Emmeline groaned and rolled her eyes. "Oh, Gran." Subtlety was *not* one of Helen's strong suits. "I thought you said you weren't going to interfere."

"I'm not interfering, merely inquiring."

Emmeline started to laugh. "Thanks, Gran."

"For what?"

"For being you." Her voice softened. "Did I ever tell how much I love you?"

"I believe you might have mentioned it upon occasion, but I don't mind hearing it again." Helen was chuckling now too.

"I love you. Now, I have to go. I'll try to make it down to Swaley next weekend."

"Bring you-know-who with you, and I can have a chat with him. To set him on the right path, so to speak. Bye, love. I'll see you next week." And, with that, her grandmother rang off.

An amused smile still played about Emmeline's lips ten minutes later as she locked her office for the night. Gran was one in a million, and she was so lucky to have her.

"Good night, chaps," Emmeline tossed out to the newsroom at large as she crossed the floor to get to the lift. "I'll see all of you in the morning. Henry is the editor on duty tonight."

A chorus of "Right, boss." and "Good night, Emmeline." floated to her ears and mingled with the usual hum of voices, ringing telephones and tapping of keyboards. She shot a look over her shoulder and beamed with pride. It was all hers. Her realm.

Emmeline took one step into the corridor and was nearly knocked down by a rather stout man, probably in his late sixties to early seventies, with iron gray wavy hair and hooded dark brown eyes. He wore horn-rimmed glasses that accentuated the sharp angle of his nose, which was bracketed on either side by deep lines. "Watch where you're going, you stupid girl," he grunted as he shoved her aside unceremoniously. "Some of us have important work to do around here."

Despite the fact that this rude man was nearly a head taller than she was, Emmeline stood in his path. "I beg your pardon.

You're the one who careened into me. I think you should open your eyes and watch where *you're* going." If there was one thing that she couldn't abide, it was rudeness.

He took off his glasses and stared down his nose at her. He smiled, but it didn't touch his cold, hard eyes. "Will you listen to this? Do you know who you're talking to? I could have you sacked just like that." He snapped his fingers in front of her face, but she didn't flinch.

Emmeline squared her shoulders and took a step closer to him. In that instant, she could have been ten feet tall rather than two inches over five feet. "I could care less who you are. All I know is that you could use a lesson or two in manners and common courtesy."

"Oh, really?" the man snapped. He snatched her wrist and jerked her so hard that her head snapped back. "Well, I think you had better take care, *dear*." He shook her again, his fingers biting into her wrist as he pressed her back into the wall. "Because I'm the man who can make your life a living hell, if I've a mind to. And at this moment, it's a *very* tempting prospect."

Emmeline sucked in her breath and struggled to free herself from his vice-like grip. His features took on a nasty, lupine aspect as his lips drew back from his smoke-stained teeth. She shivered involuntarily. In the space of a few minutes, she had gained an enemy.

They stood there eyeing at one another, an unspoken challenge hanging in the air between them.

"Dad, that's enough. Let her go," a male voice called sharply.

They both looked up to find a tall, slim man hurrying down the corridor toward them. In three long strides, he was at their side.

The older man glared at him. "Brian, this is none of your concern."

"On the contrary," Brian said as he loosened his father's grip on Emmeline's wrist and stepped between them, "as managing director, it is my duty to ensure that our employees are not terrorized and harassed. Now, why don't you do what you do best? Take yourself off to your club or the nearest pub and drown your woes in a bottle like you usually do."

"Why, you ungrateful—I've a mind to—" The older man raised his hand as if to strike, but Brian grabbed it in mid-air.

He jerked his head toward the lift. "Go on, Dad. Leave now before you make an even bigger fool of yourself."

It was unnerving to watch as father and son warily engaged in a silent battle of wills. The older man's brown gaze flickered toward Emmeline for a second and then back to his son. He leaned in close and whispered in Brian's ear, "One of these days you're going to push me too far, my loving son. You're just like your mother, always sticking your nose in where it's not wanted."

"Well, luckily for Mum, she finally divorced you and is now enjoying a normal life," Brian retorted coolly.

There was a soft *ding* as the lift doors slid open. "Your car awaits, Dad."

A mirthless laugh escaped his father's lips as he stepped into the lift. "This isn't over. I'll make sure you regret showing me up like this." And then he spat at Emmeline, "In front of the help."

Brian exhaled and shook his head wearily as the doors slid closed. "Every moment that I'm near you I regret it, dear old Dad," he murmured. "Oh." He turned to find Emmeline studying him closely. He had forgotten about her in the heat of the argument. "I'm terribly sorry about all that. My father is…well, a bit difficult."

"It's all right. I've met his type before." But she wouldn't forget the malevolent look in the older man's eyes. "You're Nigel's brother, aren't you?" She mentally compared him to Nigel. Both men were in their mid- to late-forties. Both were slightly over six feet tall with slim, athletic builds. The brothers both had brown eyes that danced with intelligence and yet reflected good humor and genuineness. Whereas Brian's wavy dark hair was threaded with gray strands, Nigel was only graying at the temples, just like Gregory. Why had Gregory popped into her head again? Her thoughts always seemed to stray to *him* at inconvenient times. Well, if she were honest, he was never far from her thoughts. Emmeline sighed and tried to concentrate on the man standing before her.

For the first time since he had intervened in her little contretemps with his father, Brian smiled. "Yes, I'm Brian Sanborn. I hope little brother hasn't been speaking ill of me."

Emmeline returned his smile and shook the hand he proffered. "It's a pleasure to finally meet you, Mr. Sanborn. I'm Emmeline Kirby. I almost feel as if I know you. Nigel talks about you all the time. He's always singing your praises. He's very proud of you and looks up to you. You can do no wrong in Nigel's eyes. It's obvious he loves you very much."

"Well, the feeling is mutual. There's nothing little brother and I wouldn't do for one another. We've always been very close. But please call me Brian. Only my father is *Mr.* Sanborn. Let me warn you that he never lets you forget that you're in the presence of the *great* Max Sanborn—media mogul, political kingmaker, collector, and art connoisseur. But only his family knows him for what he truly is," he replied bitterly, a muscle pulsing along his jaw. "A bully, a heavy drinker, a womanizer, and an all-round rotter."

"Oh, I see. I'm sorry," Emmeline murmured feebly, not knowing how to respond. She was so grateful that she had her grandmother.

"No, no. Please forgive me," Brian said contritely, suddenly recollecting himself. "I shouldn't have aired the Sanborn dirty linen in public. I can't even begin to imagine what you must think of us. But that's enough of that. I'm glad that I've finally met you, Emmeline. I would have liked to have personally welcomed you to Sanborn Enterprises, but I was out of town for a fortnight, and then one thing after another seemed to consume my attention. Naturally, your reputation precedes you. I jumped at the chance to hire you when Nigel suggested we make you an offer. I hope, despite your little encounter with my father, that you'll be happy here at *The Clarion* for many years to come."

"I'm sure I will be, Brian." *Unless your father has other ideas in mind*, Emmeline thought.

CHAPTER 2

Max Sanborn was still muttering invectives against his son and that insolent woman as he plumped down heavily on the wine-colored Chesterfield sofa at his club. He signaled to the waiter and ordered a very large whiskey. He needed it. Just to settle his nerves and to help him think. He pulled out a cigarette from his gold cigarette case and slipped it between his lips as he fumbled around in his pocket for his lighter. There was a soft *click* as the lighter sparked and ignited his cigarette. Max took a long drag, inhaling deeply as he leaned back against the sofa. What was he going to do? The auditors were coming next week, despite all his attempts to prevent Brian from calling them in. Bloody, scrupulously honest Brian. Nigel was worse. Ever since they were in nappies, they stuck together. What had he done to deserve such sons?

The whiskey arrived, and Max downed it in one gulp. It burned his throat as it made its way down to his stomach. He slammed the tumbler back on the waiter's tray and ordered a second one. Some of the amber liquid had dribbled onto his chin. Max swiped at it impatiently with the back of his hand. He decided that his ex-wife, Mireille, was to blame for presenting him with such lily-livered offspring. Well, he supposed that's what he got for marrying a bloody Frenchwoman. At least Mireille had the sense to take herself off back to France as soon as the divorce was finalized. Too bad she hadn't taken Brian and Nigel with her. Then there would have been no auditors. Max chewed on his bottom lip. Had he covered his tracks carefully enough? Would anyone be able to detect the missing money?

He snatched the second whiskey off the tray, signed the bill, and dismissed the waiter with a curt nod. Max wanted to be left alone with his own troubled deliberations. He took a swig and then another long drag on his cigarette. His hand trembled slightly as he placed the tumbler on the table at his elbow. There had to be a way out of this mess. There had to be. Otherwise, he would be ruined, and the company he built would be gone overnight. He couldn't allow that to happen. It was out of the question.

Max slouched down and rested his head his against the back of the sofa. He closed his eyes. They flew open almost immediately, and he sat up bolt upright. An even more horrifying thought popped into his mind. What would happen to his collection of art and jewels if his little sleight-of-hand was discovered? They would likely be seized by the government and sold to repay Sanborn Enterprises' mounting debts, which were a testament to his machinations. How had things gotten so out of hand? If it came down to a choice, the company could go to the devil for all he cared. His collection was his priority. No one would get his hands on it. *No one.* He would kill anyone who dared to touch it.

These disturbing ruminations were interrupted by the shrill peal of his mobile. Max reached into his pocket and smiled when he saw the number. "Sanborn," he said coolly. "I hope this means that you found the…er…items we discussed."

Max listened for a minute, and his grin grew wider. "Good. When can I expect delivery? Saturday. Excellent." He licked his lips. There was the briefest hesitation before he asked casually, "What was the figure you had in mind?" He swallowed hard. The blood drained from his face. "I see. Problem? No, of course, there's no problem. It was a little more than I had anticipated but well worth it. The money's no problem whatsoever. I can lay my hands on it without batting an eye. You just make sure you keep up your end of the bargain. Because if you cross me, I'll crush you."

ფოდ

Emmeline squinted and shaded her eyes with one hand. The early evening sun momentarily blinded her as she walked out of the Sanborn Enterprises. Her brow puckered as she gazed out at the Thames. Her mind still lingered on the disconcerting encounter she had had with Max Sanborn. How could such an unpleasant and downright nasty creature have sired two such wonderful men as Nigel and Brian? She decided that the brothers must take after their mother. It was not surprising that the poor woman divorced her husband. Emmeline couldn't understand why she had married Max in the first place. Perhaps, he had been different at the beginning. Or perhaps, she thought cynically, he was always this way, and his wife didn't realize it until it was too late. After all, one never truly knows another person, does one? Couples like to think it is possible, but it's not. Someone is always hiding *something*.

"Darling, I must say that you're looking distinctly forbidding. That scowl is doing the most unbecoming things to your lovely face. It's enough to make a weaker man turn and run. But never fear, I'm made of sterner stuff."

"What?" The voice had interrupted her train of thought. Emmeline turned to find Gregory at her elbow, impeccably dressed in a light gray suit, crisp white shirt, and pale blue silk tie and looking more dashing than ever. It was unfair that he was more handsome every time she saw him. The corners of his mouth twitched into a playful smile, and there was a mischievous gleam in his cinnamon eyes.

He bent down and brushed her lips with a soft kiss. "There that's much better. I think one more and that grim look will vanish completely. What do you say? Shall we give it a try?"

Before Emmeline had a chance to respond, Gregory had slipped an arm around her waist and pulled her against his chest. He gently tilted her chin up with his other hand so that she had no choice but to look up into his face. The force of his charm was such that it was impossible not to smile back. He felt her body relax. Her arms twined themselves around his neck and pulled his head toward her. Gregory, always the gentleman, never refused a lady anything and therefore willingly obliged her with a languorous kiss.

Emmeline was the first to break their embrace, suddenly conscious of the people walking past, some with bemused expressions on their faces. "Gregory, we're making a scene." She felt her cheeks suffuse with heat.

Gregory, on the other hand, smoothed down the corners of his mustache and glanced around unperturbed. A self-satisfied grin creased his features as he murmured, "Good evening." and nodded at two men hurrying by.

Emmeline elbowed him in the ribs. "Incorrigible. I don't know what I see in you."

"Oof," he said and made a show of rubbing his side. "I'll have you know that hurt, darling. I'm quite certain that you cracked *at least* two ribs. You really must try to curb that temper of yours. One of these days, you'll do me a serious injury and then where will I be."

"Hmph," Emmeline replied, unimpressed. "You're as strong as an elephant and just as stubborn."

Gregory draped an arm around her shoulders, and they started walking along the river. "Emmy, love of my life, that is a rather unflattering comparison."

"What would you prefer? A tiger? A cheetah? A lion? No, I know. A fox. That's what you are. Wily and cunning. A fox keeps his secrets close to his breast. Just like you."

He sensed a change in her mood, felt her shoulders tensing. He stopped and turned her to face him. His brows knit together and his eyes clouded with concern. "Emmy, what is it? What's wrong? Why have you kept me at a distance over these past few weeks?"

Emmeline bit her lip and was silent for a long moment. *What's wrong? What's wrong is that I have absolutely no idea who you are? And I don't like it. Not one bit.* The journalist in her needed answers.

She cleared her throat. "If I ask you something, do you promise to answer me truthfully? It's very important to me. To us."

Gregory flashed one his most engaging smiles hoping to dispel the rather sobering turn that the conversation had taken. "Why so serious, darling? Ask me anything you like. After everything that happened in Torquay, my life is an open book to you."

Emmeline's dark eyes roamed over every line and crease of that well-loved face. She trailed a finger along his jaw. There was a slight tremor in her voice as she whispered, "Who are you?"

One eyebrow arched upward. Whatever he had been expecting, it was not this. A shadow darkened his features as anger and some other emotion chased across his face. His gaze slid toward the river.

A cold, unreasonable panic suddenly gripped Emmeline. He was shutting her out. Perhaps, she had pushed him too hard. For a fraction of a second, she thought that he was going to walk out of her life. Again. And this time, she was certain he would disappear forever. "Gregory, please. Look at me. *Trust me*," she pleaded.

He heard the catch in her voice, but when he turned back to face her, it was as if the last few agonizing minutes had never happened. He had regained his equanimity. He gave a short laugh and kissed the tip of her nose. "Silly girl, of course, I trust you. How could you doubt it?"

"Then tell me."

"Tell you what, Emmy?" he asked innocently as he brushed a stray curl from her forehead.

She swatted away his hand. "Stop playing games." Her nerves had been pulled taut and were at the breaking point. "You know perfectly well you didn't answer my question."

"Oh, *that*." He waved a hand dismissively in the air. "It was so silly I'd nearly forgotten. You know perfectly well who I am. I'm Gregory Longdon, your fiancé. The man who loves you beyond reason. The man who would walk to the ends of the earth for you."

"I don't want you to walk to the ends of the earth. I just want you to trust me. Why is that so difficult? What are you hiding?"

"Hiding? What put such a notion into your head? Darling, your imagination is starting to run away with you. You've spent too much time cooped up behind your desk lately. I'm not hiding anything. You see before you a man who—"

"Who won't tell me the truth. I can't go on like this." She shrugged off his arm. "And I won't. I love you, but I will *not* marry you until you tell me who you really are."

Emmeline turned on her heel and left him there staring after her. Tears stung her eyelids. The words on a lonely tombstone in a small churchyard in the village of Wickersham floated before her eyes as she hurried away.

Gregory James Anthony Longdon
December 21, 1967-March 3, 1970
In loving memory of a beloved son taken too soon

CHAPTER 3

By the time she emerged from the Gloucester Road tube station in South Kensington, Emmeline's tears had dried but her conversation with Gregory—and his non-answers—still weighed heavily on her mind. She sighed and without even thinking she turned right. Her footsteps followed the well-worn route down the two short blocks to the white stucco, semi-detached house at the end of the southern terrace in quiet Hereford Square. Emmeline stood before the shiny black-painted door and rang the bell. Almost immediately, she heard the bolt being slipped back and tried to arrange her features into what she hoped was a smile.

The door was opened, and she was greeted by a chorus of "Auntie Emmeline, Auntie Emmeline." as two highly animated, golden-haired five-year-old twins flung themselves around her legs.

"Boys, boys," Maggie raised her voice above the excited chattering of her sons. "Auntie Emmeline is going to topple over if you go on like that. Anyone would think the two of you were never taught any manners. Now come on, stand aside and let her come inside."

Emmeline laughed. "Oh, it's all right, Maggie," she said as the boys quickly broke their hold. She ruffled their hair as she passed into the entrance hall. The minute the door was closed she bent down and gave each one a big hug and kiss. Two pairs of small arms wrapped themselves around her neck and squeezed hard.

"We missed you terribly, Auntie Emmeline. It's been ages and ages and ages since we've seen you," Henry, the elder brother by two minutes, said as he pulled away. He shyly gave her a kiss and then blushed furiously. Meanwhile, Andrew, deferring to Henry's senior status, merely nodded in agreement.

The twins were rapidly approaching that stage where girls were considered "icky," but Emmeline felt honored that she was an exception in their eyes. Apparently, she and Maggie were the only ones who fell into this special category. Janet, their nanny, however, was teetering on the border line.

"Ages and ages, is it? I don't think it's been all *that* long. I distinctly remember you two monsters—" She playfully poked each boy in the stomach, eliciting a giggle, as she stood up. "—running wild in my living room quite recently."

"Oh, Auntie Emmeline, that was a *whole* fortnight ago. *So* much has happened since then. Come up to our room, and we'll tell you all about it." Each boy grabbed a hand and started pulling her toward the staircase.

"Ahem." Maggie cleared her throat loudly, stopping them in their tracks. "Do you know what time it is?" She tapped one finger against her watch.

Two golden heads looked around Emmeline and exchanged a glance. Then the brothers lifted their blue eyes to their mother's face and smiled innocently. Henry answered for both of them. "Time to take Auntie Emmeline upstairs to play?"

Maggie's green eyes crinkled into a smile, but she shook her head. "No, it's bath time. Now, run along upstairs. Janet is waiting for you. I'll be up in a few minutes."

"Oh, Mummy, it's *not* fair." Henry stamped one foot for emphasis. "Auntie Emmeline just got here."

"Yeah," Andrew chimed in. "It's not fair." He thrust his chin in the air defiantly. In that instant, Maggie saw her husband Philip.

"Not another word. I seem to remember two boys promising me—after crossing their hearts, in this very hall not ten minutes ago—to go take their baths, *if* I allowed them to say hello to Auntie Emmeline. Do either of you remember that?"

Henry and Andrew shook their heads vehemently.

"Then you have *very* short memories, and the next time you ask me for a treat, I will think twice about it." Maggie's brow furrowed in what she hoped was a stern expression.

She was greeted by two plaintive wails, "But, Mummy—"

Emmeline tried very hard to hide the smile that tugged at the corners of her mouth. She cleared her throat. "Boys, boys, run along upstairs." She lowered her voice confidentially. "I'll have a word with Mummy. Perhaps, I can change her mind." She shot Maggie a look and winked.

Henry cupped a plump little hand around the side of his mouth and whispered in Emmeline's ear, "Please try hard, Auntie Emmeline. Mummy can be very, *very* strict."

"I will. Promise. Now up you go." She kissed the top of his head and gave him a gentle shove.

Maggie and Emmeline watched as the twins scampered up the stairs two steps at a time. Andrew stopped on the half-landing and gave a little wave. His mother jerked her head, and he quickly turned the corner to follow his brother, whose muffled voice could be heard in the distance.

Once the boys were gone, the two women broke into laughter. "Honestly, have you ever seen two such little terrors?" Maggie asked. "They become more headstrong every day. I blame Philip."

"Oh, no, Mags. They're wonderful boys. You're very lucky." Emmeline's throat constricted and a tear pricked her eyelid as she thought about the baby she had lost. "Very lucky."

Maggie saw a shadow pass over her best friend's face. "The baby?"

Emmeline nodded mutely. Maggie slipped an arm around her waist and leaned her head against Emmeline's dark curls. Silence filled the hall for a long moment. Emmeline was the first to break it. "It still hurts. It's not as bad as it used to be, but the emptiness is still there. It never goes away. Sometimes it hits me when I least expect it, and I feel like I'm suffocating. Just like now, when the boys were bounding up the stairs."

Maggie gave her squeeze. "Come on. Let's go into the kitchen for a glass of wine. Philip will be home soon. Dinner is warming in the oven. You're staying, of course?"

Emmeline hesitated and then changed her mind as she followed her friend into the airy kitchen, which was just off the entrance hall. "Yes, I'll stay. Thank you."

"Good. That's settled then." Maggie pulled a chilled bottle of Sauvignon Blanc out of the refrigerator. She busied herself at the counter with the corkscrew as Emmeline took two glasses out of the cupboard. There was a soft splash as the golden liquid spilled into the glasses.

Maggie handed one to Emmeline. "Cheers. To good friends."

"To good friends."

They each took a sip. "And to the men we love," Maggie said mischievously. Emmeline simply rolled her eyes. She knew what was coming.

"Speaking of Gregory—"

"I wasn't aware that we were speaking about Gregory. In fact, I don't remember his name coming up in the conversation at all. That is, not until this instant when *you* mentioned him out of the blue."

"Really, Emmeline. Let's not quibble. But now, that his name *has* come up. When are the two of you going to set a date? Hmm?" Maggie's green gaze was very insistent, hoping to prompt an answer.

Emmeline didn't oblige. Instead, she took another sip of wine to stall.

"What are you waiting for?" Maggie asked impatiently. "He's extremely dishy, witty, and the personification of charm. He's got a razor sharp mind. And the man adores you. What more could you want? You know you're the only woman for Gregory."

The only woman for him? What about Veronica bloody Cabot? Emmeline thought. But of course, Maggie didn't know about Veronica Cabot and what had happened in Torquay. Emmeline couldn't bring herself to tell Maggie or her grandmother.

So instead, she replied, "It's complicated."

"What's so complicated? You love Gregory. He loves you. You get married and live happily ever after." Maggie rubbed her hands together to emphasize this point.

Emmeline took a large swig of wine. "It's not that simple, Maggie. You don't understand. There are...things you don't know." *There are things I don't know*, she said silently. *Like who the bloody hell he really is.*

"So tell me. I won't judge. I'll listen and advise. That's what friends do. We've been friends since university. *Ten years*. I can hardly believe it's been that long. But there it is. *Tempus fugit*, as the Romans would say. And, in that time, you've become like a member of my family. My parents certainly look upon you as another daughter, and my brothers...well, they have another little sister to tease. So whatever 'it' is that I don't know, you can tell me. It can't be all that bad. The fact that you and Gregory are back together after two years proves that the bond between you is strong."

Emmeline finally lost her temper. First Helen this afternoon and now Maggie. She just wanted to be left alone to sort things out. "Gregory doesn't trust me. He's hiding something from me. Something very important about himself. I will *not* marry him until he tells me the truth. What kind of a marriage could we possibly have if it's not based on trust and honesty? And another thing—" She was in full spate now, the pent up anger and tension of the last couple of months egging her on. "—have you forgotten that he's a jewel thief? How can I marry a man who steals for a living?"

Maggie made a face. "It's a load of rubbish, if you ask me. I don't believe a word of it. The police have never proven that he stole all those jewels. It's merely supposition on their part."

"Hmph," Emmeline grunted incredulously. "You sound just like Gregory. Why is every woman he meets putty in his hands? You. Gran. And the millions of other unsuspecting females on this sceptered isle."

"Don't forget, Miss Hoity-Toity, that *you're* the one who fell in love with him."

"No," Emmeline whispered hoarsely as she dropped her

chin to her chest. "I haven't forgotten. That's what makes all of this so hard."

Maggie slipped an arm around Emmeline's shoulder and pulled her close. Her tone softened. "There's no reason why it has to be difficult. He's a good man, *and* he loves you. That's what counts. The rest doesn't matter, not really. We all have our faults. Gregory never asked to be put on a pedestal."

Emmeline's dark eyes were bright with unshed tears when she looked up again. "It's just that—" The thought was left unsaid.

The front door slammed. And then Philip's voice floated to their ears. "Your loving husband's home. Aren't you going to shower me with kisses and tell me how much you miss—" He was in the process of loosening his tie when he walked into the kitchen and saw them huddled together. "Ah, Emmeline. I had no idea you were here. Lovely to see you."

The two women started giggling. "Hello, Philip," Emmeline replied. He crossed the kitchen and bent down to give her a peck on the cheek.

Then, turning to Maggie, he said, "Hello, wife." He brushed a stray strand of reddish-gold hair from her brow with one finger and looped it around her ear. It was a very intimate gesture that made Emmeline blush. "Any chance you'll take pity on a poor working sod and give him a kiss?" He waggled his golden eyebrows up and down suggestively. At thirty-five, he still retained an irrepressible boyish charm.

Maggie took a step toward Philip and smiled into his deep blue eyes. She was nearly his height, not petite like her friend. "What do you think, Emmeline? Do you think he deserves a kiss after coming home late, *again*?"

Emmeline cocked her head to one side and rested her cheek against one finger. "Well, I think you should give him the benefit of the doubt. Everyone deserves a second chance."

"Why, thank you, Emmeline. It's nice to see that someone's in my corner," Philip retorted.

"Oh, all right." Maggie slipped her arms around her husband's waist and pressed a soft kiss against his lips. Then she shot Emmeline a meaningful look. "You should heed your own advice. *Everyone* deserves a second chance."

Emmeline sighed and shook her head. Maggie never gave up.

"I get the distinct feeling that I've interrupted something here. I can quietly retreat to the study, if you like," Philip said as he reached out for Maggie's glass and took a sip of wine.

"Nothing important. Just some girl talk," Emmeline replied.

"You're sure?"

"Absolutely. However, your charming wife has invited me to stay for dinner, if that's all right? And then Maggie promised to help me with a new story that I'm working on."

"It would be a pleasure. You know you're always welcome in this house." Philip cast a glance toward the hall. "Any other guests?"

Emmeline blushed. "No, don't worry. It's just me. Gregory's not here."

She saw Philip's face relax. He and Gregory had reached an unspoken détente, but they didn't exactly get along. Emmeline could understand that it was difficult for a man like Philip Acheson to come to terms with Gregory's chosen *metié*, for want of a better word. Philip had dedicated his entire professional career to upholding the law and defending the realm. However, only a very tiny circle, which included Emmeline, Gregory, Superintendent Burnell, and Sergeant Finch, knew that Philip really worked—in fact, had always worked—for MI5, Britain's counterintelligence agency, and not the Foreign Office's Directorate of Defence and Intelligence as everyone believed. Maggie didn't even know.

It was safer for her and the boys that way. But Emmeline's natural instincts to uncover the truth chafed at keeping this knowledge from her best friend. Just like she couldn't tell Maggie about that night back in February when Philip had been shot by a Russian spy in St. James's Park. No, that tale—the unadulterated official version with all the details—had been squirreled away somewhere in the cavernous regions of MI5's offices, where things could remain locked away for a very, very long time. Emmeline, Gregory, Burnell, and Finch had been forced to sign the Official Secrets Act about what had happened that night.

Emmeline pushed the guilt from her mind as she watched Philip and Maggie moving about the kitchen with the ease and comfort that comes of a happy marriage. Emmeline decided to give them a few minutes alone together. She quietly slipped upstairs and made her way to the twins' room. The boys were delighted and immediately pounced. After filling her in on all the *exciting* things that had happened to them since last they saw her, Henry and Andrew begged Emmeline to read to them. It was an unspoken rule that she could not leave the house until she had read them a story, or two, or when they were very demanding, three.

CHAPTER 4

Maggie was just serving the coffee when Philip turned to Emmeline and asked, "So Madame Editorial Director, what's this story that you need Maggie's help with?"

"Well," Emmeline said as she leaned her elbows on the table and rested her chin on her interlaced fingers, "I'd like to do a series about paintings and other treasures looted by the Nazis during the World War Two. So much still hasn't been recovered. Either it's been jealously guarded by museums, which contend that they acquired the pieces in good faith, or they're in the hands of private collectors who could care less about their provenance."

"I don't see how Maggie can help though. Surely, you haven't persuaded her to chuck her company and come to work for you as a reporter? Mind you, darling—" Philip took a sip of his coffee and raised his cup in the air in a little toast to his wife. "—I would support any decision you make. I'd be extremely surprised, but I would support you. Whatever makes you happy."

They all knew that Maggie would never give up the company which bore her name. She had built it all on her own— Roth Incorporated, one of the most prestigious public relations firms in London. Although she came from a wealthy and well-connected investment banking family and had lived a privileged life from the day that she was born, Maggie refused to accept any money from her father. She wanted to do things on her own terms. Perhaps it was being the youngest, and a girl, that had driven her. Her two older brothers had followed their father into the bank, but Maggie had no desire to join the family business. She wanted to make her own mark on the world. And she had. When she married Philip, she had decided to keep her maiden name because people in the industry respected Maggie Roth. No one could match her work ethic, scrupulous honesty, and engaging personality.

"No, silly," Maggie replied. "Emmeline wants to know about Great Aunt Sarah. You remember, I told you about her. Sarah Rothenberg. We all called her 'aunt,' but she was really Grandad's cousin. She got trapped in France when the Nazis invaded."

"Yes, of course, darling. I remember your father told me the story. It was all so tragic. But then, the whole war was tragic. The bestial cruelty. Families torn apart. Lives destroyed. Horrible."

"Yes," Maggie and Emmeline murmured quietly in unison. Being Jewish, they had a better understanding of certain things than Philip, who was not. Luckily, the two women's grandparents had all been born in England. But they had heard stories of their extended families and what they had endured.

For a moment, Emmeline's mind drifted to Ambrose Trent, the alias for Jonathan Steinfeld, the distant cousin she never knew about and now would never get to know because he had been murdered three months ago. She shook her head. A long, sad sigh escaped her lips. Jonathan's life and those of his father and grandfather had been driven by an overwhelming desire to seek revenge for what had been stolen from their family. She understood the need to mete out justice, but it had come at the cost of their lives. In her view, they had paid *too* great a price.

"Emmeline, are you all right? You look as if you're going to cry." Maggie's brow furrowed in concern. "Was it something we said?"

Emmeline gave her a watery smile and reached out to squeeze Maggie's hand. "No, just ghosts. And the unfairness of life sometimes."

Philip guessed that she might be thinking about Ambrose Trent and the sordid Sedgwick affair, but he held his tongue. No need to stir all that up again.

Maggie, on the other hand, said, "That's why we have to hold on tight to the people we love and who matter the most to us." She pinned her green gaze on Emmeline.

Emmeline groaned inwardly. They had come full circle. Gregory was once again the topic. "Don't you ever give up?"

"Never. You should know that by now. My company would have gone under long ago if I gave in every time things got a little difficult."

Philip cleared his throat loudly. "I think we're back to that girl talk again, so why don't the two of you scoot along to the study, and I'll do the washing up?"

Maggie batted her eyelashes and clasped her hands together theatrically. "My hero. Perhaps I'll keep you around after all."

Philip kissed the top of her head as he passed her chair with a handful of dirty plates. "Thank you, darling. You don't know what a relief it is to hear you say that. I'll be able to sleep to-night."

"Of course, I *could* change my mind. It really depends," Maggie tossed over her shoulder as she pushed her chair away from the table.

"You're a hard woman, Maggie Roth. A very hard woman. I didn't know what I was getting myself into when I married you. Now, it's too late," Philip called from the kitchen.

Maggie chuckled as she led Emmeline to the study, which was at the back of the house overlooking the garden. "It's always good to keep them on their toes, you know."

Emmeline smiled. *Perhaps Gregory and I could be this happy one day*, she thought. She just had to get past all the secrets first. The question was could she do it? At the moment, an answer eluded her.

Maggie and Emmeline huddled close together on the sofa, an old photo album resting across their knees. "This is Great Aunt Sarah just after she graduated from Oxford."

"She was lovely. Look at that thick dark hair and the intel-ligence in those dark eyes."

"Mmm." Maggie beamed down with pride at the photo of her relative. "Great Aunt Sarah was top of her class. She received a first in History. There were only two other women in her class."

"Amazing. Our generation tends to take things a bit for granted, but these women were the true trailblazers. What happened to her?" Emmeline asked as she flipped another page and her gaze skimmed over the photos.

"Well, according to Grandad, Great Aunt Sarah intended to continue her studies and get a doctorate and eventually teach, but she fell in love with a chap reading Art History. She was utterly besotted with him. She readily agreed to go with him to the South of France in the summer of 1934 so that he could paint. Supposedly, he promised to marry her as soon as he made enough money. She was his model by day and his lover by night. In the end, though, this bloke turned out to be an absolute rotter. His interest in Great Aunt Sarah quickly fizzled, and he came back home, alone. Sarah was devastated and couldn't bring herself to face her family, so she decided to stay on in France. She spoke French fluently and loved Nice. She ended up making a happy little life for herself."

"I'm glad," Emmeline said as she traced one finger over the black and white photo of the intrepid young woman. "I'm glad that she didn't let things get the better of her."

"Yes, very plucky was our Great Aunt Sarah. Her grandmother had left her some money, so she bought a small house and took on students. She taught English. Eventually, *Madame* Rothenberg came to the attention of the British consul. You know how it is. We British always tend to gravitate to our fellow countrymen and women. Perhaps it's that link, however tenuous, to home. Or simply safety in numbers. In any case, the consul invited Sarah to an official do. It was an opportunity for expatriates to mingle with members of the foreign diplomatic service. By the end of the evening, Sarah's keen mind and ready wit had managed to charm everyone she had met, whether they were French, German, Belgian, Spanish, or Italian. Observing the effortless way she was able to put people at their ease and coax them into talking about themselves set the wheels turning in the mind of our consul, a Mr. Archibald Thornhill. Even as early as 1934, the clouds of war were gathering. Thornhill was among a very small group who could read the writing on the wall, and he didn't want to be caught off guard when the inevitable finally happened. So he sent a wire off to London recommending that they invite Sarah to join the diplomatic service. They appealed to her sense of patriotism. A way to serve king and country. It didn't take much persuading. Sarah jumped at the chance. She was always open to new adventures."

"What was her job exactly?" Emmeline asked, fascinated by the story thus far.

"She became Thornhill's assistant. By all accounts, she was His Girl Friday. She accompanied him to all his meetings, did a little secretarial work and some research. But overall, Sarah just kept her ears open and reported everything she heard to Thornhill."

Emmeline's dark eyes widened. "Do you mean she was some sort of a spy?"

"Not exactly. She was more of a keen observer. Grandad said that she preferred the term 'intelligence gatherer.' It was so much more civilized."

"I'm surprised that she was allowed to tell her family what she was doing. Official secrets and all that."

"Actually, she never spoke to her family again after the episode with the Art History chap. It had left a bitter taste in her mouth. I think things had been said on both sides that couldn't be taken back. Grandad was the only one with whom she kept in touch during those years. He was her first cousin. They had been close since they were children. Sarah was three years older. But they had always shared their secrets and dreams with one another. Sarah never came out and said directly what she was doing. Grandad had to read between the lines—and worried. Being Jewish, Sarah ran an even greater risk. Anti-Semitism was always hovering behind the polite smiles. This prompted her to shorten her surname so that her roots weren't quite so obvious. Grandad's side of the family had already changed "Rothenberg" to "Roth" a generation earlier.

"The first couple of years Sarah wrote regularly to Grandad. A letter would arrive every couple of weeks. Usually, she included a snapshot of herself, or the house or her garden, of which she was especially proud. There were even a few holiday photos. That's why we have all these." Maggie held up the album in their laps. "Grandad kept everything. In August 1936, a letter announced that Sarah had married Edmond Lévy, a lawyer from a prominent Jewish family. Grandad said that she sounded really happy. Sarah and her new husband shared a love of literature, classical music, and art. Edmond was already an art collector when she met him, but together they acquired several Degas bronzes, some exquisite Fabergé pieces as well as paintings by Renoir, Pissarro, Corot, and Constable. Here take a look. These photos will give you an idea of what I mean."

Emmeline traced a finger along the black-and-white photos. She didn't know why, but they had a powerful effect on her. She felt as if she were there all those years ago, wandering from the elegantly appointed dining room to the salon, where men in black tie and women in long, flowing evening dresses were gathered. If she listened intently, Emmeline could almost hear the low murmur of conversation. What were they discussing? she wondered. She flipped another page. A photo of Sarah and a tall, slender man with a perfectly trimmed black mustache, whose head was thrown back in laughter. Emmeline supposed this was Edmond. A smile curled around her lips.

"They were such a striking couple, and you can tell that they were deeply in love. And just look at all those beautiful paintings, and the crystal and porcelain figurines. I wish some of these photos were in color."

"I know what you mean. Look at this." Maggie tapped a finger on a bucolic landscape hanging on the wall above Edmond's head.

Emmeline squinted. "It's a Constable, isn't it?"

"Yes, it was Sarah's favorite painting. *A Country Lane in Summer*. It was a gift from Edmond on their one-month anniversary. The first year of their marriage he gave her something every month."

Emmeline smiled. "How romantic." Her dark gaze fell once more on the album. She had never seen that particular painting before, but could well understand why Sarah had been captivated by it. Constable drew you into the painting, making you feel as if you were walking beside the farmer and his cart.

Emmeline flipped the page hoping to get more glimpses into the past, but there were no more photos. "Is that it?" she asked, disappointed.

Maggie sighed. "I'm afraid so. June 1939. War was looming, and the letters became infrequent. When the Germans occupied France, the letters stopped altogether. Grandad never heard from Sarah again. Later on, rumors trickled out that Sarah and Edmond had disappeared one night with what little was left after the Germans had confiscated everything of value. Apparently, they had fled via a circuitous route from Lyon to Paris then to Portugal and somehow had managed to make it to Canada. The family waited and hoped, and prayed, that Sarah and Edmond were safe. Weeks went by, then months. But word never came. And then grim reality set in."

"Oh, Maggie, I'm so sorry." The words sounded feeble even to her own ears. Emmeline put an arm around her friend's shoulders, and they sat there close together, heads touching. They stayed quietly like this for a long while, each lost in her own thoughts.

"Yes, well." Maggie sniffed and straightened up. "It's the old story, of course. The wandering Jew. Why wandering? Because he was never left in peace to carry on with his life and was always chased out of his home. But we can never forget. We owe that much to Sarah and Edmond, and the millions of others. That's why it's important that you write this story, Emmeline. It may make some people uncomfortable, but someone has to atone for such unspeakable injustice. You're the only one who can do it properly because you understand. Maybe you can trace some of the things that were stolen and restore them to the families." There was so much trust in those green eyes. "Perhaps that's naïve of me, and, granted, it would be a small consolation, but it's still *something*. A piece of the past. Anything is better than nothing." Her voice trailed off.

Emmeline squeezed her friend's hand. "I give you my word. I will not let this go. No matter what skeletons tumble out of the closet."

CHAPTER 5

That's enough of that." Maggie stood up purposefully and crossed the room to slip the album back onto the bookshelf above the desk. "I always get a little maudlin when I think about Great Aunt Sarah." She leaned her hip against the desk, a wistful expression on her face. "I wish I had known her. From Grandad's stories, she sounds as if she was tremendous fun."

"I know what you mean." Emmeline nodded and then glanced down at her watch. "Good Lord, is that the time?" She quickly got to her feet. "Much as I hate to, I'm afraid I must go. I've got an early morning meeting tomorrow."

"Come on. I'll walk you out."

"I'd like to pop my head round the door and look in on the boys before I go. And of course, I have to say good night to Philip."

"The boys are probably fast asleep by now, or at least they should be, or else I'll give them what for. As for Philip, if he's not watching that awful serial that he likes—" She made a face that elicited a giggle from Emmeline. "—then he's up on the roof terrace. He likes to go up there to clear his head at the end of the day."

"I don't blame him. With its view of the Rosary Gardens and the square's garden, the terrace is lovely in the summer. Well, at any time, really."

The terrace was indeed where they found Philip. He was sprawled in one of the deck chairs with his long legs resting on the railing.

"Hullo, you two." He smiled and stood up. "Got everything you need for your story, Emmeline."

"Enough to be getting on with. I'm sure other questions will occur to me tomorrow. I just wanted to say good night. I hope you don't feel that we chased you away."

Philip gave her a lopsided smile, which creased his features. He bent down and kissed her on both cheeks. "You could never chase me away. I just made myself scarce so that you could get on with your work. Our door is always open for you. You must know that. If the boys had their way, you'd never leave. We haven't seen enough of you lately."

Emmeline felt her cheeks flush. "Things have been a little hectic lately. What with the new job and…and other things."

Philip shot a look at his wife, who said briskly, "It's nothing that can't be resolved. A good chat always clears the air I find."

"Yes, but—"

"No, buts," Maggie retorted, then more gently, "Just *talk* to him."

"Ah," Philip murmured. "I take it this has to do with Longdon. I can't say that I'm surprised. I—"

Maggie gave him a quelling look, and whatever he had been about to say died on his lips. She shook her head and elbowed him in the ribs. Gregory was a sore subject between them.

Philip cleared his throat. "Yes. Right. As I was about to say, don't be such a stranger," he offered lamely.

Emmeline touched his arm lightly and smiled. "Thanks. I promise to make a better effort. Now, I must be off."

"Before you go, I wanted to share my news with both of you," Maggie said. "Roth Incorporated just signed a *very* lucrative multiyear contract with a big new client."

"Well done, darling." Philip slipped his arm around his wife's waist and pressed a kiss against her temple.

"That's wonderful, Maggie. Who is it?"

A feline smile touched Maggie's lips. "*Sanborn* Enterprises."

"What? I can't believe it. I mean, I *can* believe it because you're the tops. But why the big secret?"

"I didn't want to say anything until things were settled. Frankly, I had heard rumors about Sanborn that made me a little hesitant. However, the negotiations with Brian Sanborn and his brother Nigel couldn't have been more pleasant. Everyone got what they wanted. And now, I'll have the added bonus of seeing you a bit more often."

Emmeline squeezed her friend's hand, and they both laughed, delighted. "I can't wait. When do you start?"

"Actually, right away. Tomorrow, I have a meeting with the chairman, Max Sanborn, about the charity bash he's holding next week. He's going to auction off some paintings from his collection to raise money to build a new cancer research institute. He'll be showing off some of the architectural renderings. Naturally, a man like him doesn't do things simply out of a sense of altruism. It will be called the Max Sanborn Institute, of course. He wants to make sure the world and his brother know what a generous chap he is."

"Oh, I see," Emmeline mumbled.

Philip's ears pricked up at the tone of her voice. "Something wrong?"

"No. Nothing wrong, *exactly*. But I would watch myself around Max Sanborn. He's not like Nigel or Brian. Beneath the polished exterior lurks a hard man with a vicious temper." Emmeline rubbed her wrist. The memory of Max's fingers still burned in her flesh. "Just be careful, Maggie."

Maggie patted her arm. "Don't worry. I can handle grumpy old men. I've dealt with his type before."

"You've never met a man like Max Sanborn. He's...he's *dangerous*."

⁓⁓

Ah, Friday. Superintendent Oliver Burnell thought that was the most beautiful word in the English language. He started to hum softly to himself as he signed the report Finch had left and dumped it on top of the stack of files in his Out box. That was it. He checked his watch. Eleven o'clock. He had tied up everything with one hour to spare.

The superintendent took his glasses off and leaned back in his chair. A self-satisfied smile creased his round face. At noon, he was going to walk out of his office, and, for one blessed week, he was not going to think about Scotland Yard or London or thieves and murderers. He was going on holiday for the first time in three years. He had finally succumbed to his cousin's cajoling and decided to take that fishing holiday they had been talking about for so long. It would be heaven. The river, the sky, the clean air. *Heaven, sheer heaven.* After all, now that he had been promoted to superintendent, he deserved a little break.

Burnell leaned back in his chair and rested his hands atop his ample stomach. He looked down and patted his solid midsection. He shook his head and sighed. He would have to start that diet his doctor was always hounding him about. And he would. *As soon as I return.*

With this promise made, Burnell felt he could enjoy his holiday with an easy conscience. Nothing could ruin it. Nothing at all.

There was a soft knock at the door. "Come in," Burnell said cheerily.

Sergeant Jack Finch's reddish-brown head popped round the door. "Ah, Finch. Perfect timing. Just the man I wanted to see. There was something I wanted to go over with you regarding the Chapman case, and then I'm off."

Finch took a step into the office and quietly closed the door behind him. "Sir, I'm afraid there's a little problem."

"Problem? Nonsense. It's a small point. I wanted you to bring it to Inspector Halliday's attention."

"Sir, it's not about the case. It's about your holiday."

Burnell's deep blue eyes pierced Finch's warm brown ones. He was suddenly wary. "My...*holiday*?" There was a dangerous edge to his voice. "What about my holiday?"

"Sir, first, I would like it on record that I'm merely the messenger, and, as such, I should in no way shape or form be killed for being *ordered* to come here to tell you."

"Finch." The superintendent slammed his open palm on his desk.

"Yes, sir. The thing is...Assistant Commissioner Fenton has cancelled your holiday," the sergeant mumbled quickly.

Beneath his neatly trimmed beard, Burnell's face flushed an unbecoming shade of puce. "Fenton did *what*?"

Finch swallowed hard. "Assistant Commissioner Fenton has cancelled your holiday. He says that there's an important new case that needs the attention of a senior officer."

"Then why the bloody hell can't *he* handle it? He is the assistant commissioner after all."

Finch held his tongue. He knew only too well that uttering a single word would only serve to inflame Burnell even further. Instead, the sergeant shifted his weight uneasily from foot to foot.

Burnell waved a hand impatiently in the air. "Oh, sit down. You're making me seasick."

Finch obeyed, smiling weakly as he lowered himself into one of the chairs opposite his boss. He rested his palms on his knees and waited.

Burnell leaned back and stroked his beard thoughtfully as he contemplated Finch. An uncomfortable silence filled the small space between them. *Well, it wasn't the lad's fault, now was it?* the superintendent said to himself. No, this could only be laid on the doorstep of one person and one person alone. Assistant Commissioner Richard bloody Fenton. His polished, debonair, pompous, arrogant, and oh-so-inferior superior. Everyone knew that Fenton had only been bumped upstairs because of his wife's money and family connections.

Burnell was certain that this was Fenton's little revenge for having shown him up in the Sedgwick case and for having received a promotion over the assistant commissioner's objections. The man was a viper, an opportunist. Unfortunately, there was nothing Burnell could do to dislodge this extremely irksome thorn from his side short of murder. Granted, the superintendent admitted to himself, he *had* contemplated such drastic action, but, in the end, he dismissed the idea for fear it would complicate his life unnecessarily.

He exhaled a long, weary breath. "Sorry, Finch."

The sergeant relaxed. The storm had blown over *for the moment*. "That's all right, sir. You were understandably upset. Anyone would be in your shoes."

"Would they? It's nice to know that I'm not alone," Burnell replied sarcastically.

"Yes, well—"

"Oh, never mind." The superintendent leaned forward and rested his elbows on the desk. "Did Fenton tell you what this supposedly important case was all about?"

"No, sir. Just that he wanted to see you at once. He—" The shrill peal of the telephone cut off whatever Finch had been about to say.

The superintendent grabbed the receiver and barked, "Burnell." He didn't care if he sounded surly. If his holiday was cancelled, he hoped everyone else was having a thoroughly rotten day as well.

He listened for a moment, his thin white brows knitting together in annoyance. At Finch's quizzical look, Burnell covered the mouthpiece and whispered. "It's Bodicea giving orders before she goes into battle."

Finch bit back a smile. That could only mean one person was at the other end of the line. Sally Harper, Assistant Commissioner Fenton's officious and haughty secretary. The only thing that she and Burnell shared was their barely concealed mutual loathing of one another.

"Yes, Sally. Finch just this moment informed me. Yes, I quite understand. What? Is it convenient for me to come and see Assistant Commissioner Fenton now? Certainly, Sally." The superintendent's voice oozed an obsequiousness that was patently false to anyone who knew him. "As my holiday has been *cancelled*, I find that I suddenly have an opening in my diary, and I can squeeze in a meeting with the assistant commissioner. Isn't that fortuitous? Yes, I'll be there in ten minutes, and I'll bring Finch along with me. Lovely. I'll be counting the minutes. Ta, ta." Burnell waggled his fingers at the receiver before he slammed it back down in its cradle.

He leaned back in his chair. "As you surmised, Finch, we've been summoned for a command performance."

"Yes, sir. I take it Sally didn't give you any hint as to what this might be about."

"No, she did not. She has left that task to her lord and master."

❧❧❧

Burnell and Finch were looming over Sally's desk precisely ten minutes later. The superintendent and Sally exchanged wintry smiles. With that chestnut hair and trim figure, she would be an attractive woman, Burnell thought, if only she didn't scowl all the time and think that she was better than everyone else.

"If you'll just wait a moment, I'll see if the assistant commissioner is ready to see you."

"He bloody well better be ready to see us," Burnell murmured under his breath to Finch. Then he turned back to Sally and plastered a phony smile on his face. "Thank you."

They waited as Sally pressed a button on her phone. "Superintendent Burnell and Sergeant Finch are here to see you. Yes, I will. Don't forget, sir, that you have that luncheon at one-thirty." She listened for a few more seconds before ringing off.

"Assistant Commissioner Fenton will see you now. He's a very busy man, so don't keep him longer than is necessary."

"I wouldn't dream of it," the superintendent replied sweetly. The last thing that he wanted to do was to have a long chinwag with Fenton.

"Ah, there you are, Burnell," Fenton said as they walked into the office. His lips parted to reveal a row of perfectly white teeth, naturally. "I'm glad that you could drop by."

The man said the same damn thing every time, as if Burnell had any choice in the matter. "Well, as I wasn't doing anything frivolous like taking a holiday, I found myself at loose ends so I thought it might be interesting to pop in to see you, sir. I always find our conversations highly stimulating."

Fenton was caught off guard by this remark but completely failed to discern the underlying sarcasm behind it. "Do you, Burnell? Jolly good."

At the superintendent's elbow, Finch developed a sudden fit of coughing. "Dear, oh dear," Burnell said as he slapped his sergeant on the back, hard. "You should have that seen to. It wouldn't do to have it turning into a nasty case of pneumonia." He gave Finch a pointed look.

"Yes, sir," Finch replied hoarsely. His eyes were still watering. "I'll take your advice and see my GP straightaway. I'm sure it's nothing, though."

"Good lad," Burnell mumbled. "Now, what was it that you wanted to see us about, sir?" he asked as they dropped into the chairs across from Fenton.

"Right." Fenton rubbed his manicured hands together. "First off, I'd like to say that it was very generous of you, Burnell, to give up your holiday to supervise this case. Very generous, indeed." If there was any guile behind this statement, the plummy tones of his voice seemed to mask it, almost.

Burnell's back stiffened and his fingers tensed as they gripped his knees tightly. "Think nothing of it, sir. After all, who needs a holiday when one can be here at the Yard, protecting society from all manner of nefarious things?"

"Spoken like a true professional. We need more dedicated men like you. That's why I pushed for your promotion to superintendent."

Really? That's laying it on a bit thick. Who did Fenton think he was kidding?

Burnell cleared his throat and silently counted to ten. "The case, sir," he prompted.

"Ah, yes." Fenton beamed at them. "I'm certain you'll appreciate it. Not the sordid type of affair you're used to dealing with. Clean and very respectable. No murders or anything like that."

Burnell and Finch exchanged wary glances. "Then what

precisely *does* it entail? You haven't actually said." The irritation was beginning to creep into the superintendent's voice.

"Haven't I?" Fenton chuckled. "Well, what I'd like is for you and Sergeant Finch to oversee security for Max Sanborn's little charity auction next week. He's going to sell a number of the paintings, jewels, and other *objets d'art* from his collection to fund a cancer research institute that will be built in his name. Isn't that marvelous?"

"*What?*" Burnell shot to his feet. "You cancelled my holiday—my long-planned holiday—so that I can babysit the collection of some rich bas—"

Finch put out a restraining hand on Burnell's arm to prevent him from committing career suicide.

"What Superintendent Burnell means," Finch interjected diplomatically, "is that he is honored that out of everyone else in the department you selected us for this case. He knows that Max Sanborn is an influential man, as well as being a close friend of the prime minister and your family." He punctuated this with a weak smile.

Finch's gaze shifted between the two superior officers. For an uncomfortable moment, no one said anything. Then Burnell uncurled a fist, one finger at a time, and dropped his hand onto the sergeant's shoulder. The squeeze was a silent *Thank you* for not allowing him to lose his temper completely.

"Is that what you meant, Burnell?" Fenton asked. Was there the merest trace of a smile on that lean, smug face?

Burnell cleared his throat again and said through gritted teeth, "Yes, sir, that's exactly what I meant. Finch is simply better with words than I am."

"Ah, I see." Fenton leaned back in his chair and rested his elbows on the armrests. "Good. I knew you would be thrilled at the challenge."

"Oh, *absolutely*. How could you have doubted it for a single minute?" the superintendent replied with all the sincerity of a condemned man thanking his executioner for the privilege of dying. "I'm curious about one thing, though."

"Well, spit it out, man. Spit it out. I don't have all day, you know." Fenton flicked a pointed glance down at the Rolex on his wrist, signaling that the audience was fast coming to a close.

"Of course Mr. Sanborn is a very important man, but why waste the Yard's manpower when he could very easily hire a private security firm for the event?"

Fenton's brow furrowed slightly. "I hope that you're not questioning my judgment, Burnell."

"Heaven forbid, sir. I wouldn't dream of it. However, in view of the new budget directives that have been issued, it just seems to me an unnecessary waste of—"

"That's quite enough of that. You just follow orders."

"Like the Nazis did," Burnell murmured under his breath. Out of the corner of his eye, he saw Finch cover his mouth to stifle a smile.

"What was that?" Fenton snapped.

"I said I always follow your orders to the letter."

"Well, see that it stays that way," the assistant commissioner said, mollified slightly but not completely convinced. "Now then, you and Finch must be moving along. You have a meeting with Max at his office in an hour to discuss the event. See to it that you're not late. I don't want you giving the Yard a bad name. Off you go." He waved one hand at them impatiently as he reached for his phone with the other. "I'm a very busy man. I don't have time to hold your hand."

CHAPTER 6

I do apologize, Superintendent Burnell," Max Sanborn's long-suffering secretary murmured an hour later after they had presented themselves at Sanborn Enterprises. "I'm afraid Mr. Sanborn is running a little behind schedule this afternoon. He's still on a conference call at the moment."

They all turned their heads toward the solid oak door as a male voice raised in anger floated to their ears. The secretary smiled weakly at them. She was used to her boss's moodiness. "I'm sure it won't be much longer. Besides, the investigator from Symington's still hasn't arrived. They insisted that their top man sit in on the meeting. Mr. Sanborn's collection is heavily insured, and Symington's wants to make certain that nothing goes missing. In the interim, please have a seat." She gestured toward a chocolate leather sofa against the opposite wall. "May I get you a tea or coffee?"

"Tea would be lovely, Miss…"

"It's *Mrs.* Cooper, actually, but Angela will do just fine," she replied with another smile. "Now, I'll just pop down the hall for a minute to get that coffee for you gentlemen."

Burnell sighed as he plunked down on the sofa, the fingers of his right hand drumming impatiently on his knee. How he hated to hurry up and wait. This whole thing was a waste of his time. A less senior officer could have handled it quite competently.

He sighed again at the futility of it all. By his side, Finch picked up a magazine that lay on the coffee table in front of them and began flipping through it without really paying attention to the articles.

Five minutes later, the door to the corridor opened. Burnell and Finch both looked up, expecting to see the secretary, only to find themselves staring up into Gregory's bemused cinnamon eyes.

"Longdon, what the devil are *you* doing here?"

Gregory pushed the door closed behind him and walked into the center of the room. "Lovely to see you too, Oliver. Finch." He nodded at the sergeant.

A flush rose beneath Burnell's beard. "For the millionth time, it's *Superintendent Burnell*," he growled.

"Are we back to that again, *Oliver*? How tiresome," Gregory said as he wedged his elegant frame between the two detectives, crossed one long leg over the other and flashed one of his most disarming smiles at each in turn. "Ah, that's better. Nice and cozy, don't you agree?"

Burnell and Finch exchanged pained expressions behind Gregory's back.

"Longdon, we're here on police business. What do you want?"

"Want?" Gregory asked mischievously. "We haven't seen each other in ages—"

"An eternity wouldn't be long enough," Burnell grumbled.

"—and I missed you terribly," Gregory went on, ignoring the superintendent's comment. "So since I was coming down to see Emmy, I thought I'd kill two birds with one stone by popping along to surprise you. Are you surprised, Oliver? Tell me that you are."

"Over the moon with joy. Now, stop making a nuisance of yourself and go—"

"Go? But I just got here, *Oliver*, and we haven't had a proper chinwag. Oh, where are my manners? I didn't mean to exclude you, Finch. Of course, I'm simply *dying* to hear how you've been getting on as well."

"I can't tell you how warm and fuzzy that makes me feel all over," Finch replied facetiously.

"Does it, Finch? I knew we were of like minds." Gregory

settled himself deeper into the sofa and smoothed down the corners of his mustache.

A heavy silence descended upon the trio. The only one who was amused was Gregory. "Now, come, come, chaps. What's the matter? Don't go all coy and shy on me. This is no way for old friends to behave."

"Hmph," Burnell grunted. "I don't count thieves among my friends. We tend to be on opposite sides of the law."

A stricken look flitted across Gregory's features. "Oliver, you do know how to wound a chap. That is, if I *were* a thief, I would feel wounded, but seeing as I'm a law-abiding citizen with a clean conscience, your comment has not affected me in the least."

Finch let out a harsh laugh. "Clean conscience? Your hands are so dirty that every police force across Europe is just waiting for you to make a wrong move. Let's see, where shall I start? The Menot ruby, Nice, 2004; the Neuman diamonds, Zurich, 2006; Lady Ursula Winchcombe's emerald necklace, Mayfair, 2007; American heiress Martha Endicott's sapphire-and-diamond necklace, the Ritz, Paris, 2007. Obviously, 2007 was a busy year for you. I really don't need to say more, do I? Everyone knows that you were behind all of those heists and many, many more across the Continent."

A smile creased Gregory's features. "Oh, Finch, you've been under dear old Oliver's wing for several years now, and you still haven't learned that *suspecting* and *having actual proof* that a crime was committed are two *very* different things."

"So you admit that you were behind those thefts?"

There was a spark of wickedness in Gregory's eyes. "Now why would I do that? I admit nothing because there's nothing to admit. I'm as pure as the driven snow." He batted his eyelashes at Finch.

The two detectives nearly choked on this last statement.

Burnell leaned forward and shook his head at his sergeant. "Give it up, Finch. It's a waste of breath. He takes pleasure in running rings round you."

"Yes, sir, I know you're right," Finch mumbled. He

crossed his arms over his chest and moodily focused his gaze on the opposite wall.

The superintendent settled back and pointedly ignored Gregory, who took tremendous pleasure in needling his nemesis.

Gregory rubbed his hands together. "You know what we need, chaps? A good strong cup of tea. Then we'll all feel much better."

"We were perfectly fine, until you reared your ugly head. Don't you have someone else you can bother? Miss Kirby, for instance. Although God knows what she sees in you. I can't believe she took you back after your despicable behavior in Torquay."

Gregory's body tensed. His brow puckered as a range of thoughts chased themselves across his mind. And then the moment was gone.

"I'm sorry that took so long, gentlemen," Angela said as she came into the room with a laden tea tray. "Oh, Mr. Longdon, you're here. Good."

"Yes, I apologize for my late arrival. I'm afraid I ran into a spot of traffic. Here allow me to help you with that." As he stood and gallantly took the tray from her, Gregory could feel Burnell and Finch's eyes piercing the back of his skull.

Angela smiled. "Thank you, Mr. Longdon. As it turns out you're not late, after all, Mr. Sanborn's conference call is running longer than anticipated."

He winked, bringing a pink flush to her cheeks. "Then that's all right."

Burnell finally found his voice as he stood up and approached the secretary. "Mrs. Cooper. Angela. You were...*expecting* Mr. Longdon?" He had an uneasy feeling in the pit of his stomach and awaited her answer with trepidation.

She turned to him. "Why yes. I told you earlier. We were waiting for the man from Symington's."

Burnell swallowed hard. "The insurance investigator?"

Angela searched his face in confusion. "Yes."

Gregory beamed. "Surprise, Oliver."

CHAPTER 7

Burnell and Finch stared at one another, their jaws hanging wide open. The superintendent tried to say something, but the words would not come. It simply wasn't possible. Perhaps it was a cruel joke by Assistant Commissioner Fenton. *Yes, that must be it*, Burnell thought. He chided himself for believing even for a second that Symington's would be so...so *insane* was the only word for it.

He started laughing. "That's quite funny, Longdon. You know, for one second, you had me going there. Fenton put you up to this, didn't he?"

Angela was perplexed and remained silent. Gregory's smile only grew wider as he shook his head. "No, Oliver. I assure you it is all quite official and above-board. I embarked on my new career at Symington's on Monday. I was tickled pink to discover that I'd be working with you on my first case. I'm sure you're quite thrilled as well."

The color drained from the superintendent's face as the reality set in. Finch thought his boss might faint from the shock. The sergeant couldn't blame him. He knew exactly how he felt.

Burnell said, "This can't be happening. I think I need to sit down." He sank heavily onto the sofa. He rested his elbows on his knees and dropped his head between his hands. "This can't be happening."

"I don't understand. Is something wrong?" Angela asked.

"No, of course not, my dear Angela. Oliver simply wasn't

expecting such a big surprise. He's doing a good job of hiding his emotions, but I can tell that he's terribly pleased by the news."

Burnell winced at this remark.

"Really?" Angela looked at him dubiously. "Well, if you say so, Mr. Longdon. I suppose you must know. Now, would you gentlemen like a cup of tea?"

"Oh, yes. That's just what we all need. A nice cuppa."

After this little ceremony was carried out, the three men murmured their thanks, and Angela retreated to her desk. She resumed her work, typing away efficiently at her keyboard.

Gregory reached for a chocolate biscuit and munched on it happily. "Lovely cup of tea, Angela. It hits the spot." The secretary raised her head and favored him with a smile.

Burnell and Finch, on the other hand, sat there in gloomy silence. Their tea remained untouched.

"Come on, chaps. Drink up. Your tea will go cold."

Burnell fixed his blue gaze on Gregory's face. "I'm already cold. Chilled to the bone, in fact." He threw a sideways glance at Angela and then lowered his voice. "How did you manage it? The only thing that I can figure is that you blackmailed someone over at Symington's. Otherwise, there's no rational explanation for why anyone would be insane enough to put a fox in the henhouse."

Gregory threw an arm around Burnell's shoulder. "Oh, Oliver, I never realized what an entertaining fellow you are. Blackmail, indeed." He chuckled. "You know that I would never soil my hands with something so…so sordid. No, I heard it through the grapevine that Symington's had a vacancy, and I applied for the post, and—" He snapped his fingers in the air. "—*voilà*, here am I."

Finch leaned forward and whispered, "The grapevine? You mean you heard it from one of your criminal cronies and thought it would be an easy way to get some insider information for your next heist. I'm surprised eyebrows weren't raised when your CV slipped across the hiring manager's desk. Under skills, it probably says 'Expert at relieving unsuspecting owners of their jewels.'"

Gregory shook his head. "Finch, if I weren't such an easy-going chap, I'd have you up in the dock for slander. As it is, I'll let that unflattering remark pass. I'll put it down to the strain that you've been under lately, and we'll say no more about it, shall we?"

The sergeant rolled his eyes in disgust. It was useless. He sat back and took a noisy sip of his now-cold tea. It left a bitter taste in his mouth.

Gregory smiled at Burnell. "You really shouldn't work the poor chap so hard."

The superintendent put a hand up to stop his flow of words. "Put a cork in it. It's bad enough that we'll have to work with you *for the time being*, but Finch and I certainly do not have to put up with your insolence."

"But, Oliver—"

Burnell threw him a withering look.

"—I mean, Superintendent Burnell. I thought it would be a nice surprise."

"Well, you were wrong. I hate surprises, especially if they involve you."

Angela's telephone rang at this point. She picked it up and listened for a minute.

"Gentlemen, Mr. Sanborn is ready to see you now. If you'll follow me, please."

"It's about bloody time," Burnell groused under his breath as they all rose.

Gregory shot his cuffs and straightened his tie. The cheeky expression of a few moments ago vanished and a weary sigh escaped his lips. "We, who are about to die, salute you."

Burnell whirled round and put a restraining hand on Gregory's arm. "I'm warning you, Longdon, we had better not have any of your glib comments in there. Sanborn is not a man to be trifled with, so muzzle it. We don't need any more unpleasant surprises."

"I think you'll find that the biggest surprise is yet to come."

Burnell was about to tell him what he could do with his surprise, when Angela stepped aside to allow them to cross the threshold into the Max Sanborn's inner sanctum. Instead, he shot a look full of venom in Gregory's direction.

Like arrogant men of his ilk who feel the need to demonstrate that they are the ones in charge, Sanborn had his back toward them when they walked into the office, two walls of which were floor-to-ceiling windows that allowed the brilliant afternoon sun to stream in. Burnell couldn't help but notice two Renoirs, a Turner and a Degas drawing were hanging on the third wall.

Angela cleared her throat. "Mr. Sanborn, Superintendent Burnell and Sergeant Finch of Scotland Yard and Mr. Longdon of Symington's are here to see you." Then she slipped from the room and quietly closed the door behind her.

Sanborn kept them cooling their heels for a full a minute, before slowly turning his chair around. He put down the file in his hand and took off his glasses.

The chair groaned under his weight as he leaned back. "Superintendent...Burnell, is it?"

Burnell took a half-step forward. "Yes, sir. This is Sergeant Finch. Assistant Commissioner Fenton assigned us to oversee security for your charity auction."

"I see." Without any show of embarrassment, he took his time appraising them from head to toe. "I must say you don't inspire much confidence, but then you were probably the best that Richard could scrounge up at such short notice. I understand a number of your lot are on holiday at the moment. Oh well, needs must, I suppose."

This last comment only served to pour salt into the wound. Burnell's jaw clenched, and his fists curled into tight balls at his side. *Breathe*, he told himself, *he's deliberately trying to provoke a reaction. Don't give him the satisfaction.*

Finch's shot a sideways glance at his boss. He moistened his lips with the tip of his tongue and prayed that Burnell would not explode, not that he wasn't entitled to do so, but it would make matters that much worse.

The superintendent blew out his cheeks and replied, "Yes, I do believe there are several chaps on holiday." He was amazed at how calm and level his voice sounded.

Sanborn hid a smirk. He knew that his barb had hit its target.

Burnell shifted slightly to his right, and Gregory came into view. Sanborn's brown eyes widened in disbelief. He slammed his open palm against his desk, rattling the cup and saucer at his elbow and splattering coffee everywhere. He jumped to his feet and roared, "*You?*"

His face had turned an unbecoming shade of crimson as he came around the desk. "Is this some sort of a joke? Why did you bring this...this man here?" he shouted at the two detectives, who exchanged perplexed glances.

"Mr. Sanborn, sir, I can well understand your reaction—" Burnell stammered, but the other man cut him off.

"Can you? I don't think so. Why is *he* here?" He pointed an accusatory finger at Gregory.

"Sir, Mr. Longdon is from Symington's. He's the insurance investigator assigned to coordinate the arrangements for your auction."

"The hell he is. I don't want him anywhere near the auction. Do you hear?"

"*That* comes as no surprise. Word of your exploits appears to have gotten around," Burnell murmured out of the corner of his mouth at Gregory, who was the only one to remain detached during Sanborn's tirade.

The superintendent was trying to think of some conciliatory remark to diffuse the tension in the air, but no soothing words came to mind because he had no idea what was going on.

Sanborn was now standing in the middle of the room, his large frame trembling with rage. "How dare you show your face here?"

Gregory's silence only served to inflame him further. "What, no answer? You good-for-nothing—"

Before the detectives had a chance to react, Sanborn drew his arm back and threw a punch at Gregory. However, he wasn't as swift as he had been in his youth, and Gregory easily caught his fist and twisted his arm painfully behind his back.

Burnell and Finch both rushed forward. "Longdon, are you all right?"

"I'm fine, Oliver," he replied smoothly.

"Is *he* all right?" Max said through clenched teeth. "You've got your priorities backward, Burnell. I'd advise you to remember who you're dealing with here. One word in the right ear, and you'll be walking a beat again."

The superintendent cleared his throat and squared his shoulders. He didn't take kindly to threats, from anyone. "Mr. Sanborn, I suggest that you tread carefully. Mr. Longdon is well within his rights to prefer assault charges against you. You were the aggressor. It was a completely unprovoked attack. Finch and I were witnesses."

Sanborn began to laugh. It was a harsh, unpleasant sound that rumbled from deep within his throat. "Let go of me, you bastard," he said as he gave a violent shrug to free himself from Gregory's grasp.

For a minute, no one moved. Then Gregory unexpectedly released Sanborn, sending him tumbling to the floor in a heap.

"Why, I ought to give you the thrashing of your life," Sanborn said as he lumbered to his feet.

He brushed himself off and glared at Gregory. They were only inches from each other now. Of virtually the same height, Gregory could feel the older man's warm breath against his cheek. He didn't flinch.

His voice was low and full of menace. "I advise you not to try it. Otherwise, you might live to regret it."

Before things devolved any further, Burnell and Finch stepped between the two men. Finch grabbed a hold of Gregory's arm and pulled him toward the door, while Burnell struggled with Sanborn.

"Obviously, you gentleman are already acquainted with one another," the superintendent said.

For the first time since entering the office, Gregory's body relaxed and his eyes danced with impudence. "Know each other?" He threw his head back and laughed. "Know is a relative term. Isn't that right, *Uncle* Max?"

CHAPTER 8

Burnell swallowed hard. *Uncle Max*? He couldn't have heard properly. His eyes searched Gregory's face for confirmation that his faculties were indeed failing, but, instead, he saw that the very opposite was, in fact, true.

Sanborn seethed at his elbow like a temperamental horse chomping at the bit. The superintendent had to increase the pressure on his arm to restrain him.

God help us, Burnell groaned inwardly. One of the richest men in England was related to Longdon of all people. How was that possible? Then another thought struck him. *If Longdon comes from money, why is he a thief?* He shook his head. None of it made any sense.

Burnell cast a glance at Finch, who shrugged his shoulders and shook his head in bewilderment.

"I don't want Toby anywhere near me, my auction, these premises, *anywhere*. Do you understand me, Burnell?"

"Toby?" Burnell asked in confusion.

Sanborn waved a hand in disgust at Gregory.

Before the superintendent could say anything, Gregory replied quietly, "The name is Gregory Longdon."

"Ha. Where did you come up with that? Although I could care less what you call yourself these days. You'll always be Toby Crenshaw, my sister's good-for-nothing, ungrateful, sniveling son. You want to know something? The day you disappeared was the happiest day of my life."

Finch cast a sidelong glance at Gregory. His jaw had hardened into a tight line. But a smile still played around the corners of his mouth. "That's because you were always so compassionate and fond of children, Max. Isn't that what the world is supposed to think?"

"I'll tell you one thing," Sanborn snarled. "If you think you can waltz back in here after all these years and worm yourself into my good graces, you had better think again."

Gregory laughed, but it rang hollow. "Good graces. What good graces? You're a mean, nasty brute who thinks people are expendable. The only things that you care about are power and money."

There was a sharp indrawn breath from Finch, but Gregory ignored it. He was beyond caring at this point.

Sanborn's lips twisted into a nasty grimace. "So that's it. You want money. Why shouldn't that surprise me? You always were a greedy little bastard. Nothing was ever enough, despite the fact that I spent more money on you and Clarissa than you bloody well deserved."

At the mention of his mother's name, Gregory took a step toward his uncle and then checked himself. He kept his arms rigidly at his sides.

It was taking every ounce of willpower for him not to smash his fist into that much-hated face. He knew that if he started, he wouldn't stop until Max was an unrecognizable heap on the plush carpeting on the floor.

"Don't you *dare* mention Mum. You treated your own sister like the dirt under your feet."

"I took the two of you in after your father scarpered, didn't I? I put food in your mouths and clothes on your backs. What more did you want from me?"

"And not a single day went by that you didn't remind Mum. Made her feel guilty for turning to her *family*. You enjoyed watching her grovel at your feet, you cold, unfeeling bastard."

"Get out. *Now*," Max bellowed. "I don't want to see your face ever again. Do you understand me, Toby? Never darken my doorstep again, or I won't answer for the consequences."

Gregory started to say something, but he decided against

giving voice to his thoughts when he caught the warning shake of Burnell's head.

೮⁄ഉ೮⁄ఎ

"That went well, didn't it, chaps?" Gregory said once they were out in the corridor. He was his usual flippant self once more.

"*Well?*" Burnell spluttered. "What's your definition of a disaster, then?"

"Oh, come on, Oliver," Gregory murmured as he stopped to straighten Burnell's tie. "There that's much better. It doesn't do for one of Scotland Yard's finest to look frumpy."

"Get off." Burnell slapped Gregory's hands away.

"Anyway, as I was saying, the meeting went better than I had anticipated. Max could have called security to escort us— well, at least me—out. Thankfully, we were spared such a scene. However, I am sorry that the family laundry had to be aired out in public. But then, that's Max for you. Tact and discretion were never his strong suits. He was always more of your bull-in-the-china shop type."

Burnell and Finch couldn't believe their ears.

"Longdon, you're stark raving mad."

Gregory stopped and pivoted to face the two detectives. "Why?" The smile slipped from his lips, and his voice dripped ice. "Because I know that my dear, sainted uncle is a hypocrite and a fraud."

Burnell could see that the encounter with Sanborn had stirred up emotions that Gregory had thought buried long ago. The superintendent's tone softened. "Why, Longdon? I can understand you wanting to get away from your uncle. God help me for saying this, but you're an intelligent, good-looking chap. You could have done anything with your life. So why did you become a thief?"

Gregory flashed one of those smiles that always melted even the hardest of hearts. "Oh, Oliver, under that gruff exterior you really do care." He put a hand to his heart. "I'm touched. But you're wrong about one thing."

"What's that?"

"I'm not a thief."

Burnell and Finch groaned. *The game begins again*, the superintendent thought.

Gregory chuckled. Then his smile vanished, when Nigel and Brian came hurrying around the corner. Obviously, they had been summoned by Max.

Nigel's eyes widened in surprise, when he saw the trio standing in the middle of the corridor. He cast a sidelong glance at his brother, as Brian locked eyes with Gregory and stopped short.

"Excuse us, we were—" Brian's brows knit together as he looked at Gregory more closely. "Good God....It can't be. *Toby?*"

A weary sigh escaped from Gregory as he extended a hand toward his cousin. "Yes, Brian. It's me. But the name's Gregory Longdon these days."

Stunned, Brian shook his hand. "But how? I mean why?" He spluttered. "*Where* have you been all these years?"

"It's a long story. Too complicated to get into at the moment."

Brian turned to his brother. "Did you know?"

Nigel nodded. "I ran into Tob...Gregory when I was down in Torquay in April closing the Cabot deal."

"And all these months you didn't say a word to me?" Irritation was creeping into Brian's voice. He was quick to anger these days, and his nerves always seemed to be on edge. The recent discovery of the company's strained finances was taking a toll. And now, this unexpected little family reunion was thrown into the pot.

"I asked Nigel not to tell anyone."

Brian's head swung round. "I'm not just anyone, Toby. Gregory, or whatever you want to call yourself. I'm family or have you forgotten that?"

"No, I haven't forgotten," Gregory replied quietly. He exchanged a pained expression with Nigel.

Nigel tugged at his brother's arm. "Come on, this is not the time—"

Brian shook him off. "No. I want to know what makes a boy of seventeen run off in the middle of the night without a word. And then, twenty-five years later, he resurfaces under a new name, and I'm not supposed to ask any questions. No. I'm entitled to some answers. We searched for him for weeks. Nigel, don't you remember how frantic Mum was? We were all upset."

"All except Max I bet," Gregory muttered under his breath.

"Don't give me that," Brian said. "After Aunt Clarissa died, you had us and Mum. You were like our brother."

"Except in name. Max never let me forget that I wasn't a true Sanborn."

"Is that why you did it? Is that why you stole the Queen of the Night?"

"I didn't steal it," Gregory said impassively.

"Do you really expect me to believe that?"

"Queen of the Night?" Finch whispered to Burnell.

"One of the world's largest diamonds. It vanished without a trace. To this day, it has never been recovered," the superintendent murmured in his ear.

Burnell's blue gaze strayed toward Gregory's profile. *And to think, I could have been fishing up in Scotland at this moment*, he mused. He put another imaginary black mark against Assistant Commissioner Fenton's name. When it came time for the reckoning in the afterlife, Fenton would have a lot to answer for.

"Come on, Brian. Dad wants to see us. However, I suspect the reason why is standing before us. Tob…Gregory, go on." Nigel jerked his head toward the lift. "I'll ring you later."

No one moved. Gregory's gaze lingered on Brian's face. Nigel was right.

There was nothing to be gained by continuing this discussion right now. He nodded to his cousins.

Brian mumbled something unintelligible, as he brushed past. Nigel clapped Gregory's shoulder and followed his brother.

"Longdon, you have a unique talent for rubbing people the wrong way. Does it come naturally or did it take time to perfect your technique?" Burnell asked once Nigel and Brian had disappeared around the corner.

Gregory smiled. "You're just jealous, Oliver, because I'm more popular than you."

"Jealous of *you*? Either you're joking, or you have delusions of grandeur."

Gregory chuckled as he thrust his hands into his pockets and headed toward the lift. "Come on, chaps. I'll see you as far as the seventeenth floor. At that point, I'm afraid I will have to deprive you of my company as I have to pop in to see Emmy."

"Hmph. I'd love to be a fly on the wall when you divulge the family secrets to Miss Kirby." Burnell stopped and put a restraining hand on Gregory's arm. "You *do* intend to tell her, don't you?"

Gregory sighed. "Yes, Oliver. At this stage, I'm left with very little choice in the matter."

"I don't understand why you kept it from her in the first place. And for the millionth time, it's *Superintendent Burnell*," the detective grumbled. "When are you going to get that into your thick skull?"

Gregory threw his head back and laughed. "I'm a dull fellow, *Oliver*. You'll just have to keep reminding me. Ah, here's the lift. Shall we?" He stood aside and allowed the detectives to pass into the car.

༺ઝ༺ઝ

When the doors slid open, Maggie was standing there. Her face broke out into a huge grin. "Gregory, what a delightful surprise."

He stepped out of the lift and took both of Maggie's hands in his own larger ones. He gave her a peck on the cheek before waggling his fingers at Burnell and Finch. "It's heartbreak to leave you, chaps. But we'll see each other again soon."

The two detectives merely rolled their eyes and were glad to be shot of him for the time being.

"Maggie, you're a ray of sunshine in what has been an otherwise trying afternoon. How are you? You look absolutely radiant, as usual. Acheson better be taking good care of you, or else he'll have to answer to me."

Maggie felt her cheeks suffuse with heat. She knew Gregory was an inveterate flirt. Still, it felt nice to have a man other than her husband take notice of her. "Oh, stop that." She gave his chest a little shove. "You know I'm a happily married woman. No one could tear me away from Philip."

Gregory sighed in mock regret. "Pity. Acheson's a lucky chap."

"So are you. You have Emmeline. There's no one better. Which is why I'm happy I've run into you. There's something I wanted to talk to you about."

Gregory raised an eyebrow. "Oh, yes?"

"Yes. It's about Emmeline. And you."

"I see. And what would that be, exactly?" He crossed his arms over his chest.

"No, don't look at me like that. You know that I've always been one hundred percent in your corner—me and Helen, that is. We were absolutely over the moon when Emmeline told us that she had finally accepted your proposal. It was about bloody time. However, Helen and I are a bit concerned because the two of you have yet to set a date and Emmeline has been keeping you at arms-length ever since you got back from Torquay."

Her green eyes narrowed as she studied his face. "Something happened there. I can tell, but Emmeline won't talk about it. No—" She put up a hand to prevent him from protesting. "—I'm not going to pry. Whatever happened, it is for the two of you to sort out on your own. You don't need any outside interference. But I will say this, Emmeline is making herself scarce because she feels that you are keeping a secret. Whatever it is, it can't be that bad. The two of you love each other. That's what counts. God, haven't you fought hard enough to find your way back to one another? It's not worth throwing all that away. You know how our little Emmeline feels about lies and secrets. She won't stop until she ferrets out the truth. It's an occupational hazard with her. So I'm begging you, just tell her whatever *it* is. It will make things much simpler all the way around, and then Helen and I can start planning your wedding. We have some smashing ideas."

Gregory bent down and kissed Maggie's cheek tenderly. "Thanks for being such a good friend to Emmy and me. What would we do without you? You can tell Helen from me that everything will be all right. I promise. In fact, I was on my way to see Emmy."

Maggie clasped her hands together. "Right. That's all settled then. I just left Emmeline, and she's in a good mood." She glanced at her watch. "And now that I've done my good deed for the day, I must dash because I have to meet with Max Sanborn about his charity auction."

Gregory's ears perked up. "Oh, yes?"

"Yes. My firm has signed a multiyear contract to oversee public relations for Sanborn Enterprises. The auction is my first big assignment."

"I see." Gregory's brow furrowed as he mulled over this news.

"Something wrong?"

"Wrong? No. No, not at all. Congratulations on the contract," he replied hastily. "That's terrific news."

"Thanks. Now, I must go. I don't want to make a bad impression by being late to my first meeting."

"That wouldn't do at all." He reached out and pressed the button to call the lift, which came almost immediately.

"Good luck." He gave Maggie a little wave as the doors slid closed. His smile faded as he tried to ignore the growing sense of unease in the pit of his stomach.

CHAPTER 9

Emmeline didn't hear him knock, so Gregory stood in the doorway for a minute simply watching her tapping away at her keyboard. A smile played about his lips. She was always chasing the next big story. He admired her drive and sense of responsibility and fair play. Her dedication to uncovering the truth and seeking justice for those who couldn't fight for themselves was ingrained in her very being. From what Helen had told him, Emmeline had inherited these qualities from her parents. However, she had excelled far beyond what they had accomplished. Perhaps, it was because she had lost them at such a young age and felt she had to prove something to the world. Meanwhile, God help the unsuspecting sole who lied to her. Emmeline's temper could be lethal. As he was about to find out.

She stopped typing and leaned back in her chair, looking up at the ceiling for inspiration. He cleared his throat.

She spun round. "Gregory, I didn't know you were there. You should have said something."

He crossed the room and bent down to brush a soft kiss against her lips. "Hello, darling. I didn't want to break your concentration. You looked as if you were in the midst of a masterpiece."

Emmeline leaned against him for a moment. "Hardly a masterpiece, but it's an important story on looted Nazi art."

Gregory pressed a kiss to the top of her head and came around the desk. He lowered his elegant frame into the chair opposite her. "Very commendable. Speaking of important, there's something I need to discuss with you."

Emmeline's body stiffened. She was suddenly wary. "Oh, yes?" Her dark eyes roamed over every well-known curve and angle of his handsome face, but she couldn't read his expression. She folded her hands in front of her on the desk and sat expectantly. "I'm listening." There was a slight tremor in her voice.

Gregory held her gaze in silence for an interminable moment. He swallowed hard. "The thing is…There's something I must tell you about my past."

Emmeline held her breath. *Oh, God, not another wife, please.*

He leaned forward and rested his elbows on her desk. "You see, darling, I'm not the man you think I am. I'm not Gregory Longdon. I mean I am, but that was not the name I was born with."

She let out a long, slow breath. Some of the tension in her body uncoiled. "I know," she whispered.

His eyebrows shot up. "What do you mean you know? Nigel swore he wouldn't say anything to you."

Emmeline's brows knit together in confusion. "Nigel has refused to tell me anything, no matter how much I bullied him. Although I *knew* he was hiding something. Now, it is confirmed that my suspicions were correct." She smiled with satisfaction.

"If Nigel didn't tell you, how did you find out?" It was his turn to be baffled.

"You have your beloved Veronica Cabot to thank for that." That woman's name made the bile rise in her throat. Her ghost was still shadowing them. Would they never be free of her?

"Ronnie? What does she have to do with any of this?"

Emmeline sighed as she recalled that bus journey she took from Torquay to the tiny village of Wickersham. It seemed like another lifetime, but it had only been three months ago. "In one of her more spiteful moments, she said that I would learn the truth about you if I went to Wickersham. Of course, what she wanted me to discover was that the two of you had been married in the village church. However, I found out something that day that I don't think that she even knew. Otherwise, she wouldn't have hesitated to turn it to her advantage." Emmeline paused and held his gaze. "The words are emblazoned on my mind." She took a deep breath. "You probably don't remember, but in the churchyard there is a weather-beaten gray stone that marks the grave of a two-year old boy.

"'*Gregory James Anthony Longdon,*
December 21, 1967-March 3, 1970,
In loving memory of a beloved son taken too soon'

"Same date of birth. It *is* your date of birth?"

Gregory nodded.

"Well, at least that bit is the truth. So the question now is, *who* are you?"

Gregory reached out and picked up one of her small hands and brought it to his lips. "Emmy, my real name is Toby Crenshaw. But I haven't been Toby Crenshaw since I was eighteen."

"Toby Crenshaw? That's what Nigel called you when we first met him in Torquay. You *said* that he had been mistaken. You *said* that you didn't know him." She withdrew her hand from his grasp and crossed her arms over her chest. "Go on. I'm listening."

He recognized that stubborn look. Her chin jutted in the air, and there was an edge of irritation in her tone.

"Yes, well...I was taken by surprise," he said. "I hadn't expected to see Nigel in Torquay."

"That was obvious. But you still haven't explained why you've been living under an assumed name for twenty-five years."

"I was coming to that, darling. You know, impatience is *not* an endearing attribute."

Emmeline's smile did not touch her eyes, which were as dark as pitch. "Indeed? I'll keep that in mind, but we are not here to dissect my character flaws. I'm waiting for an answer. And so help me, you'd better give me one, or I'll throttle you."

He threw his head back and laughed. How he loved this woman. "Yes, darling. Nigel—and Brian, for that matter—knows me because we grew up together. They're my cousins. My mother was Max Sanborn's sister."

Emmeline's jaw dropped. Whatever she had been expecting, it certainly was not this. "That means—" Her gaze flickered roamed around her office. "You're a Sanborn. But I don't understand. Why the big charade? Why turn your back on your family?"

"*They* turned their back on *me*. At least Max did. He always hated me because I reminded him of my father, who ran out on Mum and me when I was three. Mum told me that the Sanborns never approved of my father, and they cut her off when she married him. When she came to Max with me in tow, he never missed an opportunity to pour salt into the wound and say 'I told you so.' Her own bloody family. Can you imagine? Mum was always so gentle and kind." There was a catch in his voice. A faint smile curled around his lips as he was swept up in his memories for a moment. Then a dark shadow fell across his face. "It's hard to believe she was related to Max."

"Oh, Gregory, I'm sorry. So very sorry for you." Emmeline reached out and caressed his cheek. He pressed a kiss against her palm. "I suppose I had better start calling you Toby. It'll take some getting used to, though."

"No, Emmy," he snapped. "The name's Gregory Longdon. The boy who was Toby Crenshaw died a long time ago. Aunt Mireille and Nigel and Brian did their best to console me after Mum died, but I couldn't stand it anymore. I had to get away from Max and his relentless badgering and criticism."

"But you were only a boy of seventeen," she said softly. "You must have been terribly frightened, *and lonely*." After hearing his story, she now could understand—mind you, only a little bit—why he would turn to someone like Veronica Cabot. A thought suddenly struck her. "Is that why you became a jewel thief? To support yourself?"

"Oh, Emmy. You and Oliver have one-track minds. How many times must I tell you? I. Am. Not. A. Thief."

"Ha—"

He cut her off before she could come up with a pithy response. "Besides, I have some other news I want to share with you."

She sucked in her breath. "Not another secret past?"

"No. To hasten our nuptials, I have heeded the hints—which you have dropped like boulders in recent weeks, I might point out—and gotten a job."

"A job?" She cocked her head to one side and gave him a penetrating look. "What kind of a job?"

"Symington's has hired me as their chief insurance investigator. I started on Monday. My first assignment is Uncle Max's charity auction."

"*What*? That's crazy. I don't believe it."

He picked up her phone. "Would you like to call my employer for verification?"

"Put that down. Why would they hire *you* of all people?"

"Darling, are you disparaging my capabilities?"

"No, but…what qualifications do you have? Don't they know about you?"

"Know what?"

"That you're a thief."

Gregory tilted his head back and shook it at the ceiling as if seeking divine intervention. "Must I tell you again?" He looked at her once more. "I am not a thief. I was hired because of the unique expertise I possess."

"Ha. I'll bet. Well, I suppose it's better to have the devil you know in your corner so that you can keep an eye on him."

"That is *not* a very flattering observation, Emmy."

"Nevertheless, it's the truth. But you must ask Symington's to give you another assignment."

"Why?" he asked, perplexed.

"After what you've just told me about Max Sanborn, he won't want you anywhere near his auction."

"He has very little choice in the matter. He insisted that Symington's assign their top man. He didn't want to deal with 'underlings.' The auction is on Monday. It's far too late now to find another insurer. He'll just have to lump it."

"From what I've seen of Max Sanborn, he won't take kindly to being backed into a corner. He'll kill you."

"Not unless I make the first move."

"What are you saying?"

"Nothing, Emmy. Nothing at all."

The hatred etched on his features sent a frisson down her spine.

CHAPTER 10

Superintendent Burnell stroked his beard meditatively as he stared out his office window. Only eleven hours to go before the charity auction. Burnell blew out his cheeks in a long, unhappy sigh. It had been a hectic, and particularly trying, weekend as they scrambled to make all the arrangements. Sanborn had been even more cantankerous than usual because Symington's told him—very politely, but quite firmly—that if he wanted the company to continue to insure his collection, then he would have to come to terms with Longdon being its representative. Officials underscored the fact that Sanborn had *demanded* that their top man be put in charge. They said that Longdon was the best of the best. Symington's wanted to assure Mr. Sanborn that Longdon had been thoroughly vetted. In fact, he had been recommended by someone high up in the government, in a secure department. Sanborn had not been mollified, but he had little recourse. So Longdon remained, much to Burnell's chagrin.

Something did not feel right, but it had nothing to do with the auction. The superintendent was quite sure that Longdon wouldn't be foolish enough to attempt anything—at least he hoped not. The auction had garnered far too much high-profile publicity, thanks to Ms. Roth and her firm. No, what bothered Burnell was Longdon's employment at Symington's. Why? That was the question that kept rattling around his brain. And who was the person "high up" in the government who had put in a good word for him?

The superintendent had done a bit of digging, but he couldn't discover the name of Longdon's mysterious benefactor. However, in a conversation only moments ago, one of his contacts had let slip that the benefactor was someone at MI5. When Burnell pressed for more information, his contact pleaded ignorance and abruptly ended the call. This unexpected tidbit left the superintendent with a great deal of unsettling food for thought. *MI5? What the devil is Longdon mixed up in?* he asked himself.

Burnell swung his chair around and snatched up his telephone again. He punched in a number he had come to know quite well in recent months. He waited a few seconds and then a pleasant male voice came on the line, "Acheson."

"Mr. Acheson, it's Superintendent Oliver Burnell."

"Hello, Superintendent. From the little I've seen of my wife this weekend, I thought you and Sergeant Finch would be knee-deep in the preparations for Max Sanborn's auction to the exclusion of all else."

"We are. Between you and me, I'm counting the minutes until the blasted thing is over. It's been quite…difficult."

Philip laughed. "That's putting it diplomatically. But you didn't ring me to discuss the auction. So what can I do for you?"

Burnell cleared his throat. "I need your assistance with a rather delicate matter…involving Longdon."

Philip's ears pricked up at the tone in the superintendent's voice. "Oh, Lord. What's he done now?"

Burnell scratched his head. "That's thing, you see. I'm not sure that he *has* done anything, yet. But something just doesn't smell right. I'd rather not discuss it over the phone. I'd like this to be an unofficial conversation, sir. Do you think you could meet me in St. James's, in let's say in an hour?"

Burnell heard paper ruffling and assumed Acheson was flipping through his diary. "Yes, that would be fine. I'll have Pamela clear my schedule for the rest of the morning. I'll see you by the duck island in an hour."

☙❧☙

Philip arrived first. A light wind dandled the graceful tresses of the willow trees surrounding the man-made lake that divided St. James's Park into two halves. The sun was being swallowed up by the clouds surreptitiously stealing across the sky. *Ah, well*, he thought. London's reprieve from the rain had been short-lived. He shrugged his shoulders in resignation and watched a mother and her toddler toss bits of bread and other sundry morsels into the lake. In an instant, they were surrounded by a throng of ducks and various other birds which had made the park their home. He smiled as the image of his boys came to mind. If they were here, they would be scaring the life out of these poor feathered creatures by chasing them all over the footpaths.

Philip felt a gentle tap on his shoulder and turned to find himself staring into Superintendent Burnell's shrewd blue eyes. "Ah, Superintendent, there you are. Good to see you."

After the two men shook hands, Burnell said, "It would be best if we walked, Mr. Acheson."

"Of course. However, as we've been thrown together quite a lot in recent months, I think it's high time that you called me Philip."

A faint smile touched Burnell's lips. "As you wish, sir. Philip."

"There, that's better. Now, let's take that stroll."

As always, there were tourists and locals alike wandering along the footpaths. The two men walked in silence, as they casually surveyed their surroundings until they were satisfied that they had not attracted any unwelcome company. Burnell guided them to the bridge midway down the lake that afforded a view of Buckingham Palace to their left and the Horse Guards Parade to their right. He stopped and leaned his forearms on the railing, his gaze focused on a fountain that had suddenly sprung to life. Philip leaned his back against the railing and faced the palace.

Burnell cleared his throat. "I'm not sure where to begin."

Philip crossed his arms over his chest. "When you rang, you said that you were concerned about Longdon. Whenever he's involved, it's always a worrisome matter."

"Yes. Perhaps your wife has told you that Longdon has been hired by Symington's as their chief insurance investigator and his first assignment is the auction."

"W—What?" Philip spluttered. "That's ludicrous."

"I thought Ms. Roth would have told you that part at least."

"Longdon is a sore subject between my wife and me. She's one of his biggest champions, while I am far from enamored of the bloke. I know that you can understand." The superintendent nodded his head sympathetically. "Therefore, we try to avoid discussing Longdon as much as possible. Consequently, Maggie did not tell me that he was working at Symington's and coordinating the auction for them."

Burnell straightened up and looked directly at Philip. "Forgive me. It was not my intention to cause any marital strife between you and your wife."

Philip shook his head and laughed. "Believe me, Superintendent, it would take a great deal more to come between Maggie and me. So have no fears on that score."

"Well, that's a relief. Now, you and I, and anyone who upholds the law, would never hire Longdon when confronted with evidence of, shall we say, his rather dubious career thus far."

"You're bloody right about that."

"Then why would someone at MI5 give Longdon a glowing reference? A reference, which reading between lines, I gather was more of a direct order to hire him."

"How? *Why*—" Philip stared at the superintendent in confusion.

"So you don't know anything about this?" Burnell probed gently.

"I'm as much in the dark as you are. But as soon as I get back to the office, I will start making some discreet inquiries to get to the bottom of it."

"Thank you. I'd appreciate your assistance. I've hit a brick wall."

"Don't mention it. I can't even begin to fathom what…" Philip shook his blond head and allowed the sentence to trail off.

"Yes, well," Burnell murmured. "There's just one other thing that I wanted to discuss with you."

Philip exhaled deeply and rolled his eyes. "Go ahead. I don't think that you can shock me anymore today, Superintendent."

"I wouldn't be too sure about that," Burnell said *sotto voce.* Then louder he replied, "It's a bit convoluted, but apparently Longdon is not Gregory Longdon."

One of Philip's eyebrows arched upward. "That's a rather cryptic statement."

"In only the past few days, it has come to light that he ran away from home at seventeen and assumed the name Gregory Longdon a year later. The name he was born with was Toby Crenshaw."

"I grant you it is a little unusual, but lots of people change their names."

"True. True," the superintendent concurred. "However, it appears said Toby Crenshaw is the nephew of Max Sanborn."

Philip opened his mouth, and his lips moved, but no words came out at first. Then he found his voice. "Bloody hell. This gets stranger by the minute."

CHAPTER 11

Emmeline walked into the newsroom to speak to one of the reporters about some edits she had made to his copy. This was her last task before she took the lift up to Max's sprawling penthouse on the sixty-fifth floor of the building. She knew she wouldn't have enough time to run home and change for the auction, so she had brought her black velvet cocktail dress with her and had changed in her office.

She earned a few whistles as she crossed the newsroom to the political correspondent's desk. "All right. All right. I thank you, but get back to work. Paul, I just wanted to discuss a couple of points in your article."

"Of course, Emmeline. Let's see." He reached out, took the copy from her, and listened to her comments. He nodded his head. "Right. I'll make those revisions and file the copy."

"Thanks, Paul. You did a brilliant job." She glanced at her watch. "Now, I must get upstairs for the festivities. Otherwise, Maggie will murder me. Good night, chaps," she called out as she hurried toward the door, the heels of her black suede pumps clicking loudly.

The guests had already started arriving by the time Emmeline was shown into Max's living room, which afforded a 360-degree view of London. She accepted a flute of champagne from a passing waiter and waved to several of her colleagues. Maggie had done a splendid job. The auction was going to be *the* black-tie affair of the year. The press had come in force. Emmeline saw reporters from *The Times*, *The Tele-*

graph, The New York Times, Le Monde, Corriere della Sera, Der Spiegel, a host of other papers and of course all the art magazines. The broadcast news media was fully represented as well.

"Emmeline, there you are. I was getting worried you weren't going to make it after all." Maggie gave her best friend a hurried peck on the cheek.

"Oh, Maggie, I'm sorry. I had a last-minute issue I had to deal with, but I wouldn't have missed your big moment for the world." She gave her friend's arm a reassuring squeeze. "Not only am I here for moral support, but I'm covering the story for *The Clarion.* From the looks of things thus far, I think the auction is going to be a smashing success."

"Oh, I hope so." Maggie's gaze roamed around room anxiously.

"Don't worry so much. You've thought of everything. What could possibly go wrong?"

"Emmy's right. You've done a marvelous job. Uncle Max has nothing to complain about. Just relax." Gregory had suddenly materialized behind them, looking resplendent in his tuxedo. "Hello, darling." He bent down to kiss Emmeline's cheek and slipped his arm around her waist. "I must say I will be the envy of every man in the room tonight."

Emmeline's cheeks flushed a becoming shade of pink as she leaned into him. "You're just biased."

"Nonsense, darling. You are the loveliest woman in the room." He pressed a kiss against her dark curls. "One of the *two* loveliest women in the room." He corrected himself as he winked at Maggie.

Maggie's silvery laughter bubbled up from her throat. "I think you should keep this one very close, Emmeline. Otherwise, an unscrupulous woman is liable to get her claws into him."

The smile faded from Emmeline's lips as the image of Veronica Cabot floated before her eyes. *She's dead,* her brain screamed. *Put the past behind you.*

Gregory saw the shadow fall across her face and guessed where her mind had drifted. He had been such a bloody fool.

"Yes, well, I'll try to heed your advice," Emmeline mumbled as she fingered the strand of pearls around her throat. Her gaze slid sideways, but she didn't look at him directly. However, Gregory was glad to see that his engagement ring was still firmly in place on her left hand. That was something. He'd do everything in his power to erase the memory of Ronnie from her mind.

As they had been speaking, the living room had filled up with the *crème de la crème* of society, all with deep pockets. Businessmen—both foreign and domestic—mingled with real estate magnates, MPs, members of the aristocracy, foreign diplomats, and several directors of the Sanborn Enterprises' board. A handful of actors had also been invited to add a dash of glamor.

The air of excited anticipation was infectious, and the buzz of conversation rose accordingly as more guests arrived.

Emmeline and Maggie were laughing at something Gregory had just said when Nigel appeared at his elbow. He inclined his head to the trio. "Ladies, Tob—Gregory. You've done a superb job, Maggie. I think we're going to raise a lot of money tonight and Sanborn is going to get a lot of positive publicity thanks to you."

Maggie nodded at him. "Thank you, Nigel. It's all in a day's work."

"I have no doubts that the evening will be an unqualified success. How can it not with Maggie overseeing the details?" Emmeline said proudly.

"Oh, Emmeline. You make it sound as if I arranged the event single-handedly. There was a whole team involved, including your devastatingly attractive fiancé, as well as Superintendent Burnell and Sergeant Finch to name but a few."

"Thank you, Maggie. Some people—" Gregory turned his nose up in the air and sniffed. "—appear to have selective memories."

"I have not forgotten the part you have played, *darling*, but I still have lingering questions about your employment at Symington's."

"Do you, Emmy?" he asked innocently.

"Yes." She swung round. "As for you, Nigel—"

"You're for it, mate," Gregory told his cousin. "I'd do a runner, if I were in your place."

Emmeline ignored this jibe. "As for you, Nigel, you have *a lot* of explaining to do."

"Really? Oh, look, there's Brian over there. I must go and speak to him about something. I'll see you all later."

"Coward," Emmeline said to his retreating back. He turned and gave her a sheepish grin, before shrugging his shoulders. Then he threaded his way through the crowd, stopping from time to time to speak to someone or shake a hand.

"Evasiveness appears to be a family trait." Emmeline poked Gregory in the ribs.

"I'll have you know that hurt, Emmy, my love."

"Hmph. You *will* answer my questions. You only have a reprieve for tonight. So consider yourself warned."

"You see, Maggie, we're not even married, and she's already a tyrant. You must save me."

Emmeline made a moue at him, and Maggie laughed.

"Don't encourage him," Emmeline said.

Maggie's mobile started ringing in her silk clutch. She quickly pulled it out and looked at the number. "Sorry," she mouthed. "It's Janet." She pressed a finger to her ear. "Yes, Janet. Are the twins all right? What about Mr. Acheson? I'm sorry I can't hear you."

She covered the phone and scanned the room for a quiet corner so that she could talk to her nanny. Her brow crinkled in concern.

Gregory said, "Why don't you go into Max's study? You'll be able to speak to Janet without all this noise." His gesture encompassed the whole room.

"Do you think it would be all right? I wouldn't want to upset Mr. Sanborn."

"Nonsense. Go on." He gave her a little shove. "Find out what Janet wants."

They watched her go. "I hope nothing is wrong with the boys."

"I'm sure everything's fine. No need to conjure up trouble where there is none, Emmy."

"Yes, but Janet wouldn't ring Maggie unless something—"

"*Darling.*" He gave her a stern look.

"You're right. I—"

"Excuse me, Mr. Longdon. I'm terribly sorry to interrupt," the auctioneer from Christie's was murmuring apologetically. "There's something that we need to consult you about."

"Of course." Then, to Emmeline, he said, "This will only take a few minutes." He blew her a kiss.

"Take your time. I'll be all right."

Her eyes followed him as he moved with masculine grace, skirting around the rows of chairs that had been set up for the auction and followed the auctioneer down the corridor. He had one hand in his pocket, and his head was tilted to one side to listen to something that the Christie's man was saying.

She was munching on an *hors d'oeuvre* when she spotted Superintendent Burnell and Sergeant Finch huddled together in conversation by the wall of windows that overlooked Tower Hill and Tower Bridge. Their eyes constantly roved about the room, keeping a professional watch for anything the least bit suspicious. Emmeline tried waving to catch their attention, but they weren't looking in her direction. She circled the perimeter of the room until she reached their side.

"I know you're both on duty, but I just wanted to say hello." Her smile grew broader when she saw that they were happy to see her.

Burnell extended his hand to clasp her smaller one. "Miss Kirby, what a pleasant surprise. I must say that the evening has suddenly perked up. We were wondering whether we would be seeing you."

Finch also shook her hand. "Good evening. It's very nice to see you, Miss Kirby."

"It's lovely to see you both. I wouldn't have missed this auction for the world. I'm covering it for *The Clarion*, but that's merely an excuse. I really came to provide moral support for Maggie and Gregory." At the look they exchanged at the mention of her fiancé, she quickly added, "And of course, your hard work."

"Yes, well," Burnell mumbled as he spied Gregory talking to Nigel. He tried to push his suspicions about Longdon's sudden employment at Symington's out of his mind by changing the subject. "From what I hear through the grapevine, you're giving the other papers a run for their money since you took over the reins as editorial director at *The Clarion*."

Emmeline blushed. "That's very kind of you, Superintendent. I had a few ideas when I took on the job and made some changes here and there...and well, they seem to be working out as I had envisioned."

"Oh, come now, the newspaper business is no place for modesty. I don't say to rest on your laurels, but you're entitled to toot your own horn a bit."

"Hear, hear," chimed in Finch. "Superintendent Burnell is quite right."

She laughed. "That seems totally unnecessary when I have two such distinguished gentlemen in my corner."

The two detectives were completely disarmed by this remark. They shifted on their feet, looking slightly embarrassed. Burnell coughed. "Thank you, Miss Kirby."

"Now, I'd like to ask you something. I wouldn't be so presumptuous as to call you by your Christian names—that would be overstepping professional boundaries on my part—but do you think you both could call me Emmeline. Miss Kirby makes me sound rather stuffy, and I'm not. After all, it's not as if we're strangers. We've worked together before so to speak." Her dark gaze eagerly searched each man's face.

"It would be an honor, Emmeline," Burnell said.

"Yes, Emmeline," Finch echoed.

"However," the superintendent cautioned, "we will do so only when we are alone together like this. In front of others, we will have to adopt a more formal manner."

"Of course, Superintendent, I understand perfectly," she replied with a smile.

"Good. Now then, Emmeline, aside from this wretched auction, what stories can we expect to see in *The Clarion*?"

"As you surmised, tonight's event is a one-off so to speak. I'm currently working on a series about looted Nazi art. You may have seen the first article. It appeared in yesterday's paper."

"I did indeed. I found it extremely insightful. There were some facts that you revealed of which I was totally unaware. Did you read it, Finch?"

"I did, sir. I agree with Superintendent Burnell. But then again, you are always very meticulous when researching your articles, Miss Kir—Emmeline. It's a shame that there aren't more journalists like you."

"Thank you, Sergeant Finch, but I assure you there are far more of us who are honest and strive to present both sides than there are those who covet titillating headlines regardless of whether the story is based on facts."

"Yes, of course. Forgive me. I didn't mean to malign an entire industry, simply because of a few rotten apples."

"There's nothing to forgive. I didn't take any offense, believe me," she said earnestly. "I just wanted to make you appreciate the hard work that the majority of us put in every day."

"Yes, I do see that. I'm glad that we can discuss things frankly. I'm certain this new series of yours on looted Nazi art will attract a great deal of attention."

"I do hope so, Sergeant. There are so many pieces that have yet to be returned to their rightful owners or their descendants. They deserve justice. If my series makes even a small contribution toward seeing that this is accomplished, it will have been worth it—"

"Damn and blast," Burnell cursed under his breath.

Emmeline and Finch were startled by this unexpected outburst. "What is it, sir?"

Burnell jerked is head over his right shoulder. "Look who's here." He didn't have time for more. "Ah, Assistant Commissioner Fenton, a pleasure to see you this evening. Of course, you needn't have come. There have been no problems whatsoever."

"Yes, I know. I was just speaking with Max. It appears that

you and Finch have things well in hand. Good show," Fenton replied grudgingly. From the expression on his face, he had been hoping that the two detectives would cock things up so that he could file a report against them.

Burnell hid a smile because he could read the thoughts passing through his superior's mind. "Sir, may I introduce Emmeline Kirby, the editorial director of *The Clarion*?"

"How do you do, Assistant Commissioner Fenton? I have heard so much about you."

Fenton took the hand she proffered and shook it perfunctorily. He really had no use for the press, unless it presented him in a good light. "Have you, Miss Kirby? Nothing bad, I hope."

"Oh, no. Certainly not. Superintendent Burnell and Sergeant Finch are always singing your praises." The two detectives exchanged looks over her head. "There isn't a man they admire more, I can assure you."

Burnell started coughing, and Finch had to slap him on the back, hard. "All right, sir?"

"Yes, fine, Finch," was Burnell's strangled reply. "Just slight a tickle in my throat."

"Is what Miss Kirby says true, Burnell?" Fenton asked.

The superintendent had recovered his equilibrium. "Oh, yes, sir. How could you doubt it?" He hoped he sounded sincere.

Fenton squared his shoulders, and a faint smile touched his lips. "Well, all I can say is that it's nice to have the support of one's subordinates." He turned to Emmeline and shook her hand again. "Pleasure meeting you, Miss Kirby. I'm afraid I must leave you now, I see my wife signaling furiously. We're here as Max's guests tonight, but her Uncle Patrick is one of Sanborn's directors, you know. Good night. Burnell, Finch, keep up the good work."

"Yes, sir," the two detectives said in unison. They were glad to see the back of him.

Emmeline watched as Fenton rejoined his wife and an older gentleman with snowy white hair who was leaning on a cane. "What a pompous ass. I despise men like that."

Burnell and Finch were stunned, and then the three of them burst out laughing.

When Emmeline could speak again, she said, "I was only speaking the truth, wasn't I?"

"Indeed, you were, Emmeline," Burnell replied, a twinkle still in his eye.

"Emmeline? You are becoming rather familiar with my ravishing fiancée, aren't you, Oliver? Is there something I should know about?"

The smile vanished from Burnell's lips. "Oh, it's you, Longdon."

"As you see, Oliver. Here I am in the flesh. Finch." He nodded at the sergeant. "The three of you looked very cozy a moment ago, and I felt terribly left out."

"We were just sharing a joke." Emmeline started giggling again.

"At Fenton's expense," Burnell said.

"Indeed? Carry on then. That man needs taking down a peg or two. But that still does not explain this Emmeline business."

"I simply asked Superintendent Burnell and Sergeant Finch to call me Emmeline. Miss Kirby makes me sound like a stern schoolmistress."

"And you are far from that, my darling." Gregory lifted her hand to his lips and brushed it with a kiss. Then he flashed a smile at the two detectives.

Burnell cleared his throat and adopted a serious tone. "Everything proceeding according to plan, Longdon?"

"Like clockwork, Oliver. Nothing could go wrong. In fact—ah yes, bang on time. There's the auctioneer."

They followed his gaze as the Christie's man took his place behind a rostrum. Gregory nodded to him as he and Emmeline made their way around the rows of chairs in the center of the room. They found a spot off to the side from which to get a good view of the items being auctioned. Burnell and Finch remained in the back where they could keep watch over the entire room.

"Ladies and gentlemen, if you can all please take your seats so that we can begin. Thank you all for coming tonight to support this wonderful endeavor that Mr. Sanborn has decided to finance. Perhaps in the not too distant future, a cure for cancer will be at our fingertips because Max Sanborn has chosen to build a new research institute." He was interrupted by a hearty round of applause, which were accompanied by several shouts of "Hear, hear."

Max smiled and raised his hands to quiet down the audience. For all the world, he appeared to be humbled and embarrassed by the praise—that was unless one knew him. And Gregory knew his uncle intimately. Max Sanborn was ruthless. Every move he made was calculated to his advantage alone.

"Before we begin," the auctioneer was saying, "it is my pleasure to introduce the man himself, Max Sanborn."

Another burst of applause followed. "Please, ladies and gentlemen, you're embarrassing me," Max asserted. "All of this is quite unnecessary. I like beautiful things, and I just feel blessed that I'm in a position to be able to help. That's what this is all about. Man helping his fellow man."

"That's pouring it on rather thick," Gregory whispered out of the corner his mouth to Emmeline. "He's never cared for anyone but himself." She tucked her hand through the crook of his arm and leaned into him. His face softened and she felt the returning pressure of his touch.

"Now, the last thing I would like to ask you," Max went on, "is to please bid generously. It's for a worthy cause." And with that, the auction began with enthusiasm.

Two studies by Degas, a sixteenth century English silver salt-cellar, a painted Sevres plaque circa 1765 and a small English sword from 1757 with an elaborate gold and silver hilt encrusted with rubies and emeralds had been sold by the time Maggie emerged from Max's study.

Gregory's attention was still captivated by the sword, but Emmeline's brow puckered in concern. She elbowed him in the ribs.

"What is it, darling?"

"First of all, your mouth is open. I suggest you shut it before you start drooling. Second, look." She gestured with her chin toward Maggie, who was walking stiffly toward them as if her legs would buckle under her at any moment. Her face was ashen.

"I hope nothing's happened to the boys or Philip," Emmeline said.

When Maggie was only a few steps away, Emmeline quietly went over and put her arm around her friend. Gregory supported her on the other side.

"What's wrong?" Emmeline whispered. "Are the boys all right?"

Maggie nodded mutely as she stared fixedly at Max Sanborn. Emmeline and Gregory exchanged worried looks behind her back. "Is it Philip? Has something happened to Philip?"

Maggie shook her head.

"Then what's the matter? What's happened? Please tell me." Emmeline could hear the desperation in her own voice.

Suddenly Maggie shrugged off their grasp and pushed her away to the front. "Thief," she yelled at Max.

The auctioneer froze. Several sharp intakes of breath reverberated through the audience. "Thief," Maggie screamed again, tears beginning to stream down her cheeks. "You're nothing but a vulture, preying on the bodies of the dead."

CHAPTER 12

A stunned hush fell over the room, and all eyes turned in their direction. Then a ripple of nervous whispering slowly spread across the audience. Emmeline and Gregory rushed to Maggie's side. Burnell and Finch were elbowing their way toward them as were Brian and Nigel from the opposite end of the room.

"Can someone get this hysterical woman out of here?" Max asked, annoyance clearly etched on his features.

"You're not going to keep me silent, Max Sanborn," Maggie vowed, her voice trembling with a mixture of rage and agony. "The world is going to know the kind of man you are."

"Maggie, what's all this about? Please tell me," Emmeline implored. "We can help you."

Maggie turned a tear-stained face toward her. "Emmeline," it was a hoarse whisper, "that man has Great Aunt Sarah's Constable. The one the Nazis stole. It's hanging bold as brass in his study."

Emmeline blinked, and her back visibly stiffened. "Are you sure?"

"Yes. Don't you—don't you *believe* me?" She tried to choke back a sob.

Emmeline smoothed a small hand over her friend's red-gold hair. "Shh," she murmured soothingly. "Of course, I believe you. We all believe you." Gregory nodded. She could see that he was doing his best not to give vent to his anger.

"We can't let him get away with this."

"No, Maggie, we can't—and we *won't*." In that instant,

Emmeline's dark gaze locked on Max Sanborn. "I promise you I won't let this go."

Sanborn recognized her from their ugly encounter in the corridor the other day. His eyes narrowed as they shifted between Emmeline and Maggie, tying the two of them together in his mind. He would make them pay for ruining his evening in the spotlight. By God, he would make them pay.

෴

"This is a very serious accusation, Mr. Sanborn," one of the members of the press called out. "Do you have anything to say?"

Sanborn laughed. "You must be joking. Obviously, this woman is delusional."

"So you categorically refute the allegation?"

"Of course, I refute it. Although, I don't have to justify anything to you or anyone else."

"A court of law will make you answer," Maggie shouted.

"Finch, get Ms. Roth out of here, *now*," Burnell ordered quietly. "See that she gets home safely."

"Yes, sir." Then to Maggie, he said gently, "Won't you come with me please, Ms. Roth?"

Maggie didn't budge. Finch turned to his superior and raised an eyebrow.

"Please, Maggie, listen to Sergeant Finch," Emmeline intervened. "You'll only make things worse if you stay. My colleagues are waiting to pepper you with questions that are best not asked just at the moment. The best thing that you can do is to go home to the boys and Philip. I promise I will keep you informed about whatever happens. I'll give you a ring in the morning, and I'll pop over some time tomorrow."

"Me too," Gregory added, as he touched Maggie's arm lightly. He jerked his head in the direction of the door. "Now, go on."

A weary sigh shook Maggie's body. "All right. I'll go."

Finch smiled and took her by the elbow. He could feel that she was still trembling as they started to weave their way through the crowd. "That's it, Ms. Roth. You just stick with me, and we'll get you home with the least amount of fuss. All right?"

Maggie nodded and gave him a weak smile.

Emmeline relaxed slightly once she was sure Maggie and Finch were gone. "Right," she said to no one in particular.

"Darling, aren't you going with Maggie?" Gregory queried.

She cast a glance over the crowd. Everyone was still attempting to make sense about what had occurred. She turned back to Gregory. "No, Maggie's in safe hands. They don't need me hanging about. Finch wouldn't allow any harm to come to her. So no one need worry on that point. Well, good night." She reached up, gave him a hasty peck on the cheek, and started to walk away.

"Wait a minute, Emmy." He grabbed her arm. "Where are you going?"

"I'm going to join my colleagues over there to see whether they've been able to get anything out of Max Sanborn and then I'm going down to my office?"

"Why?"

"*Why?* Didn't you see what happened here? I've got work to do. I have to change the front page of tomorrow's *Clarion*."

"Do you think that's wise?"

Her dark eyes flashed. "Just because you're a member of the family, I'm *not* going to hush up this story."

"Darling, that's rather unfair. You know me better than that."

"Do I?" she snapped, her nerves raw from the night's revelations. "What I *know* is that you're still hiding something and I don't like it."

"Emmy—"

"No." She raised a small hand in the air to forestall any further argument.

Gregory sighed and stood aside so that she could pass. He silently cursed his uncle. After all the years that had passed, nothing had changed. Nothing. Max was still destroying other people's lives. *The world would be a far better place if Max Sanborn were not in it*, he thought.

eɔeɔ

"Mr. Sanborn, I've contacted the Yard's Arts and Antiques squad. I think that they would be best suited to investigate Ms. Roth's accusations," Burnell said.

By this time, Finch had returned and had his notebook open, pen poised.

"In the interim, I'm afraid we will have to confiscate the Constable until—"

"You *what*?" Sanborn bellowed. He poked the superintendent's chest with his finger. "Who do you think you are? Over my dead body will you get your filthy paws on my painting, or anything else, for that matter. Do I make myself clear?" He shook his head. "All this trouble because some deranged female craved attention. I'd like to know what she was doing in my study in the first place. You should arrest her for trespassing."

Burnell's hands curled into tight fists at his sides. "Sir," he replied through clenched teeth, "apparently Ms. Roth was given permission to go into your study."

"Permission? Who gave her permission? It certainly wasn't by me."

Burnell coughed. "I believe Mr. Longdon told her she could go in there to ring her nanny."

"Toby?" Sanborn's hard gaze sought Gregory out across the room. Gregory looked up suddenly, as if sensing he was the subject of their conversation.

"Yes, sir," the superintendent replied, trying to regain Sanborn's attention. "So you see, Ms. Roth was not in your study under false pretenses. Therefore, if you refuse to allow us to take your painting, it could be construed that you have something to hide. I assure you things would go much more smoothly, if you cooperated." He paused. "Of course, we can always get a search warrant."

"How dare you speak to me like I'm a criminal? I'd watch my step if I were you, Burnell."

Finch marveled at how cool and unruffled his boss appeared. He knew Burnell must be seething on the inside.

"Mr. Sanborn, this is a very grave matter, and threatening a police officer in the course of his duty will not help the situation."

"Duty? Ha. Harassment is more like it. Ah, Richard, at last someone with a bit of sense. Can't you do something about these…these men of yours," Sanborn said with disgust as Assistant Commissioner Fenton approached with his wife's Uncle Patrick close on his heels.

"What's the problem, Max?" Fenton asked.

"Your men are the problem."

"Oh, yes?" One of Fenton's perfectly curved eyebrows arched upward, and he gave Burnell a penetrating look.

"Yes, apparently, Burnell has called the Arts and Antiques squad to 'investigate' that nutter's claims *and* he wants to take away my Constable."

"I see," the assistant commissioner mumbled. "Burnell, let's not overreact."

The superintendent's eyes widened in disbelief. Finch stopped scribbling notes.

When Burnell found his tongue again, he said, "What do you mean, sir?"

"Well, it's really not necessary to go to all that trouble. After all, it's not like Mr. Sanborn is an underworld criminal. This is merely some sort of silly misunderstanding. That woman—Ms. Roth, is it?—is obviously mistaken. Probably indulged in too much bubbly, I'd say."

The superintendent couldn't believe his ears. His nails dug deeper into his palms the more Fenton droned on. "But, sir, the fact is—"

"That's just it. There are no facts. Just hearsay. Do you really believe that a man like Max Sanborn, who has such a high standing in the community, would be involved in something as sordid as acquiring looted Nazi art? It's laughable when you think about it." He gave a little chuckle to emphasize his point.

"The voice of reason at last," Sanborn said as he clapped a beefy arm around Fenton's shoulders.

Burnell and Finch remained stone-faced.

"This is *not* a laughing matter," Gregory said. No one knew how long he had been standing there. "It's very serious. And I assure you, it will be looked into *thoroughly*."

"And who might you be?" Uncle Patrick asked.

"My name's Gregory Longdon. I'm Symington's chief investigator."

"Ah, Symington's. I see. Patrick Kildare is the name." He extended a bony hand toward Gregory. "I'm a Sanborn board member. My niece Cynthia is married to Richard here." He patted Fenton on the shoulder.

"Investigator, *hmph*," Sanborn grunted. "He's also my disreputable nephew and a bloody thorn in my side."

Fenton's brows shot up. "What? Longdon is your...*nephew*."

Sanborn sighed. "It's a long story, and I would rather not get into it at the moment, Richard. What's important is my Constable."

"Of course. Well, don't worry on that score. I think we're all in agreement that it was a simple misunderstanding, aren't we?"

Burnell cleared his throat. "No, sir, we are *not* in agreement. It would be in Mr. Sanborn's best interest if he allowed us to take the painting to the Yard, *now*. Otherwise, we will get a warrant."

"I most certainly will not allow it. Richard, is a warrant really necessary?"

Fenton's gaze flitted from Burnell's determined face to Sanborn. "I'm afraid I can't be seen to be giving you preferential treatment, Max. You understand. Why not let Burnell and Finch take the painting? They'll give you a receipt for it."

Sanborn's face turned a mottled crimson and the muscle in his jaw pulsed. His voice dripped ice. "Then get a bloody warrant. You'll be hearing from my lawyers."

"I suppose it's what you chaps do," Kildare said, scratching his head in bafflement. "But if you ask me, it's a waste of time in this case. I mean, it's not like anything has actually been stolen."

Gregory's head snapped up. "The Nazis were no better than common street thugs," he replied through gritted teeth. "They stole everything they could from the Jews. And when there was nothing left of material value, they murdered them."

"Yes, young man, don't get your back up. We know all that." Kildare waved his cane, his tone patronizing. "But if it turns out that this painting belonged to Ms. Roth's aunt—and I do stress *if*, because I have serious doubts about that point— Max bought the painting in good faith. He *paid* for it."

"Some collectors are driven by obsession to own a particular piece of art and are more than willing to turn a blind eye to its murky past to possess it." Although Gregory spoke to Kildare, his gaze was locked on his uncle.

"Why, you dirty bastard," Sanborn spluttered. "Richard, can't you have him arrested for slander or anything else that you can think of? I don't really care what the charge is. I'll agree to anything."

"Your own nephew? That's the last thing you need after everything that's happened tonight," Fenton countered, seeking to diffuse the situation.

"What's the matter, Max? Did I touch a raw nerve?" Gregory pressed.

Burnell lowered his head and bit back a smile. He secretly admired Longdon for not allowing the matter to drop.

"Get out," Sanborn roared. "All of you get out of my sight."

"Max, old man, really you must calm down," Kildare said.

"*Get. Out. Now*," Sanborn shouted again. "My lawyers are going to crush you, Burnell. And as for you, Toby, you are going to wish that you had never been born."

CHAPTER 13

Brian slammed the file shut and in a single, angry motion swept everything off his desk. Then he hurled his cup across the room, where it shattered into a thousand pieces.

"I had no idea that you wanted to redecorate your office. That's an interesting design," Nigel said as he inspected the coffee slowly dripping down the wall.

"What?" Brian turned around, startled. "Oh, it's you."

"Yes, it's me. I'm glad to see that you remember who I am. Now, can you tell me what all this in aid of?" Nigel asked as he stooped to pick up the papers that had been scattered all over the carpet.

"Sorry. I allowed my temper to get the better of me for a second. I'm all right now," Brian muttered, as he lowered himself on his haunches and waved his brother away. "Go on. I've got it."

He straightened up, dumping the pile of papers and files on the corner of his desk. Then he dropped into his chair with a grunt. Nigel took the chair opposite him. He crossed one leg over the other and waited in silence until his brother was ready to talk. *He looks older somehow and tired, very tired*, Nigel thought. *More than that, he looks* worried.

Brian ran a hand distractedly through his hair. His eyes were bloodshot, and a web of fine lines seemed to have sprouted overnight at the corners. He attempted a weak smile. "It's no good looking at me like that, little brother."

"I wasn't aware that I was looking at you in a particular way."

"Yes, you were, and you know it. I can also hear the wheels turning in that legal brain of yours."

"Are you going to tell me what this is all about? Or am I going to have to guess?"

A mournful sigh escaped Brian's lips as he shook his head. "Nigel, we're in trouble. Very big trouble." There was a tremor in his voice. "Sanborn is about to plunge off a very steep cliff, and there's nothing I can do to stop it."

Deep lines of concern furrowed Nigel's brow. He rested his elbows on the desk and leaned forward. "Because of Dad and the painting? Then it's true about the painting? It was looted?"

"Yes. No. I don't know about the painting. For all I know, it's true. Maggie doesn't strike me as someone who would lie about something so serious. I certainly wouldn't put it past Dad. From what I've discovered in the last twenty-four hours, he's capable of anything," he replied bitterly.

"Well, that's a comforting thought, I must say. But then, we've always known that our dear papa wasn't quite top shelf. So," Nigel prompted.

"The company is virtually bankrupt. If Sanborn doesn't get a cash infusion fast, we'll be ruined. The proverbial lock, stock, and barrel."

"*What*? How's that possible?" Nigel asked incredulously.

"It's Dad. He's been embezzling from the company for years. The last three at any rate. It's all here in the auditor's report. Millions vanished mysteriously." He patted the jumbled stack of papers on his desk.

"I don't understand. Sanborn is everything to Dad. Why would he risk bringing the company to its knees? And how did he manage to embezzle the money without anyone being the wiser? How come *we* didn't notice anything?"

"According to the report, it was very cleverly done. Only someone who knew what they were looking for could have discovered what Dad was doing. He transferred the money he stole to one of his accounts in Switzerland. And we all know how the Swiss banks pride themselves on keeping their clients' secrets."

"But still. I can't believe it."

"Believe it, little brother. When the City finds out, Sanborn's stock is going to plummet. And if that were not bad enough, now we have Maggie's bloody accusation to deal with. The press is already baying like a pack of wolves on our doorstep after last night's debacle. Mark my words, they are out for blood. They're going to say that the cancer research institute was a sham and that Dad never intended to build it. They're going to say that the auction was really a way for him to make some money quickly so that he could cover up the embezzlement before anyone noticed." Brian slammed his palm against the desk. "And they're going to say that *we* knew about the whole thing. I can take care of myself, but what about Tessa and the boys? How am I going to protect them? We'll probably lose the house in Belsize Park."

Nigel reached out and gave his brother's arm a squeeze. "Steady on. Let's not get ahead of ourselves. One problem at a time. For the moment, the only ones who know about the embezzlement are us and the auditors, right?"

Brian nodded. "Good. That gives a little room to maneuver, but we have to work fast, and if we're very lucky, no one will be the wiser. Everyone respects you. You have a reputation for being honest and fair in all your business dealings. Now it's time for you to use that goodwill and call in all the favors you have squirreled away over the years. You're going to need them to arrange several *very* large loans to keep Sanborn afloat until we can sort out this mess. Discretion is key. Not a whisper of this must get out. The people you approach must understand that. You have to be able to trust them implicitly."

Brian leaned back in his chair and steepled his hands over his stomach. "Yes," he murmured, his expression thoughtful. There was a glimmer of hope in his brown eyes for the first time since his brother entered his office. "Yes, it could work."

"It's *got* to work. It's Sanborn's only chance."

"But what about Maggie and her aunt's painting?"

Nigel sighed. "We'll just have to deal with it. As you said, I don't think she would lie. Of course, you do realize that her claim has opened a Pandora's box? Dad's entire collection—paintings, sculptures, jewels, porcelain, silver, the lot—is going to become the subject of intense scrutiny. As will his Swiss accounts."

"Bloody hell."

"Yes, I think that sums up the situation quite accurately."

The unexpected peal of Brian's telephone jarred both them. "Please not another crisis," Brian pleaded to the ceiling as he snatched up the receiver. He listened for a minute. "Right. We'll be there in five minutes." He carefully returned it to its cradle, gathered up his files and stood up. "That was our illustrious father. He wants us to come to his office. *Now*."

℮ↄ℮ↄ

Brian and Nigel could hear Max's raised voice before they even entered the outer office, where Angela was diligently carrying on with her work. The brothers both said hello to her and walked straight into their father's inner sanctum without knocking.

"She can rot in hell for all I care, Arthur. I want you to sue Maggie Roth for everything she's got. I want her company bankrupted. Throw everything you can at her. I want her to become a pariah. Spread the word throughout the City that if anyone comes within ten feet of her, he will feel my wrath. Do you understand?" Max pounded a curled fist against his open palm. Before his personal lawyer could respond, he rushed on, "She's going to learn the hard way, what it means to go up against Max Sanborn. And as for Superintendent Burnell, he's got to go *at once*. I want you to have a quiet word with Richard Fenton and see to it that Burnell is off the force by this afternoon. Then—"

"That's enough, Dad," Brian interrupted. "Sanborn is already in tremendous trouble without you pouring more oil on the fire."

"At last, the voice of reason," Arthur Galbraith, Sanborn's personal lawyer, said. "Talk to your father, Brian, Nigel. Make him see sense. My advice has fallen on deaf ears this morning." He clapped Brian on the shoulder and shook Nigel's hand before quietly leaving the office.

An uncomfortable silence descended upon the room. Five pairs of eyes stared at Sanborn, who sat fuming behind his desk. Patrick Kildare sat in a wing chair, his hands resting on top of his cane, and Harold O'Shaugnessy, his brother-in-law as well as a fellow board member, sat tensely on the edge of the Chesterfield sofa. Meanwhile, Gregory stood in the corner with his arms crossed over his chest and one shoulder leaning against the wall.

"Why are all of you looking at me like that?" Sanborn asked, imperiously.

"Dad, how come you're the only one who can't see that we're in this mess because of you and your obsession to amass 'the greatest art collection in Britain'?"

"How dare you? I ought to thrash you right here and now." His glance flickered over toward Nigel. "Both of you. You're both like your mother. Useless. No stomach for the difficult decisions."

Brian sighed wearily. "We're not children anymore, if you haven't noticed. You can't resort to a beating to avoid an unpleasant topic."

Max's fists curled into tight balls on his desk. "I'd advise you to have a care, my darling son. I'm still the chairman of this company."

"And I'm the managing director," Brian retorted, his voice rising in irritation. "I'm responsible for Sanborn's day-to-day operations. My duty is to protect our shareholders, who at this moment are running scared and will desert us if this situation isn't handled with the greatest of delicacy."

"I didn't create this 'situation' as you call it. It was that deranged woman and her bloody lies."

"Maggie Roth is not deranged, nor does she lie," Gregory said through clenched teeth as he strode into the middle of the office. He rested his palms on Max's desk and looked down at his uncle. "Maggie is a well-respected businesswoman. Respect is something one earns. But of course, you're not even on nodding terms with the word, are you, Max? You just plot and cheat to get what you want, like an alley cat rummaging through the rubbish heap, and you don't care who you hurt in the process."

Max jumped to his feet. His face was only inches from Gregory. "I'd like to know why you're here at all, Toby—"

"Gregory. The name's Gregory Longdon."

"You can call yourself Peter Pan for all I care. Nothing will change the fact that you'll always be my sniveling nephew Toby Crenshaw. You were nothing but trouble from the day I allowed you and Clarissa under my roof."

A smile played around Gregory's mouth, but his eyes were hard and full of hatred. He was about to reply with some choice words, when Nigel squeezed his shoulder.

"That's enough, Toby. You're only fanning the flames."

Gregory straightened up, shot his cuffs, and adjusted his tie. "You're right. I won't sink to his level. However, I will not stand by and allow Max to malign Maggie's good name."

"What I'd like to know is why you're all so concerned about this Roth woman? I'm the real victim here. Have you seen today's papers? I'm the one being pilloried across all the front pages. Look at these." He scooped up several papers. "'MAX SANBORN'S DIRTY LITTLE SECRET,' 'CHARITY AUCTION OR GETTING RID OF THE EVIDENCE?' 'THE SANBORN COLLECTION: A PACK OF LIES AND SHAME.' And here's the best one—" He brandished the offending paper in the air. "'BLOOD ON HIS HANDS?' That's from *The Clarion*. Our own bloody paper. I expected this sort of salacious gossip from the others, but our *own* paper. Look." He shoved the paper at Brian. "You couldn't have hushed it up?"

Brian glanced down at the byline and passed the paper over to Nigel. "No, Dad. We couldn't have hushed it up. How would it have looked if *The Clarion* was the only paper not carrying the story? People would have said that we have something to hide."

"Let them think whatever they like."

Nigel cleared his throat. "It's a fair and well-balanced story. The correspondent has interviewed Scotland Yard officials, art and legal experts, and she's even spoken to Arthur, who—"

"Fair and well-balanced? Are you out of your bloody mind? Who's this Emmeline Kirby?"

Nigel paused for a fraction of a second to cast a glance at Gregory before replying, "She's the editorial director of investigative features."

"Not any more. She's sacked."

"Dad, we can't sack her. Emmeline is damn good at her job. She's the best writer we've ever had. In the three months that she's been here, she has turned *The Clarion* around and made it a leader in the industry. She's intelligent and works harder than anyone I know."

"Get her in here. I want to see what this paragon of virtue has to say for herself."

"I don't think that's a good idea."

"Really, Nigel? I don't remember asking for your opinion." He turned his back on them and picked up the phone. "Angela, I want to see Emmeline Kirby *immediately*." He replaced the receiver and crossed his arms over his chest. "For my part, I can hardly wait to meet her."

CHAPTER 14

There was a soft tap, and then the door swung open. The first person Emmeline saw was Nigel, who gave her a sheepish smile. Brian was standing next to his brother. He inclined his head, but a frown crinkled his brow.

Then her gaze fell on Max. Her jaw tightened, and she clenched her fists at her sides. "You wanted to see me, Mr. Sanborn?"

Sanborn rose from his chair and came around the desk. He wagged an accusatory finger at her. "*You're* Emmeline Kirby?"

"Yes, sir," she replied, her voice steady.

"But you're…you're the friend of that lying lunatic." His eyes narrowed. Emmeline didn't flinch under his intense scrutiny. "Yes, and you're the one from the corridor the other day. The one with the big mouth. You've got a lot of nerve. Now, it all makes sense. It's some scheme you and that Roth woman cooked up. Well, my dear, the game is up. Whatever the two of you thought you were going to get, you can forget it. How dare you print such lies about me?" He waved the paper in the air. "You're a Sanborn employee. Don't you have any loyalty?"

Emmeline had kept her temper in check throughout this diatribe, but she could no longer hold her tongue. She thrust her chin in the air and squared her shoulders. "As a journalist, my first loyalty has always been to the truth. I will never, *never* keep quiet simply because the truth could be inconvenient."

"Well, if that doesn't beat all." Sanborn shook his head incredulously and walked around the desk. For a long moment, he didn't say anything. He simply stood there, his cheeks flushed, a slight sheen of perspiration on his forehead and a menacing glint in his eye. He towered over her, making her look smaller than her five-foot-two-inch height. However, Emmeline was completely still. She looked directly up at him. She would *not* be intimidated by this man. Sanborn's eyebrows arched upward. He had not expected to encounter the defiance so clearly etched upon her features. He was used to people trembling in fear of him.

"That spectacle that your friend put on last night and the lies that the two of you have put about are a damn sight more than *inconvenient*. Do you know what the two of you have done? *Do you?*" He shouted. Emmeline could feel his warm breath against her cheek with every word. "The wolves are howling on the doorstep ready to pounce. They're out for blood. And the future of Sanborn Enterprises hangs in the balance. All because of you and your friend."

She swallowed hard. "This situation is of your own making, Mr. Sanborn. You're the one with a painting of questionable provenance in your collection. If you purchased the painting 'in good faith' as you *claim*, then why don't you turn it over to Scotland Yard's Art and Antiques unit? Better still, why not have it checked with the Art Loss Register, the Lost Art Internet Database or the Holocaust Art Restitution Project in Washington for a start?"

"Are you stark raving mad? I'm not having every Tom, Dick, and Harry prying into my private affairs."

Emmeline ignored this outburst. "Of course to truly redeem your reputation, you could simply give Maggie her aunt's painting as an act of *good faith*."

A mirthless laugh trespassed Sanborn's lips. "Now, I know you're mad. *Give* that woman a painting that's worth millions of pounds? The two of you can forget it."

"Then I'm afraid you'll have to prepare yourself to face a lot of awkward questions in the coming days and weeks. And not just by me."

Sanborn smiled, but it did not reach his eyes. "Well, there you're wrong, *my dear*," he said sweetly. "I won't have to answer any more of *your* questions because you're sacked, effective immediately."

Emmeline blinked twice. "You can't sack me for doing my job."

"I just did. Now, get out."

She stood her ground. "My contract explicitly states that I have *complete* editorial control without *any* interference from management."

Nigel came to her defense. "Emmeline's right, Dad. I executed it myself. If you sack her, she can sue for breach of contract."

"*What?*" Sanborn's wrath was momentarily directed at his son. His jaw clenched in a tight line. His whole body was shaking. "Then sue." He spat the words at Emmeline.

Gregory saw Max's hand twitch at his side. In one stride, he interposed himself between them. He pushed Emmeline slightly behind him and grabbed Max's wrist just as he started to raise his hand to strike.

Gregory heard Emmeline's sharp intake of breath, but he focused his attention—and his outrage—on his uncle. "Did no one teach you that *you—don't—hit—ladies*?"

"Hmph. She's no lady," Max sneered in disdain. "She's just a scheming little bitch."

"Ah, Ah, language, Max," Gregory replied through gritted teeth as he increased the vice-like pressure on his uncle's wrist. "Now, are you going to apologize to Emmeline for your boorish behavior, or do I have to break your arm? The choice is entirely yours. I have absolutely no qualms should you choose the latter. Actually, I rather wish you would."

"That's enough, Toby," Brian intervened. "Let him go."

The two cousins eyed each other warily for an interminable moment. "I said let him go," Brian repeated softly.

"Please, Gregory. He's not worth it," Emmeline implored. "Don't make things worse. *Please*." She touched his arm lightly.

Gregory looked down into those dark eyes so filled with

concern and his grip slackened. He dropped Max's wrist in disgust. "Count yourself lucky, *this time*." His voice was laced with venom. "But if you *ever* try something like that again, I will kill you."

Max's brown eyebrows rose, and then a harsh laugh burst forth from deep within his throat. "Come off it, Toby. You don't have it in you, and we both know it. It's all hot air to impress this...this—" He cast a disdainful glance at Emmeline.

"I'd choose my words very carefully if I were you," Gregory warned.

Max's eyes glinted with malevolence as they once again settled on his nephew. A sardonic smile played around his lips. "—lady. You simply wanted to impress this lady." He stepped back and cocked his head to one side. His insolent gaze raked over Emmeline from head to toe. "She's not bad looking, I'll admit. If you like that type, that is. Tell me, Toby—" He lowered his voice conspiratorially. "—has she already invited you into her bed or was this little display of bravado intended to further your cause in that direction?"

The first crack was silent. It was Gregory's frayed nerves being stretched beyond the breaking point. The second crack, which reverberated around the office, was his fist connecting with Max's jaw.

Everyone froze as Sanborn fell to the floor in a heap. But far from being cowed, the incident seemed to amuse him. He sat there laughing and rubbing his jaw. "Feel better, do you, Toby?"

"What an utterly vile pig of a man you are," Emmeline said, incensed.

"I'd watch my tongue, *my dear*. I may not be able to sack you, but I'm still the chairman of this company, and I can make your life extremely uncomfortable. I'd remember that if I were you. Of course, you can always *leave* Sanborn."

"Get up, Max," Gregory snapped. "Get up and apologize to Emmeline."

Sanborn laughed again as he lumbered to his feet, his knees cracking. "You can bloody well forget it."

Nigel stepped into the fray. "Dad, your behavior this morning has been appalling, and that's putting it mildly. There is nothing, *nothing* in Emmeline's story that is biased." He slapped the folded newspaper against the palm of his hand. "In fact, it is an exemplary piece of journalism. Second, Emmeline is Tob...Gregory's fiancée, and I, for one, am mortified on her behalf for your deeply offensive and insulting remarks. Even if she weren't engaged to Gregory, it is beneath contempt for you to speak to anyone in such a manner."

Brian's ears perked up. His glance shifted from his brother to Gregory. "Fiancée? Is this true, Toby?"

Gregory nodded. "Yes, Brian." He went to Emmeline's side and tucked her arm through the crook of his elbow. This showed off her pink sapphire engagement ring to the best advantage. For the first time that morning, he smiled. "I'm a very lucky man because this beautiful, incredibly talented, and intelligent woman has consented to become my wife."

"Well, I...this has been an eventful morning," Brian stammered. "I don't know what to say."

"Congratulations are usually in order," Gregory murmured, but not unkindly.

"Yes. Yes, of course. Congratulations to you both," Brian replied warmly. He clapped Gregory on the shoulder and extended a hand to Emmeline, who returned his smile.

Patrick Kildare and Harold O'Shaugnessy, who everyone had forgotten during the heated family row, came forward to offer their best wishes. They shook hands with both Gregory and Emmeline. "May you have a long and happy marriage with many children," Kildare said, his very faint trace of an Irish brogue giving a musical lilt to these felicitations.

Sanborn started clapping his hands. "How very, very touching. For my part, the two of you can go to the devil."

"Dad, haven't you caused enough trouble this morning?" Nigel hissed.

"No, I don't think so, my loving son. Not nearly as much trouble as these two deserve. Now, I want all of you to get out of my office, most especially the happy couple."

"With pleasure," Emmeline mumbled under breath.

She had her hand on the doorknob when Max's voice stopped her. "Emmeline, is it?" She turned around slowly. "I'd watch my step if I were you. I'm going to keep a *very* close eye on you. You may have won the battle, but I will win the war—of that, I can assure you."

Emmeline's spine stiffened. "Your threats don't frighten me, Mr. Sanborn. I'm going to continue to do my job to the best of my ability. I *am* going to find out the truth, no matter where it leads me."

She swept out of the office before Max could say anything else.

"On that happy note," Gregory said as he glanced down at his watch, "I must be off as well. I have a meeting with Superintendent Burnell. Like the police, Symington's has a lot of questions about your collection."

"Get out," Sanborn growled.

Gregory flashed one of his most charming smiles and gave a little salute. "Your wish is my command, *dear* Uncle Max. I wouldn't want to overstay my warm welcome."

Max grunted something unintelligible.

"But just remember," Gregory tossed over his shoulder. The smile had disappeared, and there was a hard edge to his voice. "If you harm Emmeline in *any* way, you won't live to regret it." Brian's lips parted, but Gregory cut him off with a wave of his hand. "That's it. I'm going. Good day, gentlemen." He nodded his head to the grim circle gathered around his uncle.

Sanborn stalked back to his desk and dropped heavily into his chair. "What are the rest of you waiting for? Stop gawking at me with your mouths open and get back to work," he said impatiently. Kildare cleared his throat. "Yes, Patrick?" Sanborn demanded. "Was there something you wanted?"

Kildare shifted his weight on his feet and leaned more heavily on his cane. "As the most senior members, Harold and I wanted to express the board's concerns about the serious allegations brought against you and displeasure at the resulting negative media attention. We, the board that is…" He paused, searching for the right words, "We feel that—"

"Come on. Spit it out, old man."

Kildare's eyes narrowed as his green gaze fixed on Sanborn's face. "The board thinks it would be in the company's best interest, if you would step down as chairman."

"Oh, the board does, does it? Well, you and Harold can go back to the board and tell them that I'm not going anywhere. This is *my* company, and no one is going to push me out. Do I make myself clear? However, if you or your fellow board members have issues with my leadership, you are perfectly welcome to tender *your* resignations. Otherwise, keep your heads down and stay out of my way."

Kildare's lips pursed. "Hmm. Max, you're a smart, but unscrupulous businessman who runs too many risks. Thus far, you've managed to tread inside the law, *just*. But one of these days your ego and your impolitic tongue will send Sanborn on the slippery slope to ruin. Your enemies are waiting for that day."

"You wouldn't be threatening me by any chance, would you, Patrick? I sincerely hope not. Because I'd take *great* exception to that."

"Threaten you? Now, why would I do that?" Kildare replied mildly. "Consider it a little friendly advice."

"I see," Sanborn murmured. He was silent for a moment. "Well, I've considered it. You can tell the board I'm staying. If any of you ever *dare* to offer me such unsolicited advice again, I promise you, you will regret it. Not one of you has a right to judge me. Remember, I know *everything* about all of you. All the dirty secrets."

Their eyes locked. In that instant, some unspoken message passed between the two men. Kildare's brow furrowed. "You've made a mistake," he observed matter-of-factly.

"No, I think you'll find you're the one who has overstepped his place, *old man*."

Kildare stiffened and then turned on his heel without another word. The door rattled on its hinges, when he slammed it behind him.

"Next." Sanborn folded his hands and asked brusquely, "Harold, did you have anything else to add?"

"No, no, no," O'Shaugnessy replied nervously, his brogue heavy on his tongue as he uttered his hasty reply. "I just wanted you to know that it was entirely Patrick's idea to speak to you. I tried to dissuade him, but he was very determined."

"I see." Sanborn leaned back in his chair and bestowed a cold smile upon him. "At least someone knows which way his bread is buttered. If I were you, Harold, I would remind your colleagues that they are on the board because of my largesse."

"Y—Yes, I will," he stammered obsequiously as he quickly crossed the room. "You can count on me. I know you must be busy, so I think I'll leave now."

"That's the first intelligent thing that you've said today. Give my regards to your fellow board members." Sanborn waggled his fingers at the man in farewell.

Once O'Shaugnessy had finally gone, he shook his head and grumbled, "Spineless weasel. I always despised that man."

"Then why did Sanborn offer him a place on the board?" Nigel asked.

"Because of his connections. Why else? Now, why are the two of you still here?" Max snapped at his sons.

"There's something we need to discuss," Brian said. He exchanged a knowing look with his brother.

"Do you want me to stay?" Nigel asked quietly.

Brian shook his head. "No, I can handle it. You go on. I'll pop by your office later."

"You're sure?"

"Yes, go on." Brian jerked his head in the direction of the door. "On your way out, tell Angela we're not to be disturbed for any reason." Nigel nodded and slipped quietly from the room.

"Look here, you can't come in here tossing your weight about. Angela answers to me."

"Dad, for once in your life you're going to listen," Brian retorted wearily. "You're going to issue a press release today announcing that you've decided to step down as chairman until this whole sordid affair with Maggie Roth is sorted out. Something to the effect that you care about Sanborn too much to see its reputation sullied in any way. Do you understand?"

"Not you too. I will *not* resign. It would only make it look as if there's some truth behind that woman's lies."

"Frankly, I'm inclined to believe Maggie over you."

Max jumped to his feet, knocking over his chair in the process. "Why you disloyal, ungrateful....Go to the devil."

"You're going to resign. Today," Brian replied sententiously. "You have no choice in the matter."

He dropped the auditor's report on the desk. It landed with a *thud*.

Max fingered the document. "What's this?"

CHAPTER 15

Emmeline had temporarily hit a dead end in her research. She had spent the entire morning either on the phone with some of her contacts or checking various databases of looted Nazi art to see if she could find the trail that led to the Constable painting. All of her instincts told her that it was indeed the same painting that she had seen in those old photo albums tucked away in Maggie's study. However, she had to prove it. For Sarah and Edmond Lévy. For Maggie. And to right an unspeakable wrong that had been perpetrated against millions of others.

Arhhh, Emmeline growled inwardly in frustration. *There has to be a clue* somewhere. *But where?*

Thoughts chased each other through her mind, but she couldn't focus. She needed to get some air and clear her head. She stretched her arms above her head to try to loosen the knots in shoulders. It had just gone half past one. She decided that she would take a late lunch and drop by to see how Maggie was getting on. When she rang Maggie's office earlier, she had been told that her friend was working from home today.

Emmeline was deeply troubled about Maggie, and the concern only seemed to grow as she took the Northern Line from London Bridge station and switched at Monument for the District Line, which would take her to the Gloucester Road station. She bit her lip as the events of last night played out again in her head. Maggie was always in control and supremely organized. But last night—last night she completely fell apart. And that frightened Emmeline.

What would happen next? Maggie was no match for a ruthless man like Max Sanborn. An involuntary shiver slithered down Emmeline's spine as his contorted, red face suddenly blurred her vision. *'I'm going to keep a very close eye on you. You may have won the battle, but I will win the war—of that, I can assure you.'*

No indeed, no one was safe from a man like Max.

c∕ɔc∕ɔ

A cluster of journalists, photographers, and television cameramen were camped outside Maggie and Philip's door, disturbing the drowsy quiet of Hereford Square. A sigh escaped Emmeline's lips. She understood that her colleagues had a job to do and was among the first to vigorously defend freedom of the press. But this was Maggie they were talking about, and she wished they would all just go away.

Am I being hypocritical? she asked herself. *Or am I too close to this story? Should I step aside and allow someone else to cover it? Can I be objective?*

She stopped halfway down the block. Her brow puckered. This last question led to several minutes of uncomfortable soul-searching. In the end, she decided that she could be objective. She always had been and would continue to be. Otherwise, she would have to seriously rethink her choice of careers.

Emmeline took a deep breath and squared her shoulders. She pushed her away through the throng and rang the bell. She recognized many of the faces. Some voiced annoyance and resentment at the perceived favoritism she was being granted. She couldn't blame them.

The shiny black door opened a crack, and Philip's watchful eyes peered out at her. He pulled the door back just enough to give her space to cross the threshold.

A volley questions were hurled at him, and the furious clicking of a dozen cameras was heard before he shut them all out. Philip bent down and kissed Emmeline's cheek. "It's been a bit of a rough day keeping the wolves at bay."

"Yes, well…I'm sorry," she replied, shamefaced.

"Not your fault. You're not like most of them." He jerked his thumb over his shoulder. A ghost of a smile touched his lips. There were purple shadows under his eyes.

Emmeline touched his arm lightly. "How…Has it been really awful?"

"As you can imagine. It was a very long night—with very little sleep. First thing this morning, I took Janet and the boys to Charing Cross and put them on a train to Aylesbury. They're going to spend a few days with my parents. I wanted them well out of the way until things settle down."

"That was a good idea. The boys probably viewed it as an unexpected adventure. The train journey alone must have been cause for excitement. I'm sure your parents are thrilled at the prospect of having the boys down for a visit."

"Dad most likely is barricaded in the study, girding himself for the invasion. Mum, of course, was delighted when I rang this morning. As we were talking, she was already planning a long list of outings and treats for Henry and Andrew. She spoils them rotten." Philip shook his blond head. "No matter how many times I've told her, she doesn't seem to understand that giving in to their every whim makes it that much harder when they come back home. Then Maggie and I are subjected to days of 'But Granny lets us do this.'"

Emmeline laughed.

"You think I'm joking," he said. "But I'm being perfectly serious. In our sons' eyes, Maggie and I are ogres who take pleasure in saying 'No.'"

"That's not true, and you know it." The smile faded from her lips, and her mood sobered. "How's Maggie?"

Philip ran a hand distractedly through his hair as he led her into the living room. His blue eyes were clouded by concern and helplessness. "Not good," he said, plunking down heavily on the sofa. "She's barely eaten anything all day. I managed to get her to drink a couple of cups of strong, sweet tea, but that's it. She dragged several boxes of her grandfather's things down from the attic and closeted herself in the study. I felt as if I was intruding somehow so I left her to it. She didn't really seem to notice whether I was there or not."

"Oh, I'm certain that's not the case. Maggie knows how much you love her. Why, your rearranging your schedule to work from home today proves that."

"I'm worried. Really worried. I've never seen her like this." He reached out for her hand and squeezed it. "I don't know what to do to help her. I made a few discreet calls this morning to some colleagues, but no one was able—or willing—to tell me anything about what happened to Sarah Lévy, née Rothenberg. It's unclear why she and Edmond fled to Paris after their home and possessions in Nice were confiscated by the Nazis. Why not make their way directly to Spain or Portugal? It's all rather a jumble."

Emmeline then told Philip about her efforts to try to trace the Constable painting. "Don't worry, between us we'll find something. I'm not going to stop until that Constable is sitting above the mantelpiece in this room. First—" She started enumerating on her fingers. "—we have to find evidence that the painting belonged to the Lévys. Next, we have to follow the trail backward from the shady art dealer who sold the Constable to Max Sanborn to when it was initially stolen. I promise you I will find the Nazi bastard or collaborator, and then—"

"Then what? The men responsible are either dead or well into their eighties or nineties by now."

She went on as if he hadn't interrupted. "—I'm going to see that justice, at last, takes its course."

"I think you've set yourself a Herculean task. Besides, I don't imagine that your employer will take too kindly to you pursuing this story further."

"You're right there. Max Sanborn tried to sack me today. But he can't—" A smug smile curled around her lips. "—not unless he wants a lawsuit on his hands. My contract explicitly states that I have complete editorial control without any interference from management. I had Nigel insert that clause when we were negotiating the contract. Max is absolutely livid."

"I wouldn't be quite so gleeful about making a man like Max Sanborn your enemy. You told Maggie only the other day that he was dangerous. Why antagonize him? We both know from past experience that sometimes your...shall we say, zeal?...to uncover the truth has placed you in harm's way." Philip gave her a knowing look, which made her squirm slightly. "Why continue to work in such a hostile environment?"

She jumped to her feet. "I can't believe my ears. Are you saying that I should quit?"

"Please sit down, Emmeline. *I'm* not the enemy here. I'm your friend, and, as such, I don't want to see you get hurt." He patted the sofa. "Please sit down."

She hesitated a moment and then reluctantly sat down next to him again. She crossed her arms over her chest mutinously, which made Philip laugh. "Well, that's a little better. You were making me rather nervous. I could feel the daggers shooting from those dark eyes straight into the delicate parts of my anatomy."

Emmeline laughed too. "Sorry for being a bit prickly. My nerves have been on edge ever since the auction last night. The nasty confrontation with Max Sanborn this morning only made matters worse."

"That's all right. But that's exactly what I was getting at before. Why continue working at *The Clarion* if it's going to turn you into a bundle of nerves?"

She sighed. "Because I love my job and I'm damn good at it. In any case, Brian and Nigel are on my side. Despite the negative publicity it has brought to Sanborn Enterprises, they both defended my story and rejected their father's efforts to oust me as editorial director. Philip, my story was balanced. Even though Maggie is my dearest friend and this is *very* personal for me, I presented both sides. I interviewed legal experts, representatives from organizations specializing in finding looted art, and I even spoke to Arthur Galbraith, Max Sanborn's personal lawyer."

"I know you did. I read the article. It was very thorough, as are all your articles. I never questioned your objectivity. Please don't think that." He took her hand in his again. "It's just that sometimes your determination to find the truth makes you impetuous, and then you forget about your own safety."

"Philip, you are a dear to worry, but I know how to take care of myself."

"Hmph" was his only response to this remark.

She thrust her chin in the air. "I do. Besides, you're one to talk." She lowered her voice. "You work for MI5, for Pete's sake, and Maggie doesn't even know the truth. If that's not dangerous, I don't know what is. There will be hell to pay, if she ever finds out."

"And that's why she *never* will. But you're deliberately trying to change the subject. We were talking about you."

"No, you're wrong. We finished that conversation. And now—" She stood up. "—I'm going to see Maggie."

౭ာ౭ာ

Maggie was sitting cross-legged on the floor in the middle of the study, surrounded by several boxes. Her red-gold hair was pulled back in a ponytail, and she was wearing an old polo shirt and jeans. She was hunched over reading a sheaf of papers.

"Maggie," Emmeline said quietly as she closed the door behind her.

Her friend jumped. Maggie had been so engrossed in what she had been reading that she hadn't heard Emmeline come in. "Oh, hello, Emmeline. You startled me. Did Philip ring you?" Her voice sounded tense. Her face was devoid of the little make-up she usually wore, making every line of strain and worry more pronounced.

"No, Philip didn't ring me. I dropped by to check on you." She took a tentative step forward, unsure whether Maggie would send her away. "I was concerned about you."

Maggie didn't say anything for a long uncomfortable moment. She simply stared at Emmeline. Those normally luminous green eyes today appeared clouded and held a troubled expression.

Finally, she replied, "I'm fine." She turned her attention back to the papers in her hand. "Aren't you supposed to be at work? At work for *that* man?"

Emmeline didn't like her friend's clipped tone. "I took a late lunch so that I could come check on you," she said defensively.

Without looking up, Maggie said, "You needn't have bothered. I have things well in hand."

Emmeline crossed the room and plopped down next to Maggie. "Look at me. Please, Maggie. You are not fine." She shook her friend by the shoulders. "You can't fight Max Sanborn by yourself, and you don't have to. Did you see my story in *The Clarion* today? It was about last night's auction."

Maggie shook off Emmeline's grip. "You think I have time to read the paper. I have more important things to think about. There has to be something here. I just know it." She turned away from Emmeline and started rummaging around in the box closest to her. "There must be some mention of the Constable. A bill of sale. Something. Granddad kept all the letters and papers from Great Aunt Sarah. But where is it? I've looked and looked. I can't find anything. Emmeline, I can't find anything." Her voice cracked. "All I have is that old photo from Sarah and Edmond's apartment in Nice. What am I going to do?"

She dropped her head in her hands and began crying. "It's hopeless." Her shoulders trembled as all the pent-up emotions of the last twenty-four hours tumbled out in a cascade.

"Shh. Shh. Everything will be all right in the end. You'll see." Emmeline pulled Maggie toward her, rocking her gently back and forth. They stayed that way until all Maggie's tears had been spent.

Maggie was the first to pull away. She wiped her eyes with the back of her hand. "Better now?" Emmeline asked.

Maggie nodded. "Thanks. I'm sorry about before. I didn't mean to be so churlish. You're my best friend, and I love you dearly. I hope you know that." She took Emmeline's hand in her own.

Emmeline smiled and squeezed it. "Of course I know that, and I feel the same way. You're stuck with me, whether you like it or not." This made them both laugh. "So don't push me away. On that same token, don't shut Philip out. He loves you. The poor man is worried sick about you, but he's walking on eggshells because he doesn't want to upset you any further. Do you know that he rearranged his entire schedule so that he could work from home today to be with you? And what have you done? You've locked yourself in here."

Maggie made a moue. "I was rather horrible to him. Poor Philip. I'll have to make it up to my darling husband. I married a wonderful man."

"Indeed, you did. You were very lucky. No one could have asked for a better husband and father."

"Yes. Oh, dear." Maggie scrambled to her feet suddenly.

"What is it?"

"I've been so wrapped up in all this—" She waved a hand at the boxes. "—that I forgot about the boys. They're probably driving Janet mad. I'd better go upstairs and check on them."

Emmeline smiled. "Sit down. They're fine. Philip packed Janet and the boys off to his parents for a few days to get them out of London until things settle down."

The tension eased in Maggie's body. "I *really* have to make it up to him. He thinks of everything."

They heard a light tapping and the next second Philip's blond head popped round the door. "Sorry to disturb you, darling. I'm afraid that I have to go back to the office. Will you be all right here on your own?"

Maggie crossed the room, took her husband's face between her hands, and gave him a tender kiss. "I'm sorry, and I love you," she said after they pulled apart.

Philip smiled down at her. "I never doubted it for a minute. But if you'd care to prove it with another kiss, who am I to stop you?"

"Beast." Maggie giggled and swatted his arm, but she kissed him again anyway. "Now, off you go. I'll be fine."

Philip traced his finger along Maggie's jaw and smiled. "Emmeline, if this is the effect you're going to have on my wife, you're welcome in this house at any time. Day or night. No need to ring ahead. Just pop by."

"I thought you said that you had to go to the office," Maggie retorted. She put her hands on her hips and arched an eyebrow at him.

"I do, darling, but I didn't want to be rude to our guest. Emmeline, are you staying?"

Emmeline glanced at her watch and got up hurriedly. "No, I have to be getting back to the office too. However, I could stay if you need me, Maggie?"

Maggie shook her head. "No, go. I'm fine. Thanks to both of you, I'm thinking more clearly now. What I'm going to need is a good lawyer. I'm going to ring Barry Sykes. Perhaps he can recommend someone. And then I'm going to make Max Sanborn wish he had never set eyes on Great Aunt Sarah's Constable."

CHAPTER 16

Ah, there you are, Acheson. Bang on time, too. I like punctuality," Laurence Villiers, the deputy director of MI5, murmured as he continued to peruse *The Times* as Philip lowered himself onto the opposite end of the bench and stared out across the Serpentine in Hyde Park. To the casual observer, the two men were oblivious to one another.

"Good afternoon, sir," Philip said as he tilted his head toward the sky, for all intents and purposes to allow the sun to warm his face. "You made it sound rather urgent."

Villiers flipped a page. "I wouldn't say urgent, but I did want a quiet word with you before the situation devolved any further."

"Situation? What situation?"

"Let's not be coy, Acheson. You know exactly what I'm referring to. Your wife and the rather incendiary accusations she made about Max Sanborn last night. I'm afraid that she's stirring up a cauldron of trouble. We feel that it would be in everyone's best interest, if she dropped the matter. *Immediately.*"

Philip's head whipped round, but he was confronted only with Villiers calm profile. "May I ask why?"

"I'm afraid it's need-to-know, old chap. I'm sure you understand."

Philip's hands clenched into tight balls. He said through gritted teeth, "But *I* need to know. We're talking about my wife."

Villiers sighed wearily and folded the paper in his lap. The hard angles of his face were taut with annoyance. For a long moment, he remained silent. Only the sound of people chatting as they strolled along the water and a burst of children's laughter somewhere off to their right could be heard.

He cleared his throat and put an arm along the back of the bench as he turned his head of thick silver hair toward Philip. There was something elusive lurking in those intelligent brown eyes. "It is precisely because she is your wife that I accorded you the courtesy of a private word. Suffice it to say that there are delicate issues hanging in the balance and your wife's emotional allegations—" He put up an elegant hand to forestall the protests bubbling on Philip's tongue. "—whether they have any merit, threaten to do a lot of damage. Therefore, it is in your wife's and the country's best interest if the matter is allowed to die quietly. I trust I make myself clear and no more need be said."

Philip shot to his feet. "I'm afraid that's not possible, sir. My wife has every right to seek restitution of her aunt's painting—"

"It has yet to be proven that it *is* her aunt's painting."

Philip went on as if there had been no interruption. "—even if it means taking Max Sanborn to court."

Villiers shook his head sadly. "Legal action would be a grave mistake."

"With the greatest respect, sir, there is nothing left to be said." His blue gaze locked on the older man's brown eyes. "My wife has my complete support and loyalty on this issue."

"I must say that your attitude disappoints me tremendously, Acheson."

"I'm sorry, sir. I'm prepared to tender my resignation—"

Villiers rose as well and made an impatient gesture with his hand. "We don't need any more melodramatics. God knows the situation is rife with them as it is."

"Then I'm afraid that we're at an impasse."

"Yes, it would seem so. Think about it, Acheson. Your wife is out of her league. And that's always dangerous. If I were you, I'd keep a close eye on her."

Philip's eyes widened in surprise. He opened his mouth to say something else, but Villiers started to walk away. However, he had only taken a few paces when he turned round again. "Of course, Emmeline Kirby poses an even bigger threat. She has a tendency to dig up things that are better left buried. If she were my friend, I would do everything in my power to dissuade her from pursuing this crusade of hers any further. Otherwise, she could very easily wind up dead."

Philip's brow furrowed as myriad thoughts raced across his brain. In three strides, he was standing next to Villiers. He grabbed the older man's arm. "What do you know?"

"Know? What should I know?" he asked blandly.

Philip lost his temper. "You're the bloody deputy director. You're the *eminence grise* of the United Kingdom. You know *everything*. If you didn't, then I'd start worrying."

Villiers's mouth twisted into an enigmatic smile. "You give me too much credit, old chap. Too much credit, indeed. I'm just an ordinary Englishman trying to serve queen and country to the best of my ability. That's all."

"That's rubbish, and we both know it. Why are you deliberately keeping me out of the loop? If two women that I care about deeply are in trouble, then surely I deserve to know what—"

The smile vanished from Villiers's lips. "That's precisely why you are being kept in the dark."

"Then how can I protect Maggie and Emmeline?"

"By making the matter go away."

"Sir, they're both very strong-willed and determined. Nothing will stop them."

"Nothing except murder. That would be a most regrettable outcome." Villiers eased his arm from Philip's grip. "One more piece of advice before I go. I suggest that you and Superintendent Burnell stop asking questions about Gregory Longdon."

Then he turned on his heel and didn't look back.

⁊ʕ⁊

"Sir, I've got it," Sergeant Finch said as he burst into Superintendent Burnell's office the next day waving a piece of paper in the air. "I've got the warrant for Mr. Sanborn's painting."

"Right." Burnell tossed his glasses onto the file he had been reading. He pushed himself to his feet, straightened his tie and shrugged himself into his blazer. "Let's go pay the ever-charming Max Sanborn a visit."

"Going somewhere, Oliver?" Gregory's voice floated to their ears from the doorway.

Burnell scowled at him. "What do you want, Longdon? I don't have time for any of your nonsense today. As you can see, we're on our way out."

Gregory took a step into the office, effectively blocking their path. He flashed a smile at the two detectives. "That's not very polite, Oliver. Friends always have time for one another."

Burnell's eyes narrowed. "First of all, it is *Superintendent* Burnell. And second, we have never been, nor will we *ever* be, friends. Now, stop wasting my time and get out of my office. We have important business to attend to." He tried to shove past, but Gregory put out a hand to check him.

"Not friends? You do know how to hurt a chap. And here I was thinking that you would be as delighted to see me as I always am to see you."

"I am never happy to see you," the superintendent growled. "What—do—you—want?"

Gregory chuckled softly. "Oh, all right, *Oliver*. Out of professional courtesy, as we are colleagues, I came to inform you about a line of inquiry that I would like to pursue since we are supposed to be coordinating our efforts on this case."

"Professional courtesy? Colleagues?"

"Yes, of course. You're handling things from Scotland Yard's end, while I, as Symington's chief investigator—"

Burnell's rolled his eyes. "Chief investigator. That's a laugh," he griped under his breath.

"More like a wolf in sheep's clothing," Finch said. "If Symington's isn't careful, in a month their top clients will find that they've been robbed blind."

Gregory clucked his tongue at him in disapproval but

pressed on undaunted. "While I, as Symington's chief investigator, am exploring a less official angle that I hope will prove fruitful."

Burnell snorted. "You mean you're going to talk to one of your many cronies who hail from the criminal classes."

"Oliver, I must say I'm shocked by your attitude. I never took you for a snob. Who are we to judge our fellow man? Every man must have some form of employment to be fulfilled spiritually and to feed his family."

"What a load of rubbish. Let's call a spade a spade, shall we, Longdon? Speak to whoever you need to speak to. Whatever I think about you—and believe me, I try to think about you as little as possible—I know that you have a certain code of honor and will do everything you can to see that Ms. Roth receives justice."

Gregory's flippant manner evaporated. He extended a hand toward Burnell, who shook it. At times they may be on opposite sides, but, in this instance, they were united. There was no doubt in either man's mind about the painting's true owner. They just had to find the evidence to prove it. "Thanks, Oliver."

"Yes, well," the superintendent mumbled. "Finch and I must be going."

Gregory stood aside to let them pass. "Anything I should know about?" he asked as he followed them out into the corridor.

Burnell waved the warrant under Gregory's nose. "We're going to see Max Sanb...your uncle." The words sounded strange on his tongue. He still couldn't believe the family connection. "We got the warrant for the Constable."

"Ah. Be prepared for a fight. Max is not going to let it go quietly."

There was a smug glimmer in Burnell's eyes. "I'm afraid he has no choice. We have the law on our side."

"Max doesn't have any respect for the law. Or anything else for that matter. That's what makes him dangerous. He generally destroys anything that stands in his way."

"Not this time."

"For Maggie's sake, I hope you're right."

The lift came at this point, and they all got in. "You'll let us know how you get on with your...inquiries, won't you?" Burnell asked.

"You'll be the first to know. Of course, you are aware that Emmy is ferreting about and making Max extremely uncomfortable."

Burnell smiled. "Yes, the bombshell dropped at the auction and the subsequent questions being raised about his entire collection have been all over the news. Finch and I are eagerly looking forward to the next installment in Emmeline's series."

Gregory raised an eyebrow at the superintendent's unexpected use of Emmeline's Christian name, but let it pass without making a glib comment because they had more important things to discuss at the moment. "What you don't know is that Max tried to sack her yesterday. But he can't because of a clause in her contract. It was a very nasty set-to. Max doesn't like being cornered. He tends to lash out. If I hadn't stepped in, he would have struck Emmy."

"Good God," Finch exploded, his fists balled at his sides. "She must press charges."

"We all know that she *won't* do that. And Emmy being Emmy, she won't resign. She wants to be a thorn in Max's side, which—"

"Makes her a threat," Burnell concluded for him. "Mmm." His brows knit together in concern.

"Exactly. I can't be with her all the time."

"Don't worry, Longdon. I'll have a couple of plainclothes detectives keep an eye on her."

The lift's doors slid open. Gregory clapped Burnell on the shoulder. "I knew I could count on you, Oliver. Well, happy hunting. Give my regards to dear Uncle Max."

જાજી

For the second time in as many days, Superintendent Burnell and Sergeant Finch found themselves losing patience as they waited in Max Sanborn's outer office.

"Mrs. Cooper, you did tell Mr. Sanborn that we are here on police business?" Burnell asked Angela. He did his best to keep the irritation from his voice.

The secretary stopped tapping away at her keyboard. "I did, Superintendent. You heard me yourself call through to Mr. Sanborn. I'm terribly sorry, but as you can imagine things have been in a bit of a muddle today. I'm afraid he cannot be disturbed just now. Could I get you some tea in the meantime?"

Burnell slapped the magazine that he had twisted into an unrecognizable mess onto the table. "No, thank you. If we wanted afternoon tea, we would have booked a table at the Ritz. We came to see Mr. Sanborn, and that's what we're going to do. Come on, Finch."

"Right, sir."

They shot to their feet and were halfway across the room before Angela could stop them.

"You can't just barge into Mr. Sanborn's office," she said in dismay as she hurried after them.

With his hand on the knob, Burnell stopped and glanced back at the distressed secretary. "This little piece of paper gives me every right, Mrs. Cooper." He waved the warrant at her.

He flung the door open.

Sanborn was out of his chair in a flash. "What's the meaning of this, Burnell? Angela, I thought I told you I was not to be disturbed."

"I'm sorry, Mr. Sanborn. They just—"

"Oh, never mind. I don't want to hear your excuses," Max bellowed. "Just get back to work."

The color drained from Angela's cheeks. Her back stiffened and she swallowed her pride. "Yes, Mr. Sanborn." The door closed softly behind her.

"Now, what do the two of you want? I'm a busy man." Sanborn folded his arms across his chest and fixed a hard brown stare on the detectives.

"We've come for the Constable, Mr. Sanborn. Here's the warrant for it." Burnell handed him the paper. Sanborn made no effort to take it. "You'll find that it's all in order. I took the liberty of informing your lawyer. Therefore, I would appreciate it if you would turn over the painting to us immediately. We will accompany you up to your penthouse."

Sanborn didn't utter a word. A crimson flush spread across his cheeks and two vertical lines formed between his brows. He swatted the warrant out of Burnell's hand.

They watched as it fluttered to the floor. "That's what I think of your bloody warrant."

The superintendent calmly stooped to pick it up. "You can think what you like, but the fact is that you are being compelled *by law* to turn over the Constable to Scotland Yard until such time as its provenance can be determined."

"You and your warrant can go to the devil."

Burnell threw a frosty smile at him. "Mr. Sanborn, you are being foolhardy. If you persist in this manner, I will have no choice but to arrest you for perverting the course of justice."

A harsh bark of a laugh erupted from Sanborn's throat. He took a step forward and leaned so close that their noses were nearly touching. He was slightly taller so he peered down at the superintendent. "Try it, and you'll be out on your ear. I'll see that you never work again."

With the smile still plastered on his face, Burnell replied, "I'd advise you to ring your lawyer. Before you dig yourself into a *deeper* hole. Please go ahead. Finch and I will wait right here."

No one moved. The tension was so palpable that it crackled in their ears.

Surprisingly, Sanborn was the first to blink. "Right." He stalked over to his desk and viciously punched in his lawyer's number. He had to wait only a few seconds. Foregoing any attempt at pleasantry, he snarled, "Arthur, it's Max. Don't play the fool. You know exactly why I'm calling. Burnell's here and he—"

The lawyer must have cut him before he was allowed to give full vent to his opinions. He listened for a moment, before exploding, "*What?* I don't give a damn that the warrant's in perfect order. We're talking about *my* painting. I'm not going

to allow the police to get their grubby paws on it simply because that bloody woman—" He listened carefully and then
shook his head. "Why is it that no one but me can see that all
she wants is money? Hmm, Arthur, tell me that? What do you
mean I have no choice? Your precious law can go straight to
hell for all I care. You're paid to do *my* bidding, so live up to
your hefty salary or else you can start looking for another
place of employment. Threatening you? No, Arthur, I'm not
threatening you. I'm just letting you know the lay of the land."
He was silent for several minutes. His face grew redder as
each second ticked by. "So what you're saying is that if I don't
turn over the Constable to these—" He gave Burnell and Finch
a disgusted look. "—these yobbos, they can arrest me? For
protecting *my* property? Well, I call that outrageous. Yes, yes,
I understand. Yes, I'll *bloody give it to them*. But I expect you
to leave your office the instant I ring off so that you can be at
Scotland Yard as soon as it crosses the threshold. You know
how these blokes are. My Constable might suddenly go missing." Sanborn shot a malevolent glance at Burnell and was
satisfied to see that his barb had hit its intended mark. He
slammed the phone down and cleared his throat. "It would
seem that my hands are tied."

"I did try to explain that to you, Mr. Sanborn," the superintendent said as politely as he could.

"Oh, shut up. I don't need any of your lip. The situation is
bad enough as it is."

Burnell curled his fists so tightly that his nails dug deeply
into his palms. The blood was thrumming through his veins.

If this dragged out any longer, he would be foaming at the
mouth, so Finch decided to take control. "Shall we go up to
your penthouse, sir?"

Sanborn simply stared at him, but there was no mistaking
the murderous look in those eyes.

"Sir," Finch prompted.

"Well, come on. I don't have all day," Sanborn said as he
crossed to the door in two strides. However before he opened
it, he turned to face them. "If anything, *anything at all*, hap-

pens to my Constable, I'm going to hold the two of you *personally* responsible."

Twenty minutes later, the door rattled on its hinges as Sanborn stormed back into his office. In his absence, Brian must have dropped by because sitting in the middle of his desk was a single sheet of paper. His darling son had taken it upon himself to draft the press release announcing that he would be stepping down as chairman, effective immediately, "to prevent Sanborn's reputation from being tarnished until this sad matter can be resolved."

Max crumpled up the press release into a ball and threw it across the room. He muttered a string of oaths. Everything was falling down around his ears.

What he needed was a drink to calm his nerves. He wrenched open the bottom drawer and pulled out a bottle of single malt Scotch and a tumbler. He poured out a finger of the smoky amber liquid and downed it all at once. He felt a warm glow in his stomach. He splashed some more Scotch into his glass and took it over to the window. The sun was winking up at him from the surface of the Thames as the river traffic flowed past the building. But Max saw none of it. Thoughts were racing across his mind, the primary one being revenge. "I'll teach them all a lesson they won't soon forget," he said aloud to the empty office. And he would start right now.

Max walked over to the desk and picked up the phone. He punched in a number and tapped his fingers impatiently as he listened to the dial tone echoing in his ear. Finally, a voice came on the line. "It's Max. Just listen. If you want to continue receiving that very generous monthly retainer I deposit into your bank account, then you had better do something about this Maggie Roth business. I just had Burnell and his minion in here. They took my Constable. Stop whinging. I don't want any excuses from you. I just want you to make it all *go away*. I don't care how. After all, I ask so little from you."

He was silent for a few seconds. "Pardon, I couldn't have heard you correctly. You didn't just say that you can't get involved? You did." He shook his head gravely. "How very disappointing. And ungrateful, in view of everything that I've done to ease your way into the social circles that you so adore. Perhaps if I put it another way, you'll realize to whom you owe your loyalty. If you don't intervene, I will have no choice but to expose your dirty little family secret to the world." His mouth stretched back from his teeth into a lupine smile. "Blackmail? No, of course not. It is merely a suggestion between friends. It's up to you to make the right decision."

He severed the connection.

Now, he had to come up with a suitable way to punish Maggie Roth.

CHAPTER 17

Gregory inclined his head politely and stepped aside to allow a gentleman in a navy suit and bowler hat to leave the Maurice Boinet Gallery in Old Bond Street. As he crossed the threshold, Gregory felt as if he had stepped into a private salon. The walls were paneled in cherry, and there were several small wine-colored leather sofas positioned in strategic corners of the room so that clients could admire the smattering of Renoir, Monet, Pissaro, Mary Cassatt, and Lautrec paintings, while contemplating whether to spend several million pounds to add one of them to their collections.

The proprietor himself, a well-dressed man in his early fifties with salt-and-pepper hair, was clearly employing all his Gallic charm to persuade a middle-aged couple to dip into their deep pockets and acquire the lovely Manet hanging before them. The wife was wavering. Another minute or two and the Manet would be sold.

Gregory heard snippets of their conversation, but they had their backs to him and were completely unaware of his presence. He picked up a catalog on an upcoming exhibit and took a slow turn about the room. However, his glance kept slipping sideways to the trio discussing the painting. He stopped in front of a Degas bronze ballerina on a tall stand. He walked around it, pretending to examine the statue from all angles. Then he crossed an arm over his chest and cocked his head to the right. He leaned his cheek against his opposite hand.

A young woman with chestnut hair and clear gray eyes suddenly appeared at his elbow. "May I help you, sir?"

Gregory smoothed down the corners of his mustache and flashed a smile that caused a pink blush rise to her cheeks. "Why yes, my dear. This little piece is rather pretty." He waved a hand at the bronze. "But where are the Picasso, Matisse, and Dali paintings? I'm told Boinet has the best ones here in London."

"Oh," the woman said, flustered.

"Is there something wrong, my dear?" Gregory asked innocently.

"It's not a question of wrong exactly. I'm rather afraid that you've been misinformed, sir. Mr. Boinet only handles the Impressionists."

Gregory hoped the expression on his face was suitably crestfallen. "How disappointing. No offense to you, my dear—and your name is?"

"Nicole. Nicole Sherwood," she replied shyly.

Gregory smiled again and touched her arm lightly. "Nicole Sherwood. What a pretty name. Miss Sherwood, as I was about to say, I mean no offense but would it be possible to speak with Mr. Boinet."

"Of course, sir, but he will tell you the same thing."

"Let's see. You never know what you can learn when you chat with the owner. He might have a little treasure tucked away somewhere." His eyes narrowed as his gaze strayed to Boinet.

"Yes. I'll just let Mr. Boinet know you'd like a word. He'll see you as soon as he's finished with Mr. and Mrs. Denning. I believe he's going to take them to the main showroom on the second floor, and he'll return here directly. What name shall I give him, sir?"

"Wiggins. Cyril Wiggins."

"Right, Mr. Wiggins. If you'd like to wait over there please." She waved to a sofa that was partially obscured by the bronze. "Would you like a cup of tea?"

"Very kind of you, Nicole, but no. I do hope Mr. Boinet won't be long. I have another appointment this afternoon."

He made a show of glancing down at his watch.

"I will let him know. I'm certain he'll be with you shortly."

Gregory lowered with masculine grace onto the sofa and rubbed his hands together. "Excellent, Nicole. Excellent. Thank you very much for your kind assistance. You run along and get back to work. You needn't worry about me. I'll just run my eye through your catalog, while I wait for Mr. Boinet."

Nicole hesitated a moment. "Well, if you're sure you're all right. I do have several arrangements I have to make for next week's exhibit."

"I'm quite positive." He turned his attention to the catalog and finally Nicole went back to her desk.

Gregory had only flicked through a few pages, when Boinet came hurrying over. "Monsieur Wiggins, please forgive me. I hope—" He gasped, when Gregory stood, up, and took a few stumbling steps backward, nearly knocking over the Degas bronze. "Bloody hell, Greg. It's you." Boinet's cultured French accent suddenly deserted him, and his broad Yorkshire dialect seeped out. His blue eyes scoured the room desperately looking for a way to make a hasty escape.

Before he could make a move, Gregory reached out and grabbed his arm. The smile on his lips did not touch his eyes, and although his voice was soft, there was a menacing edge to it. "Hello, Tim old chap. You couldn't be thinking of running off somewhere, could you? I'd be extremely hurt. After all, it's been ages seen we've seen each other, and we have *so much* catching up to do. Isn't that right, Tim? Or should I say Monsieur Boinet? Nice moniker, by the way. The accent needs a bit of polishing, though."

Boinet tried to wriggle free, but Gregory's fingers bit deeper through the sleeve of his Savile Row suit and into the soft flesh on the inside of his upper arm. He laughed nervously. "Running away? Me? Not a chance, Greg. I was just surprised to see you. Yes, that's it. I was surprised. As you said, it's been a long time. At least three years, I think. But I'm afraid you've caught me at rather a bad moment. I'm a busy man these days and...well...a gallery like this does not run itself. So, it's been nice seeing you again. Do drop by any time...but not too soon because this is the busy season. I've got a lot on this afternoon, so if you'll excuse me."

Gregory stared down at the hand Tim, alias Boinet, proffered but only chuckled. Instead, he clapped an arm—hard—about the man's shoulders. "Tim, we need to talk, *now.* Or else I'm going to drop a little word in a certain superintendent's ear, and then you'll find Scotland Yard on your doorstep asking a lot of *very* awkward questions. You wouldn't want that, would you?"

Tim swallowed the lump that had lodged in this throat. For a few seconds, his Adam's apple worked furiously up and down, but no sounds came from his mouth. He gave Gregory a sheepish grin. Finally, he said, "I'm a law-abiding citizen. Why should Scotland Yard take any interest in me and my humble business?"

"Humble? You sell yourself short, Tim. All this—" Gregory's sweeping gesture took in the entire gallery. "—takes a great deal of work and persistence to achieve. Unless there is something *dishonest* about the whole enterprise. But I cannot bring myself to even contemplate such a thing about you."

"Ha." Tim laughed nervously. "Greg, you *know* that I'm as innocent as a baby in its cradle."

"Are you? You don't know how that eases my mind. Now, why don't we go to your office for a cozy little chinwag?"

Tim's shoulders slouched forward, and he exhaled a long, low breath. He accepted the inevitable. Gregory was not going to leave. "Come on then, it's this way."

"That's a good fellow. I knew you'd see reason in the end."

Tim started to lead him down a corridor and then turned back. He cleared his throat and assumed the French accent once more. "Nicole?"

The young woman popped out from around her desk. "Yes, Monsieur Boinet?"

"I'm not to be disturbed for the next hour, unless it is an extremely important client. I will be in my office with Mr—"

"Wiggins," Gregory whispered out of the corner of his mouth.

"With Mr. Wiggins."

"Right, Monsieur Boinet."

Tim's office was a smaller version of the salon. The same cherry paneling could be found here, but a large mahogany desk dominated the center of the room. The hardwood floor was covered by a plush Aubusson carpet in pastel hues.

Tim grudgingly offered Gregory a seat. He walked around the desk to a small drinks table in the corner. He picked up a bottle of whiskey and waved it in the air. "Drink?"

"I wouldn't say no." The two men were silent as Tim splashed some of the liquor into two tumblers.

He handed one to Gregory. "Cheers."

There was a wicked glint in Gregory's eyes. "Cheers. To old friends."

Tim took a swig of his drink and nearly choked on it. "To old friends," he croaked. He took a second quick sip and plunked down into his chair, steeling himself for the unpleasant interview to come.

Gregory rolled the whiskey around his mouth to savor its rich flavor, before allowing it to glide down his throat. All the while, he kept his bemused gaze on Tim, which had an unnerving effect on the other man.

"Why are you looking at me like that?" Tim asked defensively.

Gregory laughed. "I wasn't aware that I was looking at you in a particular way. However, I am getting the distinct impression that you're not happy to see me. That can't be true, can it?"

"Let's cut to the chase. What do you want, Greg? I'm a legitimate businessman now, so if you don't mind, I—"

"Legitimate? Pull the other one. A leopard doesn't change his spots. The day plain, old Tim Clarke from Thirsk became Monsieur Maurice Boinet...from Paris, is it?...there was no question of you becoming legitimate. This is merely your latest scheme. What is it this time?"

Tim took a nervous swallow of the whiskey to play for time. "I resent your tone and the insinuation."

Gregory crossed one leg over the other and brushed off an invisible piece of lint from his trousers. "You can resent it all you like. We both know it's the truth. So let's stop pretending, shall we? I could care less about what you're up to these days. In fact, I'm willing to turn a blind eye to it."

Tim's ears perked up at this, and he leaned forward in his chair. "What do you want?"

"Information."

Tim rolled the tumbler between his hands. "What kind of information?" he asked cautiously.

"Who sold the Constable painting to Max Sanborn?"

The color drained from Tim's face. He jumped to his feet. "I wouldn't know anything about that. I don't deal in looted Nazi art."

"Relax. I'm not accusing you of anything."

"I should hope not," Tim replied indignantly, squaring his shoulders. "A chap has to draw the line somewhere, you know."

"Of course, you do. However, the art world is a very small place. Everyone knows what everyone else is doing."

Tim hesitated. "That's true...to a certain extent."

"Oh, come off it. Just give me the chap's name, and I'll never darken your doorstep again."

Tim licked his lips. Anything to get Gregory out of his gallery was tempting, but he would be taking an enormous risk. Was it worth it? Would anyone find out that he was the one who spilled the beans?

"Well, Tim," Gregory pressed.

Instead of answering, he asked, "What's your interest in this? Jewels are your specialty. Unless you're planning to relieve Max Sanborn of some of the jewels in his collection? He does have some lovely pieces, I must say. But then you always had such refined tastes, didn't you? I wouldn't mind a crack at them myself."

A shadow fell across Gregory's features. His jaw tightened into a hard line. "I want the name, Tim," he said through clenched teeth.

"Not until you tell me what's your angle."

Exasperated, Gregory stood up suddenly and grabbed Tim by the lapels.

"Watch the suit," Tim said. "You're crushing the material."

"I'll crush more than the material, if you don't give me the chap's name who sold the Constable to Max Sanborn. I know you—" Greg shook the other man.

"I can't," Tim snapped. "You can beat me senseless if you like, but I won't tell you."

Caught off guard, Gregory loosened his grip on the other man. "What do you mean you won't tell me?"

"He'll kill me. I'm sorry, Greg, but it's not worth it. If it were anyone else, I'd tell you in a flash. My advice is to forget about the whole thing."

"I can't. The painting most likely belonged to the Great Aunt of a friend of mine. I'm Symington's chief investigator on the case and want to see—"

Tim's blue eyes widened in disbelief. "What? I can't have heard you properly. I thought you just said that you're Symington's chief investigator."

Gregory nodded wearily. "I am," he replied quietly.

Tim began to laugh so hard that his entire body shook. "Well, if that doesn't beat all. What was that you were saying earlier about a leopard not changing his spots? My hat's off to you. You'll be richer than your wildest dreams. Access to all those client lists. You always were a sly old dog. Always had something up your sleeve. That's why you've never been caught—"

"Shut up, Tim," Gregory snapped. "I'm only going to say this once. I work for Symington's now, and I'm investigating how a Constable painting confiscated by the Nazis ended up in Max Sanborn's collection. I want to see that the painting gets back into the hands of the owner's descendants. To do that, I need the name of the man who sold it to Sanborn."

"All right, I believe you about Symington's, and I'd like to help, really I would, but the answer's still the same." Gregory's hands curled into tight fists at his sides. "You don't understand. The bloke in question is a very nasty piece of work. He mingles in only the best circles and may have adopted a cultured veneer, but he's ruthless. At heart—if he has a heart, that is—he's still the same thug he was back in the war. He'd kill you in the blink of an eye. With his bare hands."

"I can take care of myself. Just give me the name."

"He won't go after you. He takes pleasure in seeing people suffer, so he'll go after those closest to you. The people you love. Are you willing to take that risk?"

The question hung in the air between for a long moment. "I can protect them. *The name.*"

"Don't be a fool, Greg. This bloke's not like you and me. There's no honor among thieves. He was a commander in the IRA. He's battle hardened."

IRA? That was unexpected, but Gregory was determined to see justice for Maggie. "The name."

Tim sighed and shook his head. "Be it on your own head. His name is Doyle."

CHAPTER 18

I RA? How was the IRA mixed up with looted Nazi art? Gregory asked himself as he left the gallery, deep in thought. Every muscle in his body was coiled tightly with apprehension as he walked the short distance down Old Bond Street and out onto Piccadilly. He did not like this revelation at all. Because if he could find out about Doyle, it was only a matter of time before Emmeline stumbled across the information. This made the hairs on the back of his neck prickle.

Or was it something else? Gregory slowed his pace and ducked into the Burlington Arcade. He whistled softly as he casually strolled up the arcade, which was quiet compared to the hustle and bustle on Piccadilly. He stopped midway down the corridor to admire an exquisite Victorian broach in the window of Johnson Walker. Out of the corner of his eye, he caught a flutter of sudden movement. Someone—*a man?* yes—had just rounded the corner into the arcade and stopped short when he saw Gregory. The man quickly pretended to be contemplating several cardigans in pastel hues on display at the House of Cashmere. Gregory smiled. *A secret admirer. How flattering. Now,* what *could your interest in me possibly be, my friend? Shall we find out?* he asked himself.

Gregory walked a few paces and stopped in front of a shop specializing in rare silver pieces. Then he turned his attention to an elegant Patek Philippe watch in the window of Armour-Winston Ltd. In both cases, he was satisfied to see that his shadow was dutifully following him at what he judged was a safe distance. However, after five minutes, this game had become tiresome. Gregory had more important things to do than to spend the afternoon playing cat-and-mouse. Therefore, he had to get rid of his little friend. But how?

The answer soon presented itself in the form of a portly middle-aged gentleman with ruddy cheeks who wore a navy suit and an Eton tie. At a glance, Gregory guessed he was an investment banker. Very rich, very proper, very stiff upper lip.

Gregory smoothed the corners of his mustache down and smiled. Mr. Banker was being extremely obliging. He stopped in front of Church's to get a better a look at a pair of well-made leather loafers. Gregory's shadow was hovering next to him, doing a poor job of trying to look inconspicuous.

Gregory waited until both men were distracted and seized his chance. He hurried down the corridor and grabbed a hold of his shadow's arm. "Oh, no, you don't, old chap," he started yelling. "You won't get away with that."

"Eh? What?" The man was completely caught off guard by this turn of events and tried to shrug himself free. "What are you on about? Let go of me."

"I say. What's all this fuss? You can't go shoving people about that way," the banker said pompously.

"Oh, no? I would have thought you would be grateful. I just saw this chap lift your wallet."

"What?" The banker's gray eyes were like huge saucers. He immediately started patting his jacket. "I say. You're right. My wallet *has* been stolen. You scoundrel, turn out your pockets. You there," he said to one of the beadles patrolling the arcade, "Call the police."

By this time, a small crowd had gathered around them. Gregory's shadow licked his lips and took a half-step backward. "Sir, I assure you this is some sort of a mistake."

"You're the one who has made the mistake. Now, turn out your pockets," the banker demanded.

The other man put up his hands. "All right. All right. Keep your shirt on. You'll see that you're wrong." He unbuttoned his jacket and pulled out one inside pocket and then the other. "Satisfied?"

The banker mumbled, "Now, your trousers."

"This is a bit ridiculous."

"We'll see. Come on, hurry it up."

"You are quite wrong. I never took—" The man's face became ashen when he thrust his hand into the second pocket. To his horror, he felt the very solid bulk of a wallet. Not his wallet.

"Well?" the banker pressed. "What's the matter?" His eyes narrowed. "Let me see your hands. I said take your hands out of your pocket."

The other man hesitated for a moment longer and then sighed in resignation. As he removed his hand, the wallet tumbled out and landed on the floor with a muted *thud*.

"Aha," banker said victoriously.

"There's been a mistake. I've been framed—"

The banker snorted. "Save it for the police, my lad."

As if on cue, a constable materialized at his elbow. "What's the problem here?"

"The *problem*, constable, is that this fellow here attempted to steal my wallet."

"Oh, yes?" the constable said as he took a hold of the alleged culprit's arm. "Not your day is it."

"It's all a misunderstanding. I didn't—"

The constable cut him off. "I know. I know. You're innocent. All these witnesses are mistaken. Well, you can explain it all down at the station."

"But I—"

"I'd quit while I was ahead, if I were you," the constable advised. "You wouldn't want to add resisting arrest to the charges against you."

With things satisfactorily in hand, Gregory quietly pealed himself away from the group huddled around the two protagonists of this drama and made his way down the corridor toward the Piccadilly entrance. Just as he reached the pavement, he cast a backward glance. His eyes locked on those of his erstwhile shadow, who scowled at him. The man was in no doubt whatsoever who was to blame for his present troubles. Gregory chuckled and sketched a little salute in the air, before abandoning him to his date with the law.

Gregory dashed across Piccadilly just before the light changed and went into Fortnum & Mason. He made a slow circuit of the ground floor, starting with the chocolate bonbons moving on to the jams and preserves and ending in the front by the tins of various blends of tea. After twenty minutes, he was certain that he had not attracted another unwanted friend. He left the store. Once out on the pavement again, he pulled out his mobile and punched in a number.

A male voice came on the line after the first ring. "To what do I owe this unexpected pleasure?"

"You can drop the innocent act," Gregory snapped. "You'll find your chap at the local police station. I suppose it's difficult to get good hired help these days."

There was a brief pause. "Your doing?"

Gregory smiled at the note of irritation creeping into the other man's voice. "Naturally. I'm a perfectionist. I believe in doing a job well or not at all. Sadly, your chap does not follow this philosophy." He clucked his tongue, further annoying his interlocutor. "He was very sloppy indeed. It's quite apparent that he does not take pride in his work."

"All right. You've made your point. What do you want?"

Gregory abandoned his light-hearted air. "We need to meet."

"Why?" the man asked cautiously.

"I think you know why. In fact, I think you're one the pulling strings from the shadows. As always."

"I'm quite at a loss—"

"Dammit, man, I'm not in the mood for one of your mind games. I can handle myself. But what I don't like is that Emmeline has stumbled into one of your sordid intrigues."

"Then perhaps you should persuade your intrepid fiancée to drop her crusade before she gets in over her head."

Gregory's jaw tightened. "Listen to me, you bastard, I will kill you if anything happens to Emmeline. Do you understand?" he hissed.

"It's refreshing to see that chivalry isn't dead. I'd like to meet this woman who stirs such strong emotions in you. This is the second time in two days that you've threatened to kill someone. I agree that your uncle's demise would make this world a better place. But really, Longdon, playing the bully with me is not quite the thing."

Gregory finally lost his temper. "I've had enough of this. Hatchards in one hour. If you don't show up, I'm going straight to Burnell with the connection I've discovered between Max Sanborn's looted painting and a former IRA commander named Doyle."

The voice on the other end calmly replied, "That would be ill-advised."

"Hatchards. One hour."

CHAPTER 19

Superintendent Burnell. Oh, Superintendent Burnell, there you are *at last*." Sally's heels clicked briskly down the corridor as she barreled her way toward him.

It was too late for Burnell to pretend he hadn't seen her. If he did say so himself, he had done an admirable job of avoiding her most of the day. But alas, all good things must come to an end. Unfortunately.

He plastered a smile on his face. "Ah, Sally. Were you looking for me?"

"I've been trying to track you down *all* morning. Sergeant Finch said that you were out pursuing a line of inquiry regarding Max Sanborn's painting."

Good thinking, Finch, Burnell said to himself. *I must put him in for a pay rise.*

"Yes, that's right I was out of the building."

"And I couldn't get you on your mobile," Sally replied in clipped tones.

Perhaps that's because I turned it off when I saw your number? Aloud Burnell said, "Really? That's odd."

"Hmm." Sally's lips formed a tight line, and she eyed him suspiciously but decided to let this pass.

"Was there something in particular that you needed? Or did you only want a little chat?"

"Hardly." She sniffed. "I have better things to do with my time."

"I'm sure you do. So what is it?"

"Assistant Commissioner Fenton would like a word with you."

"Ah, please tell him that I'm rather busy just now. But I'll try to drop by in the morning." *Unless a new lead comes to light.* "As I said, I'm very *busy* at the moment with this case and—"

Sally shook her head in disapproval and began to tap one foot impatiently on the floor. "No. That simply will not do. The assistant commissioner said that the instant you set foot back in the building you were to go directly to his office. You cannot keep an important man like the assistant commissioner waiting."

"I can't?" Burnell asked hopefully.

"No, you most certainly cannot. Now, let's go upstairs."

"Really, Sally, there's no need for you to escort me. I know the way to the assistant commissioner's office. If I get lost, I'll just follow the well-worn footsteps on the floor until I get to his door."

"No. You will come *now*."

Burnell sighed and thrust his hands deep into his pockets. There was nothing for it. He knew his defenses had been breached. "Right. Lead the way." He gestured with one arm toward the lift. "I can't imagine a more pleasant way to spend my afternoon than chatting with Assistant Commissioner Fenton. What a treat."

"Hmph," was Sally's response as she tossed her head in the air and turned on her heel. He caught a distinct glint of triumph in her cool gray eyes.

Apparently, she had exhausted her store of words for the day because they rode up in the lift in complete silence. This suited Burnell just fine. It gave him a few minutes to steel himself for the meeting with his boss.

"Come in," was the brisk response that floated to their ears after Sally tapped lightly on Fenton's door. She opened it wide and stepped aside to allow the superintendent to pass.

"Ah, there you are, Burnell," the assistant commissioner said. "Good of you to spare me a few minutes. I wanted to have a word with you about this Max Sanborn business."

"Did you, sir? If you're wondering, my inquiries are progressing. Finch and I obtained the warrant today and took away the Constable. We turned it over to the Arts and Antiques Unit, and—"

Fenton cut him short. "That's precisely what I wanted to speak to you about. Max...Mr. Sanborn has complained about your deplorable conduct in this matter. Apparently, you and Finch exhibited a lack of decorum and respect and made rather a nuisance of yourselves. As a result, I'm left with no choice but to take you off the case. Arts and Antiques will handle things from here on out. You are *not* to interfere further. And, you are not to go anywhere near Max Sanborn again. Do I make myself clear?"

The assistant commissioner's back stiffened, and he sat up straighter in his chair, looking up at the superintendent with all the disdain he could muster.

Why you bloody arrogant bastard, Burnell seethed silently. *The old boy network strikes again.*

"Burnell, did you hear me?" Fenton pressed.

The superintendent cleared his throat. "Yes, sir," he replied in a strangled voice. He couldn't trust himself to say more.

"Good. I'm glad that we understand each other." Fenton put his glasses on the bridge of his nose and opened a folder by his elbow. The interview was at an end. Burnell had been summarily dismissed. "On your way out, please ask Sally to come in. I need her to take a letter."

"Yes, sir," Burnell repeated again.

Sally beamed at him as he stopped at her desk to pass on Fenton's message. "Meeting over so soon? That was quick. Ah, well. I'll just go in to the assistant commissioner. Have a good afternoon, Superintendent Burnell."

From the smug look on her face, she had probably been listening at the door.

"Good afternoon, Sally," Burnell mumbled. *It's a pity that Jack the Ripper is no longer in business. He'd know how to wipe that smile off your face.*

⁂

Philip slammed the phone back in its cradle. "Damn, Villiers," he said aloud to his office.

He had just had an extremely disagreeable conversation with Bernard in research. To his unpleasant surprise, he was told that Villiers had given orders that no one was to talk to him about anything to do with Max Sanborn, the Constable, or Maggie's claims. "Damn the man," Philip fumed. "Why is he getting personally involved in this case? What is he trying to hide? He's afraid of something being discovered, but what? And *what* is his connection to Longdon?"

His mind was going in circles as he mulled over these questions at the expense of his Foreign Office work, which patiently awaited him in the form of a little stack of folders on his desk. Only the shrill peal of the telephone pulled him from his troubled thoughts.

"Acheson," he answered brusquely.

"Hello, Philip. I must say that I've had warmer greetings. Did I call at a bad time or is it just a case of you waking up on the wrong side of the bed this morning?"

Some of the tension in his body eased, and the corners of his mouth involuntarily curled into a smile. "Hello, Emmeline. I'm sorry. How are you?"

"I'm fine, but you don't sound as if you are. Did something else happen? Is Maggie all right?"

"No, everything's fine," he reassured her. "My incredibly strong-willed and determined wife went back to work today. She's not going to let Max Sanborn intimidate her. In fact, she's hired a solicitor, and he's filed a lawsuit against Sanborn. I believe the papers will be sent to his lawyer this afternoon."

"Good for Maggie. I wish I could be a fly on the wall to see Max Sanborn's reaction. He hasn't set foot outside his penthouse since he announced that he will be stepping down *temporarily* as chairman of Sanborn Enterprises. Well, you and Maggie know that you have my full support. I'm still on the story, but thus far I haven't discovered anything new about the Constable or Sarah and Edmond Lévy. I don't suppose you could use your influence to get me access to some of MI5's

World War Two files?" she asked coyly. "There might be a
tiny clue buried in them. Anything I find I would, of course,
attribute merely to a *government source*. No one would need
fear that I would be divulging government secrets. After seventy years, the majority of the files are probably declassified
anyway and their subjects most likely are dead. So there would
be no harm in allowing me to have a little peek at the files."

Philip leaned back in his chair and laughed in spite of himself. "Always at work, always thinking of an angle, aren't
you?"

"You make me sound rather cold-blooded and manipula-
tive," she replied petulantly.

"Not a bit of it. You are one of the most honest and ethical
journalists I know. There's no need to get all tetchy—"

"Well, it's a relief to know that I still have your good opinion of me."

"—however, the answer is no."

There was a brief silence. "What? I thought you said—"

"That I admire you greatly. Yes. But I can't give you access to any files at MI5. Maggie's allegations seem to have
stirred up a cauldron of trouble, and someone is running
scared. As a result, I appear to be *persona non grata* at the
moment. Deputy Director Laurence Villiers has given orders
that no one is to speak to me about anything remotely connected with the case. Therefore, by extension, I very much doubt
that dropping my name will help you. Villiers himself had a
quiet word with me yesterday and made it quite clear that I
was to stop asking questions. He also expects me to persuade
you and Maggie to stop your search."

"The bloody nerve of the man. I'd give him a piece of my
mind if I met him face to face."

Philip laughed. He could hear the tremor of outrage in her
voice. "I don't doubt that for a minute. Secretly, I think Villiers is trembling in his boots at the thought of finding you on
his doorstep armed with a tape recorder and a notebook. That's
why he wants me to do his dirty work for him."

"I think it's appalling. It's not fair to put you in the middle like this. I'll make an appointment to see Villiers in the morning."

"First of all, I'm a big boy and can take care of myself. Second, it would be *extremely* unwise to confront Villiers."

"Why? I'm not afraid of him. Maggie and her family deserve justice. And the public has the right to know the truth."

"The truth can be a dangerous thing." There was an edge to his voice.

"What…What are you saying? Philip, are you still there?"

After a long pause, he finally said, "Just be careful. That's all." He fell silent again, and a thought struck him. "Something just occurred to me. Someone, actually. I don't know why I didn't think of him before. He's a friend of mine. He may be able to give you the answers you're looking for. In fact, I'm sure of it. I'll ring him, if you like."

He heard the eagerness in her tone as she asked, "Who is this friend of yours?"

"Yoav Zielinski. He's the cultural attaché at the Israeli embassy."

෴

Gregory had just checked his watch for the fifth time, when a man in charcoal trousers slowly ascended the wooden spiral staircase to the upper floor in Hatchards. Within a minute, Laurence Villiers was standing next to him as he pretended to peruse the fiction shelves. They said nothing to one another because two women were standing nearby gushing over a bestselling author's latest book.

Gregory jerked his head in the direction of the next room where crime fiction was located. Villiers followed. There was only an elderly woman at the far end, and she appeared oblivious to their presence.

Villiers picked up a copy of *A Taste for Death* by P.D. James. He leaned an elbow on the shelf and started to flip through the pages. "I'm here, so what do you want?"

Gregory ran his finger along the shelf and plucked out a book. Out of the corner of his mouth, he replied, "Answers. About Max Sanborn's stolen painting and how it's mixed up with a former IRA commander named Doyle."

Villiers slipped his book back and selected another. "May I ask how you came about this knowledge?"

Gregory flashed a cheeky grin. "Sorry, old chap. It's on a need-to-know-basis. I'm sure you understand."

Villiers noisily slapped his book shut, causing the old woman to lift her head briefly. However, he quickly regained his composure. "Don't play games with me," he hissed.

Gregory put a hand to his chest and, in mock innocence, said, "*Me* play games? I wouldn't dream of it, mate. Just tell me the whole story so that I know how to protect Emmeline."

"I told you earlier. The best way to protect your fiancée is to persuade her to drop the story."

Gregory laughed in spite of himself. "Obviously, you don't know her. Anyone who is acquainted with Emmy knows that once she believes in something strongly, she will pursue it to the bitter end. Whatever the outcome. That's what makes her such a good journalist. And a loyal friend."

"Others would call that reckless," Villiers replied phlegmatically.

"I'd watch what I said if I were you. Emmeline is not part of our unorthodox arrangement, which I'll remind you *I* can terminate whenever I choose."

"Believe me, I'd like nothing more than to keep her at arm's length. Better yet, out of the loop completely. But she's beginning to make quite a nuisance of herself. Her questions are stirring up a great many things that are best left...*undisturbed*. My advice is to let sleeping dogs lie, old chap. Let the professionals handle it."

"Questions are her *modus operandi*. You can't stop her, so you had better tell me all about this Doyle character so that I know what I'm...we're up against."

Villiers put the book down and exhaled a long breath. He suddenly felt drained, and old. He shook his head as if he was warring with himself. He fixed a hard stare on Gregory's tense face. What he saw reflected in those cinnamon eyes that were so similar to his own was a mixture of love and concern. Villiers felt his chest constrict. He remembered a time when he must have looked just like that. And the memories came flooding back of the only woman who he had allowed to touch his heart.

At last, Villiers cleared his throat. "I'll tell you everything you want to know," he said in a hoarse whisper. "But not here." He glanced round. "I have an aversion to confined spaces. Besides, the walls have ears. Let's walk."

CHAPTER 20

They had agreed to meet somewhere they wouldn't attract attention. Somewhere away from prying eyes. Therefore, what better way to remain inconspicuous than in the middle of a great crowd. So at three-twenty, Emmeline strolled up the promenade and stopped before Traitor's Gate at the Tower of London. She was early because her grandmother had drilled into her since she was a little girl that it was bad manners to be late for anything. It was second nature to her. Besides, it afforded her a chance to get the lay of the land.

A tour guide was giving a group of Americans a brief overview of the gate's historical significance. Emmeline hovered on the outer fringes. She glanced at her watch. It was three-thirty on the nose, and there was no sign of the gentleman she was supposed to meet. She cast a look over her right shoulder toward the looming elegance of Tower Bridge and then swiveled her neck to the left, but all she saw were tourists. They were taking photos and flipping through guidebooks or being herded toward the entrance to the tower's grounds, which was at the other end of the promenade.

"You know they say that Anne Boleyn entered the tower through Traitor's Gate on her sad journey from favorite to outcast," a male voice whispered in her ear.

Emmeline swung her head around to find herself staring at a slender man in his early sixties, who was dressed in a light gray suit, crisp white shirt, and a yellow silk tie. He was small, perhaps no taller than five-foot-six or -seven. There was a be-mused look in his intelligent onyx eyes, which crinkled at the corners when he smiled. His white hair was slowly receding from the broad dome of his forehead.

"Mr. Zielinski, I presume?"

He proffered a hand and gave a brisk nod. "You presume correctly, Miss Kirby. I'm delighted to meet you." He spoke English perfectly, with only the merest trace of an accent.

His handshake was warm and dry. It conveyed a mixture of confidence and humility.

She found herself immediately at ease and returned his smile. "Thank you very much for agreeing to speak with me, Mr. Zielinski."

He patted her hand in an avuncular fashion and tucked it into the crook of his arm. "Think nothing of it. Shall we walk?"

He led her a few hundred feet toward an empty bench that overlooked the Thames and had a clear view of Tower Bridge.

"I was more than happy to meet with you. Philip didn't have to twist my arm at all," he said as they settled themselves on the bench. "In fact, I was quite eager to meet you. Your reputation precedes you, Miss Kirby. Your work is admirable."

She felt herself blushing. "Thank you. It's very kind of you to say so. But I'm just doing my job. And that's to find the truth." She rooted around in her handbag and pulled out her notebook, a pen, and her tape recorder.

"Mmm." He cocked his head to one side and studied her for a long moment. "Your father said nearly the same thing to me nearly thirty years ago."

"*My father*? You knew my father?"

"I wouldn't say know, but I did meet him and your mother. I was still in the army then, and we were fighting in Lebanon. Yes." He looked up at the bridge and frowned. His mind drift-ed back to that time of strife. But then, when wasn't there a time of strife for the Israelis? The Middle East conflict, would it never end? He sighed. "Yes, I met Aaron when he came to interview me. Your mother was the photographer."

Zielinski turned back to the present. He found Emmeline sitting very still. Her dark eyes fixed on his face. "They were quite a team, your parents. They complemented each other very well. You remind me of both of them. You have your father's dark coloring and eyes, but you are the spitting image of your mother." He tilted his head to one side and scrutinized her again. "Yes, they are both very much in evidence in you."

Emmeline swallowed the lump that had formed in her throat. She felt tears pricking at the back of her eyelids. This had thrown her completely off balance. She had come for a story. She had not expected to talk about her parents today.

"Are you all right, Emmeline? May I call you Emmeline? I feel that I know you already."

She nodded mutely. She couldn't make her mouth form any words. "Yes," she croaked at last. "Please feel free to call me Emmeline." It was a breach of etiquette, but she reached out and squeezed his hand. "Thank you for telling me about my parents and comparing my work to theirs. That is high praise indeed. They were the best of the best. I hope they would be proud of me. I was five when they were killed in Beirut. My grandmother was told that they had died during a clash be-tween guerillas and Israeli troops, who had been on a mission to rescue two soldiers captured in an ambush. It was chaos. Everyone scattered for cover, but my parents were caught in the crossfire. Nowadays, the official term is 'collateral dam-age.' It sounds so cold and aloof. But they were my parents. They—" She choked on this last word. She couldn't go on. She stared down at her hands as the tears rolled off her cheeks onto her lap.

Zielinski was silent as she struggled to regain her compo-sure. His brow knit together in concern.

Finally, she straightened her shoulders and lifted her head. She cleared her throat. "Yes, well...I'm terribly sorry. You didn't come here to talk about the past."

"Ah, but that's *exactly* what we're here to discuss, isn't it? You want to know about looted Nazi paintings in general and how a certain Constable ended up in Max Sanborn's collec-tion?"

"Yes." Her pen was poised over her notebook, and she clicked her tape recorder on.

He placed a hand over hers. "No notes. No tape recorder." His voice was quiet, but firm. "The conversation from this point on is completely *off the record*."

She held his gaze for a moment and then reluctantly agreed.

"Now, that we have laid the grounds rules. You may ask me anything you like."

Emmeline smiled. "Very well. I find it curious that Philip thought that the Israeli cultural attaché, who happens to be a decorated retired general, could help me with my inquiries when everyone else is dropping none-too-subtle hints that it would be in my best interest to abandon the story altogether. MI5, in particular, seems to have closed ranks. Poor Philip has been sent to Coventry because he has the misfortune of being married to Maggie and is a friend of mine."

"I'm not qualified to comment on how the different levels of British government interact with one another and the press. Philip simply believed that I had some knowledge that could help you."

"A very diplomatic answer. But I don't believe it."

Zielinski's onyx eyes widened in surprise. "I don't understand."

"I think you understand quite well. You're Mossad, aren't you? That's why Philip believes you can help me. Isn't it? Come on, Mr. Zielinski, admit it. This is off the record, remember."

The gentleman leaned back against the bench and chuckled. "You have a very vivid imagination. But please don't let it run away with you. I'm not a spy. I'm a teacher. A professor of history, in fact. The past is my specialty. I was head of the History Department at Hebrew University in Jerusalem when the prime minister asked me to become cultural attaché. It has been a great honor for me to represent my country here in London for the last thirteen years."

She gave him a knowing smile. "You can deny it all you like, but I know I'm right." She waggled a finger to prevent him from offering a disavowal. "Don't worry, though. Your secret is safe with me."

He scanned her face. Her eyes were filled with a mixture of triumph and archness. "You are a very stubborn young woman who won't take no for an answer."

"I've always felt that *determined* and *persistent* were so much nicer adjectives. *Chacun à son goût*, I suppose," she said with a little shrug of her shoulders.

Zielinski gave a low, soft laugh. "Yes, to each his own. You are under a great misconception, but I can see that no matter what I say there is nothing I can do to change that. So we move on." He became serious. "*A Country Lane in Summer.* Oil on canvas. Eighty-seven-point-nine by one-hundred-eleven-point-eight centimeters. Painted by John Constable in 1825."

"Yes," she prompted. "What can you tell me about the painting?"

"It was confiscated from Edmond and Sarah Lévy in Nice in 1943. They disappeared two days later."

She swallowed hard. "Do you—Do you know what happened to them? I have to try to find out for Maggie and her family's sake. It's better to know the truth than..." Her voice trailed off, the thought left unfinished.

He shook his head sadly. "There was a rumor that they attempted to make contact with the Free French to try to get to England, but they never did. They simply vanished. We believe that they were betrayed."

"I see," she murmured. She felt the warm sting of tears welling up in her eyes, but she was not going to give in to her emotions again. She had a job to do.

She shook her head as if to clear her mind. "Right. Please go on."

"The Constable and a number of other paintings were seized by the Nazis and taken by train to Austria, where they were hidden away in a salt mine for safekeeping until after the war when they would become part of the Hitler museum. However, the Americans discovered the spoils. Once Paris was liberated, a joint American and British unit began the painstaking process to catalogue the hundreds of pieces of artwork and to try to return them to their rightful owners. If they were still alive. It was a noble effort. However, some soldiers involved were not honest, and many pieces disappeared. After all, their owners were likely dead so who would miss them?"

Emmeline's jaw clenched into hard line. "How despicable. These poor people were victimized twice."

"Yes," Zielinski replied softly. "War and hatred corrupt the soul, until the line between good and evil is blurred."

"Is that what happened to the Constable? It walked into the night?"

"As far as we have been able to gather, yes. But we will come back to the painting in a moment. It is merely one of the many pawns in an elaborate chess game of deception, theft, and murder.

"You remember I mentioned that Edmond and Sarah Lévy were betrayed. We believe it was by someone in the resistance. An Irishman named Doyle, who spoke French like a native. He was clever, charming, and persuasive. But beneath the façade, he was a ruthless liar whose black heart beat with a deep-seated hatred for the British. He was a republican and wanted to see the British run out of Ireland at all costs. And so, Doyle joined the war on the German side in the hopes of hastening this conclusion."

Emmeline sucked in her breath. "My God. The IRA. But what does this have to do with—"

He took hold of one her small hands. "Everything will become clear. I promise."

She nodded and settled back against the bench, her gaze intent upon his face.

He resumed his story. "For months, this particular resistance group had been carrying out daring sabotage raids, which had left the Germans reeling. In addition, they had successfully prevented two caches of looted art from being sent back to the Furher. Needless to say, the Nazis were furious. They began to suspect that they had a spy in their midst. But who? And how would they root him out without tipping their hand?

"Enter our friend Doyle. He had already proven his loyalty to the Fatherland on several missions against the British. Now, the Germans would use him to unmask the spy and smash the resistance in one fell swoop. Doyle easily managed to infiltrate the group. He should have gone on the stage, that's how good he was at deception. With his fluent French and easy charm, he quickly garnered the trust of his fellow resistance fighters. They began sending him out on some of their most sensitive missions. As a result, it didn't take him long to tell his masters who was the spy.

"The Germans fed the traitor information about the transfer of another batch of paintings, knowing full well that he would pass it on to the resistance. And so the trap was set. The spy's body was found the next day in an alley. They had beaten him viciously before they put a bullet through the back of his head. Meanwhile, Doyle took pleasure in seeing to it that not a single member of that resistance band lived to see another day."

Emmeline gripped her knees to stop her hands from shaking. Bile was rising in her throat, choking her. "How...how horrible. What a monster this man Doyle was."

"Oh, yes, the very worst kind. A man without a conscience. But my dear, I haven't finished this sordid tale. Now we come to the Lévys' Constable. On that ill-fated night, Doyle and his German cronies made a deal and divided up the paintings amongst themselves. Hitler wouldn't miss a few paintings when he already had so many, they reasoned. Doyle managed to smuggle his share of the booty to Switzerland, where it would remain secreted away in the bowels of a bank vault. The Germans weren't so lucky. Their paintings fell into the hands of the Allies. The Constable was among them—"

"Then why was it never returned to Maggie's family?" Emmeline interrupted.

"Because it literally disappeared into the night. One of the soldiers responsible for cataloguing and determining the provenance of the stolen artwork took it."

She crossed her arms over her chest and fumed in silence

as Zielinski continued, "The Constable didn't surface again until 1952. The soldier in question had fallen on hard times. His wife left him for another man. Not only that, she cleaned out their bank account leaving him with nothing."

"Good," Emmeline said with satisfaction. "He got what he deserved."

Zielinski couldn't help but laugh at this reaction. "Yes, but this former soldier had never told his wife about the Constable. So, painful as it was, he decided to sell it and move to the Costa del Sol, where nobody knew him, and he could live like a king on the money. Now the problem was *how*? He simply couldn't walk into a gallery and offer the painting for sale. No, his only option was the Black Market. It took him a few months of discreet inquiries, but, at last, he was put in contact with someone who was willing to take the painting off his hands no questions asked. Can you guess who the buyer was?"

"Not Doyle?" she said, stunned.

"Oh, yes. Our friend Doyle assumed center stage once again. Since the end of the war, we believe he had assumed a new identity, becoming a businessman of sorts, and had been quietly building his stash of stolen paintings in Switzerland. He would sell them through a third party to collectors who were willing to pay anything and were unconcerned about such tedious things as provenance. These collectors would never be able to show the paintings in public, but this didn't trouble them. The important thing was to possess the paintings. Doyle was more than happy to cater to these greedy, unscrupulous men, for he had his own agenda.

"I hope you haven't forgotten that our friend was an active member of the IRA." Emmeline shook her head. "To all outward appearances, he was a legitimate businessman. However, Doyle was secretly using the proceeds from the sale of the paintings to bankroll the IRA's attacks here in England."

"Couldn't someone have stopped him? Surely if you know about Doyle, MI5 and MI6 must have known about him."

"Ah, Emmeline, this falls under the category of war making strange bedfellows. MI6 did haul Doyle in and confronted him with evidence of his activities. However, they offered him a deal. They would let him go, if he helped to identify some of his German comrades-in-arms who were now living in England under the guise of being refugees. Doyle readily agreed and turned in a few of his former allies. Then he went underground. No one heard from him again. There were rumors in the 1970s that he had died in an IRA attack, but his body was never found. I'm quite certain he was the one who started the rumors so that he could continue all of his nefarious endeavors unimpeded by the authorities, who were getting a little too close for comfort. And that's how the Constable ended up in Max Sanborn's possession."

"Then the bloody, arrogant bastard knows the painting was looted," she said.

Zielinski nodded sagely.

"Does Sanborn know who Doyle is?"

The diplomat allowed himself a small smile. "The sale was likely conducted through a third party. But a man like Max Sanborn doesn't get to where he is in life without knowing where *all* the bodies are buried."

Emmeline felt the blood thundering in her ears. Her mind was racing. The story was even bigger than she had at first anticipated.

Zielinski reached into the inside pocket of his suit jacket and drew out a grainy black-and-white photo of a group of German soldiers laughing. He handed it to her. "This is the only known photo of Doyle. That's him." He pointed a finger at a tall, fair-haired man whose head was turned in profile.

Emmeline squinted hard at the photo for a long moment. It was not much to go on. But it was a start.

Zielinski glanced at his watch. "I'm afraid that I stayed longer than I intended. I must be getting back to the embassy."

They both rose to their feet. Emmeline extended a hand. "Thank you so much for agreeing to meet with me, Mr. Zielinski. I can't tell you how much I appreciate it. And don't worry. Not even a whisper of your name will ever pass my lips. I want you to know I always keep my promises."

The older man pressed her small hand in both of his and smiled. "You are definitely your parents' daughter. It was a great pleasure meeting you. I know you will use the information that I gave to pursue Doyle with all your energy, but be careful. The man is extremely dangerous. His past is littered with bodies. I do not want any harm to come to you because of what I told you."

"I can take care of myself."

"Please see that you do."

With that, he inclined his head and turned on his heel. Within seconds, she lost sight of him as he melted into the crowd of tourists.

She remained there for a few seconds, her mind awhirl. Where to begin? She took out her notebook and jotted down a few questions as a starting point.

It was as she was gathering up her handbag that she felt— no, that she knew instinctively—that someone was watching her. There was a spot between her shoulder blades where two eyes were boring straight through her. Very casually, she slid a sideways glance to her right and then swiveled around to her left. But it was useless, there were so many people about that it could be anyone. Or she could just be paranoid? No. She was not in the habit of letting her imagination run away with her.

Someone was definitely watching.

CHAPTER 21

Gregory found Emmeline banging away at her keyboard when he dropped by her office around six-thirty that evening. He leaned against the door frame and simply watched her for a couple of minutes. She was so wrapped up in her work that she was oblivious to everything else around her. He admired her energy and focus, but one couldn't live on work alone.

"That's it, Emmy, my love. I've come to rescue from your toil and strife." He crossed the room and pressed a kiss against the top of her head.

She jumped and spun around in her chair. "Oh, there you are." She tilted her head up and absent-mindedly brushed his lips with a kiss. "I can't leave now. I'm working on a lead. I'll see you tomorrow, darling."

She attempted to turn back toward her computer, but he bent down and gripped both arms of her chair, preventing it from moving. "No, you don't. You are leaving with me this instant. I will not take no for an answer." He shook his head. "You can protest all you like, but I assure you it will fall on deaf ears. I have a seven-thirty reservation at La Normandie, and I refuse to be late. So let's go."

He pulled her to her feet and smothered whatever she had been about to say with a deep kiss.

She struggled half-heartedly at first. Then her arms slipped around his waist, and she returned it with enthusiasm.

She was a little breathless when they pulled apart. There

was roguish glint in his cinnamon eyes. "Why are you looking so smug?"

"I knew you couldn't resist my abundance of charm."

She swatted his arm. "You are an egotistical swine." But she flicked off her computer and carefully tucked her file on Doyle in her desk drawer.

He laughed as he gathered up her handbag and looped her arm through his. "Darling, do you know that it's bad manners to insult your future husband?" he asked as he led her toward the door.

"If you carry on like this, there won't be a marriage," she replied tartly as she locked her office.

"I'm afraid it's too late to change your mind. Helen and Maggie will be absolutely furious with you. So for your own protection, you have no choice but to marry me."

Emmeline rolled her eyes. "Beast. How is it that everyone is always on *your* side?"

He bent down and kissed the tip of her nose. "I already told you, darling. It's my abundance of charm."

"Hmph," she grunted. "I'm fighting a losing battle. You're capable of running rings around me all evening, so I'd better give up while I'm ahead."

"A very sensible idea." He slipped his arm around her waist as they crossed the newsroom. "Now, tell me about this new lead of yours?"

Emmeline kept him in suspense for a bit as she stopped off to discuss something with the deputy editor and chief political correspondent. Once the issue had been taken care of, she succinctly told him about her illuminating conversation with Yoav Zielinski. The only thing she left out was the name of her source.

"So you see, it's a much bigger story than I had originally imagined," she concluded as she jabbed the button to call the lift.

Gregory saw the spark of excitement in her dark eyes and his lips tightened into a grim line. Damn and blast. She found out about Doyle sooner than he had anticipated. He cleared his throat. "Emmy, are you sure that this anonymous source of yours is reliable?" he asked carefully.

"Absolutely. His credentials are impeccable."

"I see," Gregory murmured. "Do you really think it's wise to try to find this Doyle character? Why not leave it to the proper authorities?"

Her head snapped round so fast that he thought it would fall off her neck. A flash of anger ignited in her eyes. "I hope you're not suggesting that I abandon this story, because I won't. Besides the 'proper authorities' as you call them— which I find ironic coming from you—have been content for the last sixty odd years to pretend that Doyle never existed. After all, it would be quite an embarrassment to admit that members of the British Secret Service and counterintelligence had allowed a senior IRA leader to slip through their fingers. I'm going to find Doyle and expose him for the devil that he is."

Was this a surprise? No. Gregory sighed. He knew his arguments would be dismissed out of hand, so he didn't waste even a single breath trying to dissuade her. The only thing that he could do was to find Doyle before the man got the merest inkling that she was on his trail and tried to kill her.

Her dark gaze raked his face. "You know, you don't seem particularly surprised by my revelations about Doyle."

He raised an eyebrow. "On the contrary, darling, I'm fascinated. I'm hanging on every word."

"Uh-huh. It doesn't suit you playing dumb. In fact, it makes me rather suspicious." She took a step closer to him and poked him in the chest. "What *aren't* you telling me?"

He silently cursed Villiers for placing him in this position. Outwardly though, he was all easy charm. He smoothed down the corners of his mustache, and his lips curled into a smile. "I always tell you everything because you are the love of my life."

"Then why didn't you tell me about Veronica Cabot?" Emmeline sucked in her breath. She regretted the words as soon as she had uttered them. They just slipped out unbidden.

A lump lodged itself in her throat. She couldn't bring herself to look at him.

Gregory put a finger under her chin and gently lifted her head so that she was forced to look at him. "I promise I will spend the rest of my life trying to make it up to you, if that's possible. You have my word that nothing like that will *ever* happen again."

She nodded dumbly and then whispered, "I'm sorry. I didn't mean to throw it in your face like that. I am trying to get over it. Really I am. It's just very…difficult."

With his thumb, he wiped away a stray tear that had escaped from the corner of her eye. "You have nothing to be sorry about." He put his hands on her shoulders. "Nothing, do you hear me? I was a bloody fool, darling. I want you to trust me completely. What I want more than anything in this world is for you to be my wife."

"I know," she replied hoarsely. "I want that too." She reached up and pressed a soft kiss against his cheek. Then she disentangled herself from his embrace. "Right. Back to the matter at hand. Doyle." She fumbled in her handbag. "Here's the only photo of him ever taken. I'm afraid it's not very good and his face is in profile, but it's a start."

Gregory took the photo from her. His brows drew together as he studied it.

"Ah, there you are, Miss Kirby. I just popped by your office, but you weren't there. I'd like a word," Patrick Kildare said as the lift doors slid open.

Gregory tucked the photo into the inside pocket of his suit jacket and put a hand on the small of Emmeline's back as they entered the lift.

Emmeline shot him a pained look. After her confrontation the day before with Max, she knew management was not best pleased with her. She was tired and no mood to have a new argument, this time with a Sanborn Enterprises board member no less. However, the good manners her grandmother had taught her prevailed, and she replied, "Good evening, Mr. Kildare."

"Longdon." The older man inclined his head in greeting. Then he turned to Emmeline. "You've caused an awful lot of trouble for this company and Max in particular. Have you no loyalty? And all of it for what? The unsubstantiated claims of a woman who—"

Emmeline cut him off. "Mr. Kildare, I follow a strict code of journalistic ethics. It is ingrained in every fiber of my being. I am scrupulously conscientious about presenting *both* sides of any story. I had been working for several weeks on a series about looted Nazi art and then Mag—Ms. Roth's—claims came to light, and I followed up on this new lead. It's a new angle of the *same* story. If you took the time to read my article, you will have found that I consulted a number of legal and art experts. In addition, I gave Mr. Sanborn every opportunity to present his side. He refused. Therefore, I was left with little choice. As a result, I take great offense to you, Mr. Sanborn, and your fellow board members trying to impugn my professional reputation."

Kildare waved a gnarled hand dismissively in the air. "That's as may be, but your 'professional reputation' has dropped Sanborn Enterprises into a fine old mess."

She clamped her lips together before she made an impolitic retort. She bristled with indignation.

"Steady on, old chap," Gregory intervened. "Max has never been the innocent that you're portraying, and the company will come through this crisis, perhaps a bit battered and bruised, but intact nonetheless, because Brian has a strong hand on the helm."

"We'll see. You're a fine one to talk. You're as bad as she is with your questions and probing." The older man leaned on his cane and jerked his thumb in Emmeline's direction. "I've been doing a bit of checking on you. And what I've discovered is very unsavory indeed. From what I gather, you're the black sheep of the family." Gregory met the hard green stare without flinching, as Kildare went on, "I can't understand why Max hasn't had you arrested and allows you free rein to go on walk-about in the building."

The smile on Gregory's lips did not touch his eyes, which held something dangerous in their cinnamon depths. "First of all, I'm an employee of Symington's and have been assigned to this case. As the chief insurance investigator, I require full access to our clients and any relevant documents. Secondly, I'd advise you to keep your bloody nose out of my life and my dealings with the Sanborns."

The doors opened at this point, and the grim trio spilled out into the lobby. Kildare walked out ahead of Gregory and Emmeline. He turned stiffly around. "I will not stand by and watch the two of you bring down this company," he hissed.

"What's all this? Don't the three of you look serious huddled here together?" Nigel asked as he exited from the adjacent lift.

"Ah, Nigel," Kildare mumbled as he extended a hand to the younger man. "The voice of reason. Perhaps, you can knock some sense into Longdon and Miss Kirby. I'm afraid that if I remain here a minute longer, I will lose my temper. Goodnight."

He gave a curt nod and pivoted carefully on his heel, but he had only managed to get a few feet away when Harold O'Shaugnessy waylaid him. Kildare rolled his eyes. The last person he wanted to see at the moment was his brother-in-law.

"I can see that the two of you are ingratiating yourselves no end with our distinguished board members. Your names are being whispered up and down the hallowed corridors of Sanborn Enterprises," Nigel said. "And *not* in a very complimentary manner, I might add."

"The stiff-necked bastard cornered us in the lift and immediately started attacking Emmy. From what I could tell, he was already in a foul mood."

"Toby…Gregory," Nigel corrected himself hastily, "don't get your back up. I can well imagine what the old curmudgeon was spewing." His glance slid sideways toward the two Irishmen who were still deep in conversation.

"Anyway, it's lovely to see you both. Emmeline, don't allow Dad or anyone else to give you a hard time. You're doing a splendid job. Brian, with all his worries, thinks so too. Ironically, *The Clarion* is flying off the newsstands since you began your series."

Emmeline straightened her spine and allowed herself to preen for a moment. Gregory slipped an arm around her waist and pressed a kiss against her dark curls. "That's my bulldog."

She pushed him away. "I don't find that a very flattering comparison. Why does everyone keep making it?"

"Because it's accurate," Nigel noted, playfully.

Her eyes narrowed, and she shot him a withering look. "Not you too? He's corrupted you as well."

Nigel gave her a peck on the cheek. "Not a bit of it. It's just a little good-natured ribbing. After all, you're practically one of the family."

Her glance drifted between the two cousins who were grinning down at her. "I think that you're both beasts, and I may have to reassess my decision to marry." She removed Gregory's hand from her waist and turned her head away in mock anger.

"Oh, come now. That wouldn't be fair. Who would whip us all into shape?"

There was an impish glimmer in her dark eyes, and a playful smile quivered upon her lips. "Well, if you put it that way, it will be a pleasure to accept the challenge."

In mock horror, Gregory said, "Nigel, you've unleashed a monster." They all laughed.

"Seriously though, Emmeline, the Sanborns need you." Nigel touched her arm affectionately. "You are the best thing that has happened to this family. Aside from Mum. And Tessa—she's Brian's wife and the sweetest woman imaginable. Not all of us are like Dad. Brian and I both agree that you should continue with your series no matter where it leads."

"Thanks. Your and Brian's vote of confidence means a lot. Speaking of leads—" She hesitated, "I think it is only fair to warn you that things might become a bit more uncomfortable for your father and, consequently, Sanborn in the coming days."

"Oh, yes?" He raised an eyebrow and steeled himself for more unpleasant disclosures.

"Just this afternoon, a new source put me onto something that could be highly…explosive. If I can find the person in question and connect him to your father."

Nigel sighed wearily. He exchanged a long look with Gregory, whose face remained impassive. "Go ahead. Tell me the worst."

Emmeline went on to recount what Yoav Zielinski had told her that afternoon about Doyle and the connection to the Constable painting. She left nothing out, except where she had gotten the information.

"Bloody hell," Nigel said when she had finished her narrative. "*IRA*? Bloody, bloody hell." He ran a hand distractedly through his hair, and his voice rose slightly. "It wasn't bad enough that Dad had a painting of dubious origins in his collection—at least, I hope it was only the one. Now this…this new bombshell." He shook his head. "Brian will kill him for all the trouble he's caused. And he will have deserved it."

"Shh," Emmeline hissed. She shot a glance around the lobby, but she was relieved to see no one was paying the least bit of attention to them. Even O'Shaugnessy and Kildare seemed to have forgotten they were standing nearby, so engrossed were they in their own conversation as they walked toward the entrance. She tugged Nigel by the elbow to a quieter corner. "Come here."

"Sorry," Nigel mumbled. "My anger got the better of me there for a moment. I'm all right now. Honestly. Please go on. Does your source know *where* Doyle is? I'd be happy to wring his bloody neck myself."

"Doyle seems to have dropped off the face of the earth, but my source did give me the only known photo of him."

"Well, let's see the bastard," Nigel said as he waggled his fingers impatiently.

Emmeline turned to Gregory who discreetly took it out of the inside pocket of his suit jacket. "That's him." She pointed at the man in profile.

Nigel handed it back in disgust. "*This* is what you have to go on?" She nodded her head mutely. "This fiend can bring Sanborn to its knees, and all you have to go on is a blurry black-and-white photo. God help us all. It's worse than I thought."

"I admit that it may be a bit tenuous at the moment, but at least it's something," she replied. She didn't know whether she was trying to convince herself or him.

Gregory cleared his throat. "Ahem. There may be someone who could help us find Doyle."

Two pairs of eyes, one full of dark intensity and the other a sea of angry brown, locked on his face.

"Super." Nigel brightened and clapped him on the shoulders.

Emmeline, ever inquisitive, was more reserved in her reaction. "Who is this mysterious person?"

Gregory gave a nonchalant shrug of his shoulders. "Just a chap I know. He owns a gallery in Old Bond Street."

"I see. Does this chap have a name?"

Gregory smiled hoping to disarm her with his charm. "Of course, this chap has a name, darling. What a silly question? Everyone has a name."

She returned his smile, but pressed on, "So what is it?"

"His name?" She nodded. "Ah, now that I can't tell you."

"Why? Is he one of your underworld friends on the run from law?"

Near enough, he thought as his mind recalled his conversation with Tim. However, he clucked his tongue at her and tried to bluff. "Tsk. Tsk. You of all people should understand the delicate relationship one has with one's source. I simply could not break such a trust by disclosing his name."

"Hmph" was her skeptical response.

"Why not go talk to him now?" Nigel suggested.

"Yes, why don't we go see him now, darling?" Emmeline eagerly concurred as she slipped her arm through Gregory's.

Gregory cursed his cousin silently. However, he replied cheerfully, "Emmy, my love, you forget that we have a dinner reservation, and if we don't leave in the next five minutes, we'll be late."

"We can cancel the reservation."

"No, we most certainly cannot. This is the first time in weeks that we've had a chance to have an evening to ourselves."

"Go on, Emmeline. You can't disappoint your fiancé when he's gone to all this trouble. Go and enjoy yourselves. Make wedding plans." Nigel gave her a peck on the cheek.

"Eminently sensible advice." Gregory extended a hand to his cousin and bid him goodnight. "Now, come along, darling." He gave Emmeline a gentle shove toward the door. "Time to put work aside. The search for Doyle can wait until tomorrow."

☙❧

Tim's hand was trembling as he clumsily tried to insert the key in the lock. At last, he felt a click, and the door swung open. He quickly punched in the code on the keypad, turned off the gallery's alarm, and swiftly bolted the door once again. He leaned against it and drew a deep gulp of air into his lungs. His heart was hammering against his rib cage. He felt a little rivulet of sweat tracing a torturous path between his shoulder blades and down his back.

He deliberately left the lights off. He pushed the shade aside leaving only a sliver through which he could peer out at Old Bond Street. He couldn't see anyone. Was he imagining things? He didn't think so. He was certain that there had been someone following him. He had heard footsteps. Hadn't he?

Tim let the shade drop back into place. The salon was in deep shadow, but he managed to stumble across it and make his way down the corridor to his office. He ran his hand through his hair. He was trapped in a hell of his own making. He felt the first flutter of panic rising in his chest. He had played both ends against the middle for far too long, and now the game had caught up with him. What was he going to do?

Calm down and pull yourself together, Tim told himself. *Think, man. Think.*

He poured himself a large whiskey. His fingers were so unsteady that a good deal of the amber liquid sloshed out onto the drinks tray. He downed it all in one go. It burned as it traveled down his throat. He used the back of his hand to wipe away the whiskey that had dribbled out of the corner of his mouth. He poured himself another drink and took a greedy swig as he flopped down onto his chair. He banged the tumbler on his desk and squeezed his eyes shut.

He rested his head against the back of the chair and pressed the heels of his hands against his eyes. Damn and blast. Someone was watching him. He had been looking over his shoulder ever since Gregory had left the gallery that afternoon. The minute he saw Gregory he knew it was only a matter of time. *Greg and his bloody questions*, Tim grumbled. *Damn him to hell. Why did he have to get involved in all this? Why couldn't he have left it alone?*

He let loose a few choice expletives into the gloomy silence. Why did Greg care so much about the damn painting? Max Sanborn was filthy rich. He could hire a whole team of lawyers to fight that woman's claims.

Tim took another mouthful of the whiskey. This time bitterness lingered on his tongue. Or was that merely disgust at himself? How could he have allowed himself to get into such a bind? He knew it was a dirty business from the outset. And yet, the very danger was a kind of thrill.

But now, it was no longer exciting. He was scared, and there was no one he could trust.

However, he had to trust someone.

He downed the remainder of his drink and made a spontaneous decision. He picked up the telephone and punched in a number. He was relieved when he heard a male voice come on the line after the third ring. In a rush, he said, "Oh, Greg, thank God I've caught you." But he realized after a second it was only Gregory's voicemail asking the caller to please leave a message. He pounded his fist on his desk. "Greg, it's Tim. Ring me as soon as you get this message. It's a matter of life and death. Ring me the very second you get this. It doesn't matter the time. You're the only who can help me now. I'll tell you everything you want to know. For old time's sake, don't turn your back on me. *Please*."

He slammed the receiver back in the cradle. Gregory was his last hope. But who knows when he would get the message? Tim needed help *now*. He couldn't stay holed up here in the gallery. Why did he come here? It was bound to be the first place they'd look. He should have left the country. He should have…He should have done a lot of things, but he hadn't. He dropped his head between his hands, a desperate sigh escaping his lips. Who could help him?

He slowly gathered his wits about him and came to a decision. He reached for the phone again. He didn't have to wait long. The voice on the other end answered on the first ring. Tim cleared his throat. "I'm ready to deal. Yes, I understand. Just keep up your end of the bargain. I want enough money to get out of England and never look back." He listened for a few seconds and nodded his head. "Good. Ten minutes. Don't keep me waiting." Then he severed the connection.

He stared at the phone for a long time. After all, it was the only decision he could make.

Tim heard a noise out in the salon and froze. Every nerve in his body was alert.

He swallowed hard and rose from his desk. He tiptoed to the door and opened it a crack. His ears strained to hear. Perhaps it was Greg. Of course, that must be it. Instead of calling, he popped round the instant he heard his message. Good old Greg.

But his relief quickly turned to fear. He remembered that he had bolted the door earlier. And, in that moment, he knew whoever was out there was *not* Greg. Greg wouldn't have broken in, although he easily could have.

The blood was thundering in Tim's ears as he slowly walked down the darkened corridor to the salon. Everything was still in shadow. His fingers fumbled along the wall for the switch. His palms were moist with sweat, but his mouth was as parched as the Sahara.

Just as his fingers found the switch, an arm clamped itself around his throat, cutting off his breathing. A male voice hissed in his ear, "You made a big mistake by opening your mouth, laddie."

Tim struggled to free himself from the iron grasp, but found the more he wriggled the less he could breathe. So he stopped and let his body go limp against the other man.

His attacker loosened his hold slightly, allowing Tim to suck in a lungful of air. His chest was heaving, but he managed to say, "Doyle, I didn't say anything. You have my word. No one knows."

He saw stars as a large hand smacked him hard on the side of his head. Then a soft huff of laughter brushed his ear as the grip tightened once more around his neck. "Oh, Tim, you always were a poor liar. You'd sell your own sainted mother, if the price was right. You told Longdon about me, and now his bloody fiancée is sniffing about. That was exceedingly poor judgment."

Tim thrashed against Doyle, but he couldn't free himself. "Do you know how we dealt with traitors in the good old days?" The tone was soft, but it was laced with menace.

Tim shook his head. His bulging eyes darted desperately from side to side.

"Like this." It all happened in a second. There was a crack, and then Doyle allowed Tim to slip to the floor. "We broke the chap's neck."

CHAPTER 22

Surely it couldn't have been more than ten minutes? the young man reasoned as he let himself into the gallery. *How could it have happened so quickly?* he asked himself as he stared down at Tim's lifeless body sprawled on the polished parquet floor of the salon. He hunkered down and shook his head. There was no need to check for a pulse. It was abundantly clear that Tim's neck had been broken.

He put his hands on his thighs and pushed himself to his feet. His keen eye shot a practiced glance around the salon, but the only thing that was out of place was the dead body. He exhaled a long breath and pulled out his mobile. Reluctantly, he punched in the number. He only had to wait a few seconds.

"Good evening," the deep baritone voice of Lord Pembroke's butler boomed down the line.

"Ah, good evening," the young man replied. "I apologize for intruding on Lady Pembroke's birthday celebration. But it's imperative that I speak to Laurence Villiers."

"Of course, sir. Whom shall I say is calling?"

"Crichlow. He'll know what it's about."

"Very good. Please hold the line. I will get Mr. Villiers."

Crichlow tried to avoid looking at the dead body. No longer was it Tim Clarke, but rather "the dead body."

He didn't have long to wait. "What is it, Crichlow?" Villiers asked. There was a hard edge to the plummy tones of his boss' voice.

"Sir, Clarke's dead."

There was a brief pause and then, "I see. I don't suppose it was natural causes?"

"No, sir. His neck's broken."

"Doyle?"

"Yes, I think so, sir. It must have happened only a few minutes before I arrived to collect him."

"Pity he couldn't have told us where to find Doyle," Villiers intoned.

"He paid a high price for his greed."

"Ah, well," Villiers said philosophically. "I suppose if you think about it, in the end, Clarke laid down his life for queen and country. His death saves Her Majesty's Government a good deal of embarrassment over its misplaced trust in Doyle after the war. Still, it goes against the grain to have to turn a blind eye to a rogue like that."

"Yes, sir. I'll just make a quick sweep of the gallery to make sure Clarke didn't leave anything to connect him to us."

"Good thinking. We wouldn't want anyone asking awkward questions. Don't linger there too long and make sure no one sees you leave. I wouldn't want you stumbling across Longdon again. I must say it was extremely embarrassing to have to bail out one of my own men from the local police station."

Crichlow didn't respond. He was still smarting from the incident in the Burlington Arcade.

⌭

Gregory had turned off his mobile when he had arrived at the restaurant with Emmeline, so he didn't get Tim's message until the next morning.

He could hear the fear in the man's voice. What was so urgent? He checked his watch. It was a quarter past nine. The gallery didn't open until ten, but Tim had told him that he was always in his office by nine o'clock.

He dialed the number. There was no ringing, just a busy signal. He severed the connection and tried again. The same thing happened.

His lips pursed together and he shook his head. He didn't like it. Not one bit. He grabbed his car keys and flew out of his elegant maisonette in the Primrose Hill neighborhood. He merged onto the traffic on Albany Street and drove straight on as it became Great Portland Street. Then he made a left onto Oxford Street, where it was the usual chaos of buses, taxis, and cars. After what seemed an eternity, he turned onto New Bond Street. Mercifully, there was virtually no traffic here, and he was pulling up in front of the Maurice Boinet Gallery in Old Bond Street a few minutes later.

The door was unlocked. He pushed it open. The main salon was deserted. Even Nicole was nowhere to be seen. "Tim," he called out, "It's me. I received your message. *Tim*?"

The hairs on the back of his neck prickled. "Tim?" he ventured once more without success.

His footsteps seemed unusually loud against the parquet floor as he made his way down the corridor to Tim's office. The door was slightly ajar. He knocked firmly. No response.

"Right." With his jaw set in a determined line, he pushed the door open with one foot.

It took Gregory only an instant to determine why Tim had refused to answer him. He was slumped in his chair with his head drooping to one side at an unnatural angle. The man would never utter another word.

"Oh, Tim, you bloody stupid bugger." He exhaled a long weary breath.

Gregory crossed to the desk. Tim's face was still. It had already taken on a waxy pallor. He sighed again. He lifted Tim's wrist, but it dropped back stiffly onto his lap. His skin was cold, no blood thrumming through the veins beneath it. "Damn and blast," Gregory railed. If only he'd listened to Emmeline and Nigel and come to see Tim last night, he would still be alive.

However, as he wasn't a clairvoyant, he realized that everything had a clear-cut answer when viewed through the crystal lens of hindsight.

He quickly scanned the papers on Tim's desk, but they told him nothing. Then he reached into his suit jacket pocket and drew out his gold pen. With it, he pressed the button on the telephone, and a list of all recent calls appeared on the little screen.

He recognized his mobile number, but his eyebrow arched upward in surprise when he saw the call that Tim had made immediately afterward. "Well, well, well, what a small world indeed. Tim, old chap, you were a dark horse, weren't you? Now, why would you be having a cozy chat with Villiers on his personal mobile?"

He wouldn't have said that the two men moved in the same social circles. But alas, people were always full of surprises. This new wrinkle was definitely too intriguing to let pass.

Gregory took one last look at Tim and exited the office. He hurried into the salon, hastily locked the front door, and flipped the sign to *CLOSED*.

He pulled out his mobile and punched in a number. "Burnell speaking," the annoyed voice rumbled in his ear.

Gregory's lips broke into a grim half-smile. "Good morning to you, too, *Oliver*. I hope you've been keeping well."

"Longdon? Is that you?" Gregory could just picture the flush of anger suffusing the superintendent's cheeks. "It most certainly is *not* a good morning, especially now. What do you want?"

"I'm sorry to hear that, Oliver, because your morning is going to become even more unpleasant."

There was silence at the other end. "Are you still there?"

"I'm listening. What is it?"

"There's something at the Maurice Boinet Gallery in Old Bond Street that I'm certain that you and Sergeant Finch would be most interested in seeing. It's the owner. I'm afraid he's been murdered."

"What?" Burnell roared. "Are you sure? This isn't one of your jokes, is it, Longdon?"

Gregory had to hold the mobile away from his ear. "I assure you he is quite dead. As the proverbial door nail. Not a spark of life left in him."

"Bloody hell. Stay there. Finch and I are on our way. And for God's sake, don't touch anything."

છ૩૯૭

Fifteen minutes later, Burnell, Finch, a forensic team, and several uniformed constables had invaded the gallery *en masse*.

"Oliver, Finch, what took you so long?" Gregory hailed them in hearty greeting. "Standards at Scotland Yard must be slipping."

"Oh, shut up, Longdon. We'll have none of your lip. Where's the body?" Burnell snapped.

"Temper, temper, old chap. You'll burst a blood vessel, if you're not careful. You'll find the late Maurice Boinet in his office. But a word or two in your ear, if I may, Oliver?"

Burnell shot him a look full of venom. "*Superintendent* Burnell," Gregory corrected himself with an insouciant smile.

Burnell grumbled, but first, he gave two constables some instructions. The forensics team had already started on Boinet's office. They expected Dr. Meadows, the medical examiner, to arrive any minute now.

"All right, what is it?" Burnell asked. Finch was at his elbow, notebook already open.

"You know, I find it rather disheartening to be treated as a criminal. I'll remind you that I did my civic duty and rang *you* the very instant I stumbled across poor Mr. Boinet's body."

"Yes, you did indeed." The superintendent smiled, but there was no mirth in it. "But I find it rather curious that you were here on the spot. You had better have a *very* good explanation for that."

Gregory returned his smile, with a cheeky grin of his own. "Why, Oliver, you can't possibly believe that I was the cause of Mr. Boinet's unfortunate demise."

"You tell me."

"I most certainly was not. Murder is such…" He paused as if searching for the right word. "…such a messy business. I never understood why anyone would ever contemplate it."

Finch rolled his eyes in exasperation. "That remains to be seen. Now get on with it? What did you want to tell us?"

Gregory had toyed with the detectives long enough. He became serious. "You'll find that Monsieur Boinet was really plain old Tim Clarke from Thirsk. He had...how shall I put it?...a varied career. He was a sort of jack of all trades, but he did not exactly move in legitimate circles."

"And how would you happen to know that?"

Gregory spread his hands in the air and shrugged his shoulders. "Would you believe a little bird told me?"

"What a load of rubbish." Burnell turned to Finch. "However, after we have a look at the body, I want you to start looking into Mr. Clarke's background and see what you can come up with."

"Right, sir."

Gregory silently tagged along as the detectives made their way down the corridor to the distasteful sight that awaited them.

Tim's office was a beehive of activity. The forensic team was busy taking pictures, dusting for fingerprints and bagging anything that could remotely be considered evidence. The two detectives slipped on some latex gloves as they entered the room. They examined the body and carefully poked about, trying not to get in the forensics team's way.

Gregory remained in the doorway, his arms folded over his chest, surveying the scene. He left the detectives to conduct their work for a few minutes, before clearing his throat loudly. "Pardon me, Superintendent Burnell."

"I'd forgotten you were here. Yes, what is it?"

"Far be it from me to do Scotland Yard's job—"

"God help us all, if that ever happens. The criminals would be running riot."

"—but clearly Tim was not killed here. I believe he was moved afterward," Gregory continued as if he had never been interrupted.

"What are you chuntering on about?"

"You and the sharp-eyed sergeant did notice these scuff marks all along the parquet floor in the corridor? As if Tim had been dragged to the office and artfully arranged at his desk after he shuffled off his mortal coil."

Burnell and Finch exchanged a look and then joined Gregory in the doorway. They lowered themselves on their haunches and stared down the length of the corridor. Sure enough, as Gregory had remarked, there were faint scuff marks stretching all the way back to the salon.

They rose to their feet. The superintendent directed a member of the forensic team to take photos of the corridor and the salon.

"I'm glad I could be of service to you chaps. I'll leave you to your grim task," Gregory said cheerfully and started to make his way toward the salon.

"And where do you think you're swanning off to?"

Gregory turned and put a hand to his chest in mock innocence. "Was there something else you wanted, *Oliver*?" This last word was a whisper.

"Answers. That's what I want from you," Burnell said through gritted teeth. "Why were you here in the first place?"

Gregory was pleased to see that his needling had had the intended effect. However, his mood sobered quickly. "Tim left me a message last night asking to see me urgently. I had turned my mobile off when Emmy and I went to dinner, so I didn't get it until this morning. Tim sounded frightened."

"What was your friend afraid of?"

"He wasn't exactly a 'friend,' more of an acquaintance."

"We don't have time to quibble. Why was Boinet alias Clarke running scared?"

"Ah," Gregory replied noncommittally.

"That doesn't tell us anything, Longdon," Finch said.

Gregory's gaze flickered between the superintendent and the sergeant. He debated with himself whether he should withhold the information about Doyle. They waited expectantly. In the end, he threw his hands in the air in resignation. Villiers could go to the devil. If Emmeline was going after Doyle, it was more important that the police were aware of all the facts and were there to protect her.

"I think you'll find it all comes back to dear Uncle Max's disputed Constable painting and a former IRA commander named Doyle." Then another thought struck him. What if Villiers had Tim killed to keep him from babbling any further? "And it's quite possible that MI5 might have a hand in it too."

"Splendid. As if I didn't have enough trouble already," Burnell griped.

CHAPTER 23

Emmeline didn't want to cause any more problems for Philip. God knew he and Maggie were going through quite a rough patch, especially now that the lawsuit had been filed against Max Sanborn. Therefore, she discreetly approached several of her government contacts in the hopes of finding a lead on Doyle. However, her efforts were frustrated by a wall of silence. Far from discouraging her, this only made Emmeline more determined. If everyone was trying so hard to keep her from finding the truth, it meant that she was making things uncomfortable.

A smile played around the corners of her mouth. How she enjoyed making people, particularly those in power, squirm. After all, the simple expedient would be to give her the information she needed, and she would be on her merry way. But they never learned, preferring instead to place obstacles in her way. It only made her push harder.

For this reason, Emmeline planted herself outside of Laurence Villiers's club at noon. It was a well-known fact that Villiers always lunched at his club on Wednesdays. She would waylay him before he even got near the door.

At the stroke of noon, a shiny black Mercedes pulled up to the curb. The driver walked around the car and opened the rear door. Within seconds, a lean male leg emerged, and then the rest of Laurence Villiers came into view.

"Thank you, Ralph," she heard him say, "Be back at the usual time."

"Yes, sir." And with that, the driver clambered back behind the wheel and merged into traffic on Pall Mall.

Emmeline had been standing in the shadow of a Doric column, which afforded her a few moments to study Villiers before he saw her. He was tall and well-groomed. Everything about him exuded confidence. There was a masculine grace in his movements. In that instant when he turned his head and their eyes locked, she had the distinct impression that they had met before. But of course, that was nonsense. She had only seen him on television on those rare occasions when his expert opinion had been sought on a security matter.

She stepped forward and extended her hand. "Mr. Villiers, I'm Emmeline Kirby of *The Clarion*. I'd like to ask you a few questions."

Villiers shook her hand perfunctorily. If he was annoyed at being ambushed, he didn't show it. "I'm well aware of who you are. I'm afraid I don't give impromptu interviews. You'll have to make an appointment with my secretary. Now, if you'll excuse me, I have luncheon engagement."

He tried to brush past her, but she blocked his path. "I did make an appointment, Mr. Villiers. However, your secretary kept me cooling my heels all morning in your waiting room. I'm certain she was following your instructions. For the record, I don't appreciate such games. I'm a professional, and I have a job to do."

The ghost of a smile touched Villiers's lips and then was gone. "And I have mine. Unfortunately, the goals of the two are diametrically opposed and therein lies the conflict."

He tried to turn away, but she refused to be dismissed so easily. "There you're wrong. We both believe in the law and the truth, and seeing that the baddies pay for their crimes. Why won't you help me find Doyle? What are you so afraid of?"

This caught Villiers off guard. He stared down at the petite figure in front of him and saw steely determination etched in every line and contour of her pretty face. He could well understand what Longdon found so appealing about this intelligent and compassionate young woman. She reminded him of—No, he would not unbolt that door and let out those old memories that he had so carefully tucked away all those years ago. What was the point? The past was the past. Dead and gone.

"I'm not afraid of anything, Miss Kirby," he replied at last. "However, sometimes the truth can be ugly—and dangerous. In those cases, it's best to let sleeping dogs lie."

Emmeline smiled, but her dark eyes burned with resolve. She squared her shoulders. "I've always hated that expression. It's for the unimaginative. Those who lack backbone."

"Nevertheless, there's something to be said for the bland and boring."

"And what's that?"

"They'll live to see another day. On the other hand, an overactive imagination and an exaggerated sense of right and wrong can get one killed. I suggest you think long and hard about that, Miss Kirby, before you climb that particular slippery slope. It's bound to end in disaster."

Emmeline shivered involuntarily. She opened her mouth to say something else, but Villiers had already disappeared into his club.

Arrogant bastard. If he thought he could intimidate her, he had better think again.

෧෨෧

Villiers chuckled softly to himself from just inside the vestibule, as he watched her hitch her handbag higher up her shoulder and storm off. He was absolutely certain that their little chat had only served to inflame her further. Once she was out of sight, he pulled out his mobile and made a call, which went through immediately.

"Crichlow, what can you tell me about the investigation into Clarke's murder? Can the police connect him to us?"

"No, sir. I did a bit of tidying up at the gallery last night. I also moved Clarke's body into his office."

"Good. But I wouldn't underestimate Burnell. He's as sharp as a whip."

"We could have some trouble, though."

"Oh, in what way?"

"Longdon. Apparently, he's the one who found Clarke's body. He's been hanging about making a nuisance of himself. He insists that Clarke's murder is connected with Max Sanborn's disputed Constable painting. Therefore, as Symington's chief investigator, he says he must be privy to everything the police discover. I don't think he's told Burnell about Doyle yet, but it's only a matter of time."

"Damn and blast. He's always turning up like a bad penny. This sordid business is bound to come out if we're not careful. Too many people know about it. Longdon's fiancée just ambushed me outside my club asking me questions about Doyle."

"What did you do, sir?"

"I tried to fob her off with the usual official nonsense about it being wiser to allow some secrets to remain buried in the past. But that young woman is too clever by half. I'm afraid I've only succeeded in encouraging her to pursue the story further."

"At first, I thought it was strange that a woman like that would be engaged to Longdon. Now, I'm not surprised at all. They're two peas in a pod. Troublemakers, the pair of them. Who else would have them?"

"Yes, yes," Villiers said testily. "But I think that will work to our advantage in Miss Kirby's case."

"How do you figure that?"

"She won't stop until she finds Doyle. So all we have to do is sit back and wait patiently. Miss Kirby will do our job for us."

"Isn't it rather risky to let an amateur loose like that, sir? She's liable to get into trouble."

"From what I've learned about Emmeline Kirby, she's extraordinarily resilient. She's been in sticky situations before and managed to extricate herself. Then, of course, there's always Longdon. Like a knight errant, he comes charging in at the first hint of danger."

"But Doyle is a completely different kettle of fish."

"Yes, that's why you'll be sticking to Miss Kirby like glue from now on. I don't want you to let her out of your sight for *any* reason. Do I make myself clear? If anything happens to that young woman, there won't be a place on this earth where you'll be able to hide."

"Yes, sir. Message received and understood." With that, Crichlow rang off.

Villiers was slipping his mobile back into his pocket when it started to vibrate in his hand. He sighed. Dispensing with a polite greeting, he answered brusquely, "Longdon, this is becoming an intrusive habit. You know our contact is to be kept to a bare minimum. I'm already in a foul mood. Now, what is it?"

"Coincidences bother me. For instance, imagine my surprise when I discovered that the last call Tim Clarke made before he was murdered was to your number. I find that rather intriguing. You gave me no indication that the two of you were acquainted. This lapse on your part is quite disappointing. My brain is awhirl with questions about what else you've been keeping from me. And whether you had Tim killed to keep him quiet about your nefarious activities."

"Don't be absurd. You're almost as bad as your fiancée, who was just here haranguing me."

"Ah, that's my girl. What did Emmy want? She doesn't know about Tim, so it couldn't have been about his murder."

"She wanted to know about Doyle. Now, how do you suppose she found out about him? You didn't happen to let his name slip during an exchange of pillow talk by any chance, did you?"

Gregory's voice was an angry hiss in his ear. "Listen, Villiers, our private affairs are none of your business. So refrain from making such comments. It's beneath you. Besides, Emmy is a consummate professional. She discovered the information the old-fashioned way, through a source—"

"Who—"

Gregory cut him off. "Don't even bother to ask me who he is because she is keeping his identity confidential. I respect that and so should you."

"Secrets have a funny way of coming out at the least opportune moment."

"You should know. Secrets are your stock in trade."

"Yes, but a secret in the wrong hands is like a ticking time bomb. It's unstable and can wreak untold damage upon innocent victims. I would be quite distressed to read your fiancée's obituary in *The Times*. If I were in your shoes, I'd stop her before she gets in over her head."

The line went dead before Gregory could reply.

CHAPTER 24

Emmeline got off the lift and walked down the corridor to the newsroom. She was still seething from her conversation with Villiers. Well, the gloves were off now. There were a number of calls that she wanted to make to follow up on what she had discovered about Doyle. She needed the privacy of her office to do so. She had already written the first paragraphs of the article in her mind by the time she had reached her door.

She was about to slip the key into the lock when she noticed that the door was slightly ajar. That was odd. She closed her eyes and went over the scene the evening before when Gregory had come to collect her. Her eyes flew open instantly. *No, I know I locked it*, she said to herself. *In fact, I'm positive.*

Tentatively, she pushed the door open with her foot. "Bloody hell," she exclaimed as she ran toward her desk.

All her drawers had been pulled out, and files were scattered all over her desk. Some had spilled onto the floor. "Bloody, bloody hell," she muttered as she gathered up a handful of papers.

Her gaze swept over the room, but nothing appeared to have been stolen. Only her files had been ransacked. But why? How come none of the chaps in the newsroom noticed anything amiss?

Then a thought struck her. She plopped herself unceremoniously onto the floor. For the next twenty minutes, she methodically went through every file. It came as no surprise that the only one that was missing was the one on Doyle. At least, she had had the forethought to keep the photo of him with her at all times. At this moment, it was tucked into a hidden pocket in her handbag.

Emmeline pushed herself to her feet and picked up the phone. The first call she made was to security. The second was to Gregory.

She tried ringing Burnell as well, but was told that he was out on a new case. A riffled office did not merit leaving a message. Burnell and Finch had more important things to do. She would simply call back later. After all, she hadn't been hurt. Yet.

She shook her head to rid herself of this thought. She sat down in her chair and turned her computer on. Right now, she had a story to write.

ೞೞೞ

Superintendent Burnell rocked back and forth on his heels as Sergeant Finch jabbed the doorbell. They heard a soft buzz somewhere inside Max Sanborn's penthouse.

"I'm going to rather enjoy this," Burnell said, a smile of grim satisfaction playing around his lips.

"Yes, sir. But remember what Assistant Commissioner Fenton said," Finch cautioned, "we are not to harass 'such an important man.'"

"I don't intend to harass him. We are here on legitimate police business. After all, a man was just murdered. We would be remiss in our duty if we didn't question *everyone* with whom Tim Clarke alias Maurice Boinet had dealings."

Finch tried to bite back a smile. "I don't think Mr. Sanborn will see it in quite that light."

"If Max Sanborn didn't want the police on his doorstep, he should have chosen his associates with greater care. Remember, a man is judged by the company he keeps."

"If that's true, how will people interpret the fact that we've been seen running about town in Longdon's company of late?"

Burnell grunted. "An unfortunate occupational hazard. If

'people' know what's good for them, they won't dwell on it at all."

Finch chuckled. "If you say so, sir."

The conversation came to a rapid conclusion at that moment because Sanborn's housekeeper opened the door.

The two detectives flashed their warrant cards. "Superintendent Burnell and Sergeant Finch of the Metropolitan Police," Burnell said. "We have some questions for Mr. Sanborn."

The woman, who Burnell judged was in her mid-fifties, hesitated. She slid a sideways glance to her right. Then her hazel eyes returned to the superintendent's face. "I'm afraid Mr. Sanborn is not at home."

Burnell's right eyebrow shot up. "Is that so?" He turned to the sergeant. "Did you hear that, Finch? Mr. Sanborn appears to be out."

"I did, sir."

The woman gave them a half-smile and nodded. "Yes. If you'll leave your card, I'll be sure to let him know that you gentlemen would like to speak to him."

Burnell returned her smile. "How very kind, but that won't be necessary. We know for a fact that Mr. Sanborn is in." He put his palm on the door and opened it wider so that they could step inside. "Please let your employer know that we're here."

"Really, Superintendent," the woman said, aggrieved. She valiantly attempted to block their path but failed. "You can't push your way in like this."

"You'll find that we can. Now if you don't want us to take you in for obstruction, you'll get Mr. Sanborn. At once," he replied calmly.

"Well, I—The nerve—How dare you—" she spluttered.

Lesser men would have quailed if they had been on the receiving end of that hostile glare. But Burnell and Finch were not impressed. They simply waited in silence.

She looked from one to the other and realized that she had lost this test of wills. "Wait here."

Her heels echoed loudly against the parquet floor as she scurried down the hall full of righteous indignation.

"Round one to the Met," Burnell mumbled out of the corner of his mouth as he sketched a mark with his finger on an invisible scoreboard in the air. He whistled tunelessly to himself.

The next second, they heard Sanborn's voice. It was difficult not to. The man was shouting at the top of his lungs. "Bloody stupid, woman. I told you I was not to be disturbed, especially for those two interfering cretins." This was followed by a string of invectives.

Whatever the housekeeper responded they would never know. She suddenly appeared again. She walked straight past them. They could see that she was crying. She went into another room and came back out immediately with her handbag on her arm.

"Leave the keys on the hall table. I don't want to see your face back here ever again," Sanborn yelled.

The woman shot an accusatory glance at the two detectives. Her lips parted but, in the end, she didn't say anything. Instead, she gathered her pride around her and dumped her keys on the table. She slammed the door so hard on her way out that it rattled on its hinges.

"Well, that was pleasant. One could almost feel sorry for the woman. Almost, but not quite," the superintendent mused. "Now that we've cleared the air, it's time for 'the great man' to grant us an audience. Shall we, Finch?" Burnell extended an arm in the direction of the study.

When they appeared in the doorway, Sanborn snarled, "Get out. I'm busy." He was seated in a brown leather wing chair, a large whiskey in one hand and some papers in his lap. He made no move to rise.

"I'm afraid we can't do that, Mr. Sanborn. We need to ask you some questions about—"

"Stuff your questions. I thought Richard had you taken off the case. This is police harassment. I'll have you sacked. You'll be out on your ear by morning."

"—About Maurice Boinet. He was murdered last night," Burnell continued as if Sanborn had never spoken.

Sanborn froze. He took a slow swallow of the whiskey to

give himself time to digest this information. "I don't understand," he said at last. "What does this have to do with me?"

"Isn't Boinet the one who acted as your intermediary when you, uh…purchased—for want of a better word—the Constable?"

"So what if he did? I had no reason to murder the chap. This has absolutely nothing to do with me."

"You have to admit, sir, that it's rather curious that Mr. Boinet should be murdered only a few days after Ms. Roth made her claims about the painting," Finch remarked pointedly. He already had his notebook open and was taking down every word the other man uttered.

"You're grasping at straws. There's no connection. And don't mention that woman's name in my presence. Do you know that she has had the audacity to file a lawsuit against me?" He angrily waved a piece of paper at them.

Burnell did his best to smother the smile that threatened to break out across his face. "Did she? My word, you do seem to be having a rotten streak of luck this week."

Sanborn jumped to his feet. "I've had just about enough of your insolence, Burnell." He pointed at the door, "Get out."

"I assure you, we are as anxious as you are to end this interview. Please bear with us for only a few more minutes. There were one or two more questions that we wanted to ask."

Sanborn was on the verge of apoplexy. Finch saw an ugly crimson flush stain his cheeks, and the hand that gripped the paper was trembling. A gurgling sound emanated from deep within his throat.

Burnell, pretending not to have noticed anything amiss, went on placidly, "Did you know that Mr. Boinet was actually a petty con man named Tim Clarke? Apparently, Interpol was well acquainted with Clarke and quite eager to speak with him."

Sanborn said nothing. "Does your silence mean you were not aware of his criminal history?" the superintendent pressed. The other man did not move a muscle. "All right, sir. Let's try another question. Did you know that Clarke procured your

Constable from a former IRA commander named Doyle who
was a German collaborator?"

Sanborn's face remained impassive, but, for an instant,
there was a murderous spark in his brown eyes. The superintendent intrepidly pushed on with the one-sided interview. "I
must warn you, sir, that it is a crime to knowingly deal in
stolen artwork. The law looks down very harshly on such
transactions. And I'm sure I don't need to tell you that, were it
to become known that you had dealings with a Nazi collaborator who happened to be an IRA member, your life of luxury
would disappear in a flash, and your business would be ruined
overnight."

"You've made the biggest mistake of your life, Burnell."
Sanborn's voice dripped ice. He took a step closer and poked
the superintendent in the chest. "When I'm through with you
and your sergeant over there, you are going to wish you had
never been born."

Finch made a move to intervene, but Burnell waved him
back. The superintendent's blue gaze never left Sanborn's
face.

"I've found that when someone starts hurling threats about,
it's because he has something to hide. Let me assure you that
whatever it is that you're hiding, we *will* find out. Then I will
derive tremendous pleasure in arresting you." He turned to the
sergeant. "Come on, Finch, we've imposed on Mr. Sanborn's
generous hospitality quite enough for one afternoon. No need
to see us out, sir. We'll find our own way."

Burnell had the satisfaction of hearing the whiskey tumbler
crashing against the door, as he closed it behind him.

☙❧

Sanborn paced back and forth, muttering and cursing the
two detectives. He would see to it that they burned in hell
along with Maggie Roth.

It was time to put all those secrets that he had so carefully
gathered over the years to his advantage. Snatching up the
phone on his desk, he drummed his fingers impatiently as he

waited for the call to go through. One ring. Two rings. On the third, the party on the other end picked up.

Without preamble, Sanborn said, "You took your sweet time answering. I'm not interested in your excuses. I've got my own troubles to worry about. Keep your mouth shut and listen. Maggie Roth has filed a lawsuit to try to take *my* painting, and Burnell and Finch were just here. They practically accused me of murdering that bloody fool Boinet. But you haven't heard the best bit yet. They asked me about Doyle. I thought that would get your attention. Yes, the dirty little secret that you thought you could hide from me. Silly, don't you know I always find out? I've known for a very long time. I have files, dates, photos—*everything*. I was simply biding my time until I could put the information to good use. So if you don't want me spilling what I know, you're going to make this whole thing disappear. I don't care how you do it. Use your ingenuity. Pull strings. Blackmail. Just make it go away. After all, you're already an expert liar. My only concern is Sanborn Enterprises. You have until tomorrow to do something. Otherwise, I will feel the compelling need to unburden my soul about Doyle. And your world will come crashing down about your ears." He slammed the receiver down.

Alia iacta est, as Caesar had said. *The die was indeed cast*, Sanborn thought. But experience had taught him that relying on others inevitably leads to disappointment. Therefore, he had to take certain matters into his own hands. Maggie Roth was the weakest link. He would start with her.

CHAPTER 25

Maggie returned from a meeting to find a little pink message slip on her desk informing her that Max Sanborn had called in her absence. Could she ring him back at her earliest convenience?

Max Sanborn? What did that swine want? Nothing good that was for sure. Her hand hovered over her phone for a minute. She would never know unless she called. Oh, well, in for a penny, in for a pound. She picked up the receiver and dialed the number.

"Max Sanborn." His surly tone was a blend of arrogance and condescension.

"Mr. Sanborn, it's Maggie Roth. I received your message. What was it that you wanted to speak to me about?"

"Ah, Ms. Roth, so good of you to get back to me so promptly." His voice became softer, slightly breathy. He paused. "Look, I would like to discuss this lawsuit of yours—"

"All your questions should be directed to my solicitor. I have nothing to say on the matter. If that's all, I have a rather busy afternoon ahead of me."

"Please don't hang up. Hear me out. I don't think solicitors and lawsuits are really necessary. I'm certain that we can come to an amicable agreement amongst ourselves, don't you? It would be less messy and less costly. A court case could drag on for years. I'm sure neither one of us wants to go through such unpleasantness. The publicity alone would be distasteful, to say the least."

"I'm quite prepared to take you to court. Great Aunt Sarah's painting is my family's by right."

"I completely understand your feelings. But can't you see it from my point of view? I bought the Constable in good fait—"

Maggie snorted. "So you say."

"Yes, most assuredly in good faith. Won't you at least hear me out? If, after we talk, you still feel strongly about pursuing the lawsuit, I won't stand in your way. What do you say? Could you drop by the penthouse around seven this evening?"

Maggie bit her lip. She had never heard Sanborn speak in such a conciliatory manner. He sounded sincere, despite his reputation. He was right about one thing. She was not looking forward to a nasty trial. She really didn't want to drag Philip and the boys through something like that. So wouldn't it be churlish of her not to at least *try* to reach a settlement?

"All right," she said at last, "I'll meet with you this evening."

"Good. You won't regret it."

⋰⋱

Gregory, one leg crossed over the other, was ensconced comfortably in a chair as Emmeline banged away at her keyboard. He happened to look up at the precise moment that Burnell, with Finch in tow, appeared on the threshold.

"Ah, have no fear, Emmy, Scotland Yard's finest have come to the rescue."

Emmeline stopped typing and swiveled her chair around. She smiled up at the two detectives.

The superintendent returned her smile, but glared at Gregory and mumbled something unintelligible under his breath. To his chagrin, he heard the other man stifle a chuckle. *Lord*, Burnell silently entreated, *what did I do to deserve Longdon as a perpetual punishment?* The Almighty didn't deign to answer his question.

The superintendent sighed and instead turned to the matter at hand. His practiced glance swept over the office. It took in the cascade of files that had spilled onto the floor, while Finch inspected the lock on the door.

"There's no evidence of forced entry," the sergeant said.

Gregory stood and joined him by the door. "I took a look at the lock too, but I didn't see any tampering either."

"Of course, you would know, being an expert on locks and how to render them useless."

Gregory clucked his tongue. "Now, Finch, that was quite uncalled for, but just to show you how magnanimous I am, I'll let it go this time." He clapped the sergeant on the shoulder.

Finch shrugged off his hand. "I can't tell you how relieved I am," he replied facetiously.

"After all this time, you should know that I'm an easy-going fellow. You do such an important job, and I truly care if you sleep at night or not."

"Spare me the false concern," Finch tossed over his shoulder as he walked over to join the superintendent and Emmeline by the desk.

"Stop mucking about, Longdon," Burnell called.

Gregory clicked his heels together and gave him a mock salute. "Your wish is my command, *mon colonel.*"

In two strides, he was across the room. He carefully hitched one hip on the corner of the desk. "Oliver, in all seriousness now, I think it is patently obvious that there's only one person who could have done this." They all fell silent for a moment. "Doyle. He has gotten wind that Emmy is on his trail and he wanted to destroy all her notes so that she couldn't pursue the story any further."

Emmeline's mouth widened into a Cheshire cat grin. "But he was wrong."

Gregory knew that look, and it meant trouble. "What do you mean, darling?"

"Excuse me, for just a second." She turned to her computer and hit a key. "There, that's done."

Burnell and Finch exchanged a puzzled look and shrugged their shoulders. Gregory, on the other hand, knew better. "What exactly was that, my love?"

She stood and kissed the tip of his nose. "That was tomorrow's front page story. I just made my final edits. Shall I give you a hint what it's about?"

"I think I have a fairly good idea. And by the grim looks shadowing Oliver's and Finch's faces, I believe they've guessed as well."

"Jolly good. What clever men you are. I think you'll like my headline too. 'WHO IS DOYLE: COLLABORATOR, TERRORIST, MURDERER?' It really grabs you, doesn't it?"

Gregory's cinnamon gaze met Burnell's intense blue one. In that brief exchange, each man communicated his worry for this woman for whom they both cared.

Gregory was the first to look away. He cleared his throat noisily and fixed his attention on Emmeline. "Ahem. Yes, it certainly piques one's interest. I'll grant you that. If, that is, one is stark—raving—mad. Emmy, have you lost your mind? That article is only going to stoke the flames."

Emmeline leaned back in her chair, unperturbed by his anger. "We weren't getting anywhere. So I thought I'd rattle his cage a bit. Make him look over his shoulder."

"Make him look over his—" He shook his head incredulously. "Darling, Doyle is a trained killer. Last night, he added the murder of Bond Street art dealer Maurice Boinet to the long list of those who had the misfortune to cross him. He has already proven that he can get to you whenever he wants. And now, you've waved the red flag with that damned article of yours. Besides, I thought you said he stole your notes."

Emmeline blinked twice, but she didn't say anything. Her eyes seemed even darker against the ashen pallor of her cheeks. "I—I saved a copy of my notes on my hard drive as a backup. I always do," she replied lamely. "Murdered an art dealer? Why?"

The wheels were turning in her brain. Her gaze drifted to each man in turn.

"Wait a minute." She sat up straight. "Is this the art dealer who sold Maggie's Aunt Sarah's Constable to Max Sanborn?" No one answered. "Well?"

Burnell sighed. "Yes, Emmeline."

Gregory lifted an eyebrow. He had to get used this new-found familiarity between the gruff superintendent and his fiancée.

"We believe Doyle murdered Maurice Boinet alias Tim Clarke," the superintendent continued.

She frowned. "Tim Clarke?"

"Never mind, it's not important right now. Longdon can fill you in on his good friend, the career con man, at a later date."

She cast a glance at Gregory. "I have every intention of seeing that he does so."

"Thanks, Oliver," Gregory murmured.

Burnell's face broke into a broad grin. "Any time, old chap. Glad to be of service," he said, mimicking Gregory's usual flippant tone.

Finch clapped Gregory on the shoulder. "You and Emmeline can have a nice cozy chat over a cup of cocoa."

Gregory shook himself free of the sergeant's grasp. "All right. All right. You've had your bit of fun. Let's get back to the matter at hand. Doyle. And the fact that Emmy has painted the word target in bold letters across her chest."

"You're exaggerating. Doyle wouldn't dare come after me. It would be too risky."

"Nothing is too risky for a man like Doyle. He was IRA. He's accustomed to danger and flouting the law. Case in point, he broke into your office without anyone noticing," Burnell said, his tone grave.

"There you are, darling, straight from the mouth of Scotland Yard's finest. Not an opinion to be discounted lightly."

"I'll be fine," she asserted with more confidence than she felt.

Three pairs of male eyes stared down at her with skepticism.

She squared her shoulders and stubbornly tossed her head in the air. "I will. I'll be extra careful. I won't take any unnecessary risks."

Gregory snorted. "You forget that we know you. Throwing caution to the wind is second nature to you."

She jumped to her feet. "That's a lie. I have a job to do. I have to follow *every* lead no matter where it takes me to find the truth. The truth is what matters and seeing that justice is served."

"Not at the cost of your life," Finch said. "Nothing is worth that."

CHAPTER 26

Sanborn was sitting on the sofa in his living room, his elbows resting on his knees. He was hunched over the coffee table, muttering to himself as he swirled a brandy snifter in one hand. He had just had another flaming row with Brian about Sanborn Enterprises. If Brian hadn't stormed out a few minutes ago, Max would have taken tremendous pleasure in throttling him.

He took a large swig of his brandy. "It's *my* bloody company," he raged at the empty penthouse. "I built it with my own sweat. What does Brian know? Nothing. Absolutely nothing. He has no guts for the tough decisions. He's bound to fail."

He leaned back against the sofa and crossed his legs at the ankles. On the one hand, he hoped his son would fall flat on his face. He would quite enjoy seeing that. However, if that happened, it would mean that the company he loved would be ruined. He simply couldn't allow that. Then there was the little matter about Doyle and what he planned to do with his knowledge.

A vindictive smiled played around his lips. There were so many delightful possibilities. He was at a loss to choose which one would have the most dramatic impact.

He was still chuckling to himself, when the ormolu clock on the mantelpiece struck seven. Precisely half a second later, the doorbell rang.

"Well, well," Sanborn said as he pushed himself to his feet. "How refreshing. Maggie Roth believes in punctuality."

At least she was one problem he would resolve tonight.

The housekeeper was gone, so he crossed to the hall and opened the door himself.

"Ah, there you are, Ms. Roth. Bang on time."

He suppressed the urge to laugh when he saw the startled look in her large green eyes. Good. He liked it when people were off guard. "Won't you come in?" he said affably as he stepped back to allow her to pass.

"Yes. Yes, of course, Mr. Sanborn," Maggie replied, when she finally found her tongue.

Her mouth curved in a half-hearted attempt at a smile. She wanted to get this meeting over with as quickly as possible. She hadn't told Philip because she knew he would have strongly discouraged her. But she kept reminding herself that she was doing this for him and the boys. A few distasteful moments spent in Max Sanborn's presence would be worth it, if they could avoid further unpleasantness. And she got Great Aunt Sarah's Constable back.

Sanborn shot the bolt into place and turned round to face her again. He smiled, but she couldn't read the expression in his eyes.

He extended an arm outward. "I thought we could talk in my study. Less stuffy and therefore more conducive to finding common ground."

Maggie clutched her handbag tightly against her rib cage. "Fine. Lead the way." She was determined to remain cool and in control.

They were silent as they made their way down the corridor.

"Please sit down," he said as they entered the study.

Maggie lowered herself onto the chair he indicated by his desk. She sat on the edge, her back ramrod straight and her handbag in her lap.

A rumble of laughter emanated from him. "Oh, do relax, Ms. Roth. How about a nice dry sherry? It's just the thing."

"I really don't think so, Mr. Sanborn. I came here to discuss my aunt's painting, not to have an aperitif with you."

For a fraction of a second, the mask of cordiality slipped, and Sanborn's jaw tightened. The look was gone as quickly as it had come, leaving Maggie to wonder whether she had simply imagined it. "Of course, I understand. I suspect that you are as anxious as I am to settle this matter."

He hitched a hip on the corner of the desk and smiled down at her.

"Yes, it's been rather a trying few days."

He nodded sympathetically. "Of course, it has, my dear."

Was there just the merest hint of asperity in his tone?

"If you've been reading the papers, you'll know that it hasn't been easy for me either. So let's get down to business." One leg swung back and forth gently, his hand on a thigh. "Let me tell you what I think."

Maggie looked up at him expectantly. She would hear him out. If she didn't like what he had to say, she would get up and leave. It was as simple as that.

She never saw it coming. The back of Sanborn's hand lashed out and struck her on the right cheek. The blow jerked her head backward, bringing tears to her eyes. She brought a trembling hand up to her hot, stinging cheek. The salty taste of blood trickled onto her tongue from the cut on her lip.

She scrambled to her feet, knocking over the chair. "You're a deranged maniac." Her voice quavered as she backed away. "You ought to be locked up."

Sanborn stood and lunged at her. He grabbed her wrist, pulling her toward him. There was virtually no space between them.

His warm breath brushed her cheek. "And you're an interfering busybody who needs to be taught a lesson. No one. *No one* ever meddles in my business or my personal life. Do you understand?"

He shook her so hard that her teeth clattered together as her head swung wildly back and forth. "You're going to drop your lawsuit immediately." His tone was full of menace. "And you're going to issue a statement to the press in the morning saying that the whole thing has been a terrible mistake and you lay no claim to *my* painting. Is that clear?"

He shook her again, tightening his grip on her wrist. Tears were streaming from the corners of her eyes. She had to get

out of the penthouse. Away from this madman. She had to get
to the police. To Philip.

She tried yanking her wrist away, but he was too strong.
Her gaze darted from his congested face to the door. And now
she had no means of escape. She felt the edge of the desk digging into the small of her back. There was no way to get
around him.

"You didn't answer my question. Funny how you were able
to open your big mouth to the press and now you're a deaf
mute. I see I'll have to teach you manners as well."

He raised his hand to hit her again, but Maggie's blind,
frantic fingers clamped down on something hard on the desk
behind her. With all the force in her body, she swung upward.
There was a sickening crack, as the onyx bookend made contact with Sanborn's left temple.

He froze, his brown eyes staring down at her in disbelief.
Then his hand slackened and slipped from her arm. He slowly
crumpled to the floor.

Maggie drew deep gulps of air into her burning lungs. She
hadn't realized that she had been holding her breath. She was
shivering uncontrollably.

Sanborn wasn't moving, and the wound in his head was
bleeding, heavily.

"Oh my God, what have I done?" She put an unsteady hand
to her mouth in horror. "I've killed him. I've *killed* a man."
She stood there, gripping her elbows tightly to her body. After
several paralyzing seconds, she slowly lowered herself to her
knees. Despite the wave of nausea that washed over her at the
sight of the blood, she whispered into his ear, "Get up. Oh,
please, *please* get up." But he didn't.

So Maggie bolted.

Panic propelled her out of the study and down the corridor.
A primitive whimpering erupted from her throat as her clumsy
fingers fumbled with the lock. She had blood on her hands,
literally. Sanborn's blood. This thought sent a frisson down
her spine, but, finally, she managed to fling open the door and
flee the penthouse. She hastily pulled out a handkerchief from
her handbag and did her best to wipe away the blood.

Her eyes were swimming with tears. The corridor was a blur, but she ran. Ran for her life. She stumbled several times, but managed to keep herself upright. Sheer adrenaline drove her toward the lift. She pushed the button and pressed it again, and again. Where was the bloody lift? She pounded with the side of her clenched fist. *Where was it?* Fear clutched at her chest, ripping the breath from her lungs.

What if the police had been called? What if they were holding the lift? What if they were on their way up at that very moment to arrest her for *murder*?

She tilted her head back and desperately whispered a prayer for divine intervention. The doors finally slid open. Thank God the car was empty. She scurried inside and pressed a button. Her legs felt like water. She leaned her back against the car for support, grateful for its solidness. She squeezed her eyes shut, trying blot out the terrible scenes of the last quarter of an hour.

Her eyes popped open again. What was that noise? Had someone seen her? But the doors slid closed before she could find out.

☙❧☙

Maggie nearly jumped out of her skin when the lift stopped with a little bump on the seventeenth floor. She had expected—hoped—that it would go straight down to the lobby. She kept her head down, her gaze fixed on the floor. Her hair hid her bruised face from anyone who entered the car. She had no desire to make any small talk.

"What a pleasant surprise. Why didn't you tell me you were here?"

Maggie's head snapped up at the sound of the familiar voice. "Emmeline." It came out as a hoarse whisper.

The smile faded from her friend's lips. "What is it? What's wrong?"

Maggie was rooted to the spot. She opened her mouth, but then clamped it shut.

"What's wrong?" Emmeline repeated.

There was a soft *ding* as the doors prepared to close. Emmeline reached in quickly and dragged Maggie out of the lift.

She held Maggie by both arms and felt her friend's body shudder. "Tell me what's the matter. I can help. Oh, please, Maggie."

But Maggie shook her head. She refused to look at Emmeline. She couldn't bring herself to stare into those dark eyes that seemed to see everything. What would her friend think of her now that she was a murderer? A sob wracked her body. No one could help her. She was all alone. This thought brought on a fresh rush of warm tears.

"Let me go. There's nothing you can do." Despite the harsh tone, there were tears in her voice.

Emmeline didn't move. She put a hand under Maggie's chin and tilted it upward. "You can't get rid of me, so you might as well tell me—" She gasped. "You're hurt. What's happened to your face?"

Maggie remained silent. Not a muscle moved.

"Who did this to you?" Emmeline demanded. Her tone was low and urgent. A thousand disconcerting thoughts raced through her mind.

Before her friend could answer—if she had intended to answer the question—a couple of correspondents walked out of the newsroom and headed toward the lift. Maggie tucked her chin into her chest and pulled her hair forward to cover her bruised cheek.

Emmeline grabbed her unceremoniously by the elbow. "Come on. We'll go to my office."

She didn't give Maggie a chance to protest. She just pushed her forward. Luckily, the two chaps were deep in conversation and barely registered their presence. Once inside the newsroom, Emmeline guided Maggie quickly across the floor to her office.

Neither of them uttered a word until Emmeline had locked the door and pulled down the blinds to block out the view of the newsroom. "Now, you're not leaving this office until you tell me what happened tonight."

Maggie's hands twisted in her lap one minute and then she patted her red-gold strands into place the next. Her throat worked up and down, but, still, she said nothing. Her mouth was dry, so very dry.

"I'm waiting," Emmeline pressed. A knot had formed in the pit of her stomach watching her friend's palpable distress.

At last, Maggie appeared to gather her courage. She swallowed hard. Her green eyes, wide and round, didn't flinch.

There's was a slight tremor in her voice, but what she had to say came out loud and clear. "I killed Max Sanborn tonight."

CHAPTER 27

The blood was thundering in Emmeline's ears. It didn't make any sense. She couldn't have heard Maggie properly. But one look at her friend's face told her that it was indeed true.

Max Sanborn dead? And by Maggie? She simply couldn't believe it.

Emmeline reached across the desk and gave Maggie's hand a squeeze. "Tell me what happened." Her voice was a gentle caress. "Take your time."

Maggie took a deep breath and tried to collect her wits about her. "First, I want you to know I didn't go to his penthouse with the intention of killing him. Things sort of…got away from me…and it just…happened."

"I believe you. I'm on your side, no matter what."

And then, slowly, the whole ugly story started tumbling from Maggie's lips. Every detail, from the time Sanborn rang the office that afternoon asking to meet her to the moment Emmeline found her in the lift.

"I thought he was being sincere and wanted to settle the case out of court. Otherwise, I would never have agreed to meet him. Emmeline, you should have seen him. It was horrible. I've never been so frightened. I thought he was going to kill me and, in the end, I—" Maggie's body shuddered as the image of Sanborn's body lying on rug in his study flashed into her mind.

"From everything you've said, it's clearly a case of self-defense. Are you sure that he's dead? Perhaps, you only knocked him out."

"You didn't see him. The blood—He looked—And yet—Do you really think it's possible that he's still alive?" A glimmer of hope flashed in her green eyes.

"Yes, of course. It's possible." Emmeline stood up abruptly and hurried across to the door. "You stay here."

"Where are you going?" Maggie asked anxiously. She didn't want to be left alone.

"I'm going up to Max Sanborn's penthouse. Keep the door locked and don't let anyone in. I'll be back soon. Don't worry. I'm taking my key with me. In the meantime, give Philip a ring so that he doesn't start worrying."

"I couldn't. What would I tell him?"

"Tell him that you're going spend the night at my house. Tell him you want to discuss your ideas for my wedding. That won't arouse his suspicions. Tell him *anything*."

"But what if—" Maggie swallowed the lump in her throat. "—what if Max Sanborn is really—"

Emmeline cut her off. "We'll deal with that when the time comes. Don't start making problems. All right?"

"All right," Maggie whispered.

"Good. Remember to keep the door locked."

With that, Emmeline was gone. And the long wait began for Maggie.

❧❧❧

Emmeline burst out of the lift on the sixty-fifth floor. There was no one in the corridor. She half ran, half walked down to Sanborn's penthouse. The door was slightly ajar. She raised her fist and rapped firmly as she pushed it opened. "Mr. Sanborn," she called. "It's Emmeline Kirby. I just wanted to check that you're all right. *Mr. Sanborn?*"

She stepped over the threshold and pressed the door closed behind her. She leaned her back against it and listened. It was quiet, much too quiet. The hairs on the back of her neck prickled. "Mr. Sanborn?"

A cold tendril of fear coiled itself around her heart making her shiver involuntarily. There was nothing for it. Her feet slowly, unwillingly, shuffled toward Sanborn's study.

The door was closed. She knocked, but was greeted only by silence. So with a hand that was not quite steady, Emmeline reached out and turned the knob. The door creaked slightly on its hinges.

She sucked in her breath when her gaze fell on Sanborn's body sprawled on the floor by the desk.

He's not dead, she told herself. *Please God, don't let him be dead.*

She hurried across the room and fell to her knees beside Sanborn's body. "Mr. Sanborn?" she whispered. Uselessly, she shook his arm. And then she straightened up and frowned. "That's odd."

But before this thought could take seed, the back of her head exploded in a thousand daggers of pain. She saw stars for a brief instant. Then she was falling. Plunging so fast and so deep into a sea of blackness, where there was no more pain. *No more nothing.*

⌀⌀⌀

"You've taken leave of your senses. I don't care what it looks like. If she did it, then explain to me how she managed to knock herself out."

Emmeline heard the murmur of male voices as if she were at the other end of a very, very long tunnel. Why did they insist on talking so loudly? Honestly, men could be so inconsiderate at times.

Where was she? She had no idea. Why was everything so dark? It took a while for this question to reach her brain. Ever so slowly, she came to the realization that her eyes were closed. Thank heavens for that. She was beginning to worry that she had suddenly gone blind. She concentrated, hard—beads of perspiration formed on her brow with the effort—and finally managed to open her eyes a tiny sliver.

She blinked several times to clear her vision. Everything

started to sharpen into focus, both mentally and visually. She was on the sofa in Max Sanborn's living room, which was a beehive of activity. All manner of uniformed and plainclothes police officers were moving about. Not two feet away from her Superintendent Burnell, Sergeant Finch, and Gregory stood arguing with Assistant Commissioner Fenton.

Emmeline tried to push herself into a more seemly position, preferably sitting upright. However, her head filed a protest in excruciating terms, chiding her for taking such mercenary action. *You made your point. I'll never do that again.* She groaned and slumped back against the sofa.

The four men stopped quarreling. Gregory bent down beside her and folded one of her hands in his larger one. He smoothed back a dark curl from her forehead. "Emmy darling, how do you feel?"

"Like death warmed over." Her voice was a hoarse whisper. "I think Moses took a wrong turn and decided to part my head in two, rather than the Red Sea. I must say it was not very sporting of a fellow Jew, and I take great offense."

Gregory smiled, in spite of himself. Some of the tension eased from his body. He was grateful that she hadn't come to greater harm, no thanks to him. He silently cursed himself for not being more vigilant. Doyle had made it abundantly clear that he had Emmeline in his sights, but she had decided to add fuel to the fire with that damn article. Well, she got what she wanted. She drew Doyle out of the shadows. One thing they could thank Max for was that his death would likely bump the Doyle article to the back pages of the paper. He glanced down at Emmeline. Then again, they were talking about Emmy. Most likely, the articles would run side by side on the front page. He sighed inwardly.

Burnell was hovering over his shoulder now. His eyes were full of concern. "Glad to see that you're among us again."

Finch's pleasant face came into view too. "You gave us quite a scare."

Emmeline tried to smile at them, but it hurt too much. "Just lie back and relax," the superintendent said. He patted her shoulder awkwardly. "As soon as Dr. Meadows is finished with the bod—finished with his examination, he'll come over and take a look at your head. Can you tell us anything that happened—"

"Stop mucking about, Burnell," Fenton snapped. "If you don't arrest Miss Kirby this instant, I shall."

Emmeline's eyes opened wide. Her dark gaze flickered from Gregory to Burnell, before finally settling with trepidation on Fenton's angry countenance. The assistant commissioner was scowling at her. His lips were drawn into a thin, tight line, while his nostrils flared. There were two deep vertical grooves between his eyebrows. But what made Emmeline shudder was the malevolence she saw in those gray eyes.

Painfully, she pushed herself to a sitting position. Her mouth felt very dry. She cleared her throat. "Arrest *me*? But I haven't done anything."

"Don't play that game with me. We had an anonymous call into the station that a woman was seen fleeing from this penthouse a little over an hour ago. Everyone knows that you and Mr. Sanborn had several heated arguments over the course of the last few days. In fact, rumor has it that he wanted to sack you."

"But I didn't kill him." She clutched at Gregory's hand. "I didn't. You have to believe me."

He sat down next to her and put an arm protectively around her shoulders. "Hush, darling. Don't upset yourself. Just ignore Fenton. He's simply lost what little marbles he once possessed."

"And you—" Fenton rounded on Gregory. "—I'd have a care what I say if I were you. I'd like nothing better than to see your miserable hide behind bars where it belongs."

Gregory gently settled Emmeline against the back of the sofa and pressed a kiss to her temple. Then he rose slowly to his feet and took a step toward Fenton. They were only inches apart. "You forget that I'm a law-abiding citizen. The papers tend to take a dim view of police harassment. And another thing I might remind you, despite the fact that we were estranged for years, I am still Max Sanborn's nephew. The Sanborn name wields a great deal of influence. So I'd say *you're* the one who should have a care, old chap."

Burnell and Finch did their best to bite back their smiles.

"Why, you impudent bastard," Fenton blustered.

Gregory wagged his finger at him. "Ah, ah. Language. There is a lady present."

This only served to enrage the assistant commissioner even further. "I'll wipe that smirk off your face, Longdon. We both know that your fiancée is guilty. Who knows, you probably helped her do it. I'll enjoy finding out."

Gregory opened his mouth to reply, but Emmeline tugged at his sleeve. "Darling, don't. It will only make matters worse."

Burnell stepped between the two men. "Naturally tempers are running a bit high at the moment. Murder is always such a nasty business. However, sir, don't you think you're too close to the case to be objective? After all, Mr. Sanborn was your friend. Wouldn't it be wiser to allow Finch and me to handle things?"

Fenton's cheeks turned an ugly shade of crimson. "*What*? How dare you try to undermine my authority? I'll see that a note is put in your record about this…this disgraceful display of insubordination."

So what else is new, Burnell thought. *My file already makes for such colorful reading because of your literary flourishes.* However, he swallowed his pride. "I meant no disrespect, sir. I was just concerned about your professional reputation. I mean, consider how it would look to the public and the press."

Fenton was somewhat mollified, but not entirely. "I see your point." He was silent for a moment. Then another thought struck him. "Why were you still pestering Max? I heard talk at the station this afternoon that you and Finch interviewed him again. Why? I took you off this case. I told you to turn it over to the Arts and Antiques squad."

"Oh, but sir, we did. We always follow your orders to the letter. Finch and I are working on a new case. The murder of the Bond Street art dealer Maurice Boinet."

"So why were you talking to Max again?"

"As I'm sure you'll remember, sir, Mr. Boinet was the one who helped Mr. Sanborn acquire his—the disputed Constable painting. We thought Mr. Sanborn might be able to help us with our inquiries. We believe that Boinet's murder was connected to the sale of the painting. And now, the very next day Mr. Sanborn himself is found dead. It sets the curious mind to wondering. Rather a lot of coincidences are piling up. Wouldn't you say, sir?"

Fenton dismissed the superintendent's conjectures with a brusque wave of his hand. "I don't find it remotely curious. If you ask me, you're grasping at straws."

"Indeed, sir? Of course, Finch and I welcome your opinion, don't we, Finch?"

The sergeant merely nodded, as he tried hard to look sincere.

"As well you should, Burnell. Glad to see that you know your place."

The superintendent had pasted an obsequious smile on his face, and it was beginning to crack slightly. "There's just one thing that's bothering me, sir. Perhaps you can help us puzzle it out."

Fenton made a show of looking at his watch. "Just spit it out. I don't have all night."

"How do you think Mr. Sanborn and Boinet came to be mixed up with a former IRA commander named Doyle, and now they're both dead?"

CHAPTER 28

L ike a chameleon transforming itself before their eyes, Fenton's face drained of color until it was a pasty, ashen hue and then virtually the next instant a rose flush of such intensity replaced it. Through gritted teeth, he grumbled, "What the devil are you chuntering on about?" He shook his head in disgust. "The IRA? Of all the implausible theories. It boggles the mind. It really does. You don't seriously expect me to believe that the IRA murdered Max Sanborn."

"No, I did."

The voice, although soft and devoid of emotion, was like a clap of thunder in the already tense atmosphere. As a group, they turned their heads to find Maggie standing by the sofa, a woman PC by her side.

Emmeline leaped to her feet and immediately regretted the sudden movement. A sharp stabbing pain hurtled from the base of her neck straight to the top of her skull. "Maggie, no," she said as she collapsed back onto the sofa. She grabbed her head with both hands and rested her elbows on her knees. "You were supposed to wait in my office."

"What's this? A conspiracy. You see, Burnell," Fenton said, his eyes shining triumphantly, "I told you Miss Kirby was guilty up to her neck. She plotted the whole thing with her friend here." He waved a hand in Maggie's direction.

"No." The word was ripped from Maggie's throat. "Emmeline had nothing, absolutely *nothing*, to do with it. I killed Max Sanborn. I didn't mean too. It—it just happened."

"Just happened? You'll get no sympathy from me, Ms. Roth. All of London knows about your shameful attempt to get money out of poor, old Max."

Emmeline was on her feet again. "How dare you speak to Maggie as if she were a criminal?"

Fenton snorted. "Her own words condemned her. And you."

"I thought everyone under law was innocent until proven guilty. This is a case of self-defense, pure and simple—"

"Self-defense? It's just more lies."

Emmeline sucked in her breath. She couldn't believe her ears.

Burnell grabbed Fenton by the arm before he could do any more damage, or before Gregory could do him bodily harm. "Sir, I strongly advise you to leave. Now. If you go on like this, you'll only prejudice the case. And you wouldn't want that, would you?"

Fenton's gaze shifted from Burnell to Maggie and then back again. He cleared his throat deliberately and shot his cuffs, shrugging off the superintendent's hand. "You make a valid point. I want your report on my desk first thing in the morning."

With that, the assistant commissioner turned his back on them. He crossed the living room, stopping briefly to murmur something to a uniformed PC.

They drew a collective sigh when Fenton's disturbing presence had finally departed.

Burnell slipped one hand casually into his pocket and fixed his hard stare on Maggie. "Now then, Ms. Roth, why don't you tell us how you came to murder Max Sanborn."

Maggie blinked twice, unnerved by the blue intensity of the superintendent's unflinching scrutiny. Those eyes that were filled with a razor-sharp intelligence. Those eyes that missed nothing. Those eyes that were clearly displeased with her at the moment.

"We're waiting, Ms. Roth," Burnell pressed.

"Yes." She licked her lips. "Yes, of course." Her gaze strayed nervously to Emmeline, who was sitting close beside her. Emmeline squeezed her hand and gave her an encouraging smile. Maggie returned the pressure and straightened her shoulders. "Sergeant Finch, are you ready to take notes?"

Finch gave a silent nod.

Burnell held up a hand in the air. "Just a moment, Ms. Roth. I would be remiss in my duty if I didn't tell you that you are entitled to have your solicitor present."

Maggie smiled. "Thank you, Superintendent. I appreciate that, but I trust you and Sergeant Finch. You're both fair men. I'm quite prepared to give you my statement."

And so for the second time that evening, she found herself relating all the ghastly details of how the great Max Sanborn—a man larger than life itself—wound up dead at her feet.

"That's everything. The whole horrid story," Maggie concluded, as she choked back a sob. "I don't care what happens to me. I deserve to be punished for my crime, even though he was a despicable man. I'm just worried about what the scandal is going to do Philip and the boys. I've ruined their lives."

Emmeline rubbed her friend's back and cooed, "Shh. Shh. It's all over. Everything will be all right. You'll see."

"How can it be?" Maggie's eyes were brimming with tears. "I killed a man. I picked up that bookend and bashed in his brains. Max Sanborn is dead because of me."

"I hate to shatter your illusions, but you can dispense with your yoke of martyrdom," Dr. Meadows said matter-of-factly.

They had been so focused on Maggie's story that no one had heard the medical examiner approach.

"John, what can you tell us?" Burnell asked.

"Naturally I'll have to conduct a full examination back at the lab, but my preliminary findings indicate that Sanborn suffered blunt force trauma to his temple—"

Maggie took a deep shuddering breath. "You see. I told you."

"—but that injury was not what killed him. He was stabbed. I think he must have regained consciousness and was trying to stand up when a single, deliberate thrust was delivered to his corroded artery. He would have been dead instantly. The blow was particularly vicious. But that's just my humble medical opinion."

"That's it. That's what bothered me," Emmeline said as she scrambled to her feet with a wince. "Just before everything went black, I remember thinking that it was odd that there was so much blood if Maggie coshed him on the head."

"Oh, there's another thing," Meadows said. "Whoever the killer is, he's left-handed. On that happy note, I think I'll leave you. Oliver, Finch—" He nodded his head at the two detectives. "—I'll get you the results as soon as possible."

Burnell clapped him on the shoulder. "Thanks, John. Our usual drink at the pub on Friday?"

"Wouldn't miss it." Then to Emmeline, he said, "Before I go, let me have a look at that head of yours, young lady."

Emmeline smiled. "That's really not necessary, Dr. Meadows. I have a hard head. I'll be fine. Honestly. Please don't worry."

Meadows lifted an eyebrow skeptically. "It's against my better judgment, but you're not a child. Promise me you'll go to your local GP if you feel nauseous or your vision starts to blur."

Emmeline crossed her fingers over her heart. "I will. I promise. Thank you."

He hurried to catch up with one of the members of the forensic team. Their heads were bent close together as Sanborn's body was rolled out of the penthouse. There were still a few plainclothes officers milling about, but most of the constables had already gone.

Maggie rose on unsteady legs. Her eyes were as wide as saucers. "I don't understand."

Emmeline gave her a fierce hug that nearly toppled them both. "Don't you see? It means you couldn't have killed Max. Someone else did."

The two friends drew apart, still feeling a bit giddy after the mad swing that their emotions had taken that evening. However, the smile quickly faded from Emmeline's lips when she caught a glimpse of the grim expressions on the faces of the three men. "What is it?"

Gregory ran a hand through his hair in frustration as he paced back and forth. "Darling, are you even listening to yourself? We have no idea who killed Max, in a particularly vicious manner I might add." He stopped and turned on his heel, pinning her with his gaze. "But what we do know is that same person tried to kill *you*."

e/ɔe/ɔ

After Burnell dispatched a constable to take Maggie home, everyone agreed that it would be for the best if Emmeline did not go home that evening—everyone except Emmeline, that is. She protested vociferously to having her life turned upside down. She refused to give in to the fear.

These were brave words. And half of her truly believed them. It was convincing the other half that was taking some doing.

In the end, they came to a compromise. Gregory would accompany her back to Holland Park and spend the night—although he would be relegated to the guest room as a punishment—while Burnell ordered two teams of plainclothes officers to watch Emmeline's house in rotating shifts round the clock until Sanborn's murderer was apprehended.

Once Emmeline was fast asleep, and he had checked that all the locks were securely bolted, Gregory went into the living room and poured himself a large whiskey. He downed half of it in one gulp. He was not looking forward to his next task, but he had no choice. Better him than the police. He took another sip of the whiskey and lowered himself onto the sofa. He was suddenly very tired. The weariness had seeped into the marrow of his bones. He checked his watch. It had gone half past one. With a sigh, he reached for the phone and punched in the number at the house in Belsize Park.

He was surprised when it was answered on the first ring. "Hello." Brian's harried voice echoed in his ear.

"Brian, I'm surprised to find you up at this hour."

"Toby? I mean Gregory, is that you?"

"Yes, it's me. I'm…I'm afraid I have some bad news."

A soft huff of a laugh buzzed in his ear. It was an unnerving and deeply disturbing sound.

"Are you all right?" Gregory asked cautiously.

"No, I don't think I'll ever be 'all right' again. Lately, my days seem to be filled with bad news. I hurtle from one crisis to another. I don't even have a chance to breathe or even think, let alone see Tessa and the boys. So whatever this is, it'll have to wait until morning. Goodnight, Toby."

"Don't ring off. This can't wait." He paused and shook his head. Then, more quietly, he said, "Max is dead. He was murdered at the penthouse earlier this evening."

There was stunned, deafening silence at the other end of the line.

"Brian? Are you—"

"I heard you," his cousin replied at last. "My brain is…just having difficulty digesting the information. Dad…*dead*? Murdered? It doesn't make any sense. Who—"

"Superintendent Burnell and Sergeant Finch are investigating. It's too soon for them to have any viable suspects."

"Quite. Yes, of course," Brian murmured into the phone. He sounded as if he was a million miles away.

Gregory went on to recount everything that the police had been able to piece together thus far about the events of last night.

"Well, I'm glad that Richard Fenton was able to see sense in the end. It was absolutely ridiculous on his part, for even one minute, to have suspected Maggie or Emmeline. I'm relieved to hear that they're both all right. What a harrowing experience for them. And Emmeline's injury?"

"The doctor said that it's a mild concussion. She'll be as right as rain in a few days, if she takes it easy. She's fast asleep at the moment. I'm at her house. We all thought it wiser that she not be alone after her near escape. Needless to say, she was not best pleased, but she had no choice. Burnell also stationed two teams to watch her house round the clock until the killer is caught."

"Good thinking." Brian exhaled a long, low sigh. Gregory heard some papers being shuffled. "I suppose I have to draft a press statement. Then I'll have to start on the funeral arrange-ments. And then—What am I saying? The first thing I have to do is ring Nigel and—"

"Would you like me to break the news to Nigel?"

"No, that's all right. It's best if he hears it from me."

"I'm here, if—if there's anything I can do to help..." Gregory let the sentence trail off.

There was an awkward silence, then Brian said, "Thanks for the offer, Toby. It—it means a lot."

ᏋᎧᏋᎧ

On the opposite side of the square, Sergeant Haworth's ra-dio crackled to life. "Anything to report?"

"Nothing. All's as it should be in the dead of night," he grumbled.

"Let's hope it stays that way because there's someone else watching Miss Kirby's house besides us. He's very good."

Haworth sat up, suddenly alert. "Professional?"

"No question about it."

He reached for his camera in the passenger seat and swept the square. "I can't see him from my angle."

"I told you he's good. We almost missed him, almost."

"Did you call Burnell?"

"Yes. He said to hold our positions for the time being. However, if our chap makes a move we take him down. At once."

Haworth opened the glove box and pulled out his gun. He checked the magazine and slipped it back with a snap. "Under-stood."

CHAPTER 29

The next few days all of London and the international business world were abuzz with the shocking news about Max's death and speculation about Sanborn Enterprises' financial condition. Rumors were mounting that Max had been embezzling from the company. It was only through Brian's Herculean efforts—and thirty-six hours straight without sleep—that Sanborn's stock didn't plunge into an abyss.

Meanwhile, Burnell and Finch were no closer to catching Sanborn's murderer. They were convinced the murderer was the same man who killed Maurice Boinet. It was too much of a coincidence to be otherwise. However, every time the detectives thought they were onto a promising lead, it seemed to evaporate before their eyes, and they were back to where they started—with a strong theory and no evidence to back it up. It was almost as if the killer could guess what their next move would be even before they made it. To make matters worse, Fenton was breathing down Burnell's neck, demanding daily progress reports.

Gregory and Philip found themselves in similar straits. All their attempts to wheedle out information from their contacts were being frustrated at every turn. Through Crichlow, Villiers was keeping a watchful eye on how things were proceeding. He didn't deem it necessary to intervene, at this stage.

The only one who was in her element was Emmeline. The two murders and the ongoing controversy surrounding the

Constable painting were making for very good copy. Since only a small group of individuals knew Maggie had been in Sanborn's penthouse the night of his death, Emmeline saw no need to disclose that point. Her friend's name was not mentioned anywhere. As it was, *The Clarion* was flying off newsstands as fast as the paper was being printed.

What bothered Emmeline was the fact that the elusive Doyle remained out there, pulling strings and wreaking havoc from the shadows. Her instincts told her that he was the key to everything. If only she could unmask the contemptible fiend before he got to her, *again*. This thought sent a frisson down her spine.

"No." She shook her head and slammed her palm against her desk. "I will not be intimidated. Such ideas only feed the fear, and that does no one any good. Fear stops one from thinking clearly, and that leads to carelessness. Right now, I need all my wits about me."

༺༚༻

Sanborn's funeral, as per his wishes, was held at the village church near his country estate in Buckinghamshire. It was a somber occasion made even more so by the leaden sky. It had rained earlier that morning, but the angry charcoal clouds scudding overhead seemed poised for another round. However, this did not stop the mourners from coming to pay their respects to the great Max Sanborn—and to ensure that they were seen doing so. There were members of the government, financiers, titled ladies and gentlemen, fellow philanthropists, art critics, and celebrities. Of course, the entire board of Sanborn Enterprises was there to a man. All the mourners had something in common. They were all beholden to Max in one way or another. He had discovered all their secrets and had used them to his advantage over the years. The only reason that they were here today was to make certain he was really dead. They viewed his death with mixed emotions. On the one hand, it was a tremendous relief that Max's subtle form of blackmail would finally stop. But how could any of them be sure that he didn't leave a trail behind that would lead directly to their doorsteps?

While Brian and Nigel greeted the mourners outside the church, Gregory hovered on the outer fringes. He was family, and he was not. It was an untenable position. He found himself thinking of his mother. A faint smile touched his lips as the image of her face danced before his eyes. She had been lovely. She had always been delicate, but that hadn't stopped her from tramping with him through woods or going fishing in the river or chasing after him across the meadow. She had been warm and caring, ready to laugh at the silliest things, and she had always been there to listen to his childish dreams and desires. Until she became ill. Gregory had watched in fear and horror at how the cancer ravaged her body. She slowly slipped away from him until the disease finally took her at the age of forty and left him an orphan at sixteen.

Max, of course, was his usual callous self. He took Gregory aside, an arm around his shoulders, and murmured a few words of condolence. He said that Gregory would get over it. Time marches on, etcetera. And that was that. His uncle couldn't have shooed him from his study fast enough so that he could attend to his latest business venture.

Aunt Mireille, though, had been gentle and kind. She had always treated Gregory as if he were another son and had mourned his mother just deeply as he had. The sisters-in-law had been close friends, and Mireille felt that she owed it to Clarissa to take care of her son. Mireille tried very hard, but after a year Gregory couldn't bear to be under the same roof as Max any longer. His mother was dead. She had been the buffer and had borne the brunt of Max's abusive tongue. He would always be grateful to Mireille and felt sorry to leave her, but it had been time to go. He would make his own way in the world. He steeled himself for the inevitable loneliness, but it was better than living in his uncle's house with his mother's ghost as his constant companion.

Gregory sighed and shook his head. His gaze skimmed across to the churchyard. No one would miss him for five minutes. He slipped around the side of the church and crossed to the Sanborn plot. A gaping hole of freshly turned earth awaited Max, but Gregory was interested in the tombstone next to it. He bent down on his haunches and touched it gently. "Hello, Mum," he whispered. "It's Toby. I'm sorry I've been away for so long."

Naturally, there was no response. The only sound was the leaves rustling in the wind. But oh how he wished he could hear her mellifluous voice and silvery laughter just one more time.

"Gregory?" He felt a small hand touch his shoulder. "Are you all right?"

Emmeline. Of course. Who else could it have been?

He smiled at his mother's grave. "It's all right, Mum. You don't have to worry. I'm in good hands."

He rose to his feet and smiled down at the woman he loved. He pressed a kiss against Emmeline's dark curls and pulled her to him. "Emmy, meet Mum. She would have adored you."

Emmeline's mouth formed an "O." Her eyes searched his face, and her heart ached at what she saw there. She leaned in closer to him. "I'm sure I would have adored her too, very much. I would have loved to get to know her."

"Yes." Gregory's throat constricted. His Adam's apple worked up and down, but he didn't say anything else.

"Come on, darling. I'm afraid everyone's going into the church. We'll stop in the village later and buy some more flowers for your mother's grave before we go back to London. And now that we've been introduced, we have to come back often to visit. We can't leave her here on her own for another twenty-five years, now can we?" She gave him a bright smile and squeezed his arm.

At that moment, Gregory couldn't have loved her more.

He cast a last glance at his mother's grave before they left. That's when he noticed the fresh cut flowers for the first time. He frowned. Who could have left them?

അഅഅ

All the pews in the church were filled. Gregory and Emmeline were in the front row with Brian's family. Nigel sat on her left, while Gregory was on her right next to Brian. Tessa, Brian's wife, and their sons were on the end of the bench.

The hushed conversation had died away when the vicar appeared at the altar. He was just about to start when the heavy door at the back of the church creaked open. The vicar waited as the latecomer made her way down the aisle, her heels clicking against the stones. Everyone craned their necks to see who it was. Out of the corner of her eye, Emmeline saw Gregory nudge Brian in the ribs with his elbow.

"It can't be," Brian whispered.

"Well, she's not a figment of our imaginations," Gregory said.

Emmeline turned to Nigel and asked, "What's all the fuss about? Who is she?"

Nigel rose, and, out of the corner of his mouth, he replied, "It's Mum."

CHAPTER 30

Mireille's unexpected appearance at her ex-husband's funeral caused a minor stir and set tongues wagging. She certainly was not here to pay her respects. But the vicar quickly managed to quell the speculative whispers reverberating around his church. To his immense relief, the rest of the service proceeded without incident. Only the family dutifully trudged out to the open grave and watched as Max's coffin was lowered into the ground. The other mourners got into their cars and drove up to the house for the cold collation Tessa had arranged.

There had been no opportunity at the church to speak with Mireille, and, after the burial, Nigel had hustled her into his car. Now, Emmeline eyed the older woman over the rim of her teacup from across the drawing room. Mireille was tall, and her elegantly tailored navy suit emphasized her still-svelte figure.

Although Emmeline knew that Brian and Nigel's mother was seventy, she could have passed for a woman ten years younger. Her chestnut hair, which was expertly coiffed and colored, framed her oval face and fell to just above her shoulders, bouncing with every turn of her head.

When the gentleman Mireille had been speaking to had drifted off in search of something stronger than tea, Emmeline threaded her way through the crowd. "Excuse me, Mrs. Sanborn."

Mireille turned her head. "Yes?"

Emmeline proffered her hand. "I'm Emmeline Kirby. I wanted to extend my condolences."

The older woman's laugh was like a soft purr. "Condolences? Please save them, Mademoiselle Kirby. I couldn't be happier. Max is where he belongs. At last, he can no longer hurt anyone."

Emmeline raised an eyebrow.

Mireille laughed again. "Ah, I see I shock you. You have to get over your English sensibilities. At least Brian and Nigel are half French and do not suffer so much 'sensibilities.' What's the point in pretending that Max was a great man now that he is dead? He was a *cochon*—a pig—all his life. He thought about no one but himself. Yes, he could be charming when he wanted to, and he had an eye for the ladies. But underneath, he was rotten. Mean and vindictive." Her hand hovered for a second by her right cheek, a faraway look in her slate-blue eyes. "*Enfin*, a bully as you say in English. *C'est un vrai miracle* that he finally granted me the divorce."

Well, don't be shy, Emmeline thought. *Tell me what you really think.* "Yes, I see," she murmured, at a loss for a polite response to such brutal frankness.

Mireille observed Emmeline's discomfiture and asked abruptly, "*Alors*, are you one of Max's mistresses? Is that why you're here? To say goodbye to your lover." There was a frosty edge to her voice.

She heard a sharp intake of breath from Emmeline.

"I most certainly was not." Emmeline trembled with indignation.

"Ah, *bon*. Then we can be friends." Mireille flashed a broad grin and patted Emmeline's arm. "Come with me to the sofa, and you can tell me all about yourself."

Emmeline allowed herself to be dragged. Her mind was still off balance.

"*Bien*, Mademoiselle—?"

"Kirby. But please call me Emmeline."

"Emmeline." She rolled the name upon her Gallic tongue. "*C'est si charmante.* I insist you call me Mireille. So why is such a pretty girl here at Max's funeral?"

"I work for Sanborn. I'm the editorial director at *The Clarion*."

"*Mais, bien sûr*. Nigel told me about you. He was so happy when you agreed to come to the paper. He tells me that you work very hard and are doing a wonderful job. The paper hasn't sold so well in years. Brian is very pleased with you, too."

Emmeline felt her cheeks suffuse with heat at this praise. "That's very kind of them. I try my best."

Mireille patted her hand. "Don't be so modest, *cherie*. Others try and do not succeed. Obviously, you have talent. *Mais*, just because you are the editorial director at *The Clarion* is not a good enough reason for you to be here at this depressing affair. I do not see other Sanborn employees. Only the board members." She grimaced at this to indicate what she thought of them.

Emmeline suppressed a smile. She found that she liked the older woman very much. She was full of verve and wit. "Actually, I'm here because my fiancé is a member of the family."

The corners of Mireille's eyes crinkled when she smiled. "*Felicitations*. Now that Max is dead you will have an easier time as a Sanborn. When is the wedding? You must tell me. I will come."

Emmeline blushed again. "Actually, we haven't set the date yet—"

Mireille cut her off. "What are you waiting for?"

"It's…you see…It's a little complicated. We want to take things slow."

Mireille fixed her gaze, so like a roiling ocean, on Emmeline's face. "What's complicated? You love this man, *non*?"

These were virtually the same words that Emmeline's grandmother had used.

"Yes, but—"

The older woman made a dismissive gesture with her hand. "I never liked this word 'but.' *C'est stupide.* You must set a date *immediatement*." Again, just like Gran. And Maggie.

Emmeline sighed. There was no point trying to explain.

She simply nodded her head and gave her a watery smile.

Mireille folded her hands in her lap. "*Bon*. Now, you must tell me who is your fiancé?" Her brows knit together and she cocked her head to one side. "I cannot think who it can be. A distant cousin, perhaps."

Emmeline swallowed hard. "You could say that."

"Ah, Emmy darling, there you are. I've been looking—" Gregory stopped short a few feet away when he saw who was sitting next to her.

Mireille glanced up and politely inclined her head at the interruption. Gregory merely stared back at her without uttering a word. He smoothed down the corners of his mustache and shifted his gaze to Emmeline, who rose to her feet. She looped her arm through his and gave him what she hoped was an encouraging smile.

"Gregory, what a coincidence. We were just talking about you."

His left eyebrow arched upward. "You were?"

She gave an almost imperceptible shake of her head and saw the muscle in his jaw relax a little.

She turned back to the older woman. "Mireille, this is my fiancé Gregory Longdon. Gregory, this is Mireille Sanborn." Her voice trailed off as nephew and aunt stared at one another.

An awkward silence filled the space between them and Emmeline had to give him a little nudge with her elbow.

Mireille stood, her slate-blue eyes narrowing.

Gregory took a half-step forward. He cleared his throat and lifted her hand to his lips. "*Enchantée*, madame."

"How very gallant. I did not think gentlemen did that anymore these days," she said when he had straightened up. "*Mais*, forgive me. I feel sure that we have met before, but I cannot remember where. Longdon?" She leaned her head against one finger and studied him. "I'm afraid I cannot recall a Longdon side of the Sanborn family."

"No," Gregory murmured.

His aunt continued to stare at him, but his tongue seemed to be paralyzed. What does one say after twenty-five years?

Mireille's head suddenly snapped up. "*Mon Dieu, ce n'est pas possible.*" There was a tremor in her voice. Her hand was not quite steady as she reached up and touched his cheek. "Can it be? *Toby*?" This last word was barely a whisper.

Gregory swallowed the lump that had risen in his throat. At his side, he felt Emmeline's gentle touch on his arm. "Yes, Mireille, it's me," he replied at last.

Mireille's face broke out into a warm smile and tears shimmered in her eyes. She took his face in both her hands and lowered it so that she could give him a tender kiss. "*Mon chou.*" His lips twitched at the familiar endearment, long forgotten. "You finally came back." She pulled away to study him more closely and then she gave him another kiss. "My dear, dear boy. My third son. I've been waiting for this day for so long. I knew you would return."

೮⁄ು೮⁄ು

"All these years," Mireille said after closing the door to the library, where the three of them had escaped. "I kept waiting for you, Toby. Why did you stay away so long?"

"Toby Crenshaw is part of the past. Nowadays, it's Gregory Longdon."

"*Mais*, you will always be Toby to me. I've been so worried about you, *mon cher.*" She reached out and took his hand, needing to touch him to make certain he was not a dream.

"I'm sorry, Mireille. Truly I am. As much as I loved you, I had to get away from Max. I couldn't stand it anymore. You know how it was between us."

"Yes." His aunt shook her head sadly. "Yes, I know. He was always very hard on you because he hated your father for abandoning you and Clarissa. That was not right. I tried to do what I could to protect you, but Max was...was Max." She gave a Gallic shrug of her shoulders.

"I was grateful for everything, especially after Mum died. You were a brick. So were Nigel and Brian. But without Mum..." His voice trailed off.

Watching him from the wing chair opposite the sofa, Emmeline's heart ached for her fiancé and the forlorn, lonely boy that he had been. She hadn't uttered a word since they entered the library. She wanted to give Gregory and Mireille time to get reacquainted with one another.

He must have sensed that she was watching him because he looked up. He caressed her face with his eyes. She smiled back.

Mireille noticed this wordless exchange. "Toby, I see that I have a little less worrying to do about you because I'm satisfied that this young woman—" She nodded toward Emmeline. "—will take very good care of you."

Gregory flashed one of his irresistible smiles. "She already has me well in hand. If only she will set a date."

She patted his knee. "Leave it to me, *mon chou*. I will arrange things."

Gregory gave a soft, low laugh. How he had missed his aunt.

What chance did Emmeline stand when faced with Helen, Maggie, and now Mireille firmly in his corner? None. They all knew it was only a matter of time before her defenses were completely breached.

Emmeline sighed. If only it were as simple to catch the killer. Then they could all rest easy in their beds.

Ↄ

Finally, the time had come when they could leave the dreary gathering and return to London. Many of the guests had already departed. Gregory, Emmeline, and Nigel were going straight back to town. Brian and Tessa and their sons were going to remain in the country through the weekend. There were still a lot of Max's papers through which Brian had to sift. Mireille announced that she would be staying on in England for a few weeks to spend some time with her grandsons before their summer holidays came to an end. The boys were delighted by this prospect, as Granny tended to be extremely generous and was always highly amusing—not to mention she took their side in any dispute.

They were all in the hall making their goodbyes. Mireille extracted a promise from Gregory and Emmeline to dine with her before she went back to her villa on the Côte d'Azur.

Gregory bent down and kissed his aunt on both cheeks. "That's a date. I also wanted to thank you for leaving the flowers on Mum's grave. It was very thoughtful."

She patted his arm. "*Mon chou*, your mother was a very dear friend, and there is not a day that goes by that I do not miss her, *mais malheuresement* I didn't bring flowers for her grave. I should have, but I didn't."

"Then who did? Brian? Nigel?" But both his cousins shrugged and shook their heads.

As Gregory continued to mull over this little mystery, Mireille turned to Emmeline. "Now, *cherie*, we are going to have a very long talk when I get back to London. Have some dates in mind so that I can clear my schedule for your wedding."

Nigel saw Emmeline blush. He shook his head and gave his mother a pointed look. "Mum."

Mireille opened her eyes wide and asked innocently, "What? Did I say something wrong? Sometimes nature needs a little push."

Everyone was still laughing when the butler quietly sidled up to Emmeline. "Excuse me, Miss Kirby, this was left for you."

He handed her a manila envelope. Emmeline's brow puckered. "For me?"

"Yes, miss. I must apologize for not giving it to you earlier. There had been a minor problem downstairs that required my attention, and I had to step away for a few moments. It must have been delivered at that point. I found it on the hall table just now."

"It's quite all right." Emmeline stared down at the envelope. There was no return address. It had been hand-delivered. "It's very odd. Why would anyone be sending me something here?"

She slipped her index finger under one corner and slid it across. When the envelope was open, she shook it until its contents tumbled out. It was a single photo. Emmeline's face drained of blood, and her hands began to shake. "Oh, my God. What have I done?"

CHAPTER 31

Emmeline dropped the photo as if it had singed her fingers. Perplexed, the group watched it flutter to the ground. She frantically fumbled in her handbag for her mobile. "I have to ring Gran."

Gregory grabbed her by the shoulders. "What is it, Emmy?"

She shook off his grasp. "I have to ring Gran. I have to make sure—" Her voice was thick with tears. She put her fist to her lips to prevent herself from breaking down completely.

Nigel bent down and snatched up the photo. After a glance, he wordlessly handed it to Gregory.

It was a photo of Helen's home in Swaley. She was out in her garden with MacTavish, her Scottish terrier, close on her heels. There was a single line written across the bottom in red block letters:

IT WOULD BE A PITY IF SOMETHING HAPPENED TO THEM.

"Bloody bastard," Gregory swore. He pulled out his own mobile and placed a call to Superintendent Burnell. Succinctly, he told the detective what had happened. Burnell promised to ring the local police and have a unit dispatched to Helen's house at once.

In the meantime, Emmeline was at Gregory's side screaming into her mobile. "Come on, Gran. Come on. Answer the phone."

Everyone held their breath.

Emmeline nearly dropped the mobile. "Gran, is that you? Are you all right? Thank God. Thank God."

The tears were streaming unchecked down her cheeks. She was unable to make her mouth form words anymore. She slumped against Gregory, who put an arm protectively around her shoulders and gently pried the mobile from her fingers as she buried her face against his chest.

"Helen, it's Gregory. Don't worry. Emmy's fine. However, there's been a spot of bother. The police will be there shortly. I can't explain now, but please trust me. Can you stay with a friend for a few days?" He was quiet for a couple of seconds as he listened. "Good. Go pack a bag. No, I promise you Emmy's fine. I won't let anything happen to her. Now, go, love. I'll ring you later when the dust has settled a bit."

Mireille rubbed Emmeline's back and murmured soothingly in her ear, "*Ne vous inquiétez pas, cherie.* Your grandmother is all right. Shh. Everything will be fine."

Tessa stared down at the photo and cringed. "Who could have done such a cruel thing?"

Gregory met Nigel's steady gaze. "Doyle," they said in unison.

෴

"How? How could he have slipped into the house unnoticed?" Gregory demanded as he paced back and forth in Superintendent Burnell's office the next day.

"I don't know, Longdon," Burnell snapped, "but do sit down. You're causing my ulcer to do somersaults." He rubbed his stomach to emphasize his point.

"What?" Gregory stopped and swung round. "Oh, right. Sorry, Oliver." He lowered his elegant frame into the seat next to Finch, exuding a nervous tension that was quite out of character.

Burnell placed his elbows on the desk and leaned forward. His voice had none of its usual curtness when he spoke. "Look, Longdon, we're all concerned about Emmeline. I'm just as upset as you are about this nasty business. Perhaps, even more so. I feel responsible. I thought I had prepared for all eventualities. In view of Doyle's history, *I* should have known he would try something like this. He gets a sadistic pleasure out of toying with people. I suppose that we have to be thankful that it was only one of his little games."

"Games? He's a cold-blooded assassin. I don't know about you, but I'm not willing to wait around until he takes a second crack at Emmy and Helen."

"I'm not going to allow that to happen, we have—"

Gregory jumped to his feet and pounded his palm on the desk. "He's already proven that he's a step ahead of us. He was at Max's funeral bold as brass, and not one of us knew it. He's thumbing his nose at us. So how does Scotland Yard intend to stop him?"

The superintendent was on his feet now too. Lack of sleep and self-recrimination had left his nerves in tatters. He would not put up with this barrage of censure. "We're doing the best we can, Longdon," he growled.

"Obviously, it's not bloody good enough." The glacial hardness of his tone made the words sting that much more.

Burnell's spine stiffened. "You can go to the devil for all I care. I don't need a lecture from the likes of you of all people. Nor do I have to justify my or the Met's actions."

Gregory's steely gaze clashed with Burnell's equally fierce one. "Ah, now we come to the heart of the matter. You're absolutely correct, Oliver. You don't owe me anything. But Emmy deserves better. So much better. If she winds up dead because you allowed your personal opinion of me to get in the way of doing your job properly…well, all I can say is that I hope your conscience will let you sleep at night."

Finch heard his boss's sharp indrawn breath. The superintendent's face flushed an unbecoming shade of scarlet beneath his neatly trimmed beard. A tremor of outrage thrummed through his body.

"Steady on, Longdon. That's quite out of line," the sergeant said.

Gregory shot his cuffs. His glance slid sideways toward Finch and then back to Burnell, but he said nothing. After all, what was left to be said on the subject? He walked toward the door.

"Stay out of my way, Longdon." Burnell hurled the words at Gregory's back. "Any interference from you in *my* investigation, and you'll find yourself in new accommodations courtesy of Her Majesty's Government."

With his hand on the door knob, Gregory turned and flashed a smile that didn't reach his eyes. "Oh, Oliver, not that idle threat again. After all these years, I thought you would have recognized a lost cause when it was staring you in the face. I suppose some people simply never learn."

On that cheerful note, Gregory left the two detectives silently cursing.

ຕໆຕໆ

His argument with Gregory had left a bitter taste in Burnell's mouth. They had always played cat-and-mouse, but this had been different. Already irritated because he had had to come into the office on a Saturday, the superintendent took out his frustrations on poor Finch and anyone else who had the misfortunate to cross his path the remainder of the afternoon. Why is this case so difficult? His instincts told him that it was Doyle who was behind the murders of Boinet and Max Sanborn. The Constable painting clearly tied the man to both victims. But everything was so tenuous. He and Finch couldn't find any solid evidence—either to Doyle's culpability or his identity. Doyle was anticipating their every move even before they made it and then wiping the slate clean before their very eyes.

The shrill peal of the phone jarred the superintendent from these maddening thoughts. "Burnell."

"Ah, you are in. Good."

Damn, it was Fenton. "Yes, sir. Finch and I are working on the Sanborn case."

"I'm glad to hear it. That's exactly why I rang you. I'd like you to pop along to my office and give me an update."

Burnell coughed to cover his surprise. Fenton in the office?

On a Saturday? His whole weekend just went to hell in a hand basket. He swallowed down his irritation. "Yes, sir."

"That's a good chap. Shall we say in the next five minutes?"

"I'm on my way," he replied, but the assistant commissioner had already rung off.

Burnell was still staring at the receiver in his hand, when Finch burst into his office. "Sir, Assistant Commissioner Fenton is—"

"Is in the building. Yes, I know. He's summoned me for an audience. He wants me to 'pop along' for another bloody update. I'd like to know what I did that was so wrong that my life has been cursed not only with Longdon, but with Fenton as well."

Finch bit back a smile. "Shall I come for moral support, sir?"

Burnell sighed as he got to his feet. "No. I'm a big boy. There's no sense in both of us going into the lion's den." Another sigh escaped his lips. "The devil of it is that I have nothing to tell him. Do I?" He shot a hopeful glance at the sergeant, but Finch shook his head. "No, it was too much to ask. Look, while I'm in with his highness, I'd like you to go and have a quiet word with Acheson. At home today, while he's away from prying eyes at the office. Perhaps, he can help us find Doyle. I'm certain that once we find the man, everything else will fall into place." He paused for a moment, thoughtful as his stomach rumbled in turmoil. "My ulcer tells me that there's something we are not seeing. And my ulcer is never wrong."

Finch smiled. "Or is it merely protesting against your meeting with Assistant Commissioner Fenton?"

The corners of Burnell's mouth twitched. "There is that. My ulcer is a very discerning judge of character. Now, off you go. Tell Acheson I'll try to ring him later."

Finch nodded. "Right, sir. Good luck with Fenton."

"I'll need all the luck I can get. These little *tête-à-têtes* become more painful all the time. Send out a searching party if I don't surface in a couple of hours."

Finch chuckled and left his boss to his fate.

The meeting with Fenton went as expected. Badly. Despite the fact that Burnell had little new information, the assistant commissioner insisted on going over each item in minute detail—several times. Burnell gritted his teeth and tried to remain calm. Fenton's interference was muddying the waters. His personal friendship with Max Sanborn only served to cloud his professional judgment—if he had any to begin with, which Burnell seriously doubted. Meanwhile, Fenton's haughty tone and the way he looked down his nose at the superintendent did nothing to improve matters.

Fenton sat there, his fingers drumming on his desk, his gray eyes locked on Burnell's face, and shook his head. "Frankly, Burnell, I am extremely disappointed in the way you are conducting the Sanborn case."

"But, sir—"

The assistant commissioner put up a hand. "I don't want excuses. I want results."

Burnell clasped his hands together in his lap in a bid to keep them from betraying his anger. With a supreme effort, he managed to keep his voice steady. "Sir, I assure you that Finch and I are giving this case—as we do all our cases—our undivided attention. We simply have hit a brick wall. All our leads have gone cold."

Fenton jabbed an accusatory finger in the air. "That's because you have chosen to ignore the two—and only, I might add—logical suspects."

The superintendent's hands curled into tight balls. "If you are referring to Ms. Roth and Miss Kirby, there is simply no evidence—"

Fenton pounded his fist on the desk, causing his gold—Mont Blanc, of course—pen to jump. "No evidence? *No evidence*? Are you blind, man? How much more evidence do you want to arrest those two? By her own account, Ms. Roth had a violent argument with Max, and she hit him. Being a woman, she then panicked. She ran out of Max's penthouse like a bat out of hell, wiping blood off her hands. And hell it was indeed that she left in her wake. Then we have little Miss Nosey Parker, who's always stirring up a cauldron of trouble. In my opinion, she's by far the more dangerous of the two of them." Burnell rolled his eyes toward the ceiling at this reference to Emmeline. "From what I've seen, Miss Kirby is as cool as a cucumber. She very easily could have slipped into the penthouse and erased any trace of her flighty friend."

Burnell swallowed the reply that had leaped to his tongue and instead said, "Once again, sir, I must point out that according to Dr. Meadows the stab wound to Mr. Sanborn's throat and *not* the blow to the head is what killed him."

"Which bears out what I've been saying. Miss Kirby is the one who finished off the job that her friend started."

The superintendent took a deep breath. He didn't think he could stand much more of this nonsense. "If that's true, how come we didn't find the knife on her person or anywhere in the penthouse? And how do you explain the fact that Miss Kirby had been knocked unconscious by a blow to the back head?"

Fenton glowered at him with icy disdain. "That's what you're paid to find out, Burnell. Work a little harder. You can't expect me to do your job for you. Although from what I've observed, the only way that we're ever going to bring poor Max's murderer to justice is if I intervene. No need to be embarrassed, old chap. It's simply that this case is beyond your meager capabilities. You'll see. You'll benefit from my wealth of experience."

Burnell's blue eyes widened in disbelief. He must have been plunged into the deepest, darkest corner of hell. *You have to intervene? You've been breathing down my neck before Sanborn's body was even cold. And as for your "wealth of experience," I can tell you an uncomfortable part of your anatomy where you can stick it.*

He cleared his throat rather loudly—twice—before he felt sure he could respond in what passed as a reasonably rational tone. "Sir, if I might point out, although you and the deceased were friends, Mr. Sanborn had made a great many enemies over the course of his lifetime. In fact, recently, there appears to have been some tension between him and his son Brian."

One of Fenton's eyebrows rose in askance. "Oh, yes?"

"Yes, sir. Something to do with Sanborn Enterprises. Finch and I are going to interview Mr. Sanborn on Monday. Apparently, he and his father had a rather impassioned argument only a couple of hours before the murder. At the moment, Mr. Sanborn and his family are still down in Buckinghamshire. However, he did promise to go through all of his father's papers to see if there is anything in them that might give us a clue to the murderer."

Fenton nodded. "I see. All the papers. Very good," he replied distractedly. "This is rather distressing news about Max and Brian. I had no idea."

What, you mean is your "wealth of experience" failed to help you divine it from the air? I'm quite shocked. What is the world coming to? Aloud Burnell said, "Yes. So you see, sir, we *are* pursuing every avenue."

Fenton's brow furrowed. "What?" He leaned forward and folded his hands on the desk. "Yes, but you and Finch are doing a very poor job. This interview with Brian requires someone who possesses finesse and tact. Therefore, I'll handle it."

"But, sir—" The assistant commissioner shot an icy look at Burnell and the protest died on his lips. "Of course, sir."

"Besides, as a friend of the family, I will instantly put Brian at his ease. I assure you he will speak more freely to me than he ever will with you."

"I'm certain that you know best, sir," the superintendent replied through gritted teeth.

Burnell finally managed to escape after another half-hour, but not before Fenton extracted a pledge that he would report again first thing in the morning. A Sunday. In person.

The superintendent's ulcer was not best pleased, to say the least.

CHAPTER 32

Brian's eyelids started to droop, and the words in the file in front of him became a blur. His head lolled forward, and his lips parted slightly. However, he caught himself before he nodded off. He sat up straighter in his chair and shook his head briskly to expunge the fatigue that had seeped into his brain and bones over the course of the last few weeks. But, still, he couldn't prevent a yawn from escaping his lips. He blinked several times. His father's murder coming on the heels of the discovery of the embezzlement had thrown Brian's life upside down. He had forgotten what it was like to go to bed and actually sleep. Now, night was a time when the worries of the day simply swirled round and round in his head—growing, fomenting and slowly sucking every ounce of his energy. He was exhausted, but his brain could not rest.

He raked a hand through his hair. Had he covered everything? Was he safe? He wasn't sure. His greatest fear was that the truth would come out. And at all costs, he couldn't let that happen.

One shouldn't speak ill of the dead, but he silently cursed his father with every invective in the English language. Brian had never hated anyone like he had his father. He had thought that once Max was out of the way things would get better, but he was wrong. Even from the grave, his father was still ruining people's lives. His in particular.

The peal of the telephone tore his attention from these bitter ruminations. He grabbed the receiver. "Yes, Delia?"

"Assistant Commissioner Fenton is here to see you, Mr. Sanborn."

Brian grimaced. That was the last thing he needed. He sighed wearily. "Thanks. Send him in."

He was in no mood to see his father's friend. Richard Fenton was only a few years his senior, but Brian had never warmed to the man. There was something about him that rubbed him the wrong way. Or perhaps it was that the fact that he was his father's friend? But for the life of him, Brian couldn't understand it. Max and Richard couldn't have been more different.

Brian shrugged his shoulders. There was no point dwelling on it. He exhaled a long, slow breath and straightened his tie. He pushed himself to his feet at the sound of light tapping. The next second, the door swung open and his secretary was standing aside to allow Fenton to enter. "Thanks, Delia. Would you please bring us some coffee?"

She nodded and quietly withdrew.

Brian extended a hand as Fenton crossed to the desk. "Please sit down." He waved at the chair opposite him and he resumed his own seat. "Does your visit mean that your men have apprehended Dad's murderer?"

Fenton shook his head. "I'm afraid not."

"I see. Then how can I help you?"

The assistant commissioner crossed one well-tailored leg over the other. His brow furrowed as his gray gaze searched Brian's face. He didn't utter a word for a long moment.

"It's rather a delicate matter I'd like to discuss. I want you to understand that I came here today as a family friend and not in my professional capacity. Mind you, I still believe that Ms. Roth and Miss Kirby are culpable. But that oaf Burnell has a flea in his ear about a rather heated argument you had with Max only a couple of hours before his death."

Brian stiffened. He was glad Richard couldn't see his hands because he was gripping the armrests so tightly that the skin stretched tautly across his knuckles and was white, deathly white. He opened his mouth, but no words came out.

Fenton put up a hand. "I'm not accusing you of anything.

Please don't think that. However, you can see how it looks to someone as unimaginative as Burnell. That's why I came here today. I thought we could clear up the matter *entre nous*. So…what was the argument about?"

Brian's mouth felt dry. He licked his lips, as he shifted in his chair. He cleared his throat. "It has nothing whatsoever to do with the case, I assure you," he said smoothly.

Fenton smiled and leaned his elbows on the desk. "Come now, old chap. How can I make that determination if you don't tell me what you and Max argued about?"

Brian thrust his chin in the air. He felt the vein in his temple throbbing. "I'm afraid I can't do that. It was about Sanborn Enterprises. That's all I'm prepared to tell you."

"I'm not trying to pry into your business dealings. That's not my concern. But I do have a murder to solve. Don't you want your father's killer to be arrested?"

"Of course, I do."

"Well then, it's in your best interest to tell me what the fight was about," Fenton prompted.

"It wasn't a fight," Brian replied matter-of-factly. "It was a difference of opinion."

Fenton shifted in his chair restlessly. "That's a matter of semantics. You're making my job unnecessarily difficult." Irritation was beginning to creep into his voice.

"I'm sorry that you feel that way. But I cannot, and will not, disclose confidential company matters to you or anyone else. It's a nonstarter."

Fenton gritted his teeth. "Fine. Burnell mentioned that you were going through Max's papers. You can at least allow me to take a look at them. There might be a clue—"

Brian cut him off. "The answer is the same."

A faint flush tinged Fenton's cheeks. "I must say you're being quite unreasonable. I came here in the spirit of friendship."

"I appreciate that."

"Do you?" Fenton spat the words at him. "You have an odd way of showing it. If you will not speak to me or show me the papers—"

Brian sat up straighter in his chair. "I will not," he said stiffly. His tone was implacable. He would not be moved.

Fenton rose to his feet and shot his cuffs. "—then you're a fool, and I leave you to Burnell's tender mercies," he sneered in disgust.

In two strides, he was across the room. He flung the door open. He paused with his hand on the knob for a parting shot. "I wash my hands of you and your bloody family. You can go to the devil for all I care."

Fenton slammed the door so hard behind him, it rattled on its hinges. Brian stared at the door for several seconds. Then softly, so softly that his own ears barely heard what his lips were uttering, he said, "Richard, don't you know? The Sanborns are already dancing in the fiery depths of hell. Dad saw to that long ago when he made his pact with the devil and turned his back on the rest of us." He shook his head bitterly. "And now, I'm left to clean up the mess."

He pulled out a key from his pocket and unlocked the top right-hand drawer of his desk. A tremor shot through his hand as he reached for the manila envelope that had come that morning. He opened it again, although he knew its contents by heart. It was a single sheet of paper, unremarkable in itself but deadly nonetheless. It read:

I SAW YOU THAT NIGHT. YOU CAME BACK. AND THEN YOUR FATHER WAS DEAD. WOULDN'T THE PO-LICE LIKE TO KNOW?

Brian slammed his palm on the desk. It stung, the shock reverberating through his wrist and up his arm. He yanked the drawer open farther until it tottered slightly in the air. Stuffed all the way at the back was a crumpled handkerchief. He took it out and placed it in the center of his desk. His hand hesitated for a second and then he gingerly unwrapped it. The letter opener with its ugly brown crust of dried blood along both edges stared up at him, mocking him.

He should have gotten rid of it that night. But there had been no time. Now, hopefully, it wasn't too late.

❧❧❧

Villiers had arrived first. He was walking along the promenade on the South Bank at a sedate pace. His tightly furled umbrella was held in one hand, the modern gentleman's version of a walking stick. His gaze strayed from time to time across the Thames to the Houses of Parliament, but he saw none of their golden magnificence. Instead, his thoughts were fixated on the problem of Doyle and the recent murders. For the first time in his life, he felt as if he was losing control.

Damn Boinet, he thought bitterly. *If the bloody man hadn't always been playing both ends against the middle, he'd still be alive. And we would have Doyle.*

Doyle. Villiers shook his head and whacked his umbrella against the pavement as if he were skewering the elusive Irishman. And he would have gladly if the man had had the misfortune to be in front of him at that precise moment.

"I sincerely hope that was not intended as a punishment for me. That thrust looked as if you were intent on serious bodily damage. After all, I was a mere five minutes late. Such a minor transgression certainly doesn't warrant the punishment," Gregory said flippantly as he fell into step with him.

Villiers looked up startled. Gregory's eyes danced with mischief.

"I don't like my time being wasted," he replied in a clipped tone. "I've been seeing far too much of you lately. Our dealings are best conducted at a distance."

He turned on his heel and walked toward the parapet. Gregory grabbed his arm. "Don't you *dare* turn your back on me."

Villiers glanced down at the younger man's fingers biting into his sleeve. "I suggest you remove your hand. First, because you're attracting unwanted attention." He slid a glance to the right and left. "Secondly, I've just had this suit pressed, and you're wrinkling it," he hissed out of the corner of his mouth. Gregory let him go. Villers nodded. "That's better, old chap. Now, let's try to discuss this reasonably, shall we?"

He hooked his umbrella over one wrist and cast a glance at Big Ben, as it began to chime the hour with gravitas.

Gregory leaned his elbows on the parapet and watched the midday traffic rumbling over Westminster Bridge. "You promised me that Doyle would not harm Emmy in any way?"

"And he hasn't. Your fiancée has been roaming the length and breadth of London unmolested, asking all sorts of probing questions and writing articles that are certain to inflame passions in the breasts of those that move in the criminal classes. Is it my fault that Miss Kirby leaves turmoil in her wake?"

Gregory's gaze snapped back to Villiers's face. He took half a step toward him and then checked himself. "If I were you, I'd have a care for what I said."

A ghost of a smile played around Villiers's lips. "I assure you I meant no offense. Miss Kirby is quite admirable, in a way. But even you have to admit that your fiancée has done untold damage with her crusade and has hampered our efforts to find Doyle. He's probably gone underground by now."

"Then how do you explain his threat against Emmy's grandmother?"

"Ah. I think you'll find when one lies down with dogs, one inevitably wakes up with fleas, old chap."

"Don't give me that," Gregory snarled. "You should have foreseen that something like that would happen. You *know* Doyle is a ruthless monster."

"Yes, well." Villiers looked down at his manicured hand and then up again at Gregory. "A miscalculation, I grant you." That's as close he was going to come to an apology. "In any case, Mrs. Davis is perfectly fine. A team will be watching her day and night—discreetly, of course—until this sordid business is resolved. Satisfied?"

"It's a start anyway," Gregory responded grudgingly. "I've been doing a bit of digging on my own as the newly minted chief investigator at Symington's." He cleared his throat. "Ahem, as well as speaking to some old associates."

Villiers raised an eyebrow, but he didn't say anything.

"I think I may have a lead on Doyle."

Villiers was all ears and leaned in closer. "Oh yes?"

"Yes, but I need your help." Gregory reached into the inner pocket of his suit jacket. "Here's the only known photo of Doyle."

Villiers snatched it from him. "How did you get this?"

"Emmy got it. From a source. Let's just say I borrowed it from her."

"A source? Any idea who it is?"

"Sorry, old chap, I'm afraid it's confidential."

Villiers rolled eyes, eliciting a smile from Gregory. "Right. So what did you discover?"

e/ɔe/ɔ

Brian had rolled down his shirtsleeves and was just shrugging into his suit jacket, when there was a tap on the door. He barely had time to tuck the handkerchief, with its lethal burden, into his inside pocket, before Nigel burst into his office.

"I've just drawn up the papers—"

Brian cut off his brother. "Whatever it is, I'll deal with it later. I'm on my way out. I don't have time to talk now."

Nigel walked farther into the office, eyeing him suspiciously. "You're in an awful rush. Where are you going?"

"I told you," Brian replied through gritted teeth, "I'm going out. That's all you need to know, little brother."

"Don't little brother me. I wasn't aware that you had any meetings today. What's going on?"

Brian came around the desk, hoping his brother would get the hint. "Why the third degree?" he retorted without even attempting to cover up his annoyance. "If you'll recall, I'm the head of Sanborn Enterprises. I don't report to you."

Nigel's spine stiffened. His eyes raked over his brother's face. "What's wrong?"

"Nothing's wrong." There was an impatient edge to Brian's voice. "Why should anything be wrong? I simply have to take care of something—something rather urgent."

Nigel wouldn't let it go. "But you won't tell me what it is."

Brian's lips pressed together in a tight line. He clenched his fists at his sides. "It's none of your concern."

"Well, I need you to sign these papers, oh lofty head of the company. They deal with us relinquishing the Constable to Maggie."

Brian threw his hands up in the air in exasperation and groaned inwardly.

"You haven't changed your mind, have you?" Nigel asked warily.

"Of course, I haven't changed my mind about it. The painting belongs to her family by right. But do I have to do this *now*? Just leave them on my desk. I promise to sign them the instant I return."

"The Roths have waited over sixty years to get their painting back. I'd say that's quite long enough, wouldn't you?"

"Oh, all right." Brian snatched the papers from his brother and stalked over to his desk. "I see that you won't give me a moment's peace otherwise," he groused as he hastily scrawled his signature at the bottom of the three copies.

He turned on his heel and pressed them against Nigel's chest in a huff. "There. Are you satisfied?"

"Thank you," his brother replied quietly.

"Right. Well, I must be off. I'll be back—" He waved his hand vaguely in the air."—later."

His fingers had just clasped the doorknob, when Nigel put a restraining hand on his arm. Brian swung round. "Now what is it?"

Nigel's brow was puckered and his eyebrows knit together. "We've always been able to discuss anything. I can see everything is not all right. Why won't you—"

Brian gave his brother's arm a reassuring squeeze, and in a gentler tone, he said, "I'm just…taking care of the company. And the family. I promise there's nothing for you to be concerned about. Nothing. Everything will be all right. Please don't worry." His gaze locked with his brother's. They were silent for a long moment. Then he gave Nigel's arm another squeeze and whispered, "Just trust me, little brother."

A smile came unbidden to Nigel's lips. "With my life."

Yes, Brian thought. *Trust and loyalty were such fragile things. So difficult to earn and so easily lost.*

He was going to make damned sure that the Sanborns didn't lose anything else.

CHAPTER 33

Emmeline scowled at her watch. It was two o'clock already. Her cup rattled against her saucer as she pushed it away in disgust. No more cappuccino. Any more coffee and she would murder someone. In particular, the anonymous caller who had asked her to meet him at the Caffè Nero across from Trafalgar Square—at least, she thought it was a him. She couldn't be sure. The voice was muffled on the phone. However, she was out of the office in a flash at the words "information" and "Doyle." She would have agreed to meet the mystery chap anywhere. But now he had kept her waiting for over half an hour. No source. No new lead. No closer to Doyle. *Damn and blast*, she muttered under her breath. Well, that was it. She wasn't going to wait a minute longer. Her chair scraped angrily against the floorboards as she rose from the little table close to the door that had afforded her a perfect view of Trafalgar Square and anyone entering or leaving the café. She grabbed her handbag and flung it over her shoulder.

Her lips were pressed together in a tight line. She did *not* like being played for a fool. She pushed the door open and walked out onto the pavement. Right. If someone had gone to all the bother of sending her on a wild goose chase that meant she was on to something. The trouble was she didn't know what *it* was.

There was a kernel of an idea hovering at the edge of her consciousness, but it hadn't fully formed yet. She glanced at her watch again. She couldn't ring Gregory. He had mumbled something this morning about going to see "a chap I know." His tone had been clipped, and his face had been a mask of inscrutability. She knew that it would have been useless to try to pump him for information. Nothing would breach his defenses. Damn him for always playing his cards so close to the vest.

To be fair, though, Emmeline acknowledged that, eventually, he would tell her everything, unless he was trying to protect her. She stopped in her tracks as she turned onto Whitehall. Her back stiffened. She would kill him, if that were the case. She didn't need coddling or protecting.

She was perfectly capable of taking care of herself. Herself, yes, but what about Gran? Her life and her work were here in London.

What if Doyle decided to go after Gran again? This thought sent an icy frisson slithering down her spine.

She squared her shoulders. She wouldn't let that happen. Nothing would stop her.

"Look out," a man yelled.

Emmeline's head jerked round as she started to fall forward. "What?"

Her rattled mind froze when she saw the Number 24 bus barreling straight toward her. As if from a long distance away, she heard a woman who was waiting in the queue start to scream.

Everything seemed suspended. Except for the big, red double-decker. It was coming closer. Closer. Her arms flailed in the air as she tried to grasp something to break her fall. But there was nothing save for the hard asphalt of the road where she was going to land. Right in the bus's path.

She squeezed her eyes shut. The screeching of the wheels was ear-splitting. It was the most terrifying sound she had ever heard. Death came to everyone, but why did she have to die like this?

She sucked in her breath and braced for the impact. But it never came.

Suddenly, there was a crowd around her. A young man was helping to her feet. He couldn't have been more than a few years older than she was. "Are you all right?"

She stared at him dumbly. Her brain was having a difficult time focusing. She couldn't understand. "What? I—"

His clear blue eyes were full of concern. "I said are you all right? You're not hurt anywhere, are you? No broken bones?" His gaze raked her from head to toe.

Emmeline dusted herself off and gingerly made a cursory examination of her body. She was relieved that all her limbs seemed to be intact. "I—I'm fine. Thank you." Her voice was a hoarse whisper.

His face broke out into a grin, and there a collective sigh of relief from the small crowd huddled around them.

"All right, ladies and gentlemen. Let's clear a path here, shall we? We can't have all of you blocking the pavement," a constable said as he made his way to her side.

The bus driver was close on his heels. His face was flushed, and beads of perspiration had formed on his upper lip, and it had nothing to do with the warmth on this June afternoon. "I'm telling you. It was not my fault. All of a sudden there she was leaping out in front me. You can ask any of my passengers. They'll tell you. I've been on the job twenty years and not once have I had an accident. I'm a very careful driver. You can't pin this on me."

"Why don't we make certain the young lady is all right before we start laying blame on anyone's doorstep?" Then, to Emmeline, he asked gently, "Shall I have an ambulance take you to hospital?"

She shook her head. "That's really not necessary, constable. I'm fine. Really."

He smiled. "Well, you look perfectly fine. But you may have a concussion, miss. I think it would be best if you went to hospital."

"What you really ought to do," the bus driver broke in unceremoniously, "is to watch where you're going and to cross a busy road like Whitehall at the zebra stripes, not willy nilly. And above all, you shouldn't have your head in the clouds."

"That's quite enough of that," the constable reprimanded sternly, putting the full weight of the law into his voice. "I could cite you for reckless driving."

"Me? *Me*?" The driver's face turned even redder, if that were possible.

"Please, constable, don't do that. I'm afraid the gentleman is right. I had a lot on my mind, and I probably stepped out into the road without looking. No harm has come to me, so can we just forget this incident. I'm sorry for all the trouble I've caused this afternoon."

An expression of vindication was reflected in the driver's eye. "I told you." Then he turned to Emmeline. "Just be more careful, miss," he chided.

Completely chastened, Emmeline lowered her head and murmured, "I will from now on. I promise."

The driver nodded and shuffled toward his bus. "I can't be wasting the whole day here. You've already set me behind schedule." He shook his head in disapproval before getting aboard his vehicle.

The crowd soon dispersed and Whitehall was again a swirl of hurried activity.

"If you don't want to go hospital," the young man said, "then allow me to put you in a taxi to make sure you get to your destination safely."

Emmeline's mouth curved into a warm smile. "That's very kind. But I was on my way to visit a friend. He works around the corner." She had already decided that she would drop by to see Philip at the Foreign Office.

The young man tilted his head to one side and studied her skeptically. "If you're sure—"

"I am." Emmeline extended her hand. "Thank you for coming to my rescue. I feel rather silly about the whole thing."

He took her hand and gave it a firm shake. "Nonsense. It happens to all of us. Just try to be a little more careful."

"I will. I'll be off then. Goodbye." She gave him another smile.

He watched her retreating figure for several minutes. Then he pulled out his mobile from his inside suit jacket pocket.

"Sir, it's Crichlow. Someone just tried to kill Emmeline Kirby."

There was silence for a long moment.

"Sir, are you there?"

Villiers cleared his throat. "I can't have heard you properly."

"It's true. She's all right. She doesn't even realize it."

"Thank God for that. What happened?"

"I had been trailing her all day, but I lost sight of her for a couple seconds after she left the Caffè Nero and rounded the corner onto Whitehall. When I caught up with her again, I distinctly saw a hand shove her in front of a Number Twenty-Four bus. I yelled bloody murder, and the driver stopped with only inches to spare."

"I see. You didn't happen to see the scoundrel?"

"In that crush? Not a chance. But it stands to reason that it was Doyle."

He heard Villiers exhale a weary breath at the other end of the line. "Yes, I'm afraid you're right. Where is Miss Kirby now?"

"I'm fairly certain that she's on her way to Acheson's office. She said that she was going to see a friend and he works just round the corner. I'll pop along in a few minutes. Sir, she's playing with fire. I was on the spot today, but she may not be so lucky next time. She's getting too close for Doyle's comfort. He has her and Longdon in his sights. It's only a matter of time, before he—"

"Yes, yes," Villiers replied hastily, his voice laced with annoyance. "There's no reason to be morbid. Our job is to see that *nothing* happens to them. We're the professionals, remember? I want Doyle. Do whatever it takes. I give you *carte blanche*. I don't care if it's an embarrassment to Her Majesty's Government. Britain has weathered other controversies, she'll get through this one. I don't want Doyle walking the streets of London a minute longer."

"Understood," Crichlow mumbled. He paused for a moment. "Sir, don't you think we should tell Longdon about today? After all, she is his fiancée. If he knew how serious the situation was, perhaps—"

"Are you mad? The last thing we need is for him to be distracted. He's already emotionally involved in this case on more than one level. No, we can't afford for him to lose his focus. I agree that he and Miss Kirby are getting close. Very close. That's precisely why we have to let them follow through on their instincts."

"Yes, sir." But Crichlow didn't agree one iota. He didn't like amateurs mucking about in things that were none of their concern. It only led to trouble. And there was no one who embodied the word trouble more than Doyle. He was a lit fuse, and he would blow up in all their faces if they were not careful.

❧❧❧

Emmeline was surprised when Pamela replaced the receiver and said that she could go straight through to Philip's office, especially since she had dropped by unannounced.

She had already been preparing her apologies in her head as she turned the knob. "Philip, thank you so much for seeing me on such short notice. I'm terribly sorry to barge in like this…" Her voice trailed off, and she came to an abrupt halt in the center of the room.

Philip rose from the claret-colored leather wing chair in the corner of the room. But he was not alone. He had a visitor. Gregory.

Her dark gaze flitted between the two men. Then her eyes narrowed and fixed on Gregory's bemused face.

"Hello, darling," he said as he crossed the room in two strides and pressed a kiss to her cheek before she could start asking questions. "A more lovely creature never graced Acheson's office. Except for Maggie, of course. You are the two loveliest creatures on this earth." His smile was infused with all the charm he possessed as he led her by the elbow to the Chesterfield sofa.

Once the three of them were settled, she rounded on him. "When you start with the purple prose, I know that you're up to something."

"Acheson, can you believe it? You see before you a man who cherishes the very ground the woman he loves walks upon and whose noble breast is filled with nothing but adoration for her. And you see how shabbily I am treated. I blame Eve and her sinister apple in the Garden of Eden. Poor Adam never stood a chance."

"Hmph," was Emmeline's response as she folded her arms over her chest.

It didn't help that Philip tried to cover up his snort of laughter with a fit of coughing.

"You are far from an innocent lamb. If you are quite finished with your juvenile antics, I would like to know when the two of you became such bosom chums?"

"Well, you see—"

"I'm warning you. I want the truth."

"Darling, it's not in our nature to lie. I'm sure Acheson is quite as offended as I am that you think that we would even contemplate such a mortal sin. You wound us to the core."

"Uh. Huh. Now, I know you're hiding something. Is Philip the mysterious 'chap I know' whom you were going to see today?"

She saw Philip shoot a look at Gregory. There was an infinitesimal shake of her fiancé's head in response.

"I'm waiting for an answer."

"Yes, I do recognize the signs, darling. Furrowed brows, dark scowl. I was planning to give you one—"

"Truth, remember."

"Of course. No, Acheson was not the chap I went to see. My...acquaintance, for want of a better word...suggested that it would be beneficial if Acheson and I collaborated on the Doyle matter. And here you find us. Heads bent together. Pooling resources. A free exchange of ideas. A common cause uniting us. I tell you it has been a most illuminating and exhilarating afternoon."

"What utter drivel. I can see that you're not going to tell me who your 'chap' is, so tell me what the two of you have come up with? Anything new?"

The smile disappeared from Gregory's lips, and he became all business. "Nothing new, unfortunately, but Acheson said that he might know which files to poke about in, based on the information you and I were able to dig up on Doyle."

Emmeline's eyes shone with a fiery eagerness. She sat on the edge of the sofa. "Really, Philip?"

"Yes, it's a start. We might be able to trace Doyle through his family—extended though it may be. It's a tedious process to wade through the various relationships. We believe our man may have been the third of twelve children. Seven girls and five boys. Apparently, the father was a drunkard who couldn't hold down a job, but whose pastime was beating his wife and children."

"Despicable bastard," Emmeline mumbled under her breath.

"Yes, well, the apple doesn't fall far from the tree," Philip continued. "It seems that one night the father was particularly drunk and beat his wife unconscious. That's when young Paddy—a lad of only thirteen—took matters into his own hands and stabbed his father to death with a kitchen knife." Emmeline gasped but sat very still. "When the eldest brother came home and saw what had happened, he immediately sent for their uncle, who was active in the IRA. Within an hour, the father's body had disappeared, and the house was spotless once again. There was no hint of the violence that had taken place. The next day, the mother and all the siblings, except for the eldest brother, had been put on a boat for England. They never looked back. The uncle took Paddy and his eldest brother, Eamon, in. From that day on, they were part of the family. They had no past. It was as if they were born again. They even took on their uncle's surname. It was a life of violence and death. Eamon had a razor sharp mind for figures and a fierce determination to see Ireland free of England's yoke once and for all. Eamon won a scholarship to Trinity College, where he studied engineering and physics. However, the only thing that he dedicated his knowledge to was terrorism, pure and simple. He quickly rose through IRA's ranks to become the youngest—and most deadly—commander. But his luck ran out, and he was killed in a raid. That was the day young Paddy took up the cause so that he could avenge his adored brother's death and wreak as much destruction as possible on the English. And that's how he joined forces with the Germans in the Second World War."

Gregory pursed his lips, a dark shadow washing over his face. "A nasty customer, indeed. And you think this Paddy is our Doyle?"

"We're fairly certain. He fits the bill."

Emmeline was excited. She sat on the edge of the sofa and leaned toward Philip. "That's wonderful. That dovetails with what we discovered, although we didn't know about the murky family history and the name change."

Philip sought to temper her enthusiasm. "The devil of it is that a lot of Doyle's past conveniently disappeared from *our* records after the war, when he was supposedly helping Britain to identify and capture his Nazi cronies. Now, he's considered an embarrassment for Her Majesty's Government."

"Yes, we encountered a good bit of the same thing." Emmeline sat back and rested her head against the back of the sofa, her thoughts awhirl.

"It's definitely tricky after the war," Gregory said. "I was able to pick up what I believe is Doyle's trail in Switzerland in 1952. This bloke, if he is our man, started his own engineering firm and was doing work all over Europe. It was rather a success. It's unclear, but I think the company was launched with the money he received from selling his wartime booty. Through some old associates—" He saw Emmeline slide a sideways glance in his direction. "—I was able to trace Doyle to a secret bank account in Zurich. That's where I came face to face with the impenetrable curtain of Swiss banking secrecy."

"I'll see what I can find out from my end. There are some chaps who owe me a few favors."

Emmeline's face broke out into a smile. "For the first time in a week, I think we're making progress. I can feel it."

Philip laughed. "Well, Doyle doesn't stand a chance with you on his tail—" He inclined his head in Gregory's direction. "—or you."

Gregory touched two fingers to his forehead in a little salute at Philip's acknowledgment.

"However—"

Emmeline crossed her arms over her chest and sighed. "Oh, Philip, not a lecture please."

"My dear girl, we cannot ignore the fact that Doyle is a dangerous man. Therefore, I don't want you two taking any unnecessary risks. At the first sign of trouble, run. Do you understand me?"

Emmeline nodded dutifully. "Yes, Philip."

His eyes searched her face. "I mean it. No playing hero. *Either of you.*"

Gregory's mobile started to ring in his pocket. "I'm terribly sorry." He pulled it out and frowned when he saw the number. "Please excuse me."

He walked over to the window and turned his back to them. "Hello, Oliver."

Philip and Emmeline exchanged looks. Philip shrugged and shook his head.

"What?" Gregory said as he swung round to face them. "Yes, I see. No, thanks for ringing. I'm on my way." He snapped the phone shut.

Emmeline stood and went over to him. She touched his arm lightly. "What did Superintendent Burnell want?"

"He said that Brian's just been arrested for Max's murder."

CHAPTER 34

Burnell was waiting for them when they stepped out of the lift. His features were haggard, and his mouth was set in a grim line. Finch was standing stiffly by his side.

"Oliver, what the devil is all this about?" Gregory asked brusquely.

For once, the superintendent ignored the over familiarity. He pulled them aside and replied in a hushed tone, "I'm afraid we're as much in the dark as you are. Fenton dragged your cousin in about three-quarters of an hour ago and told us to begin processing him for his father's murder. He said that he had evidence."

"Fenton? This is ridiculous. What evidence?" The expression in Gregory's eyes alternated between confusion and indignation. "None of this makes any sense. Fenton is a friend of the family. Clearly, the police have made a mistake."

Emmeline slipped her hand through the crook of Gregory's elbow and patted his arm gently. "Shh, darling, getting upset will not help Brian." She blushed slightly as she uttered these words because she would be the first one to acknowledge that her greatest character flaws were her short temper and her impatience. However, they had to remain calm to get to the bottom of things.

His brow furrowed as his eyes raked her face, but then he lifted her hand to his lips and grazed her fingers with a kiss.

He gave her a brief smile and turned to Burnell once again. "Right. So tell us what you know."

"Fenton went to interview Mr. Sanborn earlier today about an argument he had with his father a couple of hours before he was murdered. Finch and I were supposed to speak with your cousin, but Fenton pulled rank and insisted—as a friend of the family and a detective extraordinaire, you understand—that he would go. Obviously, we don't know exactly what occurred, but your cousin essentially told Fenton to stuff it, and he refused to cooperate. Naturally, this put Fenton's back up, and he went off in a huff. His pride was so wounded that he put Mr. Sanborn under surveillance."

"I don't blame Brian for not talking to Fenton. But what I don't understand is how that leads to him being arrested?"

Burnell looked down at the floor as he rocked back and forth on the balls of his feet. He cleared his throat as he lifted his gaze to look Gregory in the eye. "There's a bit more than that."

Gregory's jaw tightened. "What else?"

"Ahem, Mr. Sanborn…your cousin was apprehended in the midst of trying to get rid of the murder weapon."

Gregory's spine stiffened. An uncomfortable silence filled the small space between them as he glared at the detective.

"What? Now, I know you're all mad." There was a hard edge to his voice.

It frightened Emmeline how cold, so very cold, he sounded. "Gregory—"

Without even a glance at her, he put up a hand to prevent her from going on.

"Look, Longdon, I don't like it either. Frankly, it threw me for a loop. But the fact of the matter is that Mr. Sanborn had a bloody letter opener in his possession. It has been identified as his father's. Aside from that fact, Mr. Sanborn has admitted to killing his father."

Emmeline saw Gregory's face take on a sickly gray pallor. He shook his head. "I don't believe it." He pounded his fist against his palm. "I *won't* believe it. It doesn't make any sense. Brian would never….Where's his lawyer?" He looked around the corridor. "Where's Nigel? Why isn't Nigel here?"

Burnell thrust his hands into his pockets. "That's the other thing. Mr. Sanborn is causing us an awful lot of trouble. He refuses to see his brother. He doesn't even want us to ring him. And before he speaks to his lawyer, he is demanding to see one person."

"Who could Brian possibly want to see, if he doesn't want to see Nigel?"

"You. He wants to see you."

eↄeↄ

Burnell showed Gregory into one of the interrogation rooms. It was cold and gray, and utterly depressing. And there was Brian sitting at the table in the middle of the room, a uniformed constable hovering behind his chair.

"Wilson, I'm giving Mr. Longdon permission to speak with his cousin. *Alone*," Burnell told the constable. "You're to stand guard outside the door."

"But, sir, Assistant Commissioner Fenton said that no one was to—"

"I sincerely hope that you're not disobeying an order," Burnell growled.

Wilson swallowed hard, his Adam's apple working furiously up and down. "No, sir."

"Good. Because the last time I looked, I outranked you. By quite a lot. That reminds me, didn't you put in papers for detective sergeant?"

"Yes, sir." It was barely a whisper.

"It would be a pity if your application were to be rejected."

"I didn't mean any disrespect, sir. I was just following—"

The superintendent gave a brisk wave of his hand. "I'm willing to overlook it this time. We'll say no more about it."

"Thank you, sir." Relief washed over Wilson's face. He quickly crossed to the door and escaped into the corridor.

Gregory was certain if that had gone on any longer, the poor chap would have passed out. "Oliver, I didn't know you had a cruel streak in you."

Burnell grunted and wagged a finger at Gregory. "You have ten minutes." He cast a glance at Brian. "Try to talk some sense into your cousin."

Gregory clapped the superintendent on the shoulder. "Thanks, Oliver, for sticking your neck out like this. I appreciate it."

"Yes, well," Burnell replied gruffly, as he tried to cover up his embarrassment. "Don't think this is for you."

Gregory bit back a smile as he walked the detective to the door. "No, of course not. The thought never crossed my mind."

"Good." Burnell jerked his head in Brian's direction. "Get him to talk." Then he was gone.

The smile faded from Gregory's lips as he turned on his heel. He held Brian's warm brown gaze for a long moment and pursed his lips. The only sound in the room was the faint echo of his footfalls as walked over to the table and took the chair opposite his cousin.

He folded his hands on the table and cleared his throat. "Now then, if I'm to extricate you from this bloody nightmare, you had better tell me everything. And I do mean *everything*."

A tiny tremor shot through Brian's hands. A range of emotions chased themselves across his features. "Thanks for coming, Toby." Gregory waved a hand in the air. "I wasn't sure whether you would. Let's face it. I haven't exactly welcomed you back into the family fold with open arms. But there was no one else to turn to."

"Oh, come off it." Irritation was creeping into Gregory's voice. He shifted his body sideways and looped one elbow over the back of the chair. "Aren't you being just a tad melodramatic? You're not a bloody orphan. What are you playing at? I don't believe for one minute that you killed Max."

Brian's forehead puckered and he gripped his hands together until the skin was distended and showed white. Very calmly he replied, "Of course, you're entitled to your opinion."

"Don't give me that. Why did you summon me down here? I can't help you unless you tell me what's going on. And another thing, why me? Why won't you see Nigel?"

Brian slammed his palm down on the table. A dark shadow fell across his features. "No," he shouted. "I don't want to see anyone. Not Tessa. Not Mum. And I especially don't want Nigel anywhere near the police station, do you hear me? You have to do everything in your power to keep him away from here. He'll listen to you, Toby. After all, you were always closer to him than me when we were boys."

Two vertical lines appeared between Gregory's brows. The fog in his mind was starting to lift, and comprehension suddenly dawned on him. "You didn't kill Max, did you?" Brian opened his mouth to protest, but Gregory just pressed forward. "Of course, you didn't. So why would you admit to the murder? Unless you're protecting someone. Someone you love." He paused, letting the silence brood in the air between them. "Someone like *your brother*."

Brian squirmed under that intense stare and had to look away. It was as good as an admission.

The scraping of his chair against the floor grated on the ears as Gregory stood up. "Now, I understand. It's an admirable gesture." He put his palms down on the table and leaned down to whisper, "But utterly unnecessary. Nigel couldn't have killed Max any more than you could. Frankly, I'm surprised that you would entertain such a thought."

Brian dropped all attempts at pretense. "Toby—"

Gregory cut him off. "The name is Gregory nowadays."

"That's neither here or there. Although I can't begin to fathom why you found it necessary to—"

"Let's stick to the topic at hand, shall we? Namely, getting you out of this mess of your own creation."

Brian grabbed his sleeve. "Tob—Gregory, listen. I saw the letter opener slip out of Nigel's pocket, the night of the murder. He pulled out his mobile to take a call when we were all in Dad's penthouse. Richard and Burnell were arguing about something. You were hovering around Emmeline and Maggie. No one noticed. So I picked it up and quietly tucked it away. Then Dr. Meadows came along and made his dramatic announcement that a knife of some sort had killed Dad and not

Maggie's blow to his head. I was going to get rid of the letter opener, but there hasn't been time. Then today, Richard popped by, poking his nose into things that didn't concern him. He was getting too close."

"Fenton is good at making a nuisance of himself," Gregory murmured.

"Yes, well. I never liked the man, but he was Dad's friend. Don't you see? I couldn't allow him to arrest Nigel. God knows Dad had it coming to him. It was only a matter of time before his greed and shady dealings caught up with him. I don't blame Nigel. He's the best of men, and I'm certain it was self-defense."

"I'm certain that you're wrong. Nigel wouldn't allow himself to be provoked like that, not even in self-defense."

"How do you explain the letter opener?"

Gregory blew out his cheeks in a long, slow breath. "I admit that poses a bit of a conundrum. But I know Nigel and so should you. I'll let you stew on that."

He crossed the room in two strides and rapped on the door to be let out. "Where are you going?" Brian asked.

Just as Wilson opened the door, Gregory glanced over his shoulder and said, "To sort this mess out, naturally. Isn't that why you called me? We can't have you languishing in prison, now can we? I'll have a lawyer down here within the hour. Tell him exactly what you told me. And anything else you haven't."

The ghost of a smile passed over his cousin's lips. "Thanks. Take care of Nigel and keep him away from here."

Gregory rolled his eyes as Wilson once again stepped inside and firmly closed the door behind him.

"Longdon?" Burnell's voice quivered with tension.

He turned to find the superintendent barreling down the corridor toward him. He remained rooted to the spot until Burnell reached his side. The superintendent's face was slightly flushed, and his eyes smoldered. "You bellowed, Oliver?"

"Superintendent Burnell," the detective hissed through gritted teeth as he shot a glance to the right and left.

"Thank you for allowing me to see Brian. Did you want

something in particular? Because I don't have time for a chat just now. Emmy's waiting and I have to arrange a lawyer for—"

"Button it. I have an extremely excitable woman in my office prepared to chain herself to the battlements, unless we release Mr. Sanborn this instant. I have no doubt whatsoever that she can start a second French revolution all on her own."

The corners of Gregory's eyes crinkled as bemusement washed over his face. "Ah, that sounds suspiciously like Aunt Mireille. I'd have a care if I were you, Oliver. You know how fiercely protective mothers are of their offspring."

"There is nothing remotely amusing about this situation."

"I must agree with you on that point."

"I don't need your agreement. I want you to do something about your bloody family."

Gregory spread out his hands in a helpless gesture. "But what can I do?"

"You can remove your aunt so that we can get on with our job."

Gregory tilted his head to one side and smoothed down the corners of his mustache. It was a mirror image of the superintendent when he was mulling over something. "You do realize that is a tall order?"

Burnell took a step closer and lowered his voice to a dangerous hiss. "If you don't get her out of my office in five minutes, I'm going to throw all of you behind bars."

"On what charge, may I ask?"

"Breach of the peace. Get. Her. Out. Of. Here. Now."

Gregory slipped an arm around the superintendent's shoulders. "Calm down, Oliver. You shouldn't get so worked up. It's not good for your blood pressure, especially since you're carrying around a few extra pounds." He patted the detective's thickening midsection.

Burnell cheeks burned. He roughly shrugged off Gregory's arm. "You have five minutes to remove her."

Gregory gave him a mock bow. "Your wish is my command."

Burnell grunted and stormed off without a backward glance.

෨෨෨

Mireille's cultured voice, laced with anger and displeasure, drifted to his ears. "*Cherie*, I will not calm down. These stupid English policemen have thrown my son in a filthy jail cell. *C'est ridicule*. I am telling you Brian did not kill Max. Although whoever did is a hero and deserves a medal."

"Please, Mireille, all of us know that Brian didn't do it. I promise you that Gregory and I will do everything we can to sort this out," he heard Emmeline reply, her tone soft and soothing. "I mean no disrespect, but I think it would be wiser if you were to go home. Getting upset and demanding that Brian be set free '*immediatement*' is not the way to ingratiate yourself with the police."

"Ingratiate? *Oh là là*." She shook one hand in the air in typical Gallic fashion and unleashed an uninterrupted string of words in rapid French. Gregory just caught the word *cochon*, as he opened the door to Burnell's office and walked in.

Two pairs of eyes, one very dark and intense and the other a steely slate-blue, impaled him. "Ah, two beautiful ladies," he said in honeyed tones.

Mireille jumped to her feet. "There you are, Toby. At last."

Emmeline was a fraction of a second slower. She walked over to him and touched his sleeve lightly. "I'll leave you two alone to talk." She gave a helpless shrug. "I did my best."

Gregory bent down and pressed a kiss against her temple. "Thank you for understanding, darling."

She smiled and gave his arm another squeeze, before quietly slipping from the room.

The minute the door closed, his aunt started firing questions at him. "Have you seen Brian? Is he all right? That Burnell and his Sergeant Finch, *vraiment ils sont des espece d'idiots*—a special kind of idiot. Can you believe that they will not allow me to see my son? They told me some bizarre story that Brian refuses to see me. Not see his mother? Can you imagine such a lie? I—"

Gregory placed his hands gently on Mireille's shoulders and gave her a peck on the cheek. "Emmy's right. You must calm down. Shh—" He put a finger to her lips. "—Brian is perfectly fine. I assure you. Please try not to worry."

"But I'm his mother."

He threw his head back and laughed. "Yes, you've left no one in any doubt about that. Everyone in Scotland Yard is painfully aware that they are in your bad books. But, darling, Brian's not a little boy anymore. There's nothing you can do here at the moment."

Tears welled up in Mireille's eyes as she searched his face. Her fingers clutched at his sleeve. "*Mon chou*, I'm so afraid for Brian." Her voice cracked. "I don't understand anything. Why did he confess? What is going to happen to him?"

He drew her into his embrace and rested his chin on top of her head. He felt her body tremble slightly. "Nothing is going to happen to Brian." He pulled away. "I promise. I will not let anything happen to the family."

His aunt reached up and traced a finger along his cheek. Her features softened, and her mouth folded itself into a faint smile. "Yes, you were always a good boy. Very quiet, but always watching. Always aware of everything. But you kept your secrets. Isn't that right?"

Gregory became serious. "But the secret of who stole the Queen of the Night, I will take to the grave with me."

Mireille's face drained of color and her knees buckled under her. She would have slid to the floor if Gregory hadn't been supporting her. "*You knew*? All these years? And you didn't say anything?"

He nodded silently, as she stared at him incredulously.

"It was the night I ran away. I was crossing the hall. The door to Max's study was slightly ajar, and I saw you taking the Queen of the Night from the safe."

She shook her head. "Yes, since you and the diamond disappeared, I just allowed everyone to believe that you stole it. Oh, what you must think of me, Toby?"

He shrugged his shoulders. "I didn't know. Max would have believed whatever he wanted anyway."

"I am truly sorry, but I just wanted—I wanted to hurt Max. To take away something that he cared about. He made my life—the boys' lives, everyone's life—hell. But I did you an injustice. I took away your good name and your reputation. I was a coward. I should never, *never* have done such a thing. Can you forgive me, *mon chou*?"

Gregory flashed her a crooked smile. "There is nothing to forgive."

"You have a more generous heart than I do."

He gave a low huff of laughter. "Isn't that what family is all about? To be there for one another through thick and thin. Max was definitely the thin edge of the wedge."

"Yes," she replied soberly. "I made a terrible mistake when I married that man."

"One thing I'm curious about is why did you stay married to him for so long?"

Mireille sighed. "Mainly for the boys. But if I'm really honest, I became seduced by the life we had. In the end, however, that was not enough. I could not tolerate Max anymore. He was furious when I told him that I was going to file for divorce. Even though there was no love left between us, he was determined to keep me. He couldn't bear to lose one of his possessions. He said, 'I will see you burn in hell in first.' *Si charmant, n'est ce pas?*"

"So how did you finally persuade him to agree to the divorce?"

"I used the only weapon that Max understood. Blackmail."

Gregory's widened in surprise.

"I see I shock you, Toby. You have to understand that when one is backed into a corner, one's primitive instincts for survival rise to the surface."

"What could you possibly have had on Max to make him acquiesce to your wishes?"

"Files he kept on his art collection. Max was well aware that most of his paintings and other *objets d'art* were Nazi spoils. But so black was his heart—if he even had one—that it didn't bother him. I was so outraged when I found the files. I was prepared to go to the police. And then I thought, 'No, let Max's greed be his undoing.' *Enfin*, he granted me the divorce. I moved back to France, as we agreed, and that was it. He made me sign some papers saying that I would never reveal what I knew. I was perfectly willing to sign anything as long as I didn't have to spend another minute under the same roof with him."

"I see," Gregory murmured. "Everything Max touched was tainted."

"Yes, he was an ogre, a beast. But I am not such a monster, despite my selfishness. Max is dead now, and I cannot hold onto these dirty secrets anymore. My conscience will not allow it. I have decided to give the files to you and Emmeline. *La petite* has a good head on her shoulders. Perhaps it will help you to find this Doyle."

Gregory gave his aunt a kiss. "Thank you, Aunt Mireille. Now we're in with a chance."

Burnell, hands thrust deep in his pockets, was loitering by Finch's desk talking in hushed tones with Emmeline and the sergeant, when Gregory and Mireille emerged from his office. He immediately scuttled over to them, with Finch and Emmeline in tow.

The superintendent inclined his head politely toward Mireille. "Mrs. Sanborn, I'm glad to see that you've—" He was about to say *come to your senses*, but under the circumstances, he thought better of it. "—recovered from the initial shock. I assure you the Metropolitan Police's intention is to punish the guilty, not the innocent. Based on your son's—let us say, curious—actions and the evidence found on his person, we had no choice but to arrest him on suspicion of murder. You must see that."

Mireille looked up Gregory, who gave a brief nod, and then turned back to Burnell. "Yes, Superintendent. I understand that you are only doing your job. You must forgive my behavior earlier. As a mother, it is only natural for you to want to protect your children no matter how old they are."

Burnell breathed a sigh of relief. *Thank God for that. I've had quite enough theatrics and surprises for one day.* Aloud he said, "Of course. I'll have Finch drive you home. We will keep you and Mr. Sanborn's wife apprised of any breaks in the case. But I'd like to request that you not make a repeat appearance here at the station. A scene like today can only serve to prejudice your son's case."

He saw an angry spark in those slate-blue eyes and then the look was gone. She cleared her throat. "Very well, Superintendent." She wagged her manicured finger at him. "But I warn you, it will not go well for you if I find out that you have hidden things from me."

"Perish the thought, ma'am."

Mireille squared her shoulders and patted a hair into place. "*Alors*, we understand each other." She turned to Gregory and touched his cheek. "Toby, I am relying on you—and you too, Emmeline, *bien sûr*—to keep an eye on them." She jerked her head at the two detectives. Then she lowered her voice so that only Gregory could hear. "Come to the house this evening. I will give you the files."

He raised her hands to his lips and brushed them with a kiss, but out of the corner of his eye, he saw Burnell standing stiffly. The poor chap couldn't take much more of this. So he gave his aunt a gentle nudge toward Finch. "Don't worry. I promise everything will be all right."

"Yes," she whispered. Every mother's fear for her child was injected into that one little word. And then with her head held high and in a stronger voice, she said, "Shall we go, Sergeant Finch?"

Finch proffered his arm. "Yes, Mrs. Sanborn. This way." He led her down the corridor to the lift.

Once they were gone, Burnell grudgingly said, "Thanks for your help with your aunt, Longdon. She was on the verge of hysterics."

Gregory's face broke out into a mischievous grin. He clapped the superintendent on the back. "My pleasure, Oliver. Any time Scotland Yard feels a case is too much to handle, don't hesitate to ring me. I'm always prepared to do my civic duty."

Burnell glowered at him. "Don't press your luck." To his annoyance, this remark elicited a smirk from Gregory.

Emmeline intervened at this stage to prevent Gregory's needling from escalating. "So can you tell us anything about Brian's arrest?"

Burnell opened his mouth to reply, when Nigel appeared at his elbow. "You've arrested the wrong man. I killed my father."

CHAPTER 35

Gregory groaned and dropped his chin to his chest. "Not you too. Bloody fools, the pair of you," he said *sotto voce*.

The superintendent's eyes widened in disbelief. *This can't be happening to me. It's like a never-ending nightmare.* He shot a venomous look at Gregory.

Gregory shrugged his shoulders and gave a sheepish smile. "What can I say? I'm afraid insanity runs in the family."

An unintelligible gurgling sound bubbled up from deep within Burnell's throat.

Gregory put a hand on his sleeve. "Oliver, old chap, I do believe that you're on the verge of apoplexy. Take a deep cleansing breath. That usually does the trick."

Emmeline elbowed Gregory in the ribs and shook her head disapprovingly. She mouthed, "You're making things worse." She nudged him out of the way with a gentle bump of her hip.

"Please ignore him. I'm sure you can understand that the entire family is under a great deal of stress."

The superintendent rounded on her. "*Stress*? You don't know the meaning of the word stress. You don't have to contend with a bunch of lunatics—" He waved wildly in the direction of the two cousins."—as well as Assistant Commissioner Fenton all day long."

Emmeline blinked at the vehemence of his tone but soldiered on into the breach. "Yes, well. Of course, nobody has a more stressful job than you. But wouldn't it be wise to hear what Nigel has to say? That's the only way that your long years of experience can separate the wheat from the chaff to find the truth."

Still seething inside, Burnell's eyes narrowed as he stared down at her. But Emmeline didn't flinch. She understood that he was in an unenviable position and felt sorry for him.

Something in her expression must have communicated itself to the superintendent because his features softened. "You're right, of course." His voice cracked as he tried to master his emotions.

With his body still rigid with tension, he turned awkwardly to Nigel. "Now then, Mr. Sanborn, you say that you murdered your father. What epiphany prompted you to come down here today to unburden your soul? I'd also be very interested to hear why you committed the crime."

He hitched one hip on the corner of Finch's desk and folded his hands on one thigh. *This should be good.*

Nigel ignored the daggers shooting from Gregory's eyes. He straightened his spine and replied defiantly, "Brian's innocent. That's why. It's as simple as that."

"Actually, there is nothing simple about this case. Why was the murder weapon found in your brother's possession? And you've haven't explained why you killed your father."

"I—you see—Dad had always been a brute in his personal life and in business."

"Yes, yes. But why choose that *particular* moment to seize the bull by the horns?"

"I—I couldn't stand his shady dealings any more. He was setting the company down on the road to ruin." He lowered his voice. "This absolutely cannot get out, but Dad was—had been for a long time—embezzling from the company."

Gregory raised an eyebrow but kept his counsel at this revelation.

Burnell stroked his beard thoughtfully and murmured, "I see. So you felt the time had come to snuff out your father's life."

He heard a sharp intake of breath from Emmeline and a "Steady on, old chap," from Gregory, but he was in no mood to make this any easier for Nigel.

"You want to know what I think, Mr. Sanborn?"

Nigel stood very still. He didn't utter a word.

"I think that you're lying."

"But—"

Burnell put up a hand and any protest rising to Nigel's lips died on his tongue. "I suggest you go home before I charge you with perverting the course of justice, and another thing—"

Whatever he had been about to say was cut off by Sergeant Finch's return. "Sir, I ran into Dr. Meadows in the corridor. Here's the report from forensics on the murder weapon."

All eyes shifted to Finch as Burnell grabbed the report. The superintendent skimmed through the contents in silence. His eyes narrowed on a certain section before he closed the file with a weary sigh.

Emmeline shot a quizzical glance in Gregory's direction, and they both leaned in closer. "Well, don't keep us in suspense, Oliver," Gregory prompted.

"Your cousin—Mr. Brian Sanborn, that is—his fingerprints don't match the ones on the letter opener. That means he couldn't have killed his father—"

Gregory gave Emmeline a hug. "I could have told you that."

"What?" Nigel asked, stunned.

"—but it doesn't explain why he was trying to dispose of it," Burnell finished sternly.

"Ah, I believe I can enlighten you on that point," Gregory said.

"Can you? Please go ahead. I'm dying to hear the story. I'm sure it's fascinating."

Gregory cast a look at Nigel. "Brian believed Nigel killed Max."

His cousin's head whipped round. "How could Brian have—" Then he clamped his lips shut.

"Mr. Sanborn, only moments ago you were confessing to your father's murder. Don't tell me that you've had a sudden change of heart?" Burnell asked with false sweetness.

Nigel stared back at him dumbly.

The superintendent tapped the report with his forefinger. "While this exonerates your brother, it does indicate that there are fingerprints on the letter opener. Someone killed your father. The fingerprints belong to someone. But who? That's the question."

Nigel swallowed hard. "I—It wasn't—"

"Oliver, what are you insinuating?" Gregory piped up. "It's just as ludicrous to believe that Nigel could commit murder. You can't possibly arrest him."

The low hum of the police station busily carrying on business as usual thrummed all around them. But the little group had been plunged into a black hole of suffocating silence, where their already frayed nerves were being stretched even tighter. Any second now and they would snap.

Burnell's blue eyes searched each of their expectant faces in turn and came to rest on Gregory. "What do take me for? A fool? I haven't gotten to the ripe old age I am without being able to recognize a lie when I hear it."

Gregory grinned from ear to ear and pulled Emmeline closer against his side. "For my part, I never doubted your judgment for a single moment. But you are a wily devil."

For once, the superintendent returned his nemesis's smile. "It serves your crazy family right for wasting my time this afternoon. Besides, the report indicates that Mr. Nigel Sanborn's fingerprints don't match the ones on the murder weapon either."

"How do you know that?"

"I had the forensic team discreetly lift a set from everyone who was in the penthouse that night, present company included. I could have told Assistant Commissioner Fenton that this afternoon, but he was so pumped up with own efforts in apprehending Max Sanborn's killer that he refused to listen to anyone. Now, all of you get of my sight and leave me in peace. Finch."

"Yes, sir?"

"Go downstairs and see to Mr. Sanborn's release. I don't want him hanging about a minute longer than necessary."

Finch smiled. "Straightaway, sir."

"I'll come with you, if it's all right?" Nigel asked.

Burnell nodded, but his face sobered as he watched them hurry across the floor. He shook his head. "It's all well and good that your cousins are in the clear," he said more to himself than to Gregory. "But that still leaves me with a murderer to catch and no viable suspects."

"And of course, we can't forget about Doyle," Emmeline chimed in.

"Forget our good friend Doyle? You must be joking. His unsavory past gives me a warm and fuzzy glow right here." He pressed a hand to his heart. "Every time I think about him, my fingers itch to strangle him." He cleared his throat and recollected where he was and with whom he was talking. "But you didn't hear that from me."

Emmeline patted his arm. "Don't worry, Superintendent. We're all of like mind and would never betray you."

"You wouldn't, but I don't know about him." He jerked a thumb in Gregory's direction.

"Oh, Oliver."

Burnell raised an eyebrow.

"I mean Superintendent Burnell. When you're with us, you're among family."

Burnell groaned. "I would shoot myself if I were related to you."

Gregory slipped an arm around the superintendent's shoulders and gave them a rough squeeze. "We all know that under that grumpy exterior—and layer of blubber—resides the heart of a giant teddy bear."

"I'd watch that tongue of yours, Longdon. One day you're going to go too far. And that's the day I'll throw you behind bars. You see, I don't believe for a single second that you've completely given up your criminal ways."

Gregory sniffed. "You wound me to the core, Oliver. You really do. I would have thought that you'd be friendlier toward the man who will likely bring you Doyle's head on a silver platter."

The superintendent's eyes narrowed. "Come again. You've been holding out on us."

"Now, would I do that?" Gregory asked innocently.

"Yes," Burnell and Emmeline replied in unison.

CHAPTER 36

It was seven-thirty by the time Emmeline managed to leave the office. The afternoon's excitement at Scotland Yard had set her behind with her work. Technically, though, while she had been there to support Gregory and his cousins, one could say that she *was* working because it was all part of the story and the search for answers. This assuaged her conscience somewhat, but it did nothing to dispel the frustration of not being able to unmask Doyle and to bring him to justice for all his crimes. And then there were Maurice Boinet and Max Sanborn. Deep in the pit of her stomach, there was a flutter of recognition that all of these loose ends tied together.

However, she had reason to hope that they would catch Doyle soon. Thank goodness some unseen mandarins high up in the Foreign Office had seen fit to allow Philip to assist them with their inquiries. Meanwhile, Mireille—bless her heart—was going to turn over Max's files. It was a question of being patient and finding the right thread to pull until the ball of yarn unraveled. Patience, alas, was not a virtue that Emmeline possessed. But what she had in abundance was a growing unease that they were running out of time. This thought scared her more than she was willing to admit.

In this restless, nervous frame of mind, she slowly followed the throng of evening commuters as they climbed the stairs at the Kensington High Street Station. She nearly jumped out of her skin when two men jostled her as they roughly pushed their way past. The entire trip on the Underground she couldn't shake the feeling that she was being watched, although she couldn't say that anyone in the car paid undue attention to her. But now again, the cool trickle of fear made the hairs on the back of her neck stand on end. She twisted her head to the right and left, and cast a glance over her shoulder once, nearly causing her to stumble. Everyone looked as if they were going about their daily lives and could care less about her.

You're turning into a Nervous Nelly, she told herself in disgust as she emerged onto the pavement.

What she needed was a distraction. The best way to take her mind off things was to do something mundane. That's why she was planning to stop at the Tesco's just down the block. That and the fact that she had neglected to go to the supermarket the past few days and the cupboards were virtually bare.

Twenty minutes later, loaded down with groceries, Emmeline scrambled to unfurl her umbrella as the rain the weatherman had promised that morning began to spill from the sky. Fortunately, it wasn't that hard, and it was only a short walk home.

The minute she turned onto Argyll Road, she was certain. The unmistakable sound of leather soles rhythmically hitting the slick pavement floated to her ears. She quickened her pace. The footfalls behind her did as well. They were growing louder as the shower turned into a downpour. The needlelike droplets pelted her from all sides.

She dropped her shopping and broke into a run when she reached the corner with Stafford Terrace. She felt like she was going mad because now she distinctly heard a second set of footsteps. She screamed and tossed the umbrella over her shoulder at her invisible pursuers.

When she was only steps from her house, she was blinded by the strong headlamps of a car moving toward her. Warm tears mingled with the rain on her face. She backed up until her shoulder blades were pressed against the wrought iron railings of her neighbor's house.

There was nowhere else to go. From her left, the footsteps were getting closer. Closer.

The car came to a screeching halt, and two men jumped out, leaving the doors wide open. She let out a strangled cry. She was trapped.

"Inside, miss. Quick as you can," one of men shouted.

Emmeline was frozen to the spot. Her chest burned with the effort of trying to draw oxygen into her lungs. Her eyes darted wildly to the right and left.

"Go on. *Move*," he yelled over his shoulder as he and his companion ran past and down the block. "Burnell sent us. Lock the doors and don't let anyone in until we get back."

At the sound of Burnell's name, adrenaline propelled her the few yards and up the steps onto her own doorstep. Her hands were shaking violently as she tried to fit the key in the lock. At last, she inserted it and slammed the door shut behind her. It took several attempts to bolt the lock because her fingers would not cooperate. She stood there in her hallway, back pressed against the door and her heart hammering away against her ribcage. Her legs couldn't hold her weight anymore, and she slowly slid to the floor. She hugged her knees tightly to her chest to try to stop the shuddering that had wracked her body. And she waited.

Outside, wave after wave of rain was being tossed around by the wind, making it difficult to see. The two plainclothes detectives were joined by their colleagues who had been keeping watch on the opposite side of the square. When they emerged onto Phillmore Gardens, several of the streetlamps were not working. The thickened shadows combined with the low moan of the wind wreaked havoc with their senses.

One of the detectives stopped suddenly in the middle of the block and put up his hand. "Listen," Inspector Parker yelled.

The four men strained their ears. Then they heard it. It was just discernible. The faint *slap, slap* of shoes hitting the pavement.

"He's headed toward the park. Let's get the bastard."

"Bloody hell," said Sergeant Haworth as they set off again. "In this filthy weather, we've as good as lost him if he reaches the park."

With chests heaving, the police officers entered through the outer fringes of Holland Park. Inspector Manning rang for backup as they plunged into the murky gloom. He and Sergeant Rogers took the path to the right, while their colleagues made their way through the wooded area.

The trees created a sort of cocoon, and the wind and rain were not as intense among the trees. The detectives heard a twig snap somewhere to their left. They stood still and held their breaths. Once their eyes had time to adjust, they distinctly saw someone…a man?…lurking among the shadows. Manning mimed that they would separate and circle round to trap the culprit between them. Rogers nodded. The inspector counted to three on his fingers and then mouthed, *Now*. They both moved, tiptoeing so that they would have the element of surprise on their side. They clung to whatever shadows the trees afforded. They were quickly able to close the gap between themselves and their prey. They were practically upon him.

Rogers reached out a hand to grab the man's collar when the unthinkable happened. He tripped over a root, wrenching his ankle and tumbling to the sodden earth. "Oof," the word escaped his lips as the wind was knocked out of him.

This spooked the man who spun round to see what was the noise.

"Damn," the detective muttered as he tried to scramble to his feet. There was no longer any reason for subterfuge. He reached out, his fingers clamping round the man's ankle. He gave it a good tug, bringing the man down beside him. The detective pounced on the suspect. Male grunts reverberated through the woods as they thrashed about on the ground.

"The game's over, old chap," Manning said as he loomed above and pulled back the safety catch on the gun he was aiming at a point somewhere in the middle of the man's chest. "You've caused quite enough trouble for one night, so I suggest that you get up very, *very* slowly with your hands in the air. No heroics. Because I really would hate to disturb the serenity of this lovely park by having to use this." He made a brusque gesture with the gun. "On your feet. *Now*."

With his eyes trained on the suspect, he asked the sergeant out of the corner of his mouth, "All right, Rogers?"

The other detective winced as he lumbered to his feet. "I'll live. Nothing more serious than a sprained ankle. My pride, though, that's a different story. Can you do anything to restore that?"

Manning laughed. But his smile vanished as soon as it appeared. "Hands high," he told their suspect. He was surprised to see that he was a fairly young man. Based on the details Burnell had told them about the case, he thought they were looking for an older fellow. "Who are you?"

"You fools," their suspect spat in disgust. "I hope you're proud of yourselves. You've made one bloody big cock up tonight."

Both detectives exchanged perplexed looks and shrugged their shoulders.

Rogers said, "I'd be careful what I say. Resisting arrest will only serve to dig a deeper hole for yourself."

"Ha," was the man's response.

"That's quite enough of that. Now, I asked you who are you?"

The man clamped his lips together in a tight line.

"So we have a jokester, do we?" Manning said. "We'll see how bold you are when we take you down to the station. In the meantime, let's see what we can discover." He carefully patted down the man's suit jacket. "Ah, what's this?" He pulled out a nine millimeter Beretta. He clucked his tongue and wagged a finger at the man. "Naughty, naughty. Don't you know that guns are dangerous?" The man glared at him but remained silent. "Still have nothing to say? What else is here? Ah, at last." He pulled out the man's wallet and rummaged through it. His eyes widened in disbelief as he turned to Rogers. "We have a problem."

Rogers raised an eyebrow and wordlessly took the wallet from Manning.

"You most certainly do have a problem," Crichlow said. "Because of your incompetence, a ruthless Irish assassin named Doyle has gotten away."

"Sir—Mr. Crichlow," Manning stammered. "To be fair, how were we to know that *you* weren't the criminal? *You* were following Miss Kirby."

Crichlow ran a hand through his hair. "*I* was trying to protect her from Doyle. On orders, I've been shadowing her for the past week. There was definitely someone following her tonight. If you fools hadn't intervened, we would have had Doyle, and she would have been safe. As it is, well..." His voice trailed off as he threw his hands in the air in frustration.

Manning's spine stiffened at this dressing down. After all, they were professionals, and they were all supposed to be on the same side. "For the record, Crichlow—" He had dropped the deferential *Mister*, the gloves were off. "—MI5 failed to inform the Met about its operations. I can tell you right now, Superintendent Burnell is going to hit the roof when he finds out."

"Burnell and the rest of Scotland Yard can go to the devil. All I care about is neutralizing Doyle."

"And protecting Miss Kirby," Manning reminded him. "I should think that was of foremost importance."

Crichlow waved a hand impatiently. "Yes, well, that goes without saying. However, if you ask me, that woman is a magnet for trouble. Doyle nearly pushed her in front of a bus this afternoon. Speaking of Miss Kirby, do you have anyone sitting on her house?"

"Yes, I rang Burnell, and he was going to send out a new team immediately. The superintendent and Sergeant Finch are probably there by now."

"That's something anyway," Crichlow scoffed as he pulled out his own mobile. He turned his back on the two detectives to make a call to Villiers, who he already knew was going to be more than a little irked about the night's debacle. He spoke in hushed tones as Manning and Rogers's colleagues materialized. However, he was told that Villiers was in conference and couldn't be disturbed. He sighed. This was just delaying the inevitable.

"Gentlemen, I want to thank you for a most unpleasant evening." He stormed off before any of the police officers had a chance to respond.

"That's put us in our place," Rogers grumbled. "The toffy-nosed twit."

"Come on," Manning said, tugging his arm. "He's not worth it. Let's get out of this bloody monsoon. I don't know about you, but I'm soaked to the skin. I even have water slosh-ing around in my shoes." He lifted his nose in the air and mim-icked Crichlow. "I can assure you it is a *most unpleasant* feel-ing."

e∽e∽

Crichlow was muttering and cursing to himself as he turned off Phillmore Gardens onto Essex Villas where he had parked his car.

How could things have gone so wrong? He had been *so* close to capturing Doyle. So close. It would have made his career. As it was now, the bastard was still on the loose and Villiers was going to have his guts for garters.

All he wanted now was a hot shower and a *very* large tum-bler of whiskey. Or two. Why not? He deserved it after to-night.

He pressed the button on the key fob to unlock his car door and slipped in behind the wheel. He was relieved to be out of the rain at last.

Reluctantly, he pulled out his mobile and tried Villiers's number again. It was answered after the first ring.

"I hope you're going to tell me that you've finally appre-hended Doyle," Villiers said without preamble.

"Unfortunately, sir, it was an utter disaster. Doyle managed to get away."

"Again." Villiers's tone was tinged with irritation and dis-dain.

"Yes, sir. Again. It was all the fault of those imbeciles who work for Burnell. They blundered in where they didn't belong and spooked Doyle."

"I very much doubt that. A killer like Doyle doesn't 'spook' as you so eloquently put it." There was a brief silence on the line, and then Villiers sigh echoed in his ear. "The fact of the matter is he's managed to evade our grasp once again. Report to me first thing in the morning. I want a full accounting about what happened tonight."

"Yes, sir. First thing," Crichlow murmured.

There was soft click and then nothing.

Crichlow stared at his mobile for an instant before stuffing it into his pocket. He leaned back against the headrest and closed his eyes. He was suddenly exhausted. Every part of his body was tired. He could hardly wait to slip between the sheets of his bed.

Just as this thought crossed his mind, something quite rigid pressed against his windpipe. It was crushing the breath out of him. His eyes popped open, and his hands scrabbled to push the stick or whatever it was off his throat. But he couldn't.

Two very large hands were pressing down harder and harder. Blood was thundering in his ears, and he was beginning to feel light-headed.

"Ah, laddie, you've made quite a nuisance of yourself, haven't you?" The lilting voice was laced with venom and ice.

Crichlow struggled in vain, and all at once the pressure was gone. He coughed and rubbed his throat. "Doyle," he croaked as he tried to swivel around to see his tormenter.

"Got it one," the voice said cheerfully. "It's a pity that wisdom came to you too late in life."

It took only one quick twist to snap Crichlow's neck.

CHAPTER 37

B y the time Gregory arrived at Emmeline's house, she had calmed down considerably. He was grateful that Burnell and Finch had come over as soon as the call had come in about the stalker.

They were all sitting in Emmeline's cozy living room doing what the British do best in times of crisis. Drinking tea.

After taking a sip of the steaming liquid, Gregory set his cup down carefully on the coffee table and took Emmeline's small hands in his. He rubbed his thumb along the soft web of skin between her thumb and forefinger. His gaze never left her face.

She ran a finger along his jaw and then pressed her cheek against his. "I'm all right. Really. I just feel extremely silly to have caused all this commotion for nothing. But what with the two murders and Doyle on the loose—my nerves got the better of me. I suppose if I had stopped to think about it I would have—"

Burnell jumped to his feet and paced back and forth in front of the fireplace. "Rubbish. It's not your fault. This whole incident could easily have been avoided if MI5 had informed the Met that they had you under surveillance. I don't say we would have liked having them on our turf, but it's a question of professional courtesy. As it is, this agent—" He snapped his fingers at Finch. "—what was the damn fellow's name?"

"Crichlow. Alan Crichlow."

"That's the bugger. Instead, this Crichlow terrorized Emmeline for no reason."

Yes, Gregory thought to himself as his eyes narrowed. *Villiers has a lot to answer for.*

"Please, Superintendent Burnell," Emmeline implored. "I don't want to be the cause of an interagency feud. It's over. Let's chalk it up to a miscommunication and move on. Fighting amongst ourselves only plays into Doyle's hand and distracts us from finding and arresting him for the murders of Max Sanborn and Boinet."

"You're right, of course. For a moment, I allowed my anger at MI5—" His hands curled at his sides, and his features were set in hard lines. "—justified, though it may be, to cloud my judgment." He took a deep breath. "We move on. Longdon, did you get those papers from your aunt?"

For the first time since walking in the door that evening, Gregory's face broke into a broad grin. "I did indeed, Oliver. I only had time to go through one file, but if the rest of it is as damning, it will only be a matter of time before we snare Doyle. To catch a criminal, you have to follow the treasure—"

"I suppose it takes a criminal to catch a criminal," Finch murmured, eliciting a smirk from Burnell.

"—in this case, the looted Nazi art," Gregory went on as if the sergeant hadn't spoken. "There's some mention in the files of Max storing some of his pieces in a warehouse in a Geneva freeport."

Emmeline scooted to the edge of the sofa. She rested her elbows on her knees and her chin on her hands. He had aroused her curiosity. "Progress at last. What's a freeport?"

"Essentially, they're tax-exempt storage depots where wealthy collectors like Max stow many of their treasures for an unlimited period of time."

"Their treasures *and* their dirty secrets," Burnell said.

Gregory tapped the side of his nose and winked at the superintendent. "Undoubtedly. My position at Symington's will make it easier for me to follow up on Max's freeport. I'll get onto it straightaway in the morning."

Three pairs of eyes stared at him. It was still strange for them to come to terms with the fact that Gregory actually *worked* for a living. What was even stranger still was that Symington's had hired him as its chief investigator in the first place.

"Yes? Any objections to my plan?"

"No. No, not all." Burnell waved a hand at him. "You carry on."

"I'll see if I can find anything out from my contacts. I'll also speak to Philip again. He may be able to grease the diplomatic wheels in light of this new information," Emmeline said.

"Good idea. This is Acheson's milieu. He'll know which rocks to poke his nose under. We'll exchange notes in the afternoon. But darling—"

"Yes?" she responded warily. She had a feeling she knew what was coming next.

Those cinnamon eyes of his shot a stern look in her direction. "Don't, and I repeat don't, go off on your own to chase any lead. Especially after what's happened tonight. Do I make myself clear?"

She knew it. She *didn't* like what he had to say. After all, she was a professional and not a child.

She flashed a sweet smile at him. "Of course. I'm surprised you feel the need to caution me. You know that I never take any unnecessary risks."

The two detectives exchanged looks with Gregory and snorted.

Emmeline crossed her arms over chest and tossed her head in the air. *Men*, she thought to herself. *They're always so smug and full of their own opinions.*

"There's no need to look at me like that."

"Like what?"

"Oh, you know, all superior and hoity-toity."

A laugh bubbled up from Gregory's throat as he took her hand in his and brushed her knuckles with a kiss. "Darling, you forget that you're not talking to strangers. We are intimately acquainted with your past escapades."

She snatched her hand away and jumped to her feet. "Escapades?" There was a dangerous edge to her voice. "I will not have you, any of you—" Her dark gaze singed the three men with her anger as it swept over them. "—sitting here in my living room diminishing my work. My job is to find the truth. And I'm damn good at my job."

Gregory reached out a hand and pulled her down next to him again. He took her face in both hands. His voice was low and tender. "No one is disputing that fact. All of us are in awe of your many talents. We just want you to be safe and to live another day so that you can continue to right the world's wrongs. No slights were intended, darling." He kissed her forehead.

This mollified her somewhat.

"Longdon's right," Burnell concurred. "All of us would like you to take greater care of yourself."

"Yes, admirable though your dedication may be," Finch chimed in, "in your search for the truth, you often forget about your own safety."

Emmeline stared at each of them in turn as she swallowed the lump that had lodged in her throat. "Well—" It was a hoarse croak and then in a stronger voice, she said, "—that's put me in my place, hasn't it? I apologize for jumping to conclusions and losing my temper. I appreciate your concern and have taken your warnings to heart. I promise I will be more careful from now on."

"Good girl." Gregory squeezed her hand. "That's all we ask. It's a bit selfish on my part because if anything happened to you, I would have Maggie pounding on my door. demanding to discuss wedding arrangements. I would rather boil in oil."

Emmeline swatted his arm, but she was smiling. "Beast."

They all laughed, but the light mood instantly dissipated when the doorbell rang. Emmeline's body tensed.

Burnell jerked his head. "Finch, go see what that's about."

The superintendent, Emmeline, and Gregory waited in silence. They heard Finch speaking in low tones with another man. And then the sergeant said, "You'd better come inside and tell him yourself."

Two seconds later, Finch and Inspector Parker appeared in the doorway.

"Tell me what?" Burnell demanded in clipped tones.

"Sir, it's about Crichlow—"

The superintendent groaned and rolled his eyes. "What the devil has that fellow gotten up to now?"

"Not a lot. He's been murdered. Strangled in his car in the next road over."

"And here I was dreaming of a quiet evening at home with a good book and a glass of brandy."

❧❧❧

Loathe though she was to admit it, even to herself, the events of the previous evening had her rattled. However, she put on a brave face for Gregory, Superintendent Burnell, and Sergeant Finch. Worrying about her was a complication they didn't need.

Besides, she was determined not to give Doyle the satisfaction of believing that he had succeeded in frightening her. Although, he had. He was patiently waiting for the perfect moment to strike. The moment when he could cause the most damage. This sent a frisson down her spine.

Right, she thought as she squared her shoulders and sat up straighter. *That's quite enough of that. This is no time to be maudlin.*

"Miss Kirby, are you all right?" Pamela asked.

"What? Yes, I'm fine. Perfectly fine and I intend to remain that way. No one is going to frighten me."

Pamela gave her an odd look, but replied, "Bully for you. It most certainly will not do to let the other side see that they've gotten under your skin."

Emmeline nodded her head. "Exactly."

The phone buzzed on the secretary's desk. She answered it, listened for a second, and then replaced the receiver. "Mr. Acheson will see you now."

"Thanks." Emmeline rose and saw herself inside.

"My dear girl." Philip came out from around the desk and crossed the room to greet her. He bent down to give her a peck on the cheek. "Are you all right?" he asked as he led her by the elbow to the leather sofa in the corner.

"I'm fine." His eyes narrowed and scoured every inch of her face. "Really. A bit anxious, perhaps, but overall I'm fine. The same can't be said for poor Crichlow."

Philip sat opposite her in the wing chair and poured a cup of tea for her. "Yes, I had Burnell and Longdon and Vill—" He had been about to say Villiers, but caught himself at the last moment. "—they rang this morning and brought me up to date. What can I do to help?"

Emmeline took a sip of tea and perched on the edge of the sofa. "I'm sure Gregory told you about the files from Mireille that detailed Max's art collection and the Geneva freeport. He was going to check on that angle, but perhaps your Foreign Office and…other connections could help us to find the information faster."

Philip leaned back and crossed one leg over the other. "I'll see what I can do, but you know the Swiss and their secrecy laws. It might prove difficult cracking that particular nut."

"You could throw your weight about a bit. Rattle a few cages, so to speak. I'm sure that someone somewhere owes you a favor or two."

Philip chuckled. "Did anyone ever tell you that you can be quite persistent?"

"Not in such a polite manner, but the general sentiment was there. It's the only way to get to the truth."

"Indeed it is."

"Now, I thought I'd try to track down Doyle from a different angle. But I'll need your help."

"Anything. I'm at your disposal."

"We all seem to have forgotten that after the war Doyle readily agreed to help identify and give evidence against his Nazi comrades. In hindsight, we know that this was merely a ruse to dupe Her Majesty's Government until he could disappear without a trace. Over the ensuing decades, a stream of conflicting rumors floated about over whether he was alive or dead. But this is a government built upon layer upon layer of bureaucracy. There has to be a file, a recording—*something*—buried in MI5's dusty ancient vaults. You must at least be able to tell me who his control officer was—and, hopefully, allow me to peek at his files. They can no longer be bound by the thirty years rule."

Philip's brow furrowed, and he pursed his lips. "That's a rather tall order. I'll—I'll have to get back to you on that request. It's not up to me. Protocol, you understand."

Emmeline carefully set her cup and saucer down on the coffee table and stood up. "Yes, of course. I just thought I'd ask. I wouldn't want you to get into any trouble. But it would be a tremendous help."

Philip rose too and showed her to the door. "As I said, I'll have to ask."

Emmeline touched his arm. "Thanks. Give my love to Maggie. She must be over the moon since Brian decided to turn over the Constable to her family."

"Yes, Brian is a gentleman among gentlemen. And Nigel, too, of course. My wife is a new woman these days. It's all thanks to you and your bulldog tenacity."

She reached up and kissed his cheek. "I don't like the bulldog part, but I'll take the compliment in the spirit that it was intended. I'm glad that I was able to help."

෴

The minute Emmeline had left Philip was on the phone to Villiers. "Emmeline wants to see Doyle's files from after the war. I think it's about time to shine the light on this ugly piece of history and damn the embarrassment. Her Majesty's Government has weathered other scandals. It'll be a few months of negative publicity, and then the whole thing will be a distant memory."

"It's not as simple as that." Villiers's plummy voice was low and smooth.

"Respectfully, sir, that's a load of rubbish. We all know how the system works."

"Even if I were inclined to allow Miss Kirby to see Doyle's files, which I am not—it goes against the grain to have the press rooting around in the archives—there is nothing for her to see."

Philip ran a hand through his hair in confusion. "What do you mean?"

"The files vanished shortly after Baxter, the control officer, died in 1952. Therefore, Doyle remains an enigma for the ages."

"Even as he goes on killing from the shadows. Sir, you do realize that he won't stop until he silences Emmeline? She poses too much of a threat."

"Ah, the delightful Miss Kirby. She's rather an expert at stirring up hornets' nests, isn't she?"

CHAPTER 38

Burnell had his elbows propped up on his desk, his head drooped between his hands. He closed his eyes. Just for a minute. He hadn't slept all night on account of Crichlow's murder.

Such inconsideration was astounding. His eyes felt like sandpaper, and his tongue was like the Sahara. His stomach grumbled its own protest as well. But he simply couldn't will his body to get up and do something about it.

He felt himself drifting off when his telephone rudely started to scream. "Ohh," he moaned as he blindly reached out for the receiver.

With his head resting on his other hand, he mumbled, "Burnell. What do you want?"

"A little civility for a start," Sally's outraged tone grated in his ear.

"Oh, no, not *you*. I am in the deepest depths of hell, after all."

"Superintendent Burnell, if you go on in this vein, I will file a complaint against you."

"Terrific. I can't tell you how that warms the cockles of my heart. Now, what do you want? I've been up all night on a case, and I'm in no mood for your hauteur today. So tell me as quick as you can and ring off."

He heard a sharp intake of breath at the other end of the line. "Why you vile man. No one has ever spoken to me in such an insolent manner before."

Burnell opened his eyes and his mouth curled into a half-smile. "Really? There's a first time for everything."

"You—you," she spluttered.

He wished he could see her face.

"You're beneath contempt." Her voice was like an icy dagger slicing across his eardrum. "I should not have to tolerate such behavior. I am bringing this conversation to an end—"

"That's music to my ears."

"—Assistant Commissioner Fenton wants to see you *at once*." With that, she severed the connection.

Burnell stared at the receiver. He was sure he heard a vindictive snort before she rang off. "And I thought this day couldn't get any worse."

⌀⌀⌀

He shouldn't have done it. After all, Finch was a good lad, loyal to a fault. No complaints about his work. But he did it anyway. Burnell dragged the sergeant with him to see Fenton. If he had to suffer another of the assistant commissioner's diatribes, he wasn't going to do it alone. Let others share in the misery. However, when he slid a glance out of the corner of his eye at Finch, he felt a stab of guilt. He silently vowed to make it up to him somehow.

Fenton was drumming his fingers on his desk. "What's this I hear? You released Brian Sanborn behind my back."

"Sir, the forensic report indicated that he couldn't have killed his father."

"Hmph," Fenton grunted. "He was caught red-handed trying to dispose of the murder weapon."

"Yes," Burnell explained patiently as if he were speaking to someone with a mental deficiency—of which he was convinced Fenton had many. "But his fingerprints did not match those on the letter opener, neither did his brother's."

"That's impossible. The lab must have made a mistake. Have them run the tests again," the assistant commissioner blustered. "Brian was acting extremely suspiciously. He wouldn't even allow me to go through Max's papers."

Burnell cleared his throat. "I believe that's because they contained sensitive information related to Sanborn Enterprises, and he was afraid that it would somehow be leaked to the press. Information that would be detrimental to the company."

"What? The arrogant bastard. Who does he think I am?"

"It's not my place to comment on your relationship with Mr. Sanborn, sir," the superintendent replied circumspectly. *From what I've observed, Brian Sanborn's tastes appear to be very discerning*, he said to himself.

By his side, Finch bit back a smile and quickly arranged his features into a deferential expression.

"Are you having a joke at my expense, Burnell?"

"Me, sir? Perish the thought. I only have the utmost respect for you as an officer and my superior." He smiled but crossed his fingers in his lap. He hoped that he wouldn't have to pay too much for that lie in the next life. *After all, they say that God is merciful*. He was counting on that.

Fenton shot him a dubious look but decided to let it drop. "We'll leave that for the moment. There are a couple of other matters I wanted to discuss with you."

"Are there?" The superintendent tried to muster some enthusiasm, but he was quite certain that he had failed.

"I've heard that a MI5 agent was murdered last night in Miss Kirby's neighborhood."

"Yes, that's correct. An Alan Crichlow. Apparently, he was on Doyle's trail as well. Dr. Meadows said his neck was broken just like the art dealer Maurice Boinet. We're fairly certain that it was Doyle. It has to be."

"I see," Fenton murmured, leaning forward and folding his hands over one another.

"If that's all, sir, as you can imagine we have a lot of work to do." Burnell scrambled to his feet, with Finch following suit.

"Sit down. We're not finished."

Burnell and Finch reluctantly resumed their seats. "We're not?"

"No. I also heard that Longdon has some of Max's files."

"You seem to hear an awful lot that you shouldn't. I'd very

much like to know who the little bird is that is pouring these sweet-nothings in your ear so that I can throttle him or her," the superintendent said under his breath.

"What was that?" Fenton snapped.

"I said that as always you're extremely well informed, sir. Longdon's aunt gave him some of her former husband's files."

"So where are they?"

"I beg your pardon."

"Where are the files? What's in them?"

"I'm afraid we haven't seen them yet. But we're told that they deal with some of the late Mr. Sanborn's art collection. It seems that Mr. Sanborn was well aware of the questionable provenance of a number of his pieces. It didn't concern him in the least. In addition, there's mention of a warehouse at a Geneva freeport. Longdon is going to check out all of that."

"I can't believe my ears. *Longdon* is going to check it out? A known criminal. The lunatics are running the asylum." Fenton slammed his hand on the desk. "Why don't we have those papers? I demand to see all of them. Immediately."

Burnell and Finch exchanged a look. "First of all, much as I hate to admit it, Longdon is Symington's chief investigator and has complete authority to pursue the evidence. Secondly, he is a member of the family. Consequently, Mrs. Sanborn is perfectly within her rights to turn over those papers to another family member."

"But they're evidence in the case. Therefore, they should be in our possession." Fenton looked down his supercilious nose at Burnell with undisguised contempt. "You call yourself a professional. I've never seen such slipshod work in my entire career. Now listen to me—" He wagged a finger at him. "—I want those papers on my desk by tomorrow morning. Otherwise, you're going to find yourself walking a beat again." He glared at Finch. "Both of you."

✀✀✀

Emmeline slammed the receiver back in its cradle. "Blast," she said aloud. She had been convinced that with Philip's help they would be able to find Doyle. But, apparently, open government only went so far. When she returned to the office, an apologetic message awaited her from Philip saying that unfortunately she would *not* be given access to any of Doyle's files. Sorry.

She leaned back in her chair and crossed her arms over her chest, stewing in silence. After a bit, she relented. It was unfair to blame Philip. He was in an untenable position, and she couldn't jeopardize his career. He was probably only following a directive from higher ups. Her mind raced. She had to get her hands on those files. It was the only way to trace Doyle. Everything about this story was buried in the past. Boinet and Max Sanborn were killed because they were greedy and unscrupulous. They had been seduced and tainted by the illicit trade in looted Nazi art. Each in his own way enjoyed thumbing his nose at the authorities. One by smuggling the treasures to salivating collectors and the other smug in the knowledge that he possessed a piece no one else did. Doyle recognized these weaknesses and took advantage of them. All the while, he hovered in the background pulling gossamer strands of silken steel tighter and tighter until Boinet and Max were trapped in his web and there was no way out, except death. Doyle was everywhere and nowhere at the same time. He was always watching, and waiting.

This thought made Emmeline shiver involuntarily. Doyle had made it abundantly clear that he could get to her any time he liked. He had broken into her office. He had followed her home last night, and Crichlow had paid with his life because of it. She sat up straighter in her chair as realization dawned on her. That was no accident yesterday afternoon. She had been deliberately pushed in front of the bus. It's funny how everything became crystal clear through the objective lens of hindsight.

Goose bumps crept up her arms as an icy dread clutched at her heart. Even now, Doyle could be lurking about in the corridors of *The Clarion*, biding his time until he could take her unawares. She got to her feet, suddenly restless. She stalked over to the window and yanked open the Venetian blinds. All she saw was the bustling newsroom. Reporters speaking on the phone, others rushing out to cover a story, editors hunched over copy. Everyone was going about business as usual. Nothing out of the ordinary. She couldn't allow Doyle to unsettle her this way. She couldn't go on looking over her shoulder wondering whether today would be the day that he let loose his revenge on her or those she loved. That was no way to live. And live she would. That was a promise.

Anger had emboldened her and tamped down the fear. But how would she get him? Doyle was a master of deception and had killed anyone who could identify him. There must be something, though. No one was infallible.

A broad smile played around her lips. All official doors were closed to her, so she would simply have to go in through the servants' entrance and hope the element of surprise would be on her side.

She walked back to her desk, pulled out a business card from her handbag, and picked up the phone again. She crossed her fingers that he would be there. One ring. Two rings. On the third ring she heard a slightly breathless voice answer, "Yoav Zielinski speaking."

"Hello, Mr. Zielinski. This is Emmeline Kirby. I hope I haven't caught you at a bad time. I—I need your help."

There was a brief pause. "Ah, Emmeline, I'm delighted to hear from you again. Yes, I'm sure we can come to some sort of arrangement. I will have to check with the ambassador, but I'm fairly certain he would be willing to sit down for short interview within the next week."

Emmeline understood that he couldn't talk freely. "I'm afraid that this is urgent. It's about Doyle. Would it be possible to see you sometime this afternoon? I could meet you anywhere you like."

"Just a moment please." He must have covered the phone with his hand because she heard him having a muffled conversation with someone. Then his voice boomed in her ear loud and clear once more. "I'm sorry about that. As you surmised, I had someone in my office. Unfortunately, I do not think it would be wise for us to meet in public again. After last night, you must know that you're being watched."

"You know about Crichlow." She was not surprised by this fact. He seemed to have antennae everywhere.

"Yes, the news spread very quickly through diplomatic circles. I would like to help you, but my involvement must remain anonymous."

"Then give me something. A name. A date. Anything. I'll take it from there. I won't mention where I got the information. I have to find Doyle before he kills again. You, of all people, should understand."

He was silent for so long that Emmeline thought he had rung off, but at last a weary sigh echoed down the line. "PDK Incorporated. And I have a suggestion. I think your readers might find it interesting if *The Clarion* did a series on London's lost rivers."

Emmeline's brow puckered in confusion. "London's lost rivers? I don't understand."

"I think you will when you start looking into the subject. I would pay particular attention to the River Tyburn. Perhaps, that should be the first story in the series. The River Tyburn is particularly fascinating. It is steeped in history. I know how much you appreciate history."

"All right," she replied dubiously. "Thank you for your help."

"Before you go, I have one more, small piece of advice."

"Yes?"

"Our friend is a serpent. He's cornered and lashing out indiscriminately. All it takes is one bite, and his poisonous venom will kill you in an instant."

Emmeline felt a nervous flutter in the pit of her stomach. "Yes, I know," she whispered hoarsely. "But that's precisely why I have to find him. To stop him. Once and for all."

It was early afternoon before Zielinski had a free moment to himself. He closed the door to his office and placed the call.

"Acheson," Philip answered in his crisp, professional tone.

"Philip, it's Yoav."

"Hello, old chap. What a pleasant surprise. How are you?"

Zielinski couldn't help but smile. Philip was always such a cheerful fellow. To an outsider, their friendship may seem odd, but they shared so many interests and had gotten along from the first moment they had met—what was it now? six years, yes. "I'm fine. But our mutual friend is determined to see this thing through to the end."

"Yes, I know. Believe me, I tried to dissuade her from pursuing this any further. But she's stubborn and won't give up. That's what makes her good at her job. It also puts her in precarious situations."

"That is my greatest concern. She is in over her head. So is Longdon ."

Philip gave a half-hearted laugh. "I'm not surprised you know about Longdon."

"My dear Philip, by now you should realize that I hear a great many things. They are no match for Doyle. Villiers better keep a closer watch on her than he has been."

"He's keeping his cards very close to the vest. I don't know what the man is playing at. He only lets me in when it suits his purposes."

"I can tell you what game Laurence Villiers is playing. He's using our friend as bait. To him, people are expendable. Our friend doesn't deserve to be used in that way. She's an amateur. Please see to it that nothing happens to her. Or Longdon."

"I'm trying my best, Yoav. Believe me."

"You're a good man, but you have to try harder. They're running out of time."

CHAPTER 39

Gregory rapped on Burnell's door and turned the handle without waiting to be bidden.

The superintendent lifted his gaze from his monitor and scowled at him. "I don't remember asking you to come in."

"Didn't you, Oliver? You must have been so engrossed in whatever it is you're studying there on your computer—" He craned his neck to try to sneak a peek, but Burnell flicked the button in the corner, and the screen went black. "—that you forgot your manners. But no need to upset yourself, I forgive you."

He flashed a cheeky smile at the superintendent and lowered himself into the chair opposite.

"I don't need forgiveness from the likes of you. Now, you had better have a very good reason for swanning in here unannounced. If you're only here to make a nuisance of yourself, you can get out."

Gregory clucked his tongue. "Someone is rather tetchy today. Where is the cuddly teddy bear that we all know and love?"

"My patience is wearing thin," he said through gritted teeth. "What. Is. It?"

Gregory was about to counter with another witty riposte, when Finch burst in. "Sorry to interrupt, sir. Oh, it's only you, Longdon," he said when he saw Gregory.

"I rather resent your tone, Finch. It lacks a certain respect."

Finch's warm brown eyes crinkled in the corners. "Does it? I can't imagine why."

"Now, now, old chap. That's not the way to speak to a highly-regarded colleague."

The sergeant snorted. "You must be joking."

"Enough," Burnell shouted. "Longdon, why is it that you seem to irritate everyone around you?"

Gregory smoothed down the corners of his mustache. He gave a wry smile. "Everyone has hidden talents."

Burnell rolled his eyes and turned to Finch. "What is it?"

"Here's the initial report on Crichlow from Dr. Meadows. He knew you wanted to see it right away."

"Good old John. I owe him a pint. I can always rely on him, unlike others who shall remain nameless." He shot a pointed look at Gregory.

"That's rather ungenerous of you, *Oliver*." This earned him an icy blue glare from the superintendent, but he went on, "Here I am a fount of knowledge, and you're treating me like a pariah."

"Spill whatever you've learned, then go. I don't want you hanging about a second longer than is necessary."

Gregory sniffed. "They say chamomile tea is quite soothing. Perhaps, you should try to drink a cup or two a day."

Burnell started drumming his fingers on the desk.

"No?" Gregory asked innocently. "Pity, it was merely a suggestion out of concern for your well-being. I'll try to think of something else to buck you up."

"Longdon," the superintendent roared.

Gregory put up his hands. "All right. I've kept you in suspense long enough. I'm still working on trying to get into Max's warehouse in the Geneva freeport. It's rather tricky. However, I did manage to find a chink in the impenetrable wall of Swiss secrecy."

At this, Burnell leaned forward, and Finch hitched a hip on the desk. "Well?" the superintendent prompted.

"I was able to find out that Max made a number of transfers from his Swiss bank account into one belonging to PDK Incorporated. These transactions were expertly masked and bounced through several dummy corporations before ultimately being deposited. They also occurred within hours of a painting being delivered to Max's freeport."

Burnell rubbed his hands together and exchanged a grin with Finch. "I've always hated coincidences."

Gregory crossed one leg over the other, a smug smile of satisfaction creasing his face. "There I must agree with you. I've always thought coincidences were overrated."

"Good work, Longdon. I must say you came up trumps."

Gregory inclined his head. "Oh, it was nothing. You just have to know what rocks to look under. Besides, what are friends for?"

"You had better quit while you're ahead. Anything else?"

"No, that's it for the moment. I'm going to talk to a few old...associates—"

Burnell raised an eyebrow but didn't comment.

"—to see if they know anything about this PDK Incorporated."

"You do that. If there's nothing else..." The superintendent's voice trailed off.

"Oliver, I get the distinct impression that you're trying to get rid of me."

"No, no. Nothing like that at all. I'm just up to my ears in work." He lifted a stack of papers to emphasize his point.

"Isn't there some rule in Scotland Yard's handbook that policemen are supposed to be honest? Lying doesn't suit you at all, Oliver. There's something you're not telling me." Concern suddenly flooded his eyes. "Is it Emmy? Has something happened to her?" His gaze flickered between the two detectives.

"No," the superintendent said firmly. "She's fine."

Relief washed over Gregory's face. "You had me worried there for a moment. If it's not Emmy, what is it?"

Burnell sighed and stroked his beard. "Someone who is an even bigger nuisance than you."

"Ah, that can only mean one person. Fenton."

The superintendent tapped the side of his nose. "You're brighter than you look."

"So what does the illustrious assistant commissioner want?"

"He wants—no, he *demands*—to see the files your aunt gave you by tomorrow morning."

A laugh rumbled forth from Gregory's chest, as he rose to his feet. "Fenton can go to the devil."

"I was fairly certain that would be your reaction. That's why you had better make yourself scarce. We'll all have hell to pay if hears you were here. It seems he has a mole, who lately has been keeping him abreast about what's been happening in the case. When I find the culprit—and I will, trust me— he or she is going to wish they were dead. I hate disloyalty." He shook his head in disgust.

"I'm inured to Fenton's threats. They simply bounce off. Shall I pop in now to have a little chat with him to set him straight?"

"*No*," Burnell thundered. "Have you flipped your lid? Don't go anywhere near him."

Gregory chuckled as he crossed to the door. He turned back with his hand on the knob. "Oliver, you take things much too seriously. You need to relax more. Stress is not good for your ulcer. I'll let you know if I find out anything new on PDK Incorporated or Doyle. In the meantime, tell Fenton to keep his nose out of things that are none of his concern."

He waggled his fingers at them and then was gone.

"Relax he says. Ha. How can I relax when I have him in one corner and Fenton in the other?"

∽∾∽

That evening, Emmeline prepared spaghetti Bolognese, and Gregory brought a bottle of Montepulciano d'Abruzzo. Over dinner in her cozy kitchen, they shared what they had each learned.

"Hmm, all roads do lead to Rome, in this case, PDK Incorporated. The company is hidden under so many layers that I wasn't able to find out who owns it. Did you have any luck?" she asked.

He shook his head. "No, none at all."

"It has to be Doyle. I just know it. Otherwise, why all the secrecy?"

"Darling, I think you're being a little over-eager. There could be all sorts of reasons that a company would want to keep its leadership a secret."

"Really? Name one. You can't, can you?"

"I can if—"

"Never mind. There's no point arguing over it. Maybe Philip can help us. No, scratch that. Philip is only allowed to dole out select pieces of information, which is useless. I have a contact at the Financial Services Authority. Perhaps if I have a quiet word with him, he can provide some dirt on PDK. There has to be something. An international company can't be operated by ghosts. Someone has to sign the checks and make the decisions."

"Once we find the paper trail, it will lead us to the top man or woman. Now let's put that aside for the moment, tell me about the other curious tip that your source gave you. London's lost rivers? I can't make heads or tails of it. Were you able to read between the lines?"

She rested her chin on her hand and gave him a triumphant smile. "As a matter of fact, that turned out to be the easier clue—if you can call it that—of the two. I admit that I was initially skeptical. However, the River Tyburn is a topic worthy of an article in *The Clarion*, which is going to appear in tomorrow's edition by the way. But let me give you some brief background information. The Tyburn is really an ancient stream that begins in Hampstead, flows under Regent's Park, through Marylebone, Mayfair, and under Oxford Street. It crosses Piccadilly and into Green Park. It flows deep under the grounds of Buckingham Palace, before curving east through St. James's Park, splitting into two and ultimately emptying into the Thames. It once branched out to form Thorney Island on which Westminster Abbey was built. Originally, the Tyburn was used as a source of fresh water and later became a sewer. Today, it flows through a brick tunnel."

"Emmy, this walk through history is absolutely riveting, but I really don't see how it brings us any closer to catching Doyle."

She sniffed. "And you accuse me of being impatient. Just bear with me for a few moments longer. The fact that the Tyburn flows under Buckingham Palace is significant because in 1963 the IRA attempted to plant a bomb in the tunnel. But the plot was foiled at the last minute because MI5 received a tip from an informant. Naturally, the whole incident was hushed up. However, not long afterward, the informant disappeared from the witness protection program and was never seen alive again."

"Let me guess. Our friend Doyle was the mastermind behind the plot."

Her smile grew wider, and she reached out to caress his cheek. "I knew there was a sharp intellect lurking behind that handsome face of yours."

He kissed her fingertips. "Much as I love you, darling, I can see that devious mind of yours is racing, and it's making me rather nervous. What have you done?"

"There's no need to look at me like that. My article provides a thorough account of the Tyburn's rich history from ancient times to the present. I think readers will be most interested, and incensed, by the bit about the attempt to blow up Buckingham Palace, don't you?"

Gregory's grip tightened on her fingers, and the lines of his face were etched with concern. "Emmy, this is not a game. Doyle already has tried to silence you, forever. Or have you forgotten that? It was irresponsible to taunt him like that."

She pulled her hand away. "Don't lecture me. How else were we going to draw him out into the open? It's about time someone stood up to him and rattled his cage. If he's angry and feels threatened, he'll make a mistake, and then will get him."

"Unless he gets to you first. And then you'll vanish without a trace like that long-ago informant."

CHAPTER 40

The next morning, Nigel had half the Sanborn Enterprises board in his office grumbling, quite vociferously, about Emmeline's article and her work in general.

"It's disgraceful," Harold O'Shaugnessy complained. "First, it was her shameless crusade against your father on behalf of her friend and her insinuations about his ties to the IRA. Now, this—" He waved today's edition of the paper in Nigel's face. "—something must be done about her. She has to be muzzled. This cannot be allowed to go on. She's going to make us a laughingstock."

"Exactly," Hawthorne chimed in. "It is unnecessary for her to rock the boat. She's no better than those loonies who stand on a soapbox on Speaker's Corner and shout out their list of grievances to the world. As if the rest of us care what they have to say. No, we can't have this. Emmeline Kirby should be sacked."

There were a few mumbled "Here, heres" in response.

"What do you expect?" Winterbottom said. "Like all Jews, she has a persecution complex and an ax to grind with the world at large."

"Is she Jewish?" Kildare asked, his green eyes widening in disbelief.

Winterbottom nodded.

"I didn't know that, but it explains a great deal. No wonder she was so quick to champion Maggie Roth's cause with that damned Constable painting."

"They're all the same. Money-grubbing. Out for whatever they can get their greedy hands on. She's a troublemaker pure and simple. She's got to go. Nigel, you're the lawyer. There must be some loophole you can find in her contract to get rid of her."

Taylor was nodding vigorously and was about to offer his own opinion on this matter, but he was checked by Nigel, who stood up and raised his voice to be heard over the din. "Gentlemen, gentlemen, although I use that term loosely in view of the present company. I can't believe my ears." His eyes roamed around the room. "I'm utterly shocked by the vile and ugly things I've just heard spewing from your mouths."

"Oh, come off it, Nigel," O'Shaugnessy said. "Don't be blind. The evidence is right in front of your eyes, just open them."

"You're right about that, Harold. My eyes have been rudely opened. All these years, I stood in the same room with all of you and was completely unaware that you were anti-Semitic, racist, and God knows what else. I can tell you right now Emmeline Kirby will *not* be sacked. She is doing a splendid job with *The Clarion*. Absolutely first rate. Brian and I couldn't be more pleased with her. She has our complete and unequivocal support. I'd like to remind you that we, as the family, own the largest block of stock and therefore have the greatest say in how Sanborn is run. Of course, you are well within your rights to disagree with us. In that case, I—and I know I speak for Brian as well—expect you to tender your resignations from the board immediately. We cannot have divisive internal squabbles. Such views will *never* be tolerated here."

Hawthorne, Brooks, and Taylor left the office without another word.

O'Shaugnessy and Winterbottom, though, would not let the matter die quietly. "I'm certain Max is turning over in his grave," O'Shaugnessy said.

"You've allowed them to brainwash you. It's that simple," Winterbottom added.

Nigel curled his fists into tight balls at his sides. "Please leave my office. I want all of you out of my sight. *Now.*"

O'Shaugnessy snorted but turned on his heel and crossed to the door. Winterbottom's upper lip curled back in disgust. He looked as if he wanted to say something, but changed his mind. What was the use? Kildare hung back leaning on his cane and silently scrutinizing Nigel, who didn't blink. Kildare gave a pitying shake of his head and reached out for the door. As he opened it, there stood Emmeline, caught unexpectedly with her hand in the air preparing to knock.

"Oh, excuse me, Mr. Kildare," she mumbled and stepped aside to allow him to pass.

His green eyes narrowed and locked on her face. However, she squared her shoulders and stared back at him defiantly. He glanced back over his shoulder at Nigel and shook his head again before rudely brushing past Emmeline.

Finally, they were all gone. *Thank God*, Nigel thought. He was so angry his hands were trembling. He wished that they would all burn in the deepest, darkest corner of hell.

"I'm terribly sorry. I get the impression that I've interrupted something," Emmeline said, her brow furrowing in concern.

"What?" Nigel suddenly realized that he had been standing there staring at the closed door. "No, no." He sank heavily back down into his chair and gestured for her to take the seat opposite. "Frankly, I'm quite glad that you appeared when you did. Otherwise, I was about to commit murder." He gave her a lopsided smile.

"As bad as that." She nodded. "Then I'm glad I saved you. We've had quite enough murders around here lately."

"Indeed we have. Now, what did you want to discuss?"

"Actually, I was wondering if perhaps you might be able to help me. It's about the Doyle story."

Nigel leaned forward, propped his elbows on his desk, and folded his hands. He listened intently as she brought him up to date on what they had discovered about Max's warehouse in the Geneva freeport and the transfers of money to PDK Incorporated that coincided with his father's acquisition of each new piece of art in recent years.

She also voiced her suspicions that PDK was a shell company and that they would find Doyle pulling the strings in the background.

He sighed wearily. With every detail that had emerged about his father's shady dealings, Nigel had grown more and more ashamed. He knew Brian felt the same way, perhaps even more so since he was the eldest and felt the weight of responsibility on his shoulders.

"So what can I do?"

"I was hoping that as a member of the family and the corporate counsel you might be able to let me see your father's records."

"Done. You have *carte blanche*. I'll call Angela and tell her to pull any of Dad's files that you think you'll need. Although, now that I come to think of it, this PDK Incorporated sounds familiar. I'm certain I've come across it somewhere before."

Emmeline scooted to the edge of her chair, a spark of eagerness lighting up her dark eyes. "Have you? Think, Nigel. In what context have you seen it? Was it a contract that you drew up?"

She held her breath as his brows knit together in concentration. But after a moment he shook his head. "No, it's no good I'm afraid."

Emmeline was crestfallen and couldn't keep the shadow of disappointment from flitting across her face.

"Look, I'll go through all of my files and let you know if I find anything, all right?"

She rose to her feet and smiled. "That would be very helpful. Thanks. In the meantime, I'll push on with my articles. I'll check in with Superintendent Burnell to see if he can tell me anything else about Crichlow's murder. I think Doyle overplayed his hand. He's running scared. Sooner or later, he's going to make a mistake."

Nigel reached out and grabbed her wrist. "You know that you have my and Brian's complete support. But you're treading a very fine line. Doyle is just waiting for you to make one small slip. He's a cold-blooded killer, and he's gone to great lengths to eliminate anyone who could identify him. I wouldn't want to see anything happen to you. He's already come after you and your family. Please don't give him another chance. Your life is not worth a story."

Emmeline felt tears prick her eyelids. *No*, she was not going to give in to fear. How could she live with herself if she did?

She cleared her throat. "I'm touched by your concern. But I'm a grown woman, and I can take care of myself. If I drop this story, Doyle wins. That's unacceptable."

Nigel blinked and watched as she slipped from his office, her every step imbued with quiet determination. Then he whispered, "But, my dear Emmeline, we all lose if you die."

ფ

Philip folded his copy of *The Clarion* and tossed it to the side. He had reread Emmeline's article on the River Tyburn and the failed IRA plot to blow up Buckingham Palace. There was only one reason why she would write the article now. Somehow she must have gotten wind that Doyle was behind it, and she was sending him a message. To draw him out. To let him know that she wouldn't stop.

Philip got to his feet and stalked over to the window. He pulled back the curtain and looked down at King Charles Street without really seeing anything. Thoughts were chasing themselves across his mind. He let the curtain drop back into place and rubbed his neck in frustration. Emmeline was playing a dangerous game, and there was nothing he could do because bloody Villiers had tied his hands. Yoav was right. Villiers was using her as bait.

Philip paced back and forth. He couldn't sit by idly. His conscience wouldn't allow it. Not only that, Maggie would murder him if she found out. At least she was well out of things for the moment. He silently patted himself on the back for insisting that she go down to the country to be with the boys and his parents. She needed a bit of rest after the strain of the past week. So that only left Emmeline to worry about. *And Longdon*, he added grudgingly.

Longdon, he shook his head. *If anyone embodied the word enigma, it was him.* He still couldn't trust the man. What did Emmeline see in him? He was smug. He was arrogant. He was a criminal. And what was his connection to Villiers? Longdon left a trail of questions with no answers. However, Philip didn't have time for Longdon now. He had to find Doyle before he went after Emmeline, *again.*

Philip went to the desk and picked up his phone. He called a friend of his down in Research and explained that he needed to see Agent Michael Baxter's 1945-1947 debriefings of an Irish Nazi collaborator named Doyle, anything and everything. Without explicitly saying so, he gave the impression that this was on Villiers's orders. As an afterthought, he decided to kill two birds with one stone and requested information on a Gregory Longdon or Toby Crenshaw as well. He stressed that time was of the essence. *Tick, tock, tick, tock,* his mind screamed. And a matter of life and death.

CHAPTER 41

S ir, I think you'll want to see this," Sergeant Finch said as he walked into Burnell's office late that afternoon.

The superintendent's ears immediately perked up at Finch's tone. "What is it?" he asked as he extended his hand to take the file.

The only sound that could be heard in the room for several minutes was the crackle of paper as Burnell flipped pages. He took his glasses off and leaned back in his chair.

"Harold O'Shaugnessy is the head of PDK Incorporated. Why does that name ring a bell? I've heard it somewhere recently."

"He's on the board of directors at Sanborn Enterprises."

Burnell snapped his fingers and sat up. "That's right. Weasly-looking old duffer. Balding, bloodshot eyes, a paunch."

Finch nodded. "That's the one. Do you think he could be Doyle? He looks more of a drunk to me."

"Maybe he's hiding his light under a bushel. Or perhaps it's an act to throw off suspicion. Since we started this case, I've learned never to underestimate Doyle. He's cunning fiend."

"If O'Shaugnessy is Doyle, it would explain how he was able to stay one step ahead of us. Do you want me to bring him in for questioning?"

Burnell stood up and started rolling down his sleeves. "No, let's go pay an unexpected visit on Mr. O'Shaugnessy and see what he has to say for himself."

❧❧❧

Emmeline pressed the heel of her palms to her eyes. They felt dry and scratchy. She was sitting at Max's desk with a sheaf of papers in front of her. She had been scouring his files for two hours trying to find any mention of PDK Incorporated. But Max must have kept the records of his illicit business dealings somewhere else. It was frustrating, but not surprising. Max Sanborn was no fool. Still, she had hoped that she could find some link to PDK Incorporated.

She glanced at her watch and pushed herself to her feet. She had a deadline. She had to revise her update on Crichlow's murder for tomorrow's paper. She straightened the stack of papers and left them for Angela. The secretary wasn't in the outer office, so she scribbled a quick note asking her to pull all of Max's expense reports for the last two years. She knew she was grasping at straws, but perhaps the invoices might elicit a clue. Then she hurried out to the lift and took it down to the newsroom floor.

Emmeline checked in with Gordon Foster to go over a few points on his article about rumors of a Cabinet reshuffle and then spoke to the deputy editor about pulling a story because she felt it needed more corroboration. She wanted to make certain all the facts were correct before they went to press.

Once that was out of the way, she went to her office and banged out her revisions in twenty minutes. She also went over the layout for tomorrow's paper. Seasoned journalist that she was, she did these tasks by rote. But the problem of Doyle loomed large in her mind. She could almost feel him hovering over her shoulder. He seemed to know her every move even before she made it. How? He was obviously following her. But there was more to it than that. Her eyes widened as a thought struck her. *Doyle was someone she knew.* Someone here at Sanborn Enterprises. Someone who didn't arouse suspicions. Someone who was always around. Someone who could roam the corridors freely.

The heavy hand of cold fear settled in her chest, and she nearly jumped out of her skin, when there was light tap at her door. But it was only Frank from the mailroom with her post. He murmured a few pleasantries, handed her the post and was gone. She exhaled a long, slow breath. Becoming paranoid was only going to addle her mind. *This is exactly what Doyle is counting on*, she told herself. *He wants you off balance and vulnerable.*

Right. Emmeline straightened her spine. *You have to think clearly.* She drummed her fingers impatiently, trying to jog her mind to work faster. There had to be something that she had missed about Doyle? About PDK? PDK was the key. Max Sanborn transferred funds to the company. She was sure if they dug a little deeper they would link PDK to Boinet's art gallery as well, probably through a subsidiary or shell company. But *where* was the link? She slammed her fist on the desk. That's when her eye caught a glimpse of Sanborn Enterprises' glossy annual report beneath her fingers, and something suddenly clicked. PDK. They were initials. Of course. Doyle had been hiding in plain sight all these years. What a fool she had been. She had known all along but hadn't made the connection. Her pulse started racing. *If she was right.*

With trembling fingers, she pulled the annual report toward her. She took a deep breath and flipped to the last page where all the corporate officers and the board of directors were listed. And there it was large as life. PDK. She had found Doyle: IRA commander, Nazi collaborator, *murderer*.

She clamped a hand over her mouth to suppress the nervous laughter rising to her lips. She reached for the phone. She had to tell Gregory. She dialed and waited. Damn. His voicemail. Where was he? She severed the connection.

She had to tell someone. She tried Superintendent Burnell, but was told he was out on a case. She left a message to have him call her as soon as he returned to the Yard.

Bloody men, she thought. *It was fine for them to tell you to be careful and not to take risks, but where were they when you needed them? Nowhere.*

She would never hear the end of it if she went after Doyle alone. But she couldn't just sit here and do nothing. She had to tell someone. Someone who could arrest Doyle.

Philip. She crossed her fingers. *Please be there. Please.*

The phone barely rang once. "Acheson."

"Oh, Philip, thank God you're still at the office."

"Emmeline? Is anything the matter?" he asked anxiously.

"No, on the contrary. I couldn't get in touch with Gregory or Superintendent Burnell. That's why I'm ringing you. I know who Doyle is, and I—"

The line went dead.

A large male hand yanked the phone from her grasp. Emmeline's heart skipped a beat as a pair of very green eyes beamed triumphantly down at her. A killer's eyes. Doyle's eyes.

CHAPTER 42

"E mmeline? Emmeline?" Philip screamed into the phone. He stood up so quickly that his chair nearly toppled back.

Only the annoying buzzing of a severed connection echoed in his ear. "Damn and blast," he swore.

He ran a hand through his blond hair distractedly and picked up the phone again. The only thing he said when Villiers finally answered was, "Doyle has Emmeline Kirby."

There was an excruciatingly long pause. "Ah, I was rather afraid it would come to something like that."

Philip exploded, "Then why the bloody hell did you drop her into it? You knew she would never give up until she found him. You're always pulling strings. Always playing with people's lives. *With Emmeline's life.*"

"Pull yourself together, Acheson. This simply won't do. We can't let our emotions get the better of us."

Philip clenched his fist at his side and replied through gritted teeth, "Sir, respectfully, this is no time to quibble. We have to find Emmeline. That's all that counts."

"Naturally, old chap," Villiers replied smoothly. "I'll be at your office in half an hour. I have an idea where Doyle may have taken her. In the interim, call Special Branch and have a unit mobilized."

ာ

"Well, that was a wasted trip," Burnell said, his voice laced with disgust.

"Yes, sir. O'Shaugnessy is a doddering fool who doesn't know his right hand from his left."

"Ha. That's putting it politely. O'Shaugnessy's president of PDK Incorporated in name only. You saw him for yourself. He can't even read a balance sheet without instructions. He's just a figurehead. Doyle makes all the decisions from the shadows. This is Doyle's doing. He's led us on a merry chase."

"So we're back to where we started."

Burnell sighed and lowered himself heavily into his chair. "Yes. And no closer to catching Doyle. There's got to be something we missed."

There was a light tap on the door, and then Gregory entered. "Hello, chaps," he said jovially.

Burnell groaned and leaned his head against the back of his chair. "No, no, no. It's too much for one man to take in one day. Go away, Longdon."

"But I come bearing gifts."

Reluctantly, Burnell sat up and rested his elbows on his desk as he rubbed his temples. "Make it quick. We've already wasted half the afternoon on a wild goose chase thanks to Doyle."

Gregory unbuttoned his suit jacket and took the seat opposite. "As you will know from reading Emmy's article on the River Tyburn in this morning's paper, in the mid-nineteenth century it was fully buried in an underground brick tunnel. Today, it's officially known as the King's Scholars' Pond Sewer and runs directly underneath Buckingham Palace. It is three meters in diameter at that point."

"Is there a point to this?"

"Oliver, patience is a virtue that you are sorely lacking." This earned him a scowl, which he answered with a smile. "If you promise there won't be any more rude interruptions, I will continue my story. In April 1963, several cracks were discovered in tunnel, and there were concerns about its structural integrity. Its proximity to the palace prompted calls for immediate repairs. After an open bidding process, an engineering firm was awarded the contract for the work. It was a Swiss firm, whose work had garnered accolades all over Europe and especially in Germany. The firm was Irisch Engineering Limited. It took six months to complete the repairs and to reinforce the tunnel and its many side channels. It's funny that only two short months after the work had been completed, Doyle and his band of thugs tried to blow up the palace via the sewer."

Burnell sat bolt upright in his chair and exchanged a look with Finch.

"Ah, I'm gratified to see that I have your full attention at last. Now, time to connect the dots. Irisch Engineering is but one subsidiary of a much larger multinational company. I'll wager you can't guess who owns Irisch Engineering."

"PDK Incorporated," Finch said matter-of-factly.

"Bravo, Sergeant. Got it in one. By the way, in case your German is a little rusty, Irisch in German means Irish."

Burnell's face broke out into a wide grin. "The conniving bugger. Good work, Longdon."

"But, sir, the fact that we can link Doyle to the 1963 plot doesn't bring us any closer to catching him now that we've eliminated O'Shaugnessy as a potential suspect."

The superintendent's eyes clouded over as he was once again confronted with this reality. He sighed heavily.

"O'Shaugnessy? Do you mean Harold O'Shaugnessy, that pompous idiot on the Sanborn board?" Gregory asked.

"That's the one." Burnell briefly told him about their discovery that O'Shaugnessy was listed as president of PDK Incorporated and their subsequent—fruitless—interview with him.

"I could have told you that you'd be wasting your time. The only reason that twit is on the board of Sanborn is because his cousin is well known in government circles and asked Max to find a place for him in exchange for future favors. It was strictly a quid pro quo arrangement. O'Shaugnessy drinks and gambles. About seven years ago, he got into a spot of bother that had to be hushed up by Max and his cousin. O'Shaugnessy is incapable of tying his own shoes let alone devising bomb plots."

"Doyle is probably laughing his head off. He killed Maurice Boinet alias Tim Clarke, Max Sanborn, and Crichlow right under our very noses, and we can't find him. Even PDK Incorporated is turning out to be a dead end. Doyle could walk through my office door right now, and I wouldn't even know him."

Gregory's eyes widened as a memory that had been lodged in the back of his mind suddenly struck him full force. He slapped his thigh and jumped to his feet. "Of course. The arrogant bastard told us. We just weren't paying attention."

"What are you on about?" Burnell asked.

Gregory pressed his palms on the desk and fixed his gaze on the superintendent's face. "Oliver, Doyle is Patrick Kildare."

"*What*? You mean Mrs. Fenton's uncle. The old man who hobbles around with a cane."

Gregory nodded. "He's a Sanborn board member. He has free access to any part of the building. That's how he was able to get into Emmy's office so easily to look for that photo of himself from the war. The only known photo of him."

"I think he's on to something, sir," Finch added. "That's why when I conducted my interviews no one in the newsroom saw a *stranger* entering or leaving Emmeline's office. No one would have given a second thought if they saw a Sanborn board member wandering about."

Burnell was on his feet now as well. "This is a bloody nightmare. So far it's still supposition on our part."

Gregory cocked his head to one side and gave him a pointed look. "Come on. What more do you need?"

"Evidence. That's what I need. I can't go knock on Fenton's door and say, 'Oh, sir, you know we've identified Doyle. He just happens to be your wife's uncle.' He'll throw me out on my ear and probably come up with a few charges. I need hard evidence."

"But, Oliver—" The shrill peal of the telephone cut off whatever Gregory had been about to say.

The superintendent snatched the receiver. "Burnell," he shouted. "Oh, hello, Philip." He was silent for several minutes as he listened intently. Two vertical lines formed between his eyes as his brows knit together. His face flushed a deep crimson beneath his beard.

"*What?*" he exploded. "How long ago?" He paused and then said, "Right, we're on our way. I'll have a unit on standby." He slammed the phone down.

Gregory felt a flutter in the pit of his stomach. He didn't like the look on the superintendent's face. "Oliver, what did Acheson want?"

"Doyle has Emmeline."

ↄ⌀ↄↄ⌀ↄ

Emmeline shivered in her thin summer dress as Kildare dragged her along deeper and deeper into the murky depths of the brick tunnel. He was very strong. In fact, his strength quite surprised her. His cane was nowhere to be seen, neither was his limp. His infirmity and his English accent like the rest of his carefully constructed persona were just an act.

He must have drugged her because she certainly would not have come willingly to this black hole of hell. Her ribs ached from where he had kicked her ten minutes ago to unceremoniously wake her from her stupor.

In the wavering light of the torch's beam, she got a glimpse of black slime smeared on the walls. She didn't dare look at the ground. It was bad enough feeling something cold sloshing around her ankles. She didn't really want to know what it was. And the smell…well, that was too offensive to even contemplate.

Kildare grunted as she tried to resist. His fingers only bit deeper into the fleshy part of her underarm. She gritted her teeth against the scream bubbling in her throat. She would not give him the satisfaction. But she would get out of here. She was *not* going to die in this forgotten world. This lost river. She was going to fight until there was no longer a breath left in her body.

"Your time is running out. You do realize that, don't you, *Doyle*? Or do you prefer Patrick?"

The back of his hand flew out and caught her on the temple. She saw stars for a few seconds and thought she was going to faint. But she didn't. And she wouldn't.

She licked her lips and cleared her throat. "If I figured out who you are, the others will too."

He stopped and flashed the torch in her eyes, blinding her. She put up her hand to block the light and protect herself if another blow was coming.

"Always sticking your nose in where it doesn't belong. Always asking questions. Well, lass, since you love raking up the past, I'm going to make sure you become intimately acquainted with it."

Goose bumps crept up her bare arms as the clammy dampness of the tunnel seeped into her bones. It was all well and good brazening it out, but when the cold, raw ugliness of death was staring one in the face, fear suddenly became one's sole companion.

೧൭೧

Philip and Villiers were seated side by side on the Chesterfield sofa, hunched over a set of drawings when Pamela showed Gregory and the two detectives into the office.

Gregory's eyes narrowed when he saw Villiers. "I should have known that you were somehow mixed up in this." He stalked over and loomed above the older man. "I warned you that Doyle was a threat to Emmy. But did you do anything? No." He poked Villiers in the chest.

"Steady on, Longdon," Burnell mumbled from somewhere behind him.

Gregory ignored him and continued his barely controlled tirade against Villiers. "You used Emmy like you use everyone else. She was just a pawn in your grand scheme to trap Doyle. You dangled her out there like a carrot on a stick. And now that bastard has her." His voice caught in his throat, and he couldn't speak for a moment. After he collected himself, he said, "If he does anything, *anything at all* to her, I'm going to kill you. I just want you to be clear on that point."

Villiers's face was a mask of inscrutability. Not a muscle moved.

The two men glared at one another. Two pairs of cinnamon eyes locked in a silent duel as two strong wills clashed.

In the end, it was Villiers who was the first to speak. "If you've quite finished with your melodramatic display, we can get down to business." His tone was crisp and matter-of-fact. "I think I know where Doyle has taken your fiancée."

"*Think*? You had better do more than think. This is Emmy's life that we're talking about, and we won't get a second chance if you're wrong."

Philip tapped him on the arm and said gently, "Longdon, we're all just as worried as you are about Emmeline. No one wants her harmed, but we have to put personalities aside and work together."

Gregory stared at him for an instant, his body rigid. Then his natural sangfroid returned. He nodded and clapped Philip on the shoulder.

Philip's lips curled into a half-smile. "There's a good fellow. Now, come here and take a look at this." He motioned toward the drawings laid out on the table in front of Villiers. "These are engineering plans of the River Tyburn, which, as you know, is a sewer today. We believe that Doyle has taken Emmeline down there and intends—" He hesitated for a fraction of a second. "—where he intends to leave her. You see, when the tide comes in, some of the chambers can fill up with water to the roof within half an hour. She'd be swept out with tide and, eventually, into the Thames." He swallowed hard. "That's what we believe happened to Flanagan, the informant who went missing after the 1963 plot was foiled."

His gaze searched Gregory's features, which were set in harsh lines. Although Gregory's complexion took on an ashen pallor, his jaw tightened with resolve.

"Right," was Gregory's rejoinder, "if we know where he is, let's go and get the bugger."

Villiers cleared his throat. "I'm afraid that's out of the question."

A stunned, heavy silence descended upon the room.

Gregory blinked and shook his head. "I beg your pardon. I can't have heard you properly."

"You heard perfectly well," Villiers retorted calmly. "No one is going near that tunnel. It will jeopardize a delicate oper—"

Gregory took a step closer to Villiers. His voice was low and menacing. "Stuff your bloody operations. I've had enough of your cold, detached plotting. We're talking about a woman's life. The only person who is going to be in jeopardy is you, if you stand in my way. I'm going to get Emmy."

Philip and the two detectives were at his side. "No," Burnell said. "We go together."

Villiers sighed with resignation and rose slowly to his feet. "I see that I'm outnumbered." He paused. "Oh, very well, we go."

CHAPTER 43

The sound of rushing water was getting stronger. *It must mean that we're near the entrance to this damn tunnel,* Emmeline reasoned. *And that means the outside world...and help.*

She grasped at this thought and hope surged through every fiber in her body. She *would* get out of here. She *would* see Gregory and Gran again.

She had to distract Doyle somehow. It was vital that she get the torch away from him. Then she could make a break for it. He may be bigger and stronger, but no matter how fit he still was—and he appeared to be very fit indeed—he would never be able to outrun her.

The only problem was there were so many chambers shooting off in different directions she wasn't sure which one would lead her to safety. What if she took the wrong one and it brought her back to where she started? A shiver slithered down her spine as she tried to banish this thought before it fully took hold.

She dragged her feet, forcing Doyle to slow his pace. She tried to shake off his arm, but his vice-like grip remained firmly in place. There was nothing for it. She took a deep breath and dipped her head down at a slight angle. She used all the momentum her body could muster and aimed her shoulder toward his rib cage.

Caught off guard, Doyle tottered for a second and then they came crashing down together with a splash. Emmeline recovered first. Her hand groped around wildly in the foul-smelling water for the torch. Warm tears pricked her eyelids when at last she felt its hard form beneath her fingers. She seized it and used the slime-covered walls to scramble to her feet.

Doyle was groaning behind her, but he was already struggling to get up. Adrenaline gave her renewed strength. She lashed out, landing a blow on the back of his skull. He went down like a sack of potatoes.

Blood thundered in her ears and her heart hammered against her chest, but she ran toward the sound of the water—and life.

She'd only gone a couple of hundred yards when she became disoriented. Was the gurgling coming from in front of her? Or was it to her right? Or should she have taken that chamber to her left? It was difficult to tell. The sounds bounced off the tunnel walls every which way. Her mind was suddenly seized by pure, blind panic.

She turned on her heel to go back but stumbled into something large and very solid. A man. With a nine millimeter Beretta aimed straight at her heart. The scream was ripped from her throat when the torch slipped from her hand, plunging everything into darkness.

ତ∙ଡ଼∙ତ

"This way," Gregory yelled. "That was Emmy."

Philip, Burnell, and Finch were close on his heels with Special Branch officers not far behind.

"Easy, Longdon," Burnell called out to him. "We don't want to alarm him. We don't want him to do anything rash."

Over his shoulder, Gregory shot back, "Alarm him? I'm going to murder him."

"So much for appealing to his common sense," the superintendent murmured as he huffed to keep up.

Gregory stopped short when they encountered Villiers and a group of tactical officers coming from the opposite direction. They met at the halfway point of the tunnel. "Where's Emmy?" he asked, his voice breathy.

"We didn't find them," Villiers replied.

"What do you mean you didn't find them? You must have."

Villiers shook his head. "The sewer is a maze of tunnels. They could be down any number of chambers."

The angry burbling of water became more insistent. It was growing louder. The tide was rising. Time was running out. For all of them.

 espan

Doyle's husky, mocking laughter seemed to fill every inch of space, to suck every bit of air in the dark, damp labyrinth.

"You stupid, stupid girl. Haven't you realized by now that you're in over your head?" His tone was laced with contempt.

Emmeline backed away from him, but the man with the gun pressed its hard muzzle between her shoulder blades.

"Ah, forgive me," Doyle said. "Where are my manners? I haven't introduced you to Kevin. He's a good, loyal lad. His grandfather and I fought together in the old days. Kevin, say hello to Miss Kirby."

The younger man's lips curled back into a wolfish leer that revealed perfectly white, gleaming teeth. His eyes were glacial pools of blue viciousness.

Doyle droned on, "Kevin and his friends are taking up the cause once again. The Good Friday Accords are a betrayal of everything we fought for. A slap in the face. It's just you bloody English lording it over us. To hold us down. But not this time." He shook his fist at her menacingly. "This new generation is going to show you. This time, your precious Buckingham Palace is going to be blown into the sky. The way it should have been in 1963. *Erin Go Bragh*. Ireland Forever. Isn't that right, Kevin?"

This elicited another grin from Kevin. "That's right."

Emmeline swallowed hard. Her mouth was dry. "What—what," she stammered, her voice trembling, "are you going to do with me?" Not that she didn't already know the answer.

"Do? We're not going to do anything to you. We're simply going to leave you to Mother Nature's tender mercies. By the sound of it—" He cupped one hand around his ear. "—the tide is right on schedule. I always liked punctuality." He sighed with satisfaction. "Very soon now you'll cease to be a problem. To anyone."

"You can't just leave me here to die."

"I don't see why not," Doyle tossed back at her.

"Because it's not very sporting, old chap, that's why," a male voice floated to their ears.

Villiers and several Special Branch men loomed out of the shadows, guns drawn. "Now, it's about time to bring this circus to an end."

"*Villiers*," Doyle hissed in disgust.

Villiers flashed a rare smile. "In the flesh, old man. In the flesh."

As Philip, Burnell, and Finch materialized from another passage, Kevin grabbed Emmeline by the waist drew her body against his chest.

No one moved, except Emmeline. She was not going to suffer the indignity of being held captive any longer, especially since the cavalry had arrived—finally. Her arms flailed wildly as she tried to make contact with whatever fleshy part of Kevin's body she could find. Unfortunately, her efforts were for naught. He dwarfed her, and he didn't have any fleshy parts. He was one lean mass of rippling muscle. His arm seemed to be made of iron. He swatted at her hands as if she were an annoying gnat.

"Big bully," she mumbled, as she kicked him in the shin. She had the satisfaction of hearing a small grunt.

"Kill her, Kevin. Do it now," Doyle urged.

Emmeline's body went limp. It was agonizing being so helpless, waiting for death to come.

Where was Gregory? She thought he would have been here. At the end. A salty tear trailed its way down her cheek. She wished she could have seen his face one last time.

"Come on, lad. Do it," the old man yelled.

Kevin pressed the cold, hard steel against Emmeline's temple. She sucked in her breath. She didn't dare move. Out of the corner of her eye, she saw Burnell, Finch, and Philip start forward. But Villiers gave a firm shake of his head. Then no one moved. Or spoke. Only the chattering of the water slowly getting closer and closer taunted them.

Kevin released the safety catch and licked his lips. Emmeline squeezed her eyes shut and offered up a prayer, before severely reproaching God for her predicament. *Next time, leave us poor Jews alone. Why do we always have to be your chosen ones?*

Kevin raised the gun and, at the last second, pivoted, putting Doyle squarely in his sights and pushing Emmeline behind him. "I give you fair warning, I'm a crack shot. Even in this light, I can't miss."

"O'Hara is a scrupulously honest fellow, so I'd take his advice in the spirit it was given, if I were you, Doyle," Villiers remarked smoothly.

Doyle's eyes blazed with green fire. "Judas," he hissed as he pointed a quavering, accusatory finger at Kevin. "You're one of *them*. You betrayed your countrymen for these pigs."

"Easy with the insults now," Villiers scolded. "The game is over, and you lost. It's time you accepted that fact." Then to Kevin, he said, "First rate job, O'Hara."

Without taking his eyes off of Doyle, Kevin replied, "Thank you, sir. We arrested the others before they got near the tunnel. The bomb's been defused."

This elicited a string of curses in Gaelic from Doyle.

"That's quite enough of that. There is a lady present," Villiers admonished.

"She's no lady. Just a bloody interfering Jew. The Germans were right during the war. Too bad they didn't manage to exterminate every last one of you."

Doyle's body trembled with rage. He shook his fist and took a menacing step toward Emmeline. Before anyone realized what was happening, he lunged forward and slipped a stiletto knife from his sleeve to his palm with a practiced flick of the wrist. He plunged the knife into Kevin's heart. The younger man's blue eyes widened in stunned surprise. He swayed slightly for a second and then crumpled into a heap.

Emmeline stared at the dead man at her feet, his eyes, glassy and sightless. She wanted to scream. Felt the need to scream. But it would not come. Her vocal chords were paralyzed by shock.

Doyle grabbed her by the hair bending her head backward. He placed the *very* sharp point of the knife against her throat. "I have no qualms about killing her. In fact, I'd quite enjoy it." To demonstrate this, he pricked her skin with the tip until it drew a tiny drop of blood. "That's just a sample of what might happen if you don't back off."

He started to move toward the opening onto one of the side chambers.

"Calm down, Doyle," Burnell said in a soothing tone, as if he were speaking to a child. "There's no need for anyone else to get hurt. Let the girl go."

"Think about it. You know these tunnels like the back of your hand. She'd only slow you down," Philip added.

"Shut up," Doyle snarled. "I don't take orders from you. Any of you." The hand that held the knife made a broad gesture encompassing all the Special Branch and police officers. "I want all of you out of my sight."

Emmeline's dark eyes darted from side to side, silently imploring someone to help her.

Burnell and Villiers exchanged looks. Then Villiers gave a jerk of his head. "All right, chaps, get out. Quick as you can."

No one moved.

Doyle tightened his hold on Emmeline. She was drawing ragged breaths into her lungs, and her heart was pounding in her chest.

"That's an order," Villiers said more forcefully.

Reluctantly, but swiftly, all the Special Branch and Met officers withdrew. Their footfalls soon died away, swallowed up by the darkness.

Burnell and Philip, both with their hands in the air, walked toward Doyle. Finch was trying to edge his way around without spooking Doyle further.

"Stop. I'll cut her right in front of your eyes. I assure you it won't be a pretty sight." His lips curled into an ugly smile, when he heard the tiny whimper emanate from Emmeline. "What nothing to say for yourself all of a sudden?" He shook her so hard that her head rattled violently back and forth on her neck.

"Come now, aren't you tired of all this?" Burnell asked. "Don't you want to stop running?"

A harsh laugh burst from his throat. "I'll never give up the fight. I'll fight until I take my last breath."

"If you insist." Gregory came flying out from one of the side tunnels. His body crashed into Doyle with such force that the three of them toppled to the ground.

Stunned and winded, they saw stars for a few seconds.

Doyle recovered first. A primitive, animal cry rumbled forth from his chest as he rolled over and slashed wildly at Gregory, just missing his face.

Gregory's fingers locked around Doyle's throat. He squeezed with all his might, while his eye warily watched the knife hovering above him. The man was relentless. He just kept coming. The lethal sliver of steel made a soft *whoosh whoosh* as it sliced back and forth in mid-air. Coming closer and closer.

Meanwhile, Emmeline pummeled the back of the Irish-man's head with her small fists, keeping up a barrage of blows. She was no longer afraid. She was bleeding *furious*. She was not going to let anyone take Gregory away from her. She had already lost him once. She was not going to allow it to happen a second time. Certainly not like this.

Burnell and Finch sprang forward and dragged Emmeline away by her heels to the relative safety of the tunnel opening. "No," she yelled, struggling against them. But it was useless. It was two against one. And they were strong men.

Villiers and Philip pounced on Doyle just as his arm swung high in the air for another blow.

Gregory rolled out from under him, panting. He got to his knees. His breathing was husky and unsteady as he slowly pushed himself to his feet. He was wet, and there was a smudge of dirt across one cheek. But he shot his cuffs and straightened his tie. "Well, you left that a bit late didn't you, chaps?"

"That's gratitude for you," Philip grunted as he hauled the thrashing Doyle to his feet and left it to Villiers to handcuff him. "Next time, we'll leave to your own devices, shall we?" But he was smiling.

Gregory returned the smile and extended a hand to the other man. "You know what they say, 'When you save another man's life, you're responsible for him.'"

Philip rolled his eyes. "God help me. You mean I'm stuck with you until the end of my days?"

Gregory flashed cheeky grin. "I'm afraid so, old chap."

Philip sighed and shook his head.

"You have my sympathies. You've definitely ended up with the short straw," Burnell said. "*I* certainly wouldn't want to have Longdon dangling around my neck for the rest of my days. What a nightmare."

"Come now, Oliver. Do I detect the tiniest smidgen of jealously on your part? You know you'll always hold a special place in my heart." Gregory fluttered his eyelashes at the superintendent and clasped his hands together like a schoolgirl with a crush.

Burnell gave an impatient wave of his hand. "Oh, stuff it."

"I, for one, am grateful for all of you," Emmeline said as she slipped an arm around Gregory's waist and pressed her body against his side. She looked up at him, her eyes bright with unshed tears. "So very grateful."

Gregory pressed a kiss to her temple. "It's over, darling," he whispered. "Nothing to worry about anymore."

"My gun. Toby, look out," Villiers yelled as he tackled Gregory out of the way.

The gunshot exploded with a deafening crack in the confined space of that subterranean purgatory.

EPILOGUE

The bullet hit Villiers just above his right shoulder blade. He landed on the ground face first. The blood quickly started seeping through his clothing and spreading across his back. He moaned softly once, and then his body went still, and he was silent.

Gregory pressed Emmeline against the slimy wall of the tunnel and shielded her with his body as Finch launched himself at Doyle, knocking the gun out of his hand. Burnell dove for it.

"This ends now," the superintendent said. His voice was low and controlled. His eyes never left Doyle's face. "It's time to pay for your crimes."

A paroxysm of choking laughter seized Doyle. "You don't have the guts to do it, copper."

The bullet found its mark right between his eyes. And then there was no more laughing.

❦

Villiers's haggard face looked even paler against the crisp white pillow of the hospital bed. His eyes were closed.

Gregory hesitated a moment in the doorway. He didn't want to disturb the man if he was sleeping. God knew Villiers had been through the wringer the past few days. However, although his wound was quite serious, the prognosis was for a full recovery. The doctor had been amazed at Villiers's constitution. "He must have a will of iron," Gregory had overheard him murmur to one of the nurses as he passed him in the corridor.

And now here he was staring at the man who had saved his life.

In the sterile hospital bed, Villiers looked smaller somehow, and frailer. What could he say? Mere words seemed inadequate. He would go. He started to back out of the room, when Villiers stirred.

The older man opened his eyes slowly and blinked twice. He must have sensed some movement on the air because his head turned on the pillow. His eyes locked on Gregory. They stared at one another for a long moment.

The hand resting on the sheet twitched slightly, and Gregory realized that Villiers was trying to beckon him toward the bed.

Gregory nodded and crossed the room. He pulled the chair closer to the bed. "These—" He waved a bouquet of yellow and red carnations in the air. "—are from Emmy. She went to the flower stall on Kensington High Street and selected them herself. She likes bright colors and said your hospital room would probably need a little livening up."

A ghost of a smile played around Villiers's lips. With shaky fingers, he touched the flowers. He cleared his throat. "Tell her thank you." His voice was a hoarse rasp. "It was very—thoughtful."

Gregory put the bouquet down on the table beside the bed. "I'll ask a nurse to put them in water for you. As for Emmy, she's always thinking of everyone else but herself."

Villiers looked up at the ceiling and fell silent. Gregory saw a range of emotions chasing themselves across his face. He couldn't fathom what the man was thinking.

Then suddenly Villiers turned back to him. "There's no use beating about the bush, so I'll just come straight out and tell you. We've received word that Swanbeck is alive."

Gregory went very still. His face drained of color, but he didn't speak.

"He vowed to come after you," Villiers whispered. He tried

to sit up, but he was too weak and slumped back against the pillow, exhausted by the effort. "Your only choice is to disappear for a while—"

Gregory stood up so quickly, his chair nearly toppled back. "*No*. I'm not leaving. I've done too much running in my life."

"But, you fool, Swanbeck will kill you if he finds you."

Gregory walked to the door. "I'm not leaving Emmy. I'll take my chances with Swanbeck." Then in a more gentle tone, he said, "I—I came today to—to say thank you for saving my life in that damned tunnel."

Villiers sighed wearily. "What was the point, if you're going make yourself an easy target for Swanbeck?"

Gregory clenched his teeth. "I'm not leaving Emmy. Not again. *Not ever*." He flung the door open and turned on his heel without waiting for a reply.

Villiers stared at the door and murmured aloud, "You're a better man than I am. A much better man."

Philip appeared on the threshold five minutes later. He tapped lightly on the door. "Sir, am I disturbing you?"

"No, it's all right. Come in, Acheson."

Philip took the chair Gregory had occupied only moments ago. "Was that Longdon I saw getting into the lift?"

"Yes, you just missed him. He brought me those—" He pointed in the direction of the flowers. "—from Miss Kirby."

Philip smiled. "Ah, yes. That sounds very much like our Emmeline."

Villiers searched his face. "You like her a great deal, don't you?"

Philip's smile only grew wider. "There's no one like Emmeline. She has a heart of gold. If you ask me, she's too good for Longdon. But that's a matter between them."

Villiers nodded his head. "I see." Then he changed the subject. "I saw the papers this morning. Doyle is certainly making for a lot of copy."

Philip leaned back in the chair. "It'll die down in a few weeks. He'll be forgotten once the next big scandal breaks. The public is fickle that way."

"I suppose you're right."

"Uh, sir, there was—something particular I wanted to discuss with you. I know this is not the best of times, but I don't think there will ever be a good time."

Villiers's brow puckered. "Well, get on with it," he said, curiosity and annoyance vied with one another on his features.

Without a word, Philip pulled out two files from his attaché case and dropped them on the bed. Villiers pulled them toward his chest. His hand froze when he saw the names on the files: GREGORY LONGDON and TOBY CRENSHAW.

His eyes shot to Philip's face, but that blue gaze gave away nothing. A tense silence filled the space between them.

Villiers twisted the sheet between his fingers and stared at the ceiling.

"Sir, Longdon is not one of my most favorite people in this world, but don't you think he has a right to know?"

Villiers's head snapped back. "*Know*? Know what? How would knowing help? He's better off this way."

"Is he, sir? How can you know that for sure?"

"I—I did what I thought was best for him and Clarissa." His voice caught in his throat. "There's no room for a wife and child in a spy's life. I—I made the mistake of thinking it was possible to have both. I was wrong. It was all a dream. A lovely dream for a time, but a dream all the same. Dreams can't last. It was a tissue of lies from the start anyway. Two people can't make a life together based on a lie. My code name was Toby Crenshaw, and that's what I told Clarissa when I first met her that summer all those years ago." For a moment, his gaze was lost somewhere in the past. "We never legally married. It never bothered her. But for all intents and purposes, we *were* married. And then Toby came along.

"I tried. I really tried to make it all work. But in the end, it was just not possible. I was a field agent. I was being sent on more and more dangerous assignments. I couldn't put Clarissa's and Toby's lives at risk. So I did what I thought was best. I left them."

Philip swallowed hard. He thought about Maggie and the boys. Who was he to judge? No one knows how he or she will react until they are thrust into a situation. "No doubt it was a difficult decision, but surely now you can explain it to Long-don."

"No," Villiers whispered. "Too much water under the bridge. It's too late to start over. I've been watching over that young fool for years without him knowing it."

"That's what you were doing in the tunnel. Protecting your son. In all the confusion no one noticed, but you called him Toby."

"I made a promise to Clarissa after she died that I would always take care of him. You know I visit her grave every month and talk to her and tell her what Toby's been up to."

Philip nodded his head. He gathered up the files and stood. "I think you need your rest, sir."

Villiers clutched at his sleeve. "What are you going to do?"

"Do about what, sir? I'm sure I have no idea what you're talking about." He patted the older man's hand.

"Thank you, Acheson."

✒✒✒

Burnell's mouth curled into a Cheshire cat grin as he made a final note and closed the Doyle file.

He leaned back in his chair and rested his head on his inter-laced fingers. Now perhaps he could take that long-delayed fishing trip in the Scottish Highlands.

He was lost in this reverie when Finch burst into his office. "Sir, I—"

"Ah, there you are. Come in. Come in. Isn't it a wonderful day, Finch?" he said with hearty enthusiasm.

"Well, there are two schools of thought on that."

Burnell caught the undertone in the sergeant's voice, but decided to ignore it. Nothing was going to spoil his good mood. "Nonsense. Doyle is dead. The murders of Max Sanborn, Maurice Boinet, and Alan Crichlow have been solved—"

"That's what I wanted to talk to you about, sir. The mur-ders."

Burnell sat up straight in his chair. The smile vanished. "What about the murders?"

Finch hesitated. "We've made a mistake. Doyle couldn't have murdered Max Sanborn."

"What?" The word exploded from the superintendent's mouth. "What do you mean?"

"Sir, please calm down and listen to me. Doyle definitely killed Boinet and Crichlow, but *not* Sanborn. It wasn't possible. Look here." He pointed to a small article in the paper about Doyle's life, the now-nefarious aspects as well as his philanthropic activities. The piece was highlighted by a photo.

Burnell read it, and his eyes widened in disbelief.

"Now do you understand, sir?' Finch asked. "He was the guest of honor at a charity dinner that night."

Burnell sat there stroking his beard. The wheels in his head were spinning.

"Someone else has Max Sanborn's blood on his or her hands," Finch continued. "We'll have to reopen the investigation."

"What? Yes, of course," Burnell murmured. "Max Sanborn's blood, of course. How could I have been so blind?" He jumped to his feet. "Come on, Finch."

"Where are we going?"

"To catch a killer."

❧❧❧

The car crunched as it pulled into the circular drive in front of the house on West Heath Road in Hampstead, which had a lovely view of the silver birches in the West Heath. Finch turned off the ignition and rested his hands on the steering wheel. They observed an older couple leaving the house. The two detectives surmised they were probably making a sympathy call on the family.

"Sir, was it wise to rush over to Assistant Commissioner Fenton's home to inform him about Max Sanborn's murderer? Shouldn't we have waited until he was back in the office? It is a rather delicate situation, after all, what with Doyle being Mrs. Fenton's uncle."

Burnell opened the door and put one foot on the ground. He was already halfway out of the car. "Nonsense, lad. What would Fenton say if he found out that we had kept the truth from him? We'd never hear the end of it."

Finch sighed. "I suppose you're right, sir," he mumbled. But he was not looking forward to the confrontation with Fenton. Reluctantly, he detached his seat belt and walked around to the other side of the car to join his boss.

Burnell straightened his tie and gave his suit jacket a hasty brush to smooth down any wrinkles. Finch pressed the doorbell.

The door was answered by a plump butler with an egg-shaped head and a hairline that was steadily creeping upward toward his crown. "Good afternoon, gentlemen. I'm afraid the family is in mourning and is not seeing any visitors."

Burnell cleared his throat. "Superintendent Burnell and Sergeant Finch." They flashed their warrant cards. "We're sorry to intrude at such a sad time, but we need to see Assistant Commissioner Fenton on urgent police business."

The butler looked down his nose at them. "I'm afraid that's not possible. Assistant Commissioner and Mrs. Fenton are only seeing close family members and friends."

Burnell pushed his way past the butler and entered the hall, with Finch close on his heels.

"Superintendent, this is an outrage. I must ask you to leave at once."

Burnell cast an appreciative glance over the furnishings and paintings that graced the walls. Then he plunked down on a delicate silk-covered settee, which groaned under his weight. "I assure you Assistant Commissioner Fenton will want to hear what we have to say. So be a good fellow and run along and get him."

To add insult to injury, Finch took the seat next to the superintendent and folded his arms across his chest. "We're quite prepared to wait."

The butler opened his mouth to say something, recognized that it was useless, and clamped it shut. He sniffed and tipped his chin in the air.

With as much dignity he could muster, he said stiffly, "Very well. Please remain here and don't go wandering about the house." Then he shuffled off down the corridor.

Burnell leaned his head toward Finch and whispered, "Wander about? Does he think that we're going to nick something? We're the bloody police, not a couple of house breakers."

Finch smothered a smile.

Fenton appeared within minutes. The butler hovered a few steps behind him.

"What's the meaning of this, Burnell?" Fenton stopped in the middle of the hallway. "Jenkins here tells me you had the audacity to push your way into my house at a time like this. This is low even for you."

"I'm sorry, sir, but I'm afraid it couldn't be helped."

Jenkins cast a vindictive smile in the detectives' direction before swanning off to do whatever it was butlers did.

Fenton threw his hands up in the air in exasperation. "In here." He jerked his head toward a door to his left.

Burnell and Finch quickly crossed the hall and followed Fenton into a study.

Fenton rounded on them. "All right, what's all this about?"

The superintendent cleared his throat. "Sir, we were mistaken. It appears that Doyle was not culpable for Max Sanborn's murder. There is no doubt that he killed Boinet and Crichlow. But not Sanborn."

Fenton stared at him in disbelief. His nostrils flared, and he puffed out his chest. "What? Did I hear you correctly? After the plague you brought down on this house, now you have the nerve to say that you were wrong."

Burnell clenched his fists into tight balls at his sides. "Respectfully, sir, Doyle—Mr. Kildare—your wife's uncle was solely responsible for the disgrace and shame visited upon your family."

"How dare you? You were always an insolent bastard. Always trying to undermine me."

"I'm sorry you feel that way, sir. I've always done my job to the best of my ability. That's all."

Fenton took a step closer to him. They were only inches apart. "That's a load of rubbish, and we both know it."

"No, sir. My duty is to ensure that no one breaks the law and justice is served. As in this case. If you would only bear with me for a few more minutes, I think everything will become clear."

A tense silence filled the room. Finch's gaze shifted between the superintendent and Fenton, who stood there glaring at one another.

"This is a complete waste of time," Fenton said, his voice laced with irritation.

"The truth is never a waste of time. It just took a little longer to find the answer."

"And what is the answer?"

"Why, sir, I'm surprised you need to ask. You already know the answer. Because *you* killed Max Sanborn."

Finch sucked in his breath and shot a glance at his boss.

"What?" Fenton hissed, his nostrils flaring. "Have you gone mad, man?"

"Come, sir, you were maneuvering behind the scenes from the beginning. How did you know Maggie Roth wiped Sanborn's blood from her hands? Her hands were perfectly clean when she appeared in Sanborn's penthouse to confess that night. The only way you could have known that she had blood on her hands was if you were *there* and had witnessed the argument between Sanborn and Ms. Roth. You likely were concealed somewhere, waiting for your chance."

Fenton's face drained of color, and his body became unnaturally still.

Burnell went on, "After she fled the penthouse, you went into the study and stabbed Sanborn in the throat while he was still unconscious. But you were trapped when Miss Kirby came in to see what had happened. In a panic, you knocked her out and fled. However, the cruel, calculating side of your brain took over at this point, and you decided to frame Miss Kirby and Ms. Roth, thereby deflecting suspicion from yourself. So you made the anonymous call to the station to set the wheels in motion. Everything else that occurred that night was part of your big act. You made your grand entrance at the crime scene saying that you had rushed over from the station the minute you heard the shocking news. But, sir, *no one* saw you at the station that night. I checked.

"Then, on the pretext of being Sanborn's friend, you wanted daily reports on our progress in the case. That's why we made little headway because you were sabotaging all our leads. There was also the business of pressuring Brian Sanborn to turn over his father's files. I don't know of course, but I suspect, that you were terrified that Max had kept a record of how you had helped him over the years to hush up some of his illegal business ventures. Once he found out about Doyle and your family connection, he probably really put the screws to you. Am I right?"

Fenton didn't utter a word, but beads of perspiration appeared on his brow.

"Well, never mind. It will be easy enough to verify, now that we know what to look for. My guess is that in exchange for your help, Max Sanborn dropped a few quiet words in the right ears and you received promotion on top of promotion. Shall I go on, sir?"

"I—I—" Fenton rasped, "I think you've done quite enough. Get out of my house."

"No, sir. Richard William Fenton, I'm arresting you for the murder of Max Sanborn. You do not have to say anything. But it may harm your defense if you do not mention when questioned something which you later rely on in court. Anything you do say may be given in evidence."

Finch twisted Fenton's arms behind his back and placed handcuffs on his wrists.

Two ugly red stains tinged Fenton's cheeks as he struggled in the sergeant's grasp. "You'll pay for this Burnell. You'll be looking over your shoulder for the rest of your life."

"Promises, promises. My, how the mighty have fallen." Then to Finch, he said, "Get him out of here. The sight of him makes me ill."

ℯ⁄ᴐℯ⁄ᴐ

Emmeline had just finished editing an article for tomorrow's paper when Frank tapped lightly on the door.

"Hello, Emmeline. This just came for you, special delivery." He handed her a manila envelope.

She smiled. "Thanks very much. Have a good evening."

He nodded and quietly closed the door behind him.

There was no return address. Emmeline quickly slit open the envelope. It was from Yoav Zielinski. There were a letter and two files.

Dear Emmeline,

I took the liberty of looking into the disappearance of Sarah and Edmond Lévy. Unfortunately, it was as I had suspected. They were betrayed and arrested by the Nazis. I am enclosing the files. I defer to you whether to show them to Maggie Roth and her family. Perhaps, it is better to leave things as they are. However, you are a far better judge than I.

Now, there is something else I wanted to tell you. I wrestled with my conscience for many hours, but in the end, I felt you had a right to know because you prize the truth so highly. You see, our conversation last week bothered me tremendously. There was something very wrong with the story you had been told. So I made a few calls to certain people who shall remain nameless, you understand, and I discovered...

Emmeline read the letter to the very end. Then, she read it through again and a third time. She slumped back in her chair stunned and mentally winded.

"Darling, are you all right?"

Emmeline jumped at the sound of Gregory's voice. All her attention had been concentrated on Zielinski's letter.

"Darling?" he said again. His brow furrowed in concern. "What's the matter?"

She stared at him dumbly and simply handed him the letter and a file.

He took them from her and lowered himself into the chair opposite. He read the letter and then looked up at her. "I don't understand. What does this mean?"

Emmeline leaned across the desk and reached for the file with trembling hands. She cleared her throat. "It means that my parents were murdered."

Author's Note

For those readers who are history buffs, there was no 1963 IRA plot to blow up Buckingham Palace. The one discussed in this story was purely my invention. Also, if you scour art books you will not find *A Country Lane in Summer* among Constable's *chef d'oeuvres*. It's another of my creations.

About the Author

Daniella Bernett is a member of the Mystery Writers of America NY Chapter. She graduated summa cum laude with a BS in Journalism from St. John's University. *Lead Me Into Danger*, *Deadly Legacy*, and *From Beyond The Grave* are the first three books in the Emmeline Kirby-Gregory Longdon mystery series. She also is the author of two poetry collections, *Timeless Allure* and *Silken Reflections*. In her professional life, she is the research manager for a nationally prominent engineering, architectural and construction management firm. Daniella is currently working on Emmeline and Gregory's next adventure. Visit www.daniellabernett.com or follow her on Facebook or on Goodreads.

Made in the USA
Middletown, DE
30 January 2022